The bullet from the MP5 hit the camera dead centre, blasting through the lens, piercing the single eye, blowing the camera apart before it thundered into Newton's temple, shattering the frontal bone. The photographer felt a second of agonizing pain, as if he'd been hit with a burning hammer, then the bullet tore through his skull, erupting from the back, carrying a confetti of brain and pulverized bone with it. The impact lifted him off his feet and he crashed to the ground, his hands still gripping what remained of the camera. Pieces of it had been driven back into his head by the passage of the bullet. Blood spread rapidly from what was left of his shattered cranium, his body quivering madly as the muscles finally gave up their hold on life.

Also by Shaun Hutson in Sphere Books:
SLUGS
SPAWN
EREBUS
BREEDING GROUND
RELICS
DEATHDAY
VICTIMS
ASSASSIN
SHADOWS
NEMESIS

SHAUN HUTSON

RENEGADES

SPHERE BOOKS LIMITED

A *Sphere* Book

First published in Great Britain in 1991 by
Macdonald & Co (Publishers) Ltd,
London & Sydney

Published by Sphere Books Ltd 1991

ISBN 0 7474 0791 6

Photoset in North Wales by
Derek Doyle & Associates, Mold, Clwyd
Printed and bound in Great Britain by
BPCC Hazell Books
Aylesbury, Bucks, England
Member of BPCC Ltd.

Sphere Books Ltd
A Division of
Macdonald & Co (Publishers) Ltd
165 Great Dover Street
London SE1 1YA
A member of Maxwell Macmillan Publishing Corporation

This book is dedicated to Liverpool Football Club. Its players, its staff, its fans and everything it stands for. For bringing me so much pleasure over the last twenty-five years, I thank you.

Acknowledgements

As ever, no book is written without a certain amount of help, inspiration and support for yours truly. So, here are most, if not all, of the people who provided those three commodities (or who paid me money to see their names in print ... just joking).

Extra special thanks to Gary Farrow, my Manager, the man who kicks arse whether it needs kicking or not, the man whose epitaph will read 'How much' or 'Only if we get the cover' ... Thanks, mate. Also thanks to Chris and Damien at 'the office'.

Very special thanks to Mr John O'Connor, Mr Don Hughes, everyone in Sales and, most of all, to my sales teams for their untiring efforts and for putting up with me 'on the road'. To Nick Webb who'd been pursuing me for years and finally nailed me ... (you're stuck with me now, Nick). To Barbara Boote, to Nann du Sautoy, to Jane Warren and Rosalie Macfarlane and everyone in publicity, in fact thanks to everyone at Macdonald/ Futura/Sphere for their support. To John Jarrold for the first of many gut-busting lunches ... Thank you all.

Special thanks to Mr Ray Mudie and Mr Peter 'prisoner of Gotham City' Williams. Always respected, always friends. I owe you.

Very special thanks to James Hale who edits with a pencil not a hatchet. Thanks also to Vanessa Holt and Carole Blake and Julian Friedmann.

Thanks to Bill Young (No threats this time, Bill)

and Andy Wint. To Brian 'there's another one in the post' Pithers, to 'Mad' Malcolm Dome at 'RAW' and to everyone at 'Kerrang' too.

Many thanks to Gareth 'still overworked and trying to practice' James, to John 'respectable at last' Gullidge and 'Samhain', to John Martin, to Nick Cairns and Andy Featherstone (beware, these men carry tape-recorders). Thanks for your support and interest.

Thanks to Alison at EMI, to Trish at BMG (thanks and don't forget your thermals ...) to Shonadh at Polygram, to Georgie, to Susie (for keeping me fit ...). To Broomhills Pistol Club, especially Bert and Anita, Mike 'Just call me Travis' Kirby and everyone else. To Ian 'I've brought the tape back' Austin, the man with the biggest phone bill in the world ... cheers, mate. To Dave and Malcolm in Manchester (I'll tell you when it's lunch-time, Malc ...), to Roger who is probably on a boat or plane somewhere and to Dave 'I'm going to use all the tape on your answering machine' Holmes.

Many thanks to all the management and staff at The Holiday Inn, Mayfair for their friendliness. And, for no other reason but I feel like mentioning them, thanks to Fouquet's in Paris, to the Barbados Hilton, Dromoland Castle in Ireland and Bertorelli's in Notting Hill Gate.

As ever, thanks to Steve, Bruce, Dave, Nicko and Adrian for letting me repeat the experience of a lifetime. Thanks also to Rod Smallwood and everyone at Smallwood Taylor. Many thanks to 'Big' Wally Grove (get some etiquette, mate ...).

Indirect thanks to Queensryche, Great White, Thunder, Tangier, Black Sabbath, Clannad and Enya. Also thanks to Michael Mann, Sam Peckinpah and Martin Scorsese.

Thanks to Croxley typing paper for the free sheets.

This novel was, as ever, written on Croxley paper, wearing Wrangler jeans and Puma trainers (well, it worked with Croxley ...).

I don't think I've left anyone out except to say a quick word of thanks to Amin Saleh, Jack Taylor and Lewis Bloch.

The most important people I leave until last and that means my Mum and Dad without whom none of this would be possible (the day I slow down, Mum, will be the day Dad gets a treble up ...). And to my wife, Belinda, who over the past few years has saved my sanity, my soul (maybe), my national insurance stamps and my twenty pence pieces. This one is with love too.

That leaves one group of people to thank and that's *you*. To every person who has ever bought, borrowed or stolen one of my books, thank you. What follows is for you, and always will be.

Shaun Hutson.

'What does not kill me makes me stronger.'
— Nietzsche

Prologue

It was the darkness of the blind.

A blackness so impenetrable, so palpable he felt as if he was floating on it. Surrounded by it. As if the tenebrous gloom were infiltrating every pore of his body, shutting out the light as surely as if his eyes had been removed.

But amidst that darkness there was pleasure.

Pleasure he had felt before and knew he would feel again. Sometimes so exquisite it was almost unbearable.

The inability to see heightened the sensations he felt.

His sense of smell was sharpened.

The odour was strong in his nostrils, pungent, sweet, occasionally somewhat rancid.

A powerful coppery odour which he knew well and which he welcomed.

His ears seemed more sensitive than usual, too, his hearing attuned more intensely to the sounds that filtered through the blackness.

It was like some kind of chorus.

His own sighs and grunts of pleasure mingled with the other noises.

The more strident cries.

Cries of pain.

He smiled in the gloom, running his own fingers over his features, pushing one index finger into his mouth and tracing the outline of his lower lip.

He tasted the blood on it and licked it off.

His body felt as if it were on fire, despite the coldness

inside the building, and he grinned as he thought about the luminosity which his body might be giving off as that warmth seemed to intensify.

But there was no glow.

Only that blackness which he loved so dearly.

Almost as dearly as the objects that surrounded him.

He ran his hands over them with greedy relish.

He was close to ecstacy.

His own breathing was low and guttural, rasping deep in his throat as he continued to run his fingers over the thing beside him.

Then finally he lifted it. Smoothly, effortlessly.

The smell seemed to grow stronger as he brought the object close to his face.

It was invisible in the darkness but he ran his right index finger across it, feeling every fold and crease.

Every unblemished inch.

It felt like velvet.

He smiled broadly, knowing that this pleasure could continue for hours yet.

They would not come for him until morning and by that time he would be satiated. Glutted on pleasure.

Until the next time.

He shuddered with anticipation and brought the object closer to his face, feeling something run slowly down his right arm.

Fluid which dripped from his elbow onto his naked thigh.

He opened his mouth slightly, preparing himself, his tongue flicking across his own lips before snaking out to weave tight patterns over the other object.

He tasted. He smelled. He felt. He heard.

The low cries.

The dripping of fluid.

His tongue touched lips.

And those other lips were warm.

Despite the fact that the head had been severed over an hour ago.

PART ONE

'No life that breathes with human breath,
Has ever truly longed for death.'
                    – Alfred Lord Tennyson.

'For a price I'd do about anything, except
pull the trigger. For that I'd need a pretty
good cause.'
                    – Queensryche.

One

STORMONT, NORTHERN IRELAND:
They would kill him.

Chris Newton had no doubt about it.

He was a dead man.

If he fucked up on this assignment then they would kill him. He shoved a fresh roll of film into the back of the Nikon which hung around his neck, checked and re-checked the other two cameras which he carried then peered through the one with the telephoto lens that was perched on the tripod before him. He adjusted the lens, trying to bring the Parliament building into sharper focus, aware that he'd already performed this task a dozen times in the last fifteen minutes.

His hands were shaking, and not just from the chill wind which swept across the great lawns fronting the building. He was nervous. No, that was an under-statement. He was scared shitless.

Had he taken all the lens caps off? Were all his exposures set right? Was the shutter speed correct?

Check.

Check.

He felt like a bloody astronaut running through the final details of take-off prior to being fired into space. And again the thought crossed his mind that, if he didn't get the pictures he'd been sent here to obtain, space probably offered his only safe haven.

The editors of The Mail had seen fit to give him this

3

assignment on the strength of the work he'd been doing on the paper for the last seven months. He'd covered everything for them from football matches to society parties and they had been impressed. Impressed enough to send him here.

The men around him were probably just as nervous as he was, Newton tried to tell himself. Most of them were smoking; one was sipping from a hip flask. Newton could have done with sharing the liquor. Anything to calm his nerves.

The assembled politicians were expected out onto the lawn within the next fifteen minutes.

He checked his watch.

Close by a film crew were setting up, the reporter tapping the end of his microphone, complaining that it didn't work. The cameraman was swinging his hand-held camera back and forth as if it were some kind of weapon, sweeping it across the ranks of newsmen and women, pausing occasionally to wipe the odd spot of rain from the lens.

The sky was overcast, threatening a downpour. It had been raining on and off since Newton arrived in Northern Ireland two days ago. In fact, Belfast reminded him of Manchester with its almost constant rainfall, the main difference being that British soldiers didn't patrol the streets of Manchester.

Not yet, anyway, he mused.

There were soldiers ahead of him, mingling with the scores of Ulster Constabulary men, the mosaic of uniforms incongruous against the regal background of Stormont itself.

'You ready?'

The voice startled him and he glanced round to see Julie Webb looking at him.

4

She had flown out with him, reminding him all the time (as if he needed it) of the importance of getting good pictures.

The Stormont Summit was the most important meeting of its kind in the history of the Six Counties: a final opportunity to end the bloodshed which had torn the country apart for over four hundred years. At this very moment inside the building there were members of the British Cabinet, the Irish Government, Ulster Unionists. Even representatives of Sinn Fein, for Christ's sake.

A meeting of ideologies which, a year before, would have been unthinkable.

But it was happening right now and Chris Newton had been sent here to record it on film.

And if he fucked up his editors would kill him.

It was as simple as that.

Julie stamped her feet trying to restore circulation, her boots crunching gravel.

'They're coming out soon,' she told him, sipping from a plastic mug she'd taken from a thermos flask. The flask itself she held to her chest as if it were a new-born child. She poured herself another cup of the steaming coffee and offered some to Newton.

He declined, shaking his head, blowing on his hands instead, trying to induce some warmth and also to stop himself trembling.

A few feet away he heard the quick-fire rattle of several shots from a Pentax.

To his left a reporter from one of the major news shows on television was recording his location and time indent. That done, he turned towards the Parliament building and muttered something under his breath before looking at his watch again.

5

The troops and security men watched the swarms of newsmen intently. Security at the gathering was even more stringent than usual, the presence of the security forces more in evidence than Newton could ever remember. As well as troops and R.U.C., it was rumoured there were a number of S.A.S. men present, invisible amongst the crowd. Newton glanced to his right and left, wondering if the very men he stood beside were in fact S.A.S. men in disguise.

His own press card had been double-checked, the guards at the press entrance apparently unconvinced that the likeness on his card matched his actual identity. Newton had thought for one awful moment that he was going to be refused entry but the guards had finally relented and allowed him to pass.

He continued rubbing his hands together, looking around.

The media interest in the summit was, naturally, immense. Newton wondered if there were any reporters left in Fleet Street. Everyone, it seemed, was gathered here; they wanted to be part of the momentous event, irrespective of whether it was part of their job or not. There were foreign film crews from as far afield as Japan, though what they made of it all Newton couldn't imagine. Probably spies from Nikon wanting to see how sales were doing, he mused, checking his own equipment again.

Larger spots of rain began to fall sporadically and a number of the assembled throng glanced upwards towards the swollen clouds and passed less than flattering comments about the weather in the province.

Newton pulled a baseball cap from the pocket of his coat and jammed it on. He bent forward to peer through the mounted camera once more, annoyed

6

when someone bumped into it.

'Careful,' he hissed irritably, glaring at the offender.

The man met his gaze with unblinking eyes, almost challengingly. He was stocky and in need of a shave. He stood looking at Newton for long seconds before passing off into the crowd.

'Prat,' the photographer muttered, making sure the other man was out of earshot. He re-adjusted the camera, peering through the telescopic lens as a sniper might study his prey.

He was one of the first to see the main door of the building open.

'Jesus,' he muttered, noticing the armed security men who emerged ahead of the first of the politicians.

And then the whole cold, wet and irritable throng of media saw what they had come to see. The weather and the conditions were momentarily forgotten.

More politicians emerged, some joking about the weather, others wondering whether or not it might be more prudent to remain inside the building until the rain had stopped.

The air was filled with the quick-fire rattle of a hundred cameras firing off an almost synchronized volley. Reporters tried to move forward but were held back by the line of security men and now the waiting media saw that the politicians were coming towards them anyway, sticking to the pathways wherever possible.

Newton, snapping away as if his life depended upon it, caught sight of the Irish Prime Minister walking alongside two Unionist MPs. Behind them the British Foreign Secretary strode between two security guards, chatting animatedly with a member of Sinn Fein. Newton shook his head in wonderment.

The politicians drew closer, grouping together for the benefit of the posse of media. The reporters now began firing questions with a verbal rapidity that almost matched the high-speed salvos coming from the cameras. Television cameras cast cyclopean eyes over the entire gathering as the questions rained down and sound men struggled to push boom mikes close enough to catch the responses.

'How much progress had been made in the talks?'

'Is it possible that a settlement could be reached before the end of the week?'

'What do the talks mean to both Northern Ireland and Southern Ireland?'

'Will the troops be withdrawn soon?'

Newton kept firing away, happy that he was covering every angle, framing every face. His nervousness seemed to have gone. He was doing what he did best now. Moving alternately between the mounted camera and the ones he carried around his neck he expertly and swiftly changed rolls of film, not wishing to leave any possible history-making shot to chance.

The questions continued to pour forth, their answers sometimes vague, sometimes encouraging, sometimes non-committal. Newton himself realized that one summit meeting and four days of discussion were insufficient in themselves to cure a disease that had afflicted the province for so long but, if the troubles in Ulster were an open wound, then this summit was going some way to at least dress that wound. The healing process would take much longer.

He was preparing to take another photo as the politicians gathered together when he was almost knocked to the ground.

He spun round angrily.

'What the fuck ...' he snapped, seeing that it was the same unshaven man who had bumped into him a moment or two earlier. 'Watch it, mate,' Newton said angrily. 'We're all in the same boat here, you know.'

The man again said nothing. His eyes were fixed on the assembled politicians who were now all but surrounded by reporters, the heaving throng kept a respectful distance by the security forces. Maybe he was one of the plain-clothes S.A.S. men, thought Newton, his job to mingle with the crowd and check for any trouble. He carried a camera around his neck but it was not the camera he was reaching for.

It was the gun that he pulled from inside his coat.

Two

Scarcely had the barrel left the folds of the jacket when Newton heard a deafening blast of fire.

He hurled himself to the ground, covering his head, but as he looked around, the roar of the retort still ringing in his ears, he saw that the unshaven man was lying close to him on his back, a massive hole in his forehead.

Two or three other men stood around him, each with a pistol in his hand. Newton noticed the thin plume of smoke rising from the barrel of one of the hand-guns.

If the unshaven man had been an assassin, it appeared he'd been shot before he could complete his mission. The plain clothes S.A.S. men were rummaging through his pockets, ignoring the blood which was still spouting from his head.

Amazed and relieved at the speed with which they had acted, Newton scrambled to his feet.

The burst of fire from behind him sent him sprawling once more.

Away to his right another man was advancing on the group of politicians, a Skorpion machine-pistol gripped in his hands. He swept it back and forth across the line of pressmen and security men.

To the left was another man, similarly armed.

And another.

Newton had one ridiculous thought as he hugged the ground, his ears ringing from the constant rattle of automatic fire.

How the hell did they get the weapons past security?

As more and more bullets ploughed into the assembled throng Newton saw men fall, clutching wounds. There were screams of fear. Of surprise.

Of pain.

Newton saw one of the Unionist MPs hit, the bullet catching him in the chest and punching through his ribs before erupting from his back.

One of the Sinn Fein men dived for cover, yelling in pain as another bullet took off two of his fingers, the shattered digits spinning into the air. He rolled over on the wet grass. A third high-velocity shell blasted away part of his face.

Soldiers tried to force the politicians back towards the relative safety of the Parliament building. Not that many needed persuading.

Those bullets which didn't strike flesh whined up off the gravel pathways around Stormont or ricocheted off the statues that adorned the ornate gardens. Lumps of stone were blasted from the carvings, the squeal of spent cartridges mingling with the constant roar of fire and the shouts and screams of those being shot.

Another of the attackers was hit but not before he managed to send a stream of fire into the S.A.S. man who'd shot him. Both crashed to the ground. But the gunman's two companions continued pumping bullets into the fleeing politicians. Indeed, into anything that crossed their path.

Newton, who was trying to crawl to a nearby hedge, glanced behind him to see that there were already more than a dozen bodies scattered on the lawn, motionless. He finally reached the hedge and dragged himself behind it, panting like a carthorse, perspiration mingling with the rain which was falling rapidly now.

The air stank of cordite, great bluish-grey clouds of it swirling around gunmen and security men alike. Heaving banks of malevolent fog which grew thicker as the firing continued.

An R.U.C. man fell to the ground, blood jetting from a wound in his neck.

One of his colleagues was shouting into a two-way radio, shielding a member of the Irish Cabinet with his body. The same burst of fire took them both. The radio fell uselessly to the ground a few feet from its bullet-riddled owner.

Some of the politicians had managed to run back towards the building and were joined in their flight by the media.

Newton caught sight of Julie Webb, tears streaming down her face, arms clasped around her head as if to keep her safe. Curled up in a foetal position, she could only scream in terror as bullets tore up the ground around her, little geysers of earth erupting as the 9mm

11

slugs drilled patterns across the ground.

And then one hit her.

It shattered her right wrist, powering through into the top of her skull.

Newton saw her body jerk uncontrollably for a second; then she was still, like so many others around her.

Still the air was filled with the roar of machine-gun fire, spent cartridge cases spraying into the air and rattling on the gravel as they rained down from breeches now hot from so much fire. Muzzle-flashes blazed as the weapons continued to spew forth their deadly load, cutting bloody swathes across those in their path.

Another S.A.S. man was hit, catapulted backwards by the impact of the bullet which stove in his breastbone and left him writhing on the wet grass that, in places, was now slicked crimson.

Then Newton heard another sound, a loud strident wail he recognized as a siren.

Away to his left, two police cars were roaring towards the scene of carnage. It seemed like an eternity to Newton since the firing had begun. It would have surprised him to know that the slaughter was just forty seconds old.

To his right another car, this one unmarked, also sped towards the fire-fight. Its driver was hunched over the wheel.

One of the gunmen shouted something to his companion and pointed first at the police cars then at the other car. The taller of the two men jammed a fresh magazine into his Skorpion and turned it towards the onrushing R.U.C. vehicles, gritting his teeth as he kept his finger tight on the trigger, grunting in pain as an S.A.S. bullet tore through his shoulder.

Bullets spattered the windscreen of the leading vehicle and glass exploded inwards, showering the driver and his companion. The car skidded off the road and ploughed across one of Stormont's immaculate lawns, leaving great furrows in the sodden grass.

The second vehicle kept coming.

As did the unmarked one.

It was as the two cars bore down on the men that Newton suddenly forgot his fear and remembered the camera around his neck.

He fumbled for the Nikon, peering through the view-finder, pinning the two gunmen in his sights as surely as they had their victims.

He clicked off half a dozen shots.

It was the taller man who saw him.

For an agonizing second it seemed to Newton as if time had stood still. Everything was frozen.

The gunman turned towards him, a slight smile on his face almost as if he were posing for the photograph.

Then he opened fire.

The first two shots missed Newton. The third was more accurate.

The bullet from the MP5 hit the camera dead centre, blasting through the lens, piercing the single eye, blowing the camera apart before it thundered into Newton's temple, shattering the frontal bone. The photographer felt a second of agonizing pain, as if he'd been hit with a burning hammer, then the bullet tore through his skull, erupting from the back, carrying a confetti of brain and pulverized bone with it. The impact lifted him off his feet and he crashed to the ground, his hands still gripping what remained of the camera. Pieces of it had been driven back into his head by the passage of the bullet. Blood spread rapidly from what was left of his shattered cranium, his body quivering madly as the muscles finally gave up their hold on life.

The taller man spun round to see that the unmarked car was almost upon them. It skidded to a halt, great geysers of gravel flying up behind it as the rear wheels spun and the driver roared at the two gunmen to get in.

The taller man hurled himself into the passenger seat. His companion, already hit, was not so lucky. One of the S.A.S. men shot him in the back of the head and his body fell heavily on the gravel as the Granada sped off.

The R.U.C. car bore down, hurtling directly towards them, one of its occupants firing out of the window at the oncoming Granada.

The tall man gripped the Skorpion in one fist and opened up, smiling as he saw bullets ripping into the police car. He saw one pierce the windscreen and catch the driver in the face. The car immediately went out of control, skidding madly before ploughing through a hedge, its tail end spinning round.

The driver of the Granada tried to avoid the other vehicle but couldn't. He slammed into its rear end as he passed, the jolt shaking the men in the car.

The remaining policeman struggled from the car, lifting his gun, trying to get a couple of shots at the escaping assassins.

A burst from the MP5 cut him down, bullets ripping into the side of the police car, one of them hitting the petrol tank.

There was a deafening roar and the police car disappeared in a searing ball of orange and yellow flame. Pieces of chassis were sent spinning into the air like blazing shrapnel. A mushroom cloud of dense black smoke billowed upwards into the sky, darker even than the rain clouds which wept over the scene of destruction below them.

Pieces of broken equipment littered the ground, scattered amongst the bodies of the dead and dying and those who might still be too terrified to move. Moans of pain mingled with the roaring flames belching from the wreck of the police car. Politicians, security men and members of the media crawled amongst the bodies, ignoring the rain which drenched them and the blood which spattered their clothes.

A television camera, its operator dead from a wound in the back, continued to turn, recording the scene of devastation until someone inadvertently bumped into it and sent it crashing to the ground.

The sound of more sirens filled the air, adding to the cacophony. The pain, the roar of flames.

The Granada was long gone.

Three

BRITTANY, FRANCE:
Even in bright sunlight the church looked dark.

Its bell-tower thrust upwards into the air like an accusing finger, pointing at the blue sky where a blazing sun was suspended like some burnished ring. There was very little cloud in the sky and what there was appeared only as thin white wisps against the watery blue of the heavens. A light breeze stirred the long grass that grew all around the church and also on the hills that overlooked it.

15

Instead of being raised high on the hilltop, the building seemed to have been relegated to the valley floor, as if it were something to be hidden from view; to be shunned instead of exalted.

A house of God where few had been and which, it seemed, God himself had decided to pass by.

The church was old and the passing years had not been kind to it. The stonework was worn, cracked in places so deeply that the entire structure looked to be in danger of collapsing. The remnants of a weather-vane twisted on top of a bell-tower which had housed no bell for hundreds of years. Where it was no one knew and no one cared.

No one ever visited the church.

The nearest village was over five miles away, the church itself set back from the narrow road which wound through the Brittany countryside.

No birds nested in the eaves. No rats frequented the hollow shell of the building.

Neither man, animal or God, it seemed, was interested in the place.

Carl Bressard stood on the hilltop looking down at the church, feeling cold despite the warmth of the sun on his skin. He looked up briefly as if to remind himself that the burning orb was still there and, as he did, a thicker wisp of cloud drifted slowly in front of it, casting a momentary shadow over the valley and the church.

Phillipe Roulon saw the look on his companion's face and smiled.

'You're afraid,' he said scornfully, sticking his face close to his friend's.

Carl would have liked to tell Phillipe he wasn't, but if he had he would have been lying.

But, he thought, what was there to be afraid of? The church was empty and had been for years, far longer than the ten years he had been on the earth. Hundreds of years, his parents had told him, when he asked them about it. They'd told him it had not been used for more than two hundred years.

Then they had told him to keep away from it.

He had asked why, but they had told him not to question their word. He was to keep away from it. It was as simple as that.

Phillipe had been told the same thing by his mother. He had no father. In fact he could scarcely remember the man who had died when he was just five years old. The intervening six years had served to blur the vision of the man in much the same way as an old photo gradually fades.

He had seen the church himself before but, as now, only from a distance. As he looked down at it he felt the goose pimples rise on his flesh. But he couldn't back out. Not now. They would go in together.

Into this place which had been forbidden to them.

Perhaps to discover why it was forbidden.

The two boys looked at one another for a moment then set off down the hill, Carl almost tripping in the long grass as they ran. But, giggling now, they hurtled down the slope, their speed increased by the sharp decline in the land.

As they reached the valley floor they slowed their pace.

The church was less than two hundred yards away now.

It had seemed small from the hilltop but now, as they looked at it, the structure seemed massive. Its walls were dark and it looked as if it had been built not from individual pieces of stone but hewn from one single lump of rock. The monolithic edifice may well have been spewed up from the earth itself, disgorged by the land. Unwanted by nature as well as by God and man.

The two boys took faltering steps towards the church, their eyes fixed on it.

Carl could see that, where there had once been stained-glass windows, there were now only yawning holes in the rock. Wounds in the stone which had been given temporary scabs in the form of boarding, nailed haphazardly across the gaps with little care for appearance. The nails which held the boards in place were rusted and broken. Some of the boards were hanging free. One swung gently back and forth, pushed by the wind which now seemed to be much stronger.

The sun burned with continued radiance but both boys felt the chill grow more intense the closer they drew to the church.

Neither dared stop walking. Neither wanted to show his fear to the other.

Besides, what was there to fear in an empty stone building?

Carl tried to comfort himself with that thought but it did little to lessen the speed at which his heart was beating.

Another cloud passed close to the sun, throwing the valley into shadow once again. This time both boys froze until the warmth returned.

They moved closer.

The grass around the church was even longer and the boys had to lift their feet high to prevent themselves tripping over the green tendrils that seemed to grasp at their shoes.

A strong gust of wind sent the weather-vane

spinning. The dull creak of rusty metal cut through the silence like a blade. There was a narrow gravel path around the church, also overgrown with weeds and grass, but at least it made walking easier. The two boys, now moving side by side, made their way along the building towards the front of the church.

The huge double doors loomed over them. The wood was rotten in places, the metal bracing rusted and flaking like dry, scabrous skin. Two massive circular rings hung down from the doors. It was over one of these that Carl's hand hovered.

All he had to do was pull the door open and the church could be entered.

'Go on,' Phillipe said, his voice soft now, the bravado gone from it.

Carl touched the rusted ring and pulled.

The door wouldn't budge.

'I knew it would be locked,' he said, stepping back with relief.

'Try the other one.'

He shrugged, felt the colour draining from his cheeks.

'Come on,' snapped Phillipe.

'You open it,' Carl hissed, standing back, watching as his companion steadied himself and gripped the iron ring in both hands.

There was a muffled groan of protest from the rusted hinges as the door opened a fraction.

Phillipe let go of the metal ring as if it had suddenly become hot. He wiped his hands on his jeans, noticing how the rust stains looked like dried blood.

The door was open wide enough to allow them to slip inside.

Both boys stood looking up at the open door, waiting

19

for some kind of signal it seemed, to tell them what to do next.

They could see into the church now, or at least as far as the impenetrable blackness which filled it.

Phillipe was the first to move towards the door, urging Carl to follow him, snapping an insult when he hesitated.

The sun was still obscured by a cloud although Carl suspected the chill he felt was more the result of fear than from the absence of the warming rays. There was no turning back now. He had to enter. Enter this empty church which his parents had warned him not to go near.

Empty.

He tried to cling to the word, seeking comfort in it.

Empty.

He moved closer to the door.

Empty.

Both boys slipped inside.

It stank. Of neglect. Of decay. Of damp. As if the passing years had caused the very air itself to decay and rot so that each inhalation the boys took was rank. Carl felt as if he was swallowing some particularly vile medicine. He wanted to spit it out.

More than anything he wanted to be back out in the light again.

Shafts of sunlight pierced the gloom in places, poking through cracks in the boarding which covered the holes where the stained glass windows had been, casting enough light for the boys to see where they were going but not sufficient to illuminate the interior.

The watery shafts seemed incapable of penetrating such overwhelming blackness.

It was as if even the sunlight sought no access to this place.

The two boys moved slowly down the central aisle of the church, peering around them into the gloom.

Pews, unfrequented for years, were overturned on either side of them. Rotten. Broken. In places they had been piled up against the wall, like bonfires waiting to be lit.

As the boys walked they found that their footsteps were curiously muffled. Suffocated by the thick layer of dust and dirt which carpeted the church floor like a noxious rug. They left footprints in the dust.

They moved towards the chancel. Here, the air itself seemed to be black. It was more difficult to breathe.

Carl coughed, the sound echoing around the confines of the church before being swallowed by the silence and the gloom.

There was a doorway in the wall which separated the chancel from the nave.

The door was slightly ajar.

'Let's go now,' Carl said, his voice low.

Phillipe moved towards the doorway, which was momentarily illuminated by the intrusion of a shaft of sunlight forcing its way between two boards on a nearby window.

'The altar is through here,' Phillipe said. 'That's where it happened.'

'You go,' Carl said, finally unashamed of his fear.

He stood watching. He didn't care if Phillipe and all his friends called him a coward when he got back to the village.

He did not want to go through that door. Even if the church was empty.

Empty.

Perhaps just a quick look.

Empty.

Phillipe was about to push open the door.

Encouraged by his friend's bravery and curiosity, Carl moved alongside him and they prepared to pass through together.

The door suddenly swung open, a particularly bright shaft of sunlight slicing through the darkness.

And in that moment they both saw the figure.

The figure moving towards them.

Four

He had heard the sounds inside the church and wondered who had come to disturb his work.

Now Mark Channing watched as the two small boys ran screaming from the building.

He stood still for a moment, scratching his chin, wondering why his appearance had so terrified the visitors. Hadn't they noticed his car parked on the Western side of the church? Obviously not, he reasoned, watching as the two figures hurtled from the door and out into the sunshine beyond. The church was silent again, the way Channing liked it. He smiled to himself and turned back into the chancel, pushing the door shut behind him.

Two battery-powered lights illuminated the chancel itself, throwing out a cold white glow which cast everything into deep shadow. Channing poured himself a cup of tea from the thermos flask in his bag and stood sipping it, looking around him.

To his left the stairs which led up into the belfry

thrust upwards into even more cloying darkness. To his right, supporting the two lamps, was the altar. Or what had once been an altar.

It was a piece of flat stone, marble-smooth and relatively unmarked. He had spread several of his notepads out on it. A package of sandwiches and the remains of a half-eaten pork pie he'd consumed about half an hour ago also lay there, like offerings to some culinary deity.

The windows on either side of the chancel were, like the windows in the remainder of the church, now missing. Boarded up like those in the nave.

Channing's work on the church had revealed that the stonework around the windows had been chipped away, indicating that the windows had been removed. Actually physically taken from their place in the stone, frames and everything. Their absence was not the result of an act of vandalism but of careful, reasoned thought.

But thought which had its basis in superstition and fear.

Channing knew the church and the surrounding area well. He knew them by association. By what he'd read and what he'd written. This was the first time that he'd ever been inside the place, though.

He'd arrived in France five days earlier and he'd been working at the church for the last three. He didn't have to seek anyone's permission to enter the building. No one in any of the towns or villages close by seemed to care that he was going to be working there and Channing had been unable to discover who owned the land on which the old building stood. The church was one of the few remaining testaments to the fact that, at one time, this part of Brittany had been the domain of that province's richest inhabitant.

23

But that had been over four hundred years ago.

Channing had sought out the church for a number of reasons. He had been owed some holiday from his post as a senior lecturer at Balliol, so he'd taken the opportunity to come to Brittany for a break as much as anything else. But his main objective had been to see the church he'd previously only read about.

Its owner, however, was more familiar to him, having been the subject of a treatise he'd written two years earlier. It had been featured in a book produced by one of the country's top publishers. The book's title escaped him (although he remembered it as a flippant, under-researched tome; apart from his own piece, of course). The name of his subject didn't.

The former owner of this dank, deserted place had been Gilles de Rais.

During the fourteenth century, de Rais had been responsible for the ritual murders of over two hundred children, many of them in the church where Channing now stood. The church had merely been part of de Rais' vast estate called Machecoul. The man had been a hero in his native country; he was made a Marshal of France for his part in the fighting against the English during the Hundred Years War and, at the height of his power, he had been rumoured to be the richest nobleman in all of Europe. But his love of expensive living and a horde of parasitic advisers, all syphoning money from de Rais' coffers, had eventually turned him from rich man to bankrupt.

It was then that he had turned to alchemy.

Then that the killings had begun.

Channing sipped more tea and again glanced around the chancel, his attention focused on the boarded-up windows.

As he turned he saw something glinting dully; one of the rapier-like spears of sunlight, forcing its way into the gloom, bounced back off something to his left.

The historian put down his cup and crossed the chancel, careful not to obstruct the shaft of light.

Below a gap in the stone left by the removal of a window there was a tiny square of luminosity, as if something within the stone itself were burning.

Channing took a small chisel from the bag which lay beside the altar and began tapping at the area around the glowing square, gradually realizing that the sunlight was striking glass.

Coloured glass.

He frowned.

The stonework was old and brittle but still remarkably strong and resistant to the chisel, so much so that Channing hit it with the heel of his hand.

A crack appeared in the wall, running rapidly from one part of the stonework to another for a distance of about two feet. Several small pieces of rock fell to the floor, their sound amplified by the silence within the chancel.

Channing reached for the small mallet that lay on the altar and, steadying himself, used it to strike the chisel.

Another crack appeared in the stone.

A larger lump fell away.

He was breathing heavily now as he continued to chip away at the crumbling stonework.

More rock came away, falling at his feet.

Then finally he saw what the stone had hidden.

Channing swallowed hard, his eyes widening as he peered through the gloom, the sunlight which had forced its way into the chancel now fading.

25

Only the light from the battery lamps illuminated what he saw.

He licked his lips, his heart thudding hard against his ribs as he stared.

Only two words escaped him, muffled by the darkness and silence within the church, but low because of his own shock. He stared on, unblinking.

'Jesus Christ,' he murmured.

Five

Channing's hands were shaking as he twisted the key in the ignition.

The car roared into life at the first attempt and the historian jammed it into gear, guiding it over the gently undulating land towards the road that would lead him back to the nearby village of Machecoul. The sun was still high in the sky but more clouds were beginning to fill the heavens, some dark. Every now and then they would obscure the sun and the land would be momentarily cloaked in shadow. The wind which had been blowing all day seemed to have strengthened. As he drove, Channing saw that the trees by the roadside were swaying more violently with each gust.

He gripped the wheel tightly, aware that his palms were moist. Tiny droplets of perspiration had beaded on his forehead.

Not all of them the product of the warmth inside the car.

What he'd found in the church had surprised him.

No, he corrected himself, it had shocked him. Shaken him. Not merely because he had not been expecting it but also by its nature.

The vision of what he had left behind there was still strong in his mind, seared into his consciousness like some kind of brand.

He shuddered as he drove, angry with himself for his initial reaction, but unable to shake the feeling of shock nonetheless.

He administered a swift mental rebuke, angered that his own professionalism had been tested and found wanting. His self-control had cracked just like the stonework in the church.

He turned the car swiftly along the winding road, anxious to reach the village and the small inn where he was staying. Anxious to get to a phone.

There was a call he had to make.

He slowed his speed slightly as he reached the outskirts of Machecoul, guiding the car around the stalls which occupied the market place. The residents of the village were busy going about their business. Farmers had brought produce in from local farms to sell and, as he parked the car outside the inn, Channing could hear voices filtering through the air, arguing good-naturedly, bartering, laughing.

But that scene of rural life was not for him. He had more important things on his mind.

He scuttled into the small, white-painted inn, noticing how cool it felt compared to outside. The plump woman who ran the place gave him the key to his room and was about to ask him if he was all right when he disappeared in the direction of the stairs that led up to his bedroom.

There were only about ten rooms let to guests and

27

most of those, at the moment, were empty.

Channing let himself in, crossed straight to the phone beside his bed and picked up the receiver.

He dialled, cursing under his breath when he realized he'd forgotten the international code for England. He dialled again. The international code, then the code for London, then the number he required.

His hand was shaking slightly.

He held the receiver to his ear, listening to the assortment of pops, crackles and hisses that ran down the line as his number was connected. At the far end the phone was ringing.

And ringing.

'Come on,' he murmured, impatiently.

And ringing.

'Hello,' a feminine voice began.

'Hello Cath,' he said breathlessly.

The other voice continued.

'This is Catherine Roberts. I'm afraid there's no one here at the moment …'

'Shit,' rasped Channing, slamming the phone down. Bloody answering machine. He waited a second then dialled again and waited.

The same metallic voice greeted him and he was about to replace the receiver a second time when he heard a buzz as the machine was switched off. 'Hello,' the voice repeated.

'Cath, is that you?' he said.

'Yes, who's that?' the woman on the other end asked.

'It's Mark Channing. I didn't want to talk to that bloody machine.'

'I just walked through the door,' she explained. 'I thought you were in Brittany.'

'I am. Listen to me, Cath. I've been to the church at

Machecoul,' he told her, his voice low, almost breathless. 'There's something there. You have to see it.'

'What is it?' she wanted to know.

'When can you fly out?'

'Mark, for God's sake,' she began, almost laughing. 'I can't just drop everything.'

'You have to,' he insisted, and she was aware of the anxiety in his voice. 'This is important. It's in your field.'

'My field?' she said vaguely, puzzled by his urgency.

'You're an art historian, for Christ's sake,' he snarled, as if he needed to remind her of her profession. 'A medievalist. I need you to look at what I've found. I need your help.'

Six

COUNTY CORK, THE REPUBLIC OF IRELAND:
The line of cocaine seemed almost phosphorescent in the dimly-lit bedroom.

Laura Callahan, her naked body covered by a thin sheen of perspiration, swept the long brown hair from her face and knelt beside the table where the coke was waiting. Two razor-blades lay close by.

She pressed the first two fingers of her right hand against her right nostril and carefully, lovingly pushed the tip of her nose into the line, smiling broadly as she caught the first few grains of powder. Laura inhaled, sliding over the table as she drew the fine white powder into her nostril. She writhed, her eyes closed in ecstasy, feeling the coldness growing inside her nostril as she took in more and more of the coke. As she slithered over the polished wood she looked down and saw her reflection. The sight pleased her.

Her body was firm, her breasts small but the nipples hard. She paused for a moment to admire her reflection. The flat stomach, the smooth hips and the tiny triangle of dark hair between her legs. She allowed one finger to stir the tightly-curled pubic hair, teasing herself for a second before returning to the line of cocaine.

She snorted the remainder then rolled off the table, her breath coming in gasps.

As she rolled over she pressed her legs tightly together and felt moisture beading on her upper thighs. She sat up, one finger stirring the swollen outer lips of her vagina, tracing a pattern over the warm wet flesh until she reached the hardened nub of her clitoris.

She gasped as she stroked it.

Cocaine flecked her nose and her upper lip and she flicked her tongue out to remove it, feeling the same momentary numbness in her mouth as she did in her nose. She giggled, then crawled across towards the bed, towards the man who lay there waiting for her.

He too was naked, his erection throbbing against his stomach as he lay back, a drink cradled in one of his large hands.

She kissed his right foot as she pulled up onto the bed. Then, moving higher, she kissed his shins, his knees, his thighs. Only here she paused, allowing her tongue to dart out and taste the flesh of his leg. She bit it gently then licked, leaving a trail of saliva as she moved closer to his groin.

David Callahan watched, an amused smile on his face. He reached down and slowly entwined some of her long hair around his hand, gripping it, pulling her up higher until her mouth was in line with his penis.

He grinned as she kissed the bulbous head, allowing her tongue to creep into the narrow eye of the glans, licking away a dribble of clear fluid.

As she sat up she saw the lines of coke on his body.

One ran from each of his shoulders down as far as his groin.

She looked at him and laughed, kissing his chest, careful not to disturb the precious white powder. Then, beginning with the line at his left shoulder, she snorted her way down his body until the musky smell of his pubic hair, already matted with her own secretions from earlier on, mingled with the coke.

She laid her head on his stomach this time, careful not to displace the other line with her hair. Then, slowly, she moved her head forward, her lips enveloping his penis, her tongue slithering around the shaft. With one hand she began to massage his swollen testicles, allowing her free hand to reach back between her own legs, to stir the wetness there.

She felt other fingers alongside her own and then Callahan himself was pushing first his index finger then his middle finger into her dripping cleft, his thumb rubbing her clitoris, making her moan softly as she continued to suck his erection.

She sat up, his fingers still inside her, anxious to reach the second line of cocaine.

Laura took it into her other nostril this time, breathing it in as she slid down once more towards Callahan's groin. This time, she took his penis into her mouth and kept it there. Sucking and kissing as he

31

pushed his fingers into her with increasing speed, smiling as he felt the liquid pleasure covering the probing digits.

She stroked his thighs and rubbed his scrotum, aware that he, like she herself, was reaching a climax. Laura prepared herself for his ejaculation, clamping her mouth more firmly onto his throbbing organ as she felt his penis jerk, heard him grunt with pleasure.

And then her mouth was flooded with the oily, white fluid, gouts of it shooting into her throat. She swallowed as fast as she could until her mouth was full and some of the sticky liquid dribbled from the sides of it.

She felt her own orgasm surge through her and opened her mouth to gasp her pleasure as his fingers rammed deeper into her and she too spilled her ecstacy onto his hand.

Callahan gradually withdrew his fingers from her and held them before her.

She sucked at them, licking the slicks of fluid, sucking his fingertips like a hungry child would suck a nipple.

She tasted herself. She tasted his emission on her tongue.

They laughed loudly as they embraced, both coated in sweat from their pleasure. Then they both looked towards the bottom of the bed and grinned.

The image disappeared instantly as David Callahan pressed the 'Stop' button on the video.

Lying beside him on the huge bed, Laura Callahan took a sip of Jack Daniels and smiled. She moved closer to her husband, one hand reaching for his stiffening penis.

'You were great,' said Callahan, smiling. 'You should get an Oscar.'

'I don't want an Oscar,' she purred, nuzzling his neck. 'I want you.' She closed her hand around his erection.

Callahan thrust into her hard and she raised her legs, allowing him deeper penetration, finally locking her ankles behind his back as his movements became more forceful.

The video camera at the bottom of the bed regarded them impassively this time, their lovemaking reflected in its single glass eye.

Seven

In the silence of the bedroom he could hear her breathing.

There was a slightly nasal quality to Laura's exhalations, a product of more than five years on cocaine.

Callahan didn't know exactly what it did to the nasal passages. He didn't really care. She enjoyed it. Who was *he* to deny her pleasure?

He sat up in bed, careful not to disturb his wife. For long moments he watched her sleeping: the steady rise and fall of her chest, the gentle pulse in her throat. Then, carefully, he swung himself out of bed, pulled on his bathrobe and padded across the bedroom towards the bathroom. Once inside he flicked on the light, wincing as the fluorescents buzzed into life. Callahan turned on the tap, scooped some water into his mouth and smoothed his hand through his short dark hair. He stood before the mirror gazing at his reflection, pleased with what he saw.

He was thirty-six, four years older than his wife, and his body was still lean and muscular. He opened the bathrobe to inspect his pectoral muscles. He worked out every morning in the small gym which he'd had built into the house when they'd first bought it two years ago. The house and the fifteen acres of land which went with it had been relatively cheap, certainly to a man of Callahan's means. He wasn't sure exactly how many million he was worth. He didn't think that much about money. He had more than he'd ever need so there wasn't the necessity to think about it. Only those who didn't have enough were obsessed with the stuff, he thought, amused by his own philosophy.

He splashed more water onto his face, wiping the excess moisture away with the sleeve of his bathrobe. Then he tugged on the string and the bathroom was plunged into darkness again.

Callahan moved back into the bedroom, glancing across at Laura.

She had rolled onto her side now, her legs drawn up to her chest.

Callahan stood gazing at her for a moment then crossed to the window.

Their bedroom was at the front of the house and, with the aid of the large spotlights which blazed from the roof, Callahan could see about twenty or thirty yards down the wide driveway which approached the massive house.

Visible through the gloom were the stables which housed half a dozen horses. To the right of them stood a couple of barns. Another gap of ten yards or so and the west wing of the house was visible.

34

The whole building was white-washed, in places its walls covered by ivy that grew so densely the stonework was almost totally obscured by the parasitic plant. Elsewhere dozens of windows reflected the night like scores of blind eyes.

All except one.

Callahan gazed out over the driveway in front of the house, peering close to the glass of the window to get a better view.

A light came on in one of the downstairs rooms.

He looked at his watch, the hands glowing sickly green in the darkness.

3.32 a.m.

Surely none of the staff would be up at this time of the morning.

The light went off again and Callahan relaxed for a moment.

He rubbed his eyes, as if he'd just woken.

The light came on again.

Went off.

Came on.

Callahan turned and headed for the bed, stopping short, pulling open the drawer of the cabinet beside it.

From the top drawer he pulled out a Smith and Wesson .38.

He flipped out the cylinder, checking that the weapon was full, then, satisfied that it was, he crossed back to the window and looked out.

The light was still on in the downstairs room.

Callahan gripped the revolver in his fist. Glancing back at Laura, he headed for the bedroom door.

Eight

The silence inside the house was almost oppressive, the only sounds coming from Callahan himself as he moved quickly but quietly across the vast landing towards the head of the stairs.

As he reached the balustrade he stopped and peered over, looking down into the hallway. Without lights it was like looking into a well. He thought about flicking on the switch at the top of the stairs, flooding the flight of steps and the hall beneath with bright light, and his finger hovered for a moment before he decided against that course of action. Instead he gripped the .38 more tightly and began to descend.

The fourth step creaked loudly in the silence and Callahan muttered something under his breath, pausing for a moment in the stillness.

The room where he'd seen the light, however, was well away from the stairs. Even if there were anyone in there it was unlikely they'd heard the groaning stair.

He pressed on, taking the steps more quickly now, anxious to reach the bottom.

Could it be an intruder, he wondered?

That possibility seemed unlikely.

The house itself was more than fifteen miles from the nearest village, the grounds protected by a stone wall twelve feet high.

Any intruder met a sophisticated alarm system wired to every door and window inside the house itself and there was also the distinct possibility that they might disturb one of the members of staff.

If there was an intruder in the house then they were both determined *and* expert.

Unless it wasn't a burglar.

Callahan paused a moment longer, feeling the sweat on his palms. He let go of the revolver and wiped both hands on his bathrobe before seizing the gun once more.

Not a burglar.

Maybe the intruder didn't want his money or his valuables.

Maybe they wanted *him.*

Callahan had made enough enemies in his time, on both sides of the law and on both sides of the Irish sea. He knew there were men who, even now, would pay a great deal of money to see him dead.

That was one of the reasons he'd been forced to leave London. The situation there had simply become too dangerous for him. He'd had too much to lose, his life not being the least.

He gripped the pistol tighter and moved out of the hall towards the door on his right.

It led through into a long corridor flanked on either side by more closed doors.

Callahan paused beside the door, then swiftly turned the knob and stepped through.

The room where he'd seen the light was ahead of him, around a bend in the corridor.

On the walls on both sides paintings hung. here a Matisse, there a Dali. Further down there was a Goya. They were all originals. All priceless now.

Callahan moved slowly down the corridor, his footsteps muffled by the thick carpet. He was aware of his own low breathing as he moved further towards the bend.

As he reached it he stopped again, a single bead of perspiration squeezing itself onto his forehead.

There were more light switches at hand but he resisted the temptation to flick them on. He saw the thin band of light beneath the door directly in front of him.

Callahan approached slowly, his eyes on the thin strip of luminosity.

The light went out.

He froze.

Had whoever was inside heard him?

The brightness returned.

Callahan gritted his teeth, pulled the .38 from his pocket and moved towards the door again, his hand hovering over the knob.

There was no sound from inside.

Except ...

What the hell was that noise?

He stood close to the door, listening, a frown creasing his brow.

The light went off once more.

Callahan actually had his hand on the handle now, turning it slowly, praying to a God he didn't believe in that it wouldn't squeak.

'Right, you bastard,' he whispered under his breath.

He threw the door open, the pistol raised before him.

As he did the light came flickering on and, as it did, he heard the noise again.

A buzzing, puttering sound.

It came from above him.

From the fluorescent light which was flickering on and off.

It was faulty. The bloody light was faulty.

Callahan chuckled, shook his head and exhaled deeply, annoyed with himself for having allowed fear to take such a hold on him. Christ, what the imagination could do to you! But there was also relief in his exhalation.

Relief that there had been no one in the room.

He looked at the .38 in his hand and slipped it back into his pocket. No one this time, but next time who could tell? He wondered how much longer he would have to wait.

Callahan flicked off the faulty light, making a mental note to get one of the staff to fix it in the morning. He turned and headed back down the corridor, past the Matisse and the Dali and the Goya and the sculptures. Past all the possessions that testified to the magnitude of his wealth.

As he closed the door he could not help but glance over his shoulder, as if this had been some kind of warning. A portent.

He knew they would come eventually.

But when they did, he'd be ready for them.

Nine

The house in Porten Road, Hammersmith was unremarkable; a simple terraced place badly in need of some exterior decoration.

Sean Doyle sat in the Datsun, one foot up on the dashboard, alternately glancing out of the window and flicking at the laces that hung from his baseball boots.

Doyle noticed how some of the houses, formerly council, had been bought by their occupants. Many sported the mock-stone frontages that seemed the mark of new owner-occupiers. All taking advantage of the Government's wonderful offer to own the houses they'd lived in since rent was ten shillings a week, thought Doyle, gazing at the rows of houses.

Lights burned in many front windows, promising warmth beyond their closed curtains.

It wasn't too warm inside the car and Doyle turned up the heating, massaging his left leg as he felt a twinge of cramp in his calf. He lowered his leg, raising his right instead, propping that against the dashboard.

He flicked on the radio, tired of the silence.

Doyle twisted the frequency dial but found only vacuous pop music, the same sanitized crap on every station, it seemed. There was a play on Radio Four but he skipped by that and finally found the tail end of a Black Sabbath track, but the static was so bad he decided to turn the set off again.

Doyle was bored. He'd been sitting in the car for nearly two hours already. His back ached, his arse ached and his head was beginning to ache. He fumbled in the glove compartment for the remains of a Mars Bar he'd started devouring earlier. He hadn't eaten for over six hours, apart from the few mouthfuls of chocolate. At two-thirty that afternoon he'd bought a hamburger but now his stomach was growling loudly. He patted it in a gesture of placation, then yawned and tried to stretch in the confines of the car, hearing his shoulders and elbows crack.

He coughed and looked around once more, catching sight of his own reflection in the rear-view mirror. He ran both hands through his shoulder-length brown hair. His eyes looked sunken, as if someone had coloured in the area beneath his lower lids with dark ink. His haggard look was negated somewhat, however, by the gleam of his dark grey eyes. They seemed to glow in the dull light of the street lamp, darting back and forth with an alertness and energy that seemed to have deserted the rest of his body.

He rubbed his hands together and stuck them in the pockets of his leather jacket, slumping back in his seat and gazing out into the street. He could feel the ache beginning to creep up from the small of his back. He fidgeted, trying to make himself comfortable. Thirty years old and you're a fucking wreck, he told himself, a slight smile creasing his lips.

Unlike most of the other houses in Porten Road, no light burned in the window of Number 22.

In fact, no light burned anywhere in the place. Not that he could see, anyway. He knew, however, that there were people inside. He'd seen three enter in the last thirty minutes. The first had arrived in a battered old Capri which he'd parked across the street from where Doyle now sat. He'd let himself in by the front door, glancing furtively around before opening it.

The other two had arrived together about ten minutes ago.

Doyle checked his watch.

8.36 p.m.

On this side of the road a man was walking his dog, trying to keep the wretched animal under control as it jerked and pulled on the end of the lead. Doyle smiled to himself as the man swore at the Alsatian which, it seemed, had decided to cross the street, tugging its reluctant owner with it. He watched them in the rear-view mirror and caught sight of another man.

41

The newcomer was short and stocky, hands tucked deep into the pockets of an overcoat. He glanced at the Alsatian, quickening his pace when it seemed to be making for *him*.

Doyle saw the man turn into the short pathway that led to the door of Number 22. He walked up to the door and knocked once. The door was opened a fraction and the man entered.

Quite a gathering, Doyle thought, checking his watch again.

Another five minutes.

He yawned and rubbed his eyes, blinking myopically through the gloom.

'Panther One, come in.'

The voice sounded loud in the confines of the car, despite the fact that there was a newspaper laid over the two-way radio.

'Panther One, do you read me, over?'

Doyle picked up the newspaper, glancing again at the photo of the topless model. Her name was Tina and she was a hairdresser; the caption said, 'Guaranteed to make your hair curl.' Doyle grinned and tossed the paper onto the back seat.

'Panther One, for Christ's sake ...'

He picked up the two-way.

'Panther One. Don't have a fit, I can hear you,' Doyle said quietly, eyes still scanning the street ahead of him.

'Then why didn't you answer?' the metallic voice demanded.

'I did answer. I'm speaking to you now. What the fuck do you want?'

'We're in position.'

'Good for you,' said Doyle disinterestedly, eyes still roving.

42

'Porten Road, Ceylon Road and Milson Road are all closed off,' the voice told him.

Doyle didn't answer. He'd spotted another man approaching the front door of Number 22.

'Doyle, I said ...'

'I heard what you said. Stand by.' Still gripping the two-way, Doyle watched as the man advanced towards the door and knocked twice. He bounced up and down on the balls of his feet as he waited for it to be opened. When it finally was, he walked in, disappearing from view. Doyle held on to the two-way with his left hand; with his right he reached inside his jacket.

The rubber grips of the CZ-75 automatic brushed against his finger-tips as he felt the shoulder holster.

In another holster, worn around his waist, hidden by his leather jacket, he carried a much more formidable weapon. The .44 Bulldog, despite its small size, could put a hole in a wall at two hundred yards.

'You and your men ready?' Doyle asked, eyes now fixed on the front door of Number 22.

'I told you we're in position,' the voice replied irritably.

'Well, tell them to stay out of my fucking way. Let's go. It's party time.'

Ten

As Doyle swung himself out of the car he saw other men running towards Number 22.

Some were in uniform.

43

Doyle made it to the door first, vaulting the gate as if there were some kind of prize for reaching the house ahead of his colleagues. He didn't slow his pace, merely ran at the door and launched himself at it, slamming against the wood, which creaked protestingly. He took a step back and drove a powerful kick against the lock, grinning when the door crashed back on its hinges. He dashed into the hallway, followed by two of the uniformed men.

The place smelt of damp, neglect and something more pungent which Doyle recognised as urine. But smells didn't bother him. He heard raised voices from a room to his left and he turned.

'Upstairs,' came a shout from behind him.

Two of the uniformed constables thundered up the stairs. Doyle kicked the door ahead of him open, the CZ now gripped in his fist. He stepped away from the door, heard more shouts from inside.

From the rear of the house there was the sound of breaking glass. Curses.

He ducked into what was supposed to be the sitting room. There was a battered old sofa, the stuffing spilling out of one arm. Two wooden chairs. Nothing else. The floor was bare board.

There were three men inside the room and Doyle levelled his pistol at the closest one.

The man immediately raised his hands in surrender, his face losing its colour as if the blood had been sucked from his cheeks.

Doyle heard more shouts coming from the rear of the house then, suddenly, there was the ear-splitting roar of a gun.

He glanced to his right and, in that split second, one of the men facing him dashed towards the window.

He hit the glass with the force of a steam-hammer, crashing through the dirtied panes, shattering the wooden slats and sending crystal shards flying into the air. He hit the ground, rolled over once and ran for the road.

'Watch them,' shouted Doyle and hurtled after the fleeing man. He vaulted the fence and sped after the escaping figure, who glanced over his shoulder to see his pursuer gaining.

Up and down Porten Road curtains were being drawn to one side as the commotion roused neighbours. Curious faces peered out into the night and saw the chase unfolding before them.

The man Doyle was pursuing was several years younger, but he had not counted on the other man's fitness. He ran round a car and into the street. Doyle merely leapt up onto the bonnet then launched himself at his foe, missing him by inches. He rolled over and got to his feet, seeing the other man, dressed in a blue jacket and jeans, heading across the street towards a passageway between two houses.

Doyle followed as the man battered his way through a wooden gate at the head of the passage.

Blue-jacket ran on, spinning to his right, into the garden at the rear of the house. There was a high fence partitioning the back yards and Blue-jacket began scaling it. Doyle skidded around the corner in time to see the other man scrambling over the fence. Doyle holstered his pistol, allowing himself the use of both hands, threw himself at the partition and clambered up and over it. He dropped down beside a fish pond as he continued his pursuit.

A hedge was the next obstacle and Blue-jacket leapt it easily.

Doyle followed, his eyes never leaving his quarry, homed in on the fleeing man as if they were locked on by radar.

The man looked back, surprised to see Doyle still in pursuit. He was no more than ten yards away now and Blue-jacket could feel his own breath rasping in his throat as he desperately sought some way back into the road, some passageway.

If only he could get to the car.

Ahead of him there was another fence and a greenhouse, and beyond that a much taller wall. He leapt the fence, almost falling as he landed.

Doyle saw the obstacles too but he slowed his pace.

There was no way his quarry was going to get over the wall. This was the end of the road, he thought, grinning.

He pulled the CZ from its holster and stood still.

'Stand still,' he roared, settling himself, drawing a bead on his foe.

Blue-jacket spun round, saw the gun and slowed his pace slightly.

'Fuck you,' he bellowed back, stepping slowly towards the greenhouse, not really knowing where he was going but knowing that the Englishman would not fire.

His eyes widened in a mixture of shock and terror as he realized he was wrong.

Doyle fired twice.

The first bullet hit the man in the chest, the second in the throat.

The impact lifted him off his feet and his body catapulted several feet backwards, as if punched by an invisible fist. He crashed into the greenhouse, which promptly collapsed around him, showering him with

46

huge fragments of glass. The noise was deafening as the crystal shards rained down around him, cutting his flesh. Blood from the lacerations mingled with the crimson fluid already spurting from the two bullet wounds.

Doyle walked across to the body and looked down at it, kicking one of the man's outstretched legs. He noticed that the body was lying on some tomato plants, and blood had spattered the fruit.

Doyle, ignoring the smell which rose from the corpse, pulled a tomato free and began chewing on it, looking down at the dead man.

The back doors of the house opened and a man emerged. He looked at the scene of carnage and shouted something Doyle didn't catch. Then, as the man repeated it, he heard the words more clearly.

'Call the law,' the man shouted to someone inside the house.

Doyle took another bite from the tomato, wiping the juice from his chin.

'No need,' he said, holstering the CZ. 'I *am* the law.'

Eleven

The blue lights of the ambulance turned in silence, bathing the area in a dull glow. Without its siren the vehicle seemed curiously serene. Doyle leant against the bonnet of his car, smoking. The tableau before him looked like a film to which someone had forgotten to add the sound.

There were policemen, uniformed and plain-clothes,

milling about in the road, some gathered around in groups, others talking to the occupants of other houses. Many were standing on their front doorsteps peering out at the activity. Two police cars were parked outside Number 22. Ten minutes earlier a van had arrived and the four remaining occupants had been bundled inside and driven off. The battered Capri had also been towed away by a police pick-up truck. Doyle sucked gently on his cigarette and watched the other men scuttle to and fro, his attention finally drawn to some movement off to his left.

Two ambulancemen emerged from the passageway between the two houses carrying the body of the man Doyle had shot.

His body was covered by a blanket.

A tall, slightly overweight policeman walked alongside the stretcher. He glared at Doyle as he passed but the younger man merely took a final drag on his cigarette and ground it out beneath his foot. He wandered across towards the rear of the ambulance, where the body was being lifted in.

As the men were about to lay it down inside the vehicle Doyle reached for the blanket, pulling it back.

He looked down at the waxen features, the eyes still open and staring, fixing Doyle in a blank accusatory stare.

'Any I.D. on him?' Doyle wanted to know, flipping the blanket back over the dead man.

'Why did you kill him?'

The question came from the tall man standing beside him. Chief Inspector Ian Austin drew in an angry breath and puffed out his considerable chest. He was taller than Doyle and looking down on the younger man suited him.

'Is it important?' asked Doyle matter-of-factly.

'Yes, it's important,' hissed Austin through gritted teeth. 'He was unarmed, for God's sake!'

'I didn't know that at the time.'

'Would it have made any difference if you had?'

'No. I'd still have shot him.'

Doyle dug in the pocket of his jacket for his cigarettes, pulled one out and lit it, flicking the match into the road. He stepped back as the ambulance doors were closed.

'So what *was* his name?' he asked.

'Galbraith. Martin Galbraith,' said Austin wearily. He walked with Doyle as the younger man headed for his car.

'Any form?'

'Suspected arms dealing, robbery. He did a couple of years inside, over here *and* in Ireland,' said Austin.

Doyle nodded and drew on his cigarette.

'What about the rest of the boys?' he said, slipping into an Irish accent.

'They've been taken to a police station for questioning,' Austin told him.

'Which one?'

'That's none of your business, Doyle. This is *our* game now,' said the policeman irritably.

'Bollocks,' snapped the younger man. 'Which nick have they been taken to? I want to speak to them.'

'I told you, it's *our* province. This was a joint operation between the anti-terrorist squad and the flying squad. It has nothing to do with you or your department. You were here tonight to observe and advise. Not to shoot the bloody suspects.'

'You're lucky I only killed one,' Doyle told him. 'You don't know how to handle them, Austin.'

'And I suppose shooting them is the answer?'

'It's *my* fucking answer,' snapped Doyle. 'Now, which nick have they been taken to?'

'Why do you need to know? So you can torture information out of them? You'll need official clearance before you interrogate prisoners of this nature.'

'I've got clearance. Call my superiors if you don't believe me. Why do you think I *was* here tonight? I'll tell you. Because no one trusted you and *your* boys to do this job without fucking it up.' Doyle pulled open the door of his car. 'Now, if you won't tell me where they've been taken, I'm sure someone else will.' He slid behind the wheel, winding his window down, looking up at Austin. 'What did they find in the house, anyway?' He hooked a thumb over his shoulder in the direction of Number 22. 'And don't tell me *that*'s none of my business.'

Austin regarded the younger man angrily for a moment, the knot of muscles at the side of his jaw throbbing.

'Two AK-47's, three thousand rounds of ammunition and some Semtex,' he said.

'How much?'

'About seventy pounds.'

Doyle nodded.

'Enough to make half a dozen bombs. Enough to kill Christ knows how many people.' He smiled humourlessly. 'And you moan because I shot one of the fuckers.' Doyle started his car, stepping on the accelerator, allowing the engine to roar for a moment. 'I'm going home to change. I'll probably see you later.' He let off the handbrake. 'Just for a little chat with our Irish friends.' Doyle winked at the Chief Inspector and guided his car away from the kerb, banging his hooter as two men blocked his path. They jumped aside hastily as he drove by.

Austin stood and watched the Datsun disappear around a corner. He was clenching and unclenching his large fists, his eyes fixed on the path taken by Doyle.

'Bastard,' he murmured under his breath.

Preparation

The man had been hanged three days earlier.

His body dangled from the rope, twisting gently in the breeze. The wood of the gallows creaked mournfully, offering a final lament.

It was difficult to tell his age; most of his features were gone.

The crows had done their work thoroughly.

The eyes had been taken first, devoured hungrily by the carrion birds.

Flies had feasted on the open wounds, laying eggs in the lacerations so that now portions of the face seemed to move. As if muscles were still twitching in that dead visage.

Maggots writhed beneath the flaps of skin, eating their way free.

One eye-socket was bulging with them; the wriggling forms spilled down a torn cheek like living, parasitic tears.

The body continued to turn slowly as the night breeze stiffened, hauling the clouds around the moon like a cloak, bringing an even greater darkness over the countryside.

The two men who stood looking up at the dangling corpse did so with indifference.

51

They didn't know the man's name, they didn't know why he'd been hung. They didn't care.

The first was a tall, slender individual with bony fingers which he kept shuffling together as if they were playing cards. His companion was also tall but more stoutly built.

He was the one who carried the knife.

The moon disappeared behind another bank of cloud and the darkness returned.

The second man stepped towards the corpse, noticing, at last, how low to the ground the dead man's legs were. His feet were only a foot or so clear. Indeed, whoever had tied the knot around the man's neck had been no expert. The second man glanced at the dangling body more closely, noticing how the neck was stretched. The flesh was taut over the withering muscles.

The man had been choked to death, denied the mercy of a broken neck.

The second man was aware too of the stench that came from the body. The smell of putrefying flesh.

The hanged man's clothes had been taken so there was nothing to contain the odour. He wrinkled his nose as he moved closer to the corpse, his gaze resting for a second on the ravaged, shrunken genitals.

Probably the crows again, he thought. The dead man's scrotum had been torn open, most likely by a powerful beak. The testicles had been devoured, the penis savaged.

The feet of the corpse bore several bad cuts, too. Probably foxes or badgers, unable to reach the rotting carcass, had taken bites from the most accessible part. Three toes were missing.

The man seemed to tire of his appraisal of the dangling body and, instead, set to work. He seized the left arm in one powerful hand. Then, with the other, he pressed the knife against the wrist.

52

The dead man's skin felt soft and pliant and he found it relatively easy to cut.

Until he reached the bone.

The knife blade grated against the radius and the ulna but the man persevered, smiling when he heard a dull crack. He continued with the knife, using a sawing action until finally, tugging on the appendage simultaneously, he severed the hand.

He held it up like some kind of trophy and walked back towards the first man, who had watched the whole episode unmoved.

Now he reached inside his jacket and took out a small wooden box about six inches by eight. He flipped it open and watched as his companion laid the hand inside. Then, satisfied, both men walked across to the horses that were tethered nearby, swung themselves into the saddle and rode off.

The hanged man twisted gently in the breeze.

Twelve

The green light was flashing on the answering machine when Doyle walked in.

He flicked on a light as he walked into the flat, crossed to the machine and pressed the button marked 'Incoming Messages'. As he waited for the machine to rewind he pulled off his leather jacket and tossed it onto the sofa, walking across the sitting room of the flat towards the hi-fi.

The first message began to play back.

'Is that Carol …? Is Carol there …? …' Then silence and a click.

Wrong number.

'Prat,' murmured Doyle, annoyed at the anonymous caller. There was a beep then the second message began.

'Sean, this is Angela. Angela O'Neal. I hope you remember me.' A chuckle. 'I hope you enjoyed the other night as much as I did.'

Doyle turned and headed back to the answering machine.

'I'm sure I gave you my number, but in case you've forgotten it I'll give it to you again so you can call me. The number …'

Doyle switched off the machine, turned and headed back to the hi-fi. He switched it on, the tape inside the machine turning immediately.

'… *In a hotel room I remember the way, we'd do what we do* …'

Doyle passed through into the kitchen, pulling off the shoulder holster as he did so.

'*Too long, without your touch, too long without your love* …'

The singer roared on from the sitting room as Doyle pulled a pint of milk from the fridge, removed the top and swallowed great gulps. He wiped his mouth with the back of his hand, took a glass from the draining board, blew in it to remove some dust, and filled it with the white fluid. He carried it back through into the sitting-room, putting the glass down for a moment as he undid the holster around his waist. He dropped the Charter Arms .44 onto the sofa alongside the CZ, glancing down at the two weapons for a moment before walking on through into the narrow corridor which led to the bedroom and bathroom.

Inside the bathroom Doyle turned on the shower, testing the water temperature with his hand as it spurted from the head. He sat down on the stool in the bathroom and pulled off his baseball boots and socks. Then he stood up, looking at himself in the mirror opposite. He pulled off his T-shirt.

His torso was a patchwork of scars, some running from his shoulder to his navel, others shorter, sometimes deeper, cutting across his chest and stomach. He turned, glancing at the back where there were more. One in particular ran from his left scapula, across his back, then diagonally down to his lumbar region.

It was that wound which had almost killed him.

Doyle turned round once more, running the tip of his index finger over a particularly deep scar which had bisected his right pectoral muscle. There was no nipple there either, just a ragged hole which looked dark in the brightness of the fluorescent light above.

He pulled off his jeans and tossed them to one side.

There were more scars on his legs and buttocks. Even his left shin was heavily marked, the scars looking white beneath the hair on his legs.

He looked like a road-map.

He accepted the scars now. In the beginning it had been difficult. Many times, especially when he'd first seen the extent of his injuries, he'd felt like weeping, not in self-pity but at the damage which had been wrought on his frame. He was grateful that his face had escaped relatively unscathed, but for a deep scar which ran horizontally from the corner of his left eye to his jaw. He had been lucky. His torso and legs had borne the worst of the damage.

Doyle stood staring at his body for long moments,

memories flooding back into his mind, still uncomfortably fresh even after five years.

The man he'd been after had been responsible for three murders. All politicians. He'd been one of the IRA's top hit men and it had taken Doyle more than three months to pin the bastard down. Weeks of trekking round Londonderry and Belfast looking and listening for any sight or sound of his prey until, finally, he'd found the man. McNamara. He could still remember him. Doyle had been given orders to bring the man in alive and that was precisely what he'd been trying to do when McNamara realized that he'd been cornered. The chase had taken them through the Creggan and Bogside estates but, by the time they reached the Craigavon bridge, McNamara had taken his fill of being chased by this maniac Englishman.

He'd been carrying a couple of pounds of explosive on him, possibly for an impending job. He'd jumped into a car on the bridge and, as Doyle had drawn closer to him, gun already aimed at the fugitive, McNamara had detonated the explosive he'd been carrying.

The car had been blown to pieces and the Irishman with it. Two passers-by had been killed by the flying pieces of pulverized car, many injured.

Doyle amongst them.

He could still remember lying on the bridge, unable to move, his body feeling as if it were on fire, yet being perfectly able to take in every detail of what was going on around him.

A small child had peered down at him, at the blood which he could feel running from his own wounds, which he could see puddling around him. Most ridiculous of all, there had been an empty cigarette packet lying in the gutter beside him, and all Doyle could seem to focus on were the words: SMOKING CAN SERIOUSLY DAMAGE YOUR HEALTH. *But not as much as gelignite*, he said to himself, and that had been his last thought before passing out.

He'd woken three days later in hospital (in an army hospital, he'd later learned) and he'd suffered as much pain then as he'd ever thought imaginable.

One lung had been punctured by a piece of sharp metal; fragments of it, still lodged in his back, were waiting to be removed. His left kidney had been badly damaged, perhaps irreparably, the doctors had thought at the time. Another piece of burning steel had hamstrung him. Another had torn away most of the flesh on his left quadricep and also shattered his femur in two places.

Eight ribs had been broken, two smashed beyond saving. A portion of one had been taken from inside the punctured lung. He remembered someone telling him he'd lost over thirty pints of blood. The right scapula, the left clavicle, the ulna and radius of his left arm had all been broken.

Apart from a hairline fracture of his right sphenoid bone and the gash on the left hand side of his face, his head was unmarked.

A doctor told him he'd been lucky.

With most of the bones in his body broken and more pain than he'd thought it possible to endure, Doyle had been somewhat at odds with that particular diagnosis. Let someone blow the fuck out of you, then see if *you* feel lucky, he'd thought, gazing up at the doctor through eyes clouded with pain and morphine.

Still, he'd been told, he was out of action, out of danger now. All he had to do was get well. It was a miracle he'd survived. Somebody up there liked him.

They'd rolled out the clichés for him.

Somebody liked him, did they? Well, if it was God, he had one hell of a sense of humour.

Doyle took one last look at his ravaged body in the bathroom mirror and stepped into the shower, enjoying the feel of the water on his skin.

From the sitting room the music thundered on, but beneath the stinging jets of water Doyle couldn't hear it.

He didn't hear it when the phone rang either.

Thirteen

When he finally stepped from the shower he stood, head lowered, on the towel he'd spread on the bathroom floor. It was like some kind of meditative act. Eyes closed he stood there, water running in rivulets from him, some of it coursing down the deep scars like a stream through rock. He sucked in several deep breaths and finally reached for the bath towel nearby and began drying himself. From inside the sitting room he could still hear music. Wrapping the towel around himself he headed for the source of the sound, picking up the glass of milk as he did. Water was dripping from his long hair and Doyle wiped it away as it trickled down his back.

He crossed to the stereo and eased the volume down slightly. Then he reached for the phone and jabbed out some digits.

It was picked up almost immediately. Doyle smiled as he recognized the voice.

'Yeah, who is it?'

'Ron, it's Sean.'

'Doyle, what the fuck do *you* want?' Ronald Wyatt wanted to know. 'I hear on the grapevine you've been a naughty boy.' He chuckled. 'Old Austin was spitting blood about that mick you blew away.'

'Fuck him,' snapped Doyle. 'It's the others I'm interested in. I want to know where they took them; Austin wouldn't tell me.'

'Why do you want to know?'

'Why the hell do you think I want to know? I want to talk to them.' Doyle wiped some droplets of water from his face.

'About what?'

'Come on, Ron, what is this? Twenty fucking questions? Just tell me where they took them,' snapped Doyle.

'Shepherd's Bush Road police station.'

Doyle smiled.

'Thanks,' he said.

'By the way, if anyone asks how you found out, remember ...'

'I know, a little bird told me,' Doyle chuckled.

'A little blonde bird with big tits.' Wyatt erupted into a spasm of laughter. Doyle held the phone away from his ear for a moment.

'Cheers again, Ron,' he said and was about to replace the receiver when Wyatt spoke again. There was a sudden unexpected sobriety in his tone.

'Sean, what the fuck *is* going on?' he asked. 'I mean with the IRA. You know that they were as keen on a peace plan as anyone. Now, first we've got that bloody massacre at Stormont and then piles of Semtex here in London. It doesn't make any sense.'

'Since when did any of this shit in Ireland make sense, Ron?'

'Right,' Wyatt murmured wistfully.

'I'll talk to you soon,' said Doyle. This time he did put down the receiver.

Shepherd's Bush, eh? It made sense. It was the closest police station to the scene. Doyle should have realized.

He turned and headed back towards the bedroom where he quickly dried himself. He took clean jeans and a clean T-shirt from his wardrobe, pulled them on and dragged on a pair of cowboy boots. He glanced briefly at his reflection in the mirror and wandered back into the sitting room. There he took the .44 from its holster and flipped open the cylinder, emptying the weapon. He gathered up the rounds and crossed to a cabinet next to the stereo which was still roaring out music.

'... *Let me keep on sleeping, forget that I'm alone* ...'

Doyle opened a drawer and pulled out a box which he carried back to the sofa. Then, squatting on the arm of the settee, he slid the box open to reveal the shells inside.

'... *One day of faceless living is twenty four hours too long...*'

The copper casings reflected the light, glinting as Doyle removed six of them. He glanced at the bullets admiringly for a moment and slowly pushed one into each chamber of the .44.

These were his pride and joy.

Number twelve shot suspended in liquid teflon in a copper casing.

Beautiful.

Twice the explosive power of any dum-dum bullet. These didn't need to strike bone first; they exploded

60

immediately they entered their target. One was always enough.

He pushed the final shell into the cylinder and snapped it shut, jamming the weapon into the waistband of his jeans. He pulled on his leather jacket, turned off the stereo and headed for the door, car keys already in his hand.

He was half-way down the stairs when his phone rang but he hesitated only a second, knowing that the answering machine would pick up the call.

After two rings, however, there was silence.

For the second time that night the caller had chosen not to leave a message.

What had to be said should be said to Doyle himself. For now it could wait.

Fourteen

BRITTANY, FRANCE:
It was hideous.

Channing had no idea what it was but the creature was repulsive. Despite its vile appearance he looked at it more closely, marvelling not so much at the grotesqueness of the creation but at the skill which had gone into its construction.

He had guessed that the stained glass window must be at least five hundred years old but the workmanship was remarkable. Now, as he dipped the piece of rag in surgical spirit and began working carefully on one portion of the glass, he began to see the colours more clearly.

Lit only by the glow of the hurricane lamp, the image appeared from beneath the grime with infinite slowness as Channing worked intensely to remove the dirt that obscured it. Outside the sun was sinking low behind the hills, bleeding its colour across the sky. Channing could see none of this. All he was aware of was the window before him.

And of the face which was becoming clearer by the second.

This was not right, Channing thought. He had seen enough stained glass in his time to realize that the artefact before him was not the product of a God-fearing mind. No man of God would create an image so repulsive.

Who, then, had created the window?

Ninety per cent of it was still covered by dust and dirt, much of it so thick that not even the surgical spirit would remove it.

Catherine would know how to reveal the other panels, he thought. She would know. Once the entire window could be viewed he might be able to find some answers.

Encased in stone, as it had been when he'd first found it, the window had looked as if it had been hidden. As if whoever had constructed it had secreted it away within the church at Machecoul. As if only certain eyes were meant to gaze on it.

From what he uncovered so far he couldn't think of many who would want to.

The face was becoming clearer.

The dirt of ages, the filth of neglect was thick on the rag he was using. Channing tore off another piece, discarded the first and continued with the cleaning process.

More of the face now became visible and he moved back slightly, trying to see exactly what he had discovered.

The hurricane lamp flickered and Channing looked at it warily for a moment until the full glow was restored.

The face within the panel glared back at him.

It was shaped like that of a man but the head seemed to broaden, to swell at the temples, and across the forehead there were several protuberances. *Horns, perhaps?*

The hurricane lamp flickered again.

Channing moved closer to the window, staring at the face more intently.

A large mouth yawned open, long teeth prominent in both upper and lower jaws. From inside that mouth a thick barbed tongue flickered, but there was nothing else reptilian about the appearance of the monstrosity. The most striking thing about it were its eyes.

As Channing held the hurricane lamp close to the window the glass eyes seemed to glow. Both had been formed from single chips of red glass and now, with the light on them, they seemed to burn as if lit from within, shining with a lustre that must have been quite awe-inspiring when they were first created.

Channing shuddered, aware that the hairs on the back of his neck were rising.

Even his rudimentary knowledge of stained glass told him that the windows were originally constructed as learning aids as much as offerings to God. Peasants, unable to read, would be taught by monks or priests using the panels of the windows as a kind of storyboard. But the depictions were usually Biblical or philosophical. Channing shook his head slowly as he gazed at the creature depicted in the part of the panel he had uncovered.

What kind of story would feature a beast like this?

And what kind of man had invented such a monstrosity?

Again the hurricane lamp flickered.

Channing reached out and gently touched the glass, running the tip of one index finger around the perimeter of a red eye.

The glass felt ice-cold.

He felt the goose-pimples rise on his flesh immediately.

He traced the outline of the face with his finger, finally touching the gaping mouth, running his hand over the grimy glass.

The mouth opened.

As if the glass itself had suddenly become animated, the mouth seemed to collapse in on itself.

In that second Channing felt his hand slipping through.

Through the glass.

Between those painted lips and teeth.

He jumped back in panic, his heart hammering uncontrollably in his chest, but as he moved his hand remained inside the mouth. His eyes bulged in their sockets as he tried to pull himself free.

Then he felt mounting pressure on his wrist.

As if something was biting him.

The pieces of glass that formed the lips of the mouth seemed to be closing around his arm, chafing skin.

They snapped together with a loud crack.

And finally Channing was free of the grip.

Free because his hand had been severed.

He fell back onto the floor of the church screaming,

the torn arm held before him like a bizarre trophy, blood spouting madly from the stump of the wrist.

The thick crimson fluid was pouring down the front of the window too, smeared copiously around the mouth of the creature depicted there.

The mouth was now closed.

Channing gaped at his shattered wrist and at the pieces of pulverized bone and the tendril-like lengths of vein and artery still spurting scarlet.

And he screamed again.

He was still screaming when he woke up.

Dragged from the dream by his own bellowing, he sat up, his body sheathed in sweat, his hands shaking madly.

He held them both out as if to check that he still possessed two. The residue of the nightmare was still strong in his mind.

He tried to control his breathing, realizing now that it had been a dream. Gradually he felt his heart slowing, the rushing of blood in his ears diminishing. He was aware that he was in his bedroom at the inn and not inside the church of Machecoul. Channing heard movement outside his room, a gentle tapping on the door followed by some urgent enquries about his well-being from the lady who owned the place. His screams must have awoken her, he reasoned. He called back that he was fine. It was just a nightmare.

Just a nightmare. Jesus Christ!

Channing finally slumped back onto pillows which were drenched with sweat. He ran both hands over his face, closing his eyes momentarily, relieved when he saw no more of the vision he'd witnessed in his dream.

He sucked in a deep breath, held it for a moment and let it out slowly, aware that his heart had ceased its frantic pounding. He began to relax.

Sleep came to him again, but slowly. He accepted its embrace almost unwillingly, wondering what else he might find inside his mind once the peaceful oblivion settled upon him.

He was just drifting off when the phone brought him hurtling back to consciousness.

The ringing continued for a moment or two as Channing tried to re-orientate himself. Then he reached for the receiver.

The hands on his watch showed 2.14 a.m.

Fifteen

LONDON:

The desk sergeant at Shepherd's Bush Road police station didn't look up as he heard the footsteps approaching his counter. He continued sipping at his tea and filling in names on a form he had laid out in front of him.

Only when the newcomer coughed theatrically did Sergeant Raymond Nyles deign to glance up.

His first impression was one of surprise. The man facing him was in his early thirties, he guessed, dressed in a leather jacket, T-shirt and jeans. As he took a step back, Nyles peered over the counter and saw that he wore cowboy boots, too.

What a bloody sight, the Duty Sergeant thought.

'Can I help you?' he said wearily.

'Some men were brought in earlier tonight,' Doyle

told him, as if imparting some information Nyles wasn't aware of. 'Four of them. Irish.'

Nyles was non-committal. He merely frowned slightly, pulled at the end of his nose and continued looking appraisingly at Doyle.

'If they were, what do you want to know for?' he asked.

Doyle dug inside his jacket and pulled out some I.D.

'Don't play games with me,' he snapped, tossing the slim leather wallet in front of Nyles. 'I need to see them.'

Nyles inspected the I.D., checking the photo inside against the face of the man who stood before him as if he doubted the validity of the picture.

'C.T.U.,' he muttered, his frown deepening. 'The Flying Squad are already here, they were the ones who brought them in. No one told me the Counter-Terrorist Unit were involved too.'

'Perhaps they forgot,' said Doyle, gathering up the leather wallet. 'Now can you just tell me where the men are being held?' Irritation was creeping more noticeably into his tone. Nyles regarded him a moment longer, then reached for the phone on his desk and flicked a switch. Doyle leant against the counter and lit up a cigarette, ignoring the NO SMOKING sign emblazoned on the far wall.

Nyles spoke into the phone and, a moment later, a uniformed constable appeared. He looked at the sergeant and then at Doyle.

'Take this ... gentleman through to the cells,' said Nyles, glancing once more at the counter terrorist before returning to his form. 'Stay with him.'

'There's no need for that,' Doyle said, nodding for the constable to lead on.

They walked along a wide corridor with rooms on each side, finally pausing at a heavy iron door set in the far end. The constable unlocked it and led Doyle through.

'Are you Flying Squad?' asked the uniformed man.

Doyle grunted indignantly.

'No. Why?'

'It's just that there are two or three of them here already. I thought you ...!'

'No. Not me,' Doyle interrupted.

The constable paused at a door, knocked and opened it when he heard the order from inside to enter. He held the door for Doyle.

The room smelt of cigarettes and strong coffee. There were two men inside, one of whom he recognized immediately.

'What are *you* doing here?' asked Chief Inspector Austin. 'I told you to keep out of this.'

The other man in the room glanced at Doyle, then returned his attention to the two-way mirror which looked into a small room beyond. It was about half the size of the one in which the men stood, about six feet by six, containing only a table and two chairs.

Seated in the room was a man in his early forties, greying at the temples. Red in the face, he was constantly looking round the room as if expecting a hole to open up in the wall and allow him to escape. He chewed on his thumbnail constantly.

'Who is he?' said Doyle, pouring himself a cup of coffee.

'His name is Sheehan,' said Austin. 'Thomas Sheehan. Known member of the IRA. Served three years in Long Kesh in the late seventies for possession of explosives.'

'What about the others that were brought in?'

'Same. All known IRA.'

'Has anyone spoken to any of them yet?' Doyle asked, sipping his coffee, never taking his eyes from the man in the room beyond.

'We've spoken to all of them,' said the other man with Austin. 'They won't speak.' He said it with something approaching smugness.

'I heard your boss was on his way down here,' Austin informed the counter-terrorist.

'Donaldson? What does he want?' Doyle enquired, his gaze still fixed on Sheehan.

'The same thing we all do. Information,' said the policeman. 'It seems unlikely we're going to get it just yet. Perhaps when the bastard's sat there for a few more hours without a cigarette or the chance to have a piss he'll feel like talking.' Austin and his companion smiled at each other.

'Bollocks,' said Doyle. 'It's going to take more than a bursting bladder to make him talk.'

'Why don't *you* have a word with him?' said the other policeman, a note of sarcasm in his voice. 'Perhaps he'll be so scared he'll tell you everything.' The man chuckled.

'Look, mate, I guessed you were a prick,' said Doyle. 'You don't have to advertize the fact.' He took another sip of his coffee, not even giving the other man the benefit of a glance.

The policeman was on his feet in seconds, lunging at Doyle, who merely moved to one side, allowing Austin to grab his furious companion.

'Cut it out,' the Chief Inspector snapped, holding the other man by the shoulders and finally shoving him back towards his seat. The man, Garner, looked angrily at Doyle.

'They won't talk, Doyle,' Austin said, with an air of finality. 'None of them.'

'They'll talk to me,' said the counter-terrorist, putting down his cup.

'No way. You set one foot in that room and they'll be crying police brutality.'

'Let them,' said Doyle. 'Who's going to hear?' He turned and headed for the door which led through into the smaller room.

'Doyle, I'm ordering you,' shouted Austin.

'You can't order me. Donaldson *can* but he's not here, is he?' said the younger man, one hand on the door knob. 'I told you, I just want a chat with him.'

'Go on then, big shot,' hissed Garner.

'You shut up, too,' Austin rasped, rounding on his companion.

Doyle turned the knob.

'Who do you think you are, bloody Clint Eastwood?' snapped the C.I.

The door was closed.

Doyle was inside the room.

'Mouthy bastard,' said Garner, watching Doyle as he approached the table where Sheehan sat. 'The mick won't talk to *him*. Who does he think he is, anyway?'

'Shut up, Garner,' Austin said wearily. 'Just shut up.'

Both men watched in silence as Doyle went to work.

Sixteen

Thomas Sheehan looked up as the door opened, his eyes flicking appraisingly over this newcomer. If the

70

Irishman was surprised by Doyle's appearance it didn't show in his face but for a slight narrowing of his eyes. He chewed part of his thumbnail away and spat it onto the floor in front of Doyle, who merely walked around to the other side of the table and rested one booted foot on the chair.

His eyes never left Sheehan's.

The man was sweating slightly but not, Doyle guessed, from fear. He'd seen men like Sheehan before. Hard bastards. Prepared to take it rough, if they had to. Fear of their own colleagues was sometimes a more potent obstacle to communication than fear of the authorities.

Doyle meant to change that.

'You've probably had the nice copper, bad copper routine already,' said Doyle, lighting up a cigarette and blowing the smoke in the direction of the Irishman. 'Been sitting here a while, busting for a piss, dying for a fag, wondering how much longer they're going to keep you sitting here. Well, Tommy, that's all down to you. You can sit here for another few hours, you can sit here for another few days, for all I care. You might have got time to waste but I haven't. I need to talk to you, or, more to the point, I need *you* to talk to *me*. If you want to make it easy, that's fine; if you want to make it hard on yourself I really couldn't give a fuck either way. I want some answers before I leave this room.'

'Nice speech. Go fuck yourself,' said Sheehan, looking around the room, anywhere but at Doyle.

A slight smile creased Doyle's lips.

Well, well, no wonder Austin could get nothing from him, thought the counter-terrorist.

'I'm not answering your fucking questions. Go to hell,' Sheehan said dismissively, this time looking at the younger man.

'If I go, you're coming with me,' Doyle told him, noting the surprise in the Irishman's eyes as he heard the words spoken in his native tongue. 'Now, start talking. Why the meeting?'

'Fuck you.'

Doyle drove his boot against the edge of the table, propelling it with great force and power into the chest of the Irishman who was knocked from his chair by the impact. He crashed heavily against the wall, banging his head. Doyle was on him in a second, dragging him to his feet and slamming him upright against the white tiled wall.

'What's going on?' he snarled, in English this time. 'Talk to me, you bastard.'

Sheehan felt his feet being lifted from the floor as Doyle exerted more pressure on his throat. The Irishman summoned a mouthful of spittle and spat into the Englishman's face.

Doyle's eyes blazed with rage and he drove a fist into Sheehan's stomach. The blow tore the breath from the man and also released the last shreds of control he was keeping on his full bladder. As he sank to the floor a dark stain began to spread across the front of his trousers.

Doyle placed one foot on the man's chest, watching as the urine soaked through his clothes, some of it puddling beneath him.

'Messy boy,' he chided, digging the heel of his boot into Sheehan's chest more firmly. The knot of muscles at the side of the Englishman's jaw pulsed angrily.

'Talk to me, shithead,' Doyle rasped. The acrid stench of urine reached his nostrils. 'You're starting to stink and I don't want to spend any more time in here than I have to. So, tell me what the fuck is going on?'

He slammed Sheehan back against the wall even harder.

The Irishman raised his hands and tried to pull his tormentor's arms down, anything to relieve the pressure on his throat but Doyle merely pressed his thumbs in harder, watching with relish as his opponent's face began to turn scarlet.

It looked as if Sheehan was trying to speak but the only sounds he could make were strangled gasps. Doyle held him a moment longer then hurled him across the room where he rolled once, then crashed into the other wall, right beneath the two-way mirror. Doyle took two paces and was on him again. This time he simply drove the toe of his boot into the Irishman's side, satisfied when he heard a dull crack.

One rib gone, he thought.

Sheehan groaned and reached for his injured side but Doyle dragged him upright again, staring deeply into his eyes.

'You can't do this,' the Irishman groaned. 'I've got rights.'

'You've got nothing,' Doyle hissed, slamming him back against the wall again.

This time the impact was so violent that it opened a cut on the back of Sheehan's head. Blood began to well from the gash and trickle through his hair. Doyle glanced at the crimson smear on the wall without a flicker of emotion. He slammed Sheehan down into the one seat which was still standing and grabbed the back of his head, getting a handful of hair in his fist, ignoring the blood that stained his palm. He jerked Sheehan's head back so sharply it seemed he would break his neck.

'Why don't you talk to the others?' Sheehan rasped.

'Because they're small fry. *You* organized that meeting tonight. You're the one who knows what's going on and why. Now tell me or I swear to Christ I'll break your fucking neck.' As if to reinforce the conviction of his statement, Doyle jerked even harder on the Irishman's hair, almost causing him to overbalance.

'I can't talk,' said Sheehan with difficulty. He felt close to fainting.

'Can't or won't?' snapped Doyle and suddenly hurled Sheehan forward, driving his head against the table top with such force that it broke his nose. Blood exploded from the shattered appendage and ran down the Irishman's face and shirt, mingling with the urine that had already stained his trousers.

Doyle stepped back. Sheehan was burbling incoherently now, his face was a crimson mask. He finally managed to sit up, one hand held to his face. Blood seeped through his fingers. He looked at the counter-terrorist with hatred in his eyes but Doyle saw something else there too.

Fear, perhaps?

The Irishman was breathing heavily, deep gasping breaths through his open mouth as he held his pulverized nose, occasionally taking his hand away to inspect the amount of blood on his fingers.

'You bastard,' he hissed at Doyle. 'And you expect me to talk?' He tried to grin but it appeared as a leer.

'I don't expect you to,' Doyle informed him. 'But I *advise* you to, unless you want your cheek bones and your jaw to end up like your nose.' There was no inflection in the words, no threat. Merely the statement of the inevitable.

'So what do you think I know?' Sheehan asked,

74

wincing as he wiped his shattered nose with one shirt sleeve. Blood still dripped from it, puddling beneath him.

'Just tell me what's going on.'

'What the fuck are you talking about? What *is* going on?' Sheehan said, almost mockingly.

Doyle's expression didn't change.

'Don't be a smart-arse, Tommy,' he said. 'Two days ago in Northern Ireland, as you well know, twenty-three politicians, including some Sinn Fein men, were murdered. Nobody knows *who* shot them, or why, and now, tonight, we find you and your cronies with enough Semtex to start a fucking war.' Doyle rested one boot on the edge of the chair and leaned closer to Sheehan. 'Ten days ago the Provisional IRA said that they were willing, if their leaders found the terms favourable, to stop all hostilities against the British army and to cease any activity on the mainland against military and civilian targets.' He paused a moment, glaring at the Irishman. 'Your fucking lot were ready to call it a day. No more bombings, no more shootings, no more knee-cappings. Nothing. And now what happens? In the space of forty-eight hours twenty-three people are murdered and we find your explosives store. Now tell me you don't know what's going on.'

Sheehan eyed the counter-terrorist warily, still dabbing at his nose with his shirt.

'You can't blame me for what happened at Stormont,' he said.

'I can blame you for any fucking thing I want unless you come up with some info to tell me otherwise,' Doyle snapped irritably. 'Who was behind that shooting? Who told you to call a meeting tonight?'

'What the fuck are you talking about, *meeting*?'

75

'You and the others have worked together before as a team. Thinking of going back into business?' The two men looked at each other in silence for a moment. 'Who told you to call that meeting? The same bloke who organized the shooting at Stormont?'

'Why don't you talk to the fucking Protestants?' snapped Sheehan. 'How do you know the fucking UVF aren't to blame?'

'A hunch,' said Doyle flatly. 'Now I'll ask you once more,' he stepped back a pace, one hand reaching around to the back of his jacket. 'Who ordered the shooting at Stormont?'

'You want me to turn tout?' Sheehan chuckled, dabbing at his nose. 'You know what they'd do to me if I did? A bag over the head and two bullets in the skull.'

'If you're worried about turning tout then there's somebody to grass on isn't there?' Doyle said, flatly.

'You're quick,' snapped Sheehan.

'No, I'm impatient. Give me a name.'

'No way.'

'As you want.'

It was then that he pulled the gun.

Seventeen

The Charter Arms .44 looked huge as Doyle pulled it free, aiming it at Sheehan's head.

Chief Inspector Austin saw the weapon and shouted, realizing that Doyle couldn't hear him through the two-way mirror.

'He's going to kill him,' said Garner incredulously. 'The mad bastard is going to kill him.'

Austin shouted once more then spun round, heading for the door into the small cell beyond.

This time Doyle *had* gone too far.

'Leave him.'

The voice startled Austin, both its intrusion and the feeling of power it seemed to carry. He turned to see who had spoken.

Jeffrey Donaldson stood inside the room, looking past Austin at the counter-terrorist and his adversary. He watched as Doyle pressed the gun against the remains of the Irishman's nose, fresh blood spilling down his face.

'He could kill the man, for Christ's sake,' Austin protested.

'He *could*,' said Donaldson, moving closer to the two-way mirror. Garner looked at the newcomer. He was in his mid-forties, tall and lean. His face had a somewhat pinched appearance due to his hollow cheeks. Even the greying beard he sported did nothing to make his features appear fuller. He was dressed in an open-necked shirt and trousers, with an overcoat around his shoulders. As he watched the tableau behind the glass he plucked absent-mindedly at his beard, as if trying to tease each bristle free.

'How long's he been in there?' Donaldson asked.

'About fifteen minutes,' Austin told him. 'I suppose we should be grateful Sheehan lasted *that* long.' He glanced at the two men in the smaller room once more. 'He wouldn't speak to us but Doyle insisted on trying for himself.'

'He uses different methods,' said Donaldson matter-of-factly.

77

'Brutality being the main one,' Austin snapped. 'You're his superior, *you* stop him.'

Donaldson had been head of the Counter-Terrorist Unit for the last four years. He had been one of the few in that unit who had actually encouraged Doyle to return to the fold after he'd been advised to quit for good. The injuries he'd sustained after the bomb blast had looked like forcing him into early retirement and Donaldson could still remember visiting the younger man in hospital, wondering if he would ever walk again, never mind return to the job. When, against all medical and official advice, Doyle had returned, Donaldson had seen what a changed man he was. Before, he'd been cautious. Since the blast he'd been positively reckless with regard to his own safety. He seemed to care nothing for life any more, his or anyone else's. There was a ferocity about him which was sometimes quite terrifying.

Donaldson was witnessing it now.

'Get him out of there,' Austin said. 'He'll kill Sheehan, then we'll never get anything out of him.'

'I read his file in the car on the way here,' Donaldson said. 'What makes you think you'll get anything out of him anyway?'

'There are certain procedures which must be followed …!' Austin began but Donaldson cut him short.

'Certain procedures,' he said scornfully. 'You mean, do it by the rules? Well, the rules are different with men like Sheehan. You should know that. Doyle plays by *their* rules.'

'Doyle doesn't play by anybody's rules,' Austin snapped. 'How the hell can you trust him, anyway? His family were Irish, weren't they?'

'That's one of the things that makes him perfect for the job. He understands their mentality.'

Doyle had just pushed Sheehan up against the wall. He now shoved the gun under his chin.

'I don't trust him,' said Austin.

'I don't trust anyone,' Donaldson said, looking directly at the policeman.

'He's insane.'

'He gets results.'

'That's as maybe. I still think he's insane.'

Donaldson smiled thinly.

'You could very well be right,' he said quietly.

Austin had no answer. All he could do was watch as Doyle moved the barrel of the .44 up towards Sheehan's mouth.

Eighteen

'You can't kill me.'

There was a note of desperation in Sheehan's voice as Doyle prodded the gun against his cheek.

'Who ordered the shooting?' asked the counter-terrorist flatly.

'Fuck you,' shouted the Irishman.

Doyle grabbed his hand and slammed it down on the table top, gripping the wrist firmly, spreading the fingers.

With a movement combining lightning speed and demonic force he brought the butt of the pistol down onto the tip of Sheehan's index finger.

The fingernail splintered under the impact; bone crumbled easily. Blood burst from the end of the pulped digit.

'I don't know,' Sheehan wailed.

Doyle smashed the tip of his middle finger.

A fresh scream of pain filled the room.

'Talk to me,' Doyle said through clenched teeth.

'I can't tell you,' Sheehan insisted.

Doyle smashed a third finger tip.

And a fourth.

It looked as if someone had slammed the Irishman's hand repeatedly in a car door.

Doyle aimed for the thumb.

The nail actually came free along with a small chip of bone in a spurt of blood as the thumb was pulverized.

'You've only got one hand left,' hissed Doyle. 'You won't even be able to wipe your own arse if you don't give me some answers. Who ordered the shooting at Stormont?'

He hurled Sheehan across the room once more, advancing on the fallen man who was trying to protect his injured hand.

'No more,' he gasped, blood still running from his broken nose.

'Then talk,' said Doyle flatly. He knelt beside the Irishman, the .44 pressed against his chest. 'Who ordered the Stormont shooting? Was it the IRA?'

Sheehan sucked in a deep breath.

'Jesus,' he murmured softly. 'If I tell you ...'

'Was it?' rasped Doyle.

'No.'

If Doyle was surprised it didn't register on his face.

'Not officially,' Sheehan told him.

Doyle grabbed him by the front of his blood-stained

shirt, dragged him to his feet and dumped him on one of the chairs again.

'Not officially,' he mimicked. 'What the fuck is that supposed to mean? Was it the IRA or not?'

'They *were* IRA men who did the shooting but they were acting unofficially. *Against* Sinn Fein orders.' He looked down at his hand and what remained of the finger tips.

'Tell me more,' said Doyle.

'You were right in what you said; Sinn Fein were all for this peace settlement in the six counties. They even gave orders that hostilities were to stop until the politicians had had their say. The men who did the shooting at Stormont didn't want that. They wanted the war to go on. No peace settlement. They wanted to carry on fighting. They wanted the money, too.'

'What money?' asked Doyle sharply, his attention now fully focused, his curiosity aroused.

'The group that did the shooting were privately funded. Someone paid them a huge amount of money to carry out that shooting at Stormont.'

Doyle stroked his chin thoughtfully.

'And you; where do you figure in all this?' he asked. 'Was it the same man who ordered the shooting that told you to call the meeting tonight?'

Sheehan nodded slowly.

'We were supposed to start bombing civilian targets, cause as much disruption as possible, create anti-Irish feeling again and stop the peace initiative going through,' he confessed.

'How much were the gunmen paid to do the shooting?' Doyle wanted to know.

'I heard about a million, maybe more.'

'Jesus,' muttered Doyle. 'Who paid them?'

'That I *don't* know.'

'Do you want to lose your other hand?' the counter-terrorist hissed. 'Who paid them?'

'I swear to God I don't know.'

'How many gunmen were involved in the shooting?'

'I don't know that, either. All I know is there are five or six men working in the squad.'

'Who's in charge of them?'

'His name's Maguire. James Maguire. That's all I know. I swear.'

'I need to know who paid him the million quid and why,' said Doyle.

'I told you, I don't know,' Sheehan insisted.

Doyle took a step back.

'Bullshit,' he hissed, aiming the gun at the Irishman. 'Who paid them?'

'I don't know.'

'Then you're no use to me any more,' the counter-terrorist said, drawing a bead on Sheehan. The sight was over his forehead.

'I've told you all I know,' Sheehan shouted frantically, his eyes bulging in the sockets. 'You can't kill me.'

Doyle smiled.

'Wrong,' he said quietly, and thumbed back the hammer.

It was then that Sheehan fainted.

'And you have no doubt that he was telling the truth?'

Jeffrey Donaldson's words seemed to echo around the small room inside the police station. He chewed on the stem of a pipe as he spoke, the fumes from the bowl mingling with air already heavy with cigarette smoke. It looked as though someone had draped the air with a shroud.

Doyle took a sip of his coffee, wincing when he found it was cold.

'He didn't know anything else,' he said. 'He doesn't know who hired Maguire and his men.'

'Who the hell would want to do that?' said Austin.

'Who could *afford* to do it?' Garner asked.

'Another terrorist organisation? Someone with a vested interest in seeing that there *is* no peace settlement in Ireland,' Donaldson suggested. 'Maybe even another country.'

'Like Libya or Iran?' Doyle mused.

'Or someone bigger,' Donaldson said, raising his eyebrows.

'What do you mean?' Austin said.

'Most IRA weapons and funds come from outside sources,' Donaldson told him. 'The Middle East, America, Russia. Some IRA men are even sent to the Middle East to learn their trade. What we have to find out' – he looked at Doyle – 'is who paid the money and why.' He got to his feet. 'I want you at my office tomorrow morning at ten o'clock, Doyle. We'll go over this again there.'

The younger man nodded and ground out his cigarette in a nearby ashtray.

'What about me?' Austin asked. 'I have a right to know what's going on. What you decide to do.'

'This is out of your hands now, Austin,' Donaldson told him. 'It's beyond the Flying Squad. You haven't the resources or the capabilities to deal with this situation. We'll take over from here.' And then he was gone.

Doyle also got to his feet and headed for the door.

'It might interest you to know that Sheehan is in hospital,' said Austin. 'You could have killed him.'

'I wish I had,' the counter-terrorist said flatly as he paused in the doorway. 'Maybe next time I will.' Then he too was gone.

Séance

There were five of them seated around the table, their faces cast in deep shadow.

The only light in the great hall came from the hundreds of candles arranged in various patterns on the floor. The entire room was filled by sickly yellow light and the acrid smell of a thousand burning wicks. Smoke rose in small ethereal plumes every once in a while when a gust of wind extinguished a candle. Each time it was rapidly re-lit by one of the three men who looked on.

The quintet seated at the table remained where they were, heads bowed, fingertips touching gently.

In the centre of the table, framed by yet more candles, lay the body of a child.

The boy was naked. Unconscious.

The drug had taken a very short time to work on him and now, exposed to their prying eyes, he lay spread-eagled in their midst.

One of the men kept looking at the boy but a word from one of his companions forced him from his pleasure and he closed his eyes once more.

Outside the wind was whipping around the building, screaming at the windows and snuffing out more candles. Again they were re-lit.

The man who had been staring at the unconscious child

heard movement to his right but did not look up. He knew what was happening. Knew that one of his companions had risen and was now standing, arms outstretched in a gesture designed to encompass all those who sat at the table.

The man standing began to speak but his words were not always easy to understand. Not because of any speech impediment but because of their nature.

Strange, apparently meaningless phrases spilled from his lips. The others heard the words but did not understand.

It began to get colder in the room.

In the centre of the table the child stirred for a moment, perhaps momentarily roused by the chill, but after a short moan he drifted into oblivion again.

The cold intensified.

It was as if every ounce of warmth was being sucked not only from the room but from the men who sat at the table. They began to shiver, not least the one who sat at the head of the massive oak table. He raised his head to see that his companion was still speaking but his words now seemed to have changed from a series of phrases into a chant.

The chant grew louder.

The cold grew more palpable.

A breeze seemed to sweep through the room and many of the candles were blown out, their yellow lights snuffed as surely as if invisible fingers had nipped the wicks.

As the men who looked on made to re-light them the individual who was chanting held up a hand to stop them. They sank back into the shadows, grateful to hide in the gloom.

The chanting stopped.

There was a low rumbling sound which seemed to come not from one particular source but from all around the table.

All around the hall.

It was as if the entire place and all its occupants were

about to be engulfed by an earthquake.

A candlestick fell to the ground, clattering noisily on the stone floor. It was followed by another.

And another.

As each fell so their candles went out and the darkness in the room deepened.

So did the cold.

The man at the head of the table, squinting through the gloom, saw something.

At the far end of the hall, even through the tenebrous darkness, he could discern a shape. Somehow blacker than the night itself, it was as if a portion of the umbra had taken on tangible form and detached itself from the remainder of the shadows.

That shape was now moving towards the table.

The man narrowed his eyes, both to see through the gloom and also to try and pick out exactly what the shape was.

He swallowed hard as he realized that the one they had sought was among them.

Nineteen

Bright shafts of sunlight thrust their way through the windows of the Mayfair office. Motes of dust caught in the golden shafts as if magnetized.

The sunlight was shining onto Jeffrey Donaldson's polished desk top. He was sitting back in his swivel chair, puffing contentedly on his pipe. Smoke rose in small clouds, dissipating high above him, swirling around the huge crystal chandelier which hung from the centre of the ceiling.

The chair made little noise as he moved back and forth in it. In fact the entire room seemed unnaturally silent; even the footfalls of the other man in the room were muffled by the thick pile of the carpet.

Tom Westley wandered back across the office and set down a crystal tumbler close to Donaldson, who glanced up from the file he was reading and inspected the contents of the glass.

'It's a bit early for this, isn't it, Tom?' he said, smiling.

'If you don't want it I'll drink it,' Westley said, sipping his own Scotch.

He was a year or two older than Donaldson, and much more powerfully built; a broad, muscular man with a tanned face and large hands that not only dwarfed the glass but threatened to crush it if he squeezed too hard. He stood at the window, looking out over the paved area beneath. There was a patio and a small pond which boasted a fountain. Sunlight glinted on the surface of the pool, the warmth of the water coaxing movement from the fish which populated it.

Westley took another sip of his drink, then wandered back across the room and added a squirt of soda.

'What's wrong?' Donaldson asked.

'I don't like this situation, Jeff. This business with the IRA,' he said, turning to face his companion. 'I read Doyle's report too.' He shook his head. 'This ... antagonism between himself and the IRA seems to go beyond the job. He treats the fighting as if it's something personal between *him* and the Provisionals.'

Westley drained the contents of his glass and poured himself another.

This time he didn't bother with the soda.

Donaldson eyed his companion guardedly for a moment, watching as he downed half of the fiery liquid in one gulp. He had always disapproved of his companion's sometimes excessive drinking habits but, as they never interfered with his work, he thought it churlish to make an issue of it. When his twenty-year old daughter had been killed in a car accident two years earlier Westley had hit the bottle hard; even now, when he felt too much stress he was a little too easily tempted to reach for the Scotch.

Donaldson smiled thinly.

'Doyle's *passion* for his work might be to our advantage,' he said.

Westley grunted.

'If you ask me, the bastard is insane,' he said. 'Since he was injured he's changed. His attitudes, his methods, everything.'

'He was always a little over-zealous,' Donaldson said, reaching for his own drink and taking a sip. 'Even before the accident.'

'Well, he's much more than that now. I think he's dangerous to others as well as himself. Some of the other agents think he has divided loyalties.'

Donaldson raised one eyebrow quizzically.

'I mean, with his family being Irish,' Westley continued.

'His family are dead. He has no one. That might account for his state of mind.'

'Does it account for his death-wish, too?' asked Westley cryptically.

The two men looked at each other for a moment.

Then Donaldson leant forward and flicked a switch on the console on his desk.

'Send Mr Doyle in, please,' he said and sat back.

Westley held his companion's gaze a moment longer, then poured himself another drink.

There was a knock on the door and Doyle entered. Greetings and handshakes were exchanged and Doyle sat down opposite Donaldson. He also accepted the drink Westley offered him, cradling the fine crystal glass in his hand as he sat there, waiting for the older man to take up his position on the other side of the desk. It was as if Westley felt he needed that distance between himself and Doyle.

'We'll keep this as brief as possible, Doyle,' said Donaldson, flipping open another file. He glanced at it, then turned it towards the younger man. On top of a pile of papers was a photograph. The man in the picture was in his mid-twenties, strong-featured, his face framed by a mop of curly hair. There was a sparkle in his eyes which looked like defiance.

'James Maguire, the man responsible for the shootings at Stormont,' said Donaldson. 'That's the man we want. Him and as many of the men operating with him as possible.'

Doyle glanced at the photo and nodded almost imperceptibly. Then he looked at his superiors.

'He'll never let himself be taken alive,' he said.

'We know that,' snapped Westley. 'But you could at least try.'

Doyle shrugged.

'I'm telling you, he won't let himself be taken, and if that's the way he wants it ...' He allowed the sentence to trail off.

'You'll be working with another agent,' Donaldson

told him.

'No way,' Doyle snapped. 'I work alone. I don't need anyone else getting in the way.'

'This isn't a bloody western, Doyle,' Westley reminded him, 'or some bad American cop show. All this maverick crap doesn't wash here. You're working with another agent.'

'Then find some other prat to do the job,' snapped Doyle, getting to his feet.

'Wait,' hissed Westley.

'Who *is* the other agent?' Doyle demanded.

'Willis,' Donaldson told him.

A thin smile flickered on Doyle's lips.

'Why Willis?'

'Because no one else will work with you,' Westley said. 'And quite frankly I don't blame them.'

Again Donaldson flicked the switch on his console.

'Tell Willis to come in,' he said.

Doyle turned as the door opened, the smile hovering once more on his lips.

'You know Doyle, don't you?' Donaldson said as the other agent approached the desk.

Georgina Willis nodded.

Twenty

The four of them sat in the office while Donaldson ran over the briefing. Doyle seemed uninterested, his attention fixed more firmly on his companion.

Georgina Willis was three or four years younger than

Doyle. She had a thin face which tapered off into a neatly pointed chin. Blonde hair flooded onto and beyond her shoulders, and every so often she would run a hand through it, occasionally glancing at Doyle. When she did, he looked deeply into her green eyes, noting how clear and alert they were. She was dressed in a sweatshirt and jeans, and as she sat listening to Donaldson she curled the lace of one trainer around her index finger. She was pretty and Doyle couldn't help but wonder how the hell she had ever come to be in this line of work. Maybe he'd take the time to find out, he promised himself.

Maybe.

Donaldson finally finished speaking and looked at the two agents as if expecting some response from them.

They merely looked at each other. Then Doyle glanced at his watch.

'If the lecture is over, I think I've heard enough,' he said.

'Take the files on Maguire. Study them,' said Westley. 'Find out all there is to know about him.'

'He's the enemy,' Doyle said flatly. 'What more do we *need* to know?' He got to his feet.

Georgina picked up one of the manilla files and followed Doyle towards the door.

'You'll leave for Belfast on separate planes tomorrow morning,' Donaldson told them. 'Once you get there, you're on your own. How you find Maguire, that's your problem. There's nothing more we can do for you.'

'Nice to know we've got your support,' Doyle said acidly and walked out. Georgina followed him, closing the door behind her.

Westley waited a moment then slammed his fist down on the desk top.

'Insubordinate bastard,' he snarled. He wandered across the room to another door in the oak-panelled wall. He opened it and two men stepped into the office. Both were dressed casually, both in their mid-thirties. One was smoking a cigarette he'd rolled himself. Peter Todd took the cigarette from his mouth and removed some tobacco from the tip of his tongue.

George Rivers glanced down at the file on the polished desk top, catching sight of the pictures of Maguire.

'Nasty piece of work, isn't he?' he said, smiling.

'You heard what was said in here?' Westley asked.

Both men nodded.

'You will follow Doyle and Willis until they've tracked down Maguire and his renegades,' Westley said. 'Then you will kill Doyle *and* Willis. Clear?'

The two men nodded.

Twenty-One

There were relatively few people in the pub. It was still too early for the office lunchtime trade, and for that Doyle was thankful. He didn't like crowds, didn't like people crowding him. He picked up the drinks from the bar and made his way across to the table where Georgina Willis sat. She thanked him, then watched as he wandered across to the juke-box, fed in some change and punched in his selections. He returned to the table and sat down just as the first swelling roar of guitars began to blast from the speakers. One or two other drinkers looked up irritably.

Georgina glanced at him as he sipped his drink, studying the hard lines of his face, her eyes finally alighting on the deep scar which marked the left side of his features. Doyle scratched at it unconsciously and took another swallow from his glass. He'd asked her if she wanted a drink when they'd left the office but he didn't seem to be in the mood for conversation, she thought, sipping at her own drink and running one index finger around the rim of the glass.

'If we're going to work together we might as well try and get on,' she said finally, tiring of the silence between them and Doyle's apparent indifference. He seemed distant, his mind focused on something far beyond the pub and the music that filled it.

He nodded slowly.

'Is it me?' she asked.

He looked puzzled.

'You've hardly said a word since we left Westley's office,' she told him.

'I was thinking about something,' he told her.

'Maguire?' she wondered.

'Maguire. His renegades. This whole fucking job.' He took another swallow from his glass. 'Westley and Donaldson are crazy if they think we'll be able to catch him.'

'You think he's going to be that hard to track down?' she said.

'Finding him won't be a problem, but I'm damned if I'm going to waste valuable time trying to make him see the error of his ways.' Doyle emphasised the words with scorn. "Or that it would be in his own interests to give himself up. When the time comes I'm going to kill him, because you can bet your arse he's going to try and kill *us*.'

'Donaldson and Westley won't like it.'

'Then let *them* find him and bring him in.' Doyle finished what was left in his glass, then got himself another. Georgina watched him as he stood at the bar, telling the barman to make it a double Scotch this time. He paid and returned to the table.

'How do you want to play this one?' she enquired. 'Once we're there.'

He shrugged.

'Married couple,' he suggested. 'Boyfriend-girlfriend. Something like that. Mr and Mrs Average.'

She nodded and ran a hand through her hair, her green eyes fixed on him.

'I heard they wanted you to retire after what happened,' she said. 'Why didn't you?'

'Retire to what? Sitting around in some fucking nursing home counting my scars and drawing a disability pension once a month?' He shook his head. 'They wanted me to retire because they didn't like my methods. When I got hurt it just gave them some extra leverage to get me out. So they thought.'

'You were lucky to survive. Why put your life on the line again and again? And don't tell me it's patriotism.'

'I never pretended it was. I enjoy what I do.' He looked directly at her, almost surprised when she held his gaze. 'What about you? Why did you get into this line of work in the first place?'

'I went through the usual channels,' she told him. 'Undercover, plain-clothes. When the chance came to join the Counter-Terrorist Unit I took it.'

'Why?'

'My brother was killed by the IRA two years ago. A bomb had gone off in Belfast city centre; he was helping get people into an ambulance when one of

94

their snipers shot him. He was only twenty.'

'So it's a revenge thing for you?'

'I suppose you could say that. Isn't it with you?'

'It's not revenge, it's hatred,' he told her flatly. 'I should have died that day in Londonderry. The doctors said I didn't have any right to survive, considering the extent of the injuries.' He looked down into his glass, as if seeking his next sentence in the liquor. 'I've been living on borrowed time ever since. It's just a matter of how long before that time runs out. That's why I live life day to day. I could be dead tomorrow, why worry about it? There's no point looking beyond tomorrow.'

'I can see it's going to be a bundle of laughs working with you, Doyle,' she said, smiling thinly.

'Then don't work with me. Why did you volunteer in the first place?'

'Because no one else would work with you.'

'And what makes you so different?'

'I know how you feel.'

'Because of what happened to your brother?' He shook his head. 'No one knows how I feel, Georgie. I don't expect them to. I don't want them to *try*.' He tapped his temple. 'What goes on in here is my business, nobody else's.'

She sipped her drink, studying him over the rim of the glass.

'So we're agreed, then,' she said finally.

'On what?' he asked, looking puzzled.

'When we find Maguire, we kill him.'

Doyle smiled, and for the first time she saw something approaching warmth in the gesture.

It passed as rapidly as it had appeared.

'Cheers,' he said, raising his glass.

They left the pub together, separated on the corner

of the street and went in different directions, Doyle towards Hyde Park corner, Georgie towards Green Park.

It was 12.36 a.m.

And that time was duly noted by the figure who had sat patiently at the wheel of the Granada since they'd entered the pub.

Watching.

Waiting.

PART TWO

'We are born into a world where alienation awaits us.'
— R.D.Laing

'Eternity! thou pleasing, dreadful thought.'
— Joseph Addison

Twenty-Two

BRITTANY, FRANCE:

The cyclist tottered uncertainly, swaying from side to side as he struggled to negotiate the hill.

Catherine Roberts slowed down, watching the man warily in case he fell off into the path of her car, then finally accelerated past him, glancing at his face in the process. He looked ready to drop.

Not surprising in this heat. It poured through the windscreen as if the Peugeot were some kind of mobile greenhouse. She wiped a hand across her forehead, annoyed that the window on her side was stuck fast and could not be wound down. The air being blown into the car was hot and dry. She shifted uncomfortably in her seat as she drove, feeling the perspiration on her back and her legs. She drove barefoot, the pedals of the car warm beneath her skin.

She'd rented the car at the airport when she'd landed about an hour ago; now she was nearing the end of her journey.

Signposts, standing there like count-down markers, told her that the village of Machecoul was close.

On the back seat of the car was a small suitcase containing the bare minimum of clothes and necessities. She didn't know how long she was going to be in France.

She didn't even know why she was here, or what she was going to see.

Channing's brief phone conversation with her hadn't exactly been exhaustive in its detail.

The call had come unexpectedly; she hadn't seen him for months. She wondered what had made her agree to come. Curiosity? Perhaps she wanted to see him again. She shook her head, answering her own unspoken question. No, it wasn't that. What had happened between them was in the past now, dead and buried, and she, for one, had no wish to resurrect it. Her journey, she told herself, was in the pursuance of professional interest. It was an answer pretentiously contrived enough to persuade her.

Despite the heat that filled the car, ahead of her the clouds were dark, looming over the hills that surrounded Machecoul like gloomy portents of rain to come. Perhaps the weather would break up. She hoped it would, right now, so that she could be free of the stifling heat inside the car. Her long dark hair was tied back, pulled back a little too severely from her thin face. Yet to enter her thirty-fourth year, she was a little concerned to see the lines around her eyes. Some were uncomfortably deep to be passed off as laugh-lines. There were others under her chin, too. Irritated by her own vanity she drew her attention away from the rear-view mirror and concentrated on the road once more.

She passed a sign which proclaimed she was just five kilometres from the village she sought.

Again the thought slipped to the forefront of her mind.

What did Channing want her to see?

What had he found here that was so important?

She noticed that the road was beginning to slope downwards now. She could see the tops of houses as she turned a corner. The hills levelled out beneath her, sloping down towards the village itself. Most of the buildings were on the valley floor, others clung to the hillsides as if some frantic architect had flung them there.

Two children playing by the roadside glanced inquisitively at the car as she passed. One waved and Cath smiled and waved back. She wondered if all the natives would be as friendly.

She drove slowly through the centre of the village, glancing around the market square, looking for the inn where she knew Channing was staying and where he had booked her in, too. She finally found it and parked, glad to be out of the baking confines of the Peugeot. She picked up her suitcase and wandered into the small reception area which was delightfully cool and smelt of freshly-picked flowers.

The plump woman who owned the place greeted her warmly and Cath responded, using what little French she could remember to good effect.

She asked if Mr Channing was around.

He wasn't, she was told, as she was led up to her room. Once inside she thanked the plump woman, closed the door and headed straight for the bathroom, where she stripped and stepped beneath the shower, washing away the perspiration and also the grime of the flight and drive. She dried her hair quickly, wrapped a towel around herself and padded back into the bedroom where she began unpacking.

She had just pulled on a clean blouse and skirt when there was a knock on the door. Cath crossed to it and found she had a visitor.

Mark Channing smiled thinly when he saw her, stepping into the room, pulling her to him and kissing her on the cheek.

The greeting of a friend, not a former lover.

He asked how her flight and the drive from the airport had been. He told her she looked well. The usual bullshit, she thought, polite conversation.

She thought how terrible he looked.

Channing looked pale and his eyes were sunken, the lower lids puffy. He hadn't shaved for a couple of days.

'Are you feeling ok?' she asked him, genuinely concerned at his haggard appearance.

He smiled but it looked more like a sneer.

'I haven't been sleeping very well,' he told her, the smile fading as if even the recollection of the nightmares was painful.

'Well,' she said, 'are you going to put me out of my misery? Tell me what you dragged me over here for?' She smiled.

The gesture wasn't reciprocated. Channing got to his feet. Already he was heading for the door.

'Mark,' she said, surprised. 'What have you found?'

He swallowed hard.

'It's simpler if I show you. Come on.'

Twenty-Three

COUNTY CORK, THE REPUBLIC OF IRELAND:
The accident had happened less than ten minutes ago.

Looking at the wreckage, Callahan could only guess at what had happened.

The road which led past his estate and into the nearby village of Glengaire was narrow, flanked on

102

both sides by tall hedges and trees. Scarcely wide enough to accommodate two cars side by side, let alone a car and an articulated lorry.

The huge Scania had skidded across the road, flattening about twenty yards of hedge in its wake.

It looked as though it had hit the car head-on.

He thought it was a Sierra but, from the damage the vehicle had sustained, it was virtually impossible to tell. The car looked as if it had been put into a huge vice and crushed.

As yet, there was no sign of the passengers.

The only signal that there had even been anyone in the pulverized car was the amount of blood on the road.

Callahan sat intently behind the wheel of the Mercedes, window wound down, eyes fixed on the scene of carnage before him.

In the passenger seat Laura wriggled slightly, her short skirt pulled up almost to her thighs. Beneath it she wore no underwear and, as she too looked at the scene of devastation, she felt a warm glow spreading between her legs. She leaned forward to get a better look, her breath coming in low gasps as she watched the blood running across the road.

A member of the Garda walked across to the cab of the lorry and looked up into it.

The windscreen was shattered, spider-webbed where the driver's head had connected so forcefully with it. There was blood inside the cab, smeared on the shattered glass.

The Garda man opened the driver's side door and peered in.

The driver was slumped across the seats, blood pouring from his face and head. Both his eyes were closed, sealed shut by the congealing gore, it seemed.

103

Laura shifted in her seat once more, aware of the growing wetness between her legs. She glanced quickly across at her husband and smiled, one hand slipping onto her own thigh, stroking the smooth flesh, increasing her excitement.

From where they were parked, the Mercedes was hidden from the view of those on the road by a low hedge, but the Callahans had an excellent sight of all that was unfolding before them. One of their gardeners had heard the crash while working out by the perimeter wall which ringed their estate. He had mentioned it in passing to Callahan and the Englishman and his wife had driven to the scene immediately.

It had been worth it.

They had even beaten the ambulance and fire brigade to the crash.

'I wonder how many are in the car?' said Laura quietly, one hand now gliding up between her thighs, the fingers brushing her tightly-curled pubic hairs.

How ever many there were, Callahan thought, there wasn't going to be much of them left.

'I wonder if the driver's dead in the lorry,' Laura breathed, taking her index finger and slowly licking the moisture from its tip. She could see the Garda man walking back to his car, speaking into his radio. His feet left bloodied imprints on the tarmac where he'd walked through the blood that had spilled over the road.

In the distance they heard a siren.

The ambulance had come from the village, Callahan reasoned. It pulled up beside the lorry and two uniformed men jumped out, hurrying across to the cab. One climbed up into it, the other crossed to the car and inspected the wreck. He turned away swiftly, his face pale.

104

Laura felt the wetness between her legs increase.

More sirens.

Another ambulance. A fire engine.

They too pulled up next to the stricken vehicles, their crews spilling out, swarming around the wreck like ants round a piece of raw meat.

Callahan looked on intently as two of the firemen began cutting into the wreck with oxy-acetylene cutters, working their way around a shape in the front of the car.

The Garda man had taken off his hat and was leaning back against the bonnet of his car, breathing heavily into one hand as he watched the rescue operation.

The fireman removed a panel in the side of the car about four feet square.

The body didn't so much fall as ooze out.

From the shape of the corpse, Callahan guessed that nearly every bone in the man's body must have been crushed in the horrendous impact with the lorry. The steering column had been driven back into his chest, shattering his ribs. The top half of his body looked as if it had been wrapped in a crimson blanket. And yet his eyes were open as they pulled him out. Stretched wide in terror, perhaps, as he'd realized the inevitable end seconds before it had happened?

One arm had been almost severed at the shoulder.

Laura rubbed her thighs more tightly together, her breathing growing deeper, the wetness from her vagina now beginning to seep onto the material of the seat beneath her.

When the driver was lifted onto the roadside she could see that his stomach had been split open as surely as if it had exploded from inside. Thick lengths of intestine throbbed in the hole, spilling free as he was laid on the grass beside the road.

The Garda man finally lost his battle of will and vomited down the side of the car.

The firemen began to remove the second body.

It was a woman.

At least Callahan thought it was.

Glass from the smashed windscreen had flown back into the car and effectively shredded her face, ripping the skin beyond recognition. Portions of her features merely slid from her skull as she was lifted free.

The force with which she had been thrown forward had ensured that her body had been crushed up against the dashboard, her hips and legs pulped, one of them little more than tendrils of dripping muscle and flesh. But her head was where the worst damage had occurred.

As she was laid on the blood-spattered road, part of the top of her skull seemed to fall away and a thick slop of brain spilled from the mashed cranium. The fireman holding her head wiped his hands on his tunic and turned away. It must have been like touching an overripe rotten peach, Laura thought, watching as more sticky brain matter dribbled onto the road.

Laura was breathing loudly now, rubbing her thighs together with almost rhythmic precision as the feeling grew more powerful. She could feel the sensations building, the moisture between her legs flowing freely. Her nipples were achingly erect and she leant forward an inch or two more, her eyes fixed on the wrecked car, her body now quivering all over.

She sucked in a breath which rasped in her throat; she wanted to close her eyes, to enjoy the feeling more fully but she did not want to deprive herself of the

106

sights before her widening eyes. She ground herself more strongly into the seat, her thighs clenched tightly together as she rocked back and forth, flicking her lips with her tongue, knowing that the moment of supreme pleasure was almost upon her.

Callahan glanced across at her and smiled.

As they lifted the remains of the baby from the wreckage, she climaxed.

Twenty-Four

BRITTANY, FRANCE:

'How did you find it?'

Catherine Roberts' voice echoed inside the still confines of the church. Her eyes never left the object before her.

'Virtually by accident,' Channing explained. He described how he had inadvertently uncovered the window.

She took a step closer, touching the small section of exposed glass with her index finger.

'What is that thing?' Channing wanted to know, indicating the features of the creature on the window.

Cath could only shake her head. She peered closer, gazing at the glass itself rather than the shape that had been exposed.

'I won't be able to tell which method was used to make the window until we've uncovered it fully,' she said, still gazing at it.

'What do you mean?' Channing was rubbing his hands together, feeling cold.

'Once I've determined the method, I'll be able to give you a more accurate dating. Some of this seems to have been constructed using the *cloisonné* technique.' She tapped the glass. 'Coloured glass would actually be poured into compartments that were shaped to form images. But the rest of it ...' She allowed the sentence to trail off.

'I'm still not with you,' Channing said somewhat irritably, annoyed that Cath had not taken her eyes off the window since first meeting it.

'If some of the glass was prepared using the *cloisonné* method and some was done by painting onto glass then it means the window was put together by more than one man. And possibly over a period of years.'

'Is that so unusual?' he wanted to know.

She frowned and nodded.

'A window was as individual to its maker as, say, a novel is to its writer. It was unusual to find glass-makers working together on one window,' she told him, her eyes still fixed on the glass.

'What about that image?' he persisted, pointing at the grotesque creature depicted on the piece of window visible. 'I don't recognize it. I realized that the windows were used as teaching aids but that figure isn't biblical or mythological.' Channing found himself looking at the dull red, glass eyes. His mind flickered briefly back to his nightmare of the night before.

The mouth opening.

His hand disappearing into that yawning, fanged chasm.

He shuddered.

The dream had come to him almost every time he \sed his eyes for any length of time. He knew it was a \m but the ferocity of the nightmare had not

108

abated. If anything, each successive experience burned it more vividly into his mind. He turned away for a moment.

Catherine, on the other hand, remained crouched before the glass.

'We have to uncover the rest of it,' she said.

'I agree with you. If we come back in the morning …'

'No, Mark, I want to start now,' she said sharply, still not looking at him.

'You mean drive back into the village for your tools?'

She cut him short once again.

'You called me out here to work on the bloody thing,' she rasped, finally turning on him angrily. 'So let me work on it.'

They faced each other in silence for a moment, the cloying solitude of the church wrapping itself around them like a blanket. 'You go back, fetch my tools. Now,' she said. Then her tone softened a little. 'Please, Mark. It *is* important. You were right when you called me. I have to see it all. The sooner I can start, the sooner I can uncover it, decipher it.' She even managed to smile. 'Maybe even tell you what the significance of this little darling is.' She pointed to the image of the creature etched in glass.

Channing stood looking at her, then nodded and left the chancel.

Cath heard his footsteps echoing away. She turned back to look at the piece of glass he had uncovered.

At the monstrous face.

The red eyes seemed to fix her in a blank stare.

She reached out to touch one with her finger.

As she did, she smiled.

Twenty-Five

Channing yawned and looked at his watch.

10.34 p.m.

They'd been at the church for more than four hours now. Outside, the pleasant sunshine had long since been forced away by the onset of evening then the thick blackness of night, and with that blackness had come a cold wind that seemed to permeate even the stone of the church. He could hear it whistling around the old building as he stood in the chancel. It rattled the boarded-up windows too, poking cold fingers through into the church interior. Yet despite the cold Channing's shirt was damp with perspiration.

The effort of moving so much stone, so carefully, had drained him.

Upon returning from the village with some of Cath's tools they had set to work on the window, on the most important task first.

It had to be freed from the stonework which held it in place. They had no way of knowing if the window wasn't, like the others in the church, already smashed. Or perhaps they were only dealing with a fragment of a much larger window, the rest perhaps destroyed. Only by removing the encasing stone would they know the first of many answers posed by the discovery.

The work had not been strenuous so much as nerve-wracking. Encased in stone as it was, the window was still highly vulnerable to any over-zealous attempt to free it. It was like, Channing thought, trying to free a human body from ice with a pneumatic drill.

This task was ten times more delicate.

The glass was old, fourteenth or fifteenth century, Catherine was sure of that now. One slipped chisel or misplaced mallet blow and the entire thing could be smashed into a million pieces.

They had worked diligently, almost nervously, to chip away the stone from around the prized discovery, laying pieces of masonry on the floor of the church, occasionally stepping back to see how far their work had progressed.

After an hour they had uncovered the top three panels of the window.

The section now exposed to the dull light of the hurricane lamps was virtually impossible to see, however. The covering of masonry, the ravages of time and some defects in the glass itself served to ensure that they could not see through the patina of muck which coated the glass. The iron and lead strips used to separate the coloured panels were rusted and discoloured, too.

But they worked on, satisfied that the window was standing up to their attentions adequately, although Channing couldn't banish from his mind the thought that when they removed the final piece of stone the entire structure would topple forward and shatter on the church floor. He pushed the thought to the back of his mind.

As they worked, certain puzzling anomalies began to emerge.

Not only was the glass apparently the work of more than one glazier, but the stone which held it so firmly was of a different period to that from which the building itself had been constructed.

111

'It was added at a later date,' Channing had said.

'But why hide it?' Catherine had wanted to know, her attention riveted to the window and growing as more of it was revealed.

Channing had no answer to that particular question. Perhaps once it was uncovered and deciphered that riddle would be solved.

As more panels were revealed it became obvious that the glass so far discovered was not merely part of a larger window.

What Channing had found was complete.

The window was about forty-eight inches wide, perhaps anything up to six feet in height. Catherine had paused for a moment, wiping perspiration from her face with the back of her hand, then, with infinite care, she had scraped away some dirt from one of the panels, examining the glass beneath with the aid of a jeweller's eye-piece and a spot-light.

'It's crown glass,' she had told him. 'At least, this part is.' Without waiting for his question she had continued. 'A bubble of glass was blown onto an iron tube and then spun until it formed a disc. Then they'd use a grosing iron to chip away the edges until they'd formed the glass into the right shape.' She prodded the glass with a tracer, indicating the tiny bubbles still visible in the glass. 'The bubbles in crown glass always run in concentric circles.'

'Does that tell you anything about the man who made it?' Channing had wanted to know.

'That's one of the oldest methods of making stained glass. Other parts of it seem to have been made by other means. That's what makes me think it was constructed by more than one glazier.' She had uncovered another part of the design beneath the film of dirt.

A clawed hand had been revealed.

The huge claw was holding a child.

Channing had frowned, but somehow it made sense.

If this window had indeed been commissioned for Gilles de Rais then the inclusion of a child in its design was almost predictable.

What else could be expected of a man responsible for the deaths of over 200 children?

'The colouring methods are different, too,' Catherine had said, looking first at the clawed hand then up at the red eyes which still seemed to glow so luminously from the face of the first creature. 'That,' she pointed at the creature's face, 'looks as if it was fixed. The glass was coloured before it was put into the panel. This,' she tapped the claw very gently, 'looks as if it was painted onto the glass once it had cooled.'

'How did they colour the glass?' Channing had enquired.

'They added different metal oxides to the pot metal, that's what they called the molten glass.' She wiped her face once more. 'If they wanted red glass they added copper oxide. For green they'd add iron oxide. Cobalt oxide, blue. Manganese oxide, purple. If they wanted yellow they added sulphur.'

He had listened intently, his eyes flicking alternately between the window and Catherine.

Now, as the hands of his watch crawled round to 11.00, he leant back against the altar and looked at the window.

The glass might as well have been opaque for all they could see.

Just the claw and the face of the other creature; the rest was still encrusted by a thick layer of dirt.

Channing was tired, more tired than he could

113

remember. He felt as if the strength had been sucked from him, as if, instead of blowing wind into the church, the elements outside were drawing it away, creating a vacuum inside the chancel which made it difficult to breathe. He attributed it to the clouds of dust which hung in the air.

It was getting colder.

He rubbed his arms and shivered, looking again at his watch.

'We ought to get back to the inn,' he suggested.

Cath continued staring at the outline of the window, amazed that it was intact.

'Cath,' he said quietly, 'I said …'

'I heard you,' she snapped, not looking at him, not taking her eyes from the casement.

'We can carry on working tomorrow morning,' Channing persisted.

Still she didn't answer him, her eyes fixed on the face of the creature in the top left-hand panel. Every now and then she would glance at the clawed hand which clutched the child but it was the red eyes that held her gaze. Finally she managed to tear her attention from it. She massaged the bridge of her nose between her thumb and forefinger and nodded.

'Maybe you're right. A good night's sleep wouldn't hurt,' she said, even managing a thin smile.

A *good night's sleep.* Channing couldn't remember when he'd last enjoyed that luxury.

They began to gather up their tools.

'Something's been puzzling me, Mark,' she said. 'About the church itself. How did you manage to get permission from the local authorities to work here?'

He shrugged.

'They class it as a derelict building,' he told her.

114

'They don't care who comes here or what they do when they get here. If it fell down tomorrow I don't think it would bother them.'

The wind seemed to increase in intensity. Channing shivered.

It was definitely getting colder.

Through a gap in one of the boarded-up windows he saw the moon appear momentarily in the sky before a bank of black cloud swallowed it up.

One of the hurricane lamps flickered and died, then glowed again.

Channing looked across at the window.

A dull thud reverberated throughout the church, the sound carried on the stillness.

He must have forgotten to secure the church door when they'd first entered, he told himself.

'Leave it for tonight, Cath,' he said.

The thud came again.

Twice in quick succession.

What the hell was going on here?

Twenty-Six

Channing looked around towards the door which led into the chancel. Perhaps the main door of the church had been slammed shut by the powerful wind. He crossed to the chancel door, opened it and peered out, his torch beam cutting a swathe through the gloom, picking out the main door.

It was shut tight.

115

Another thud, this time from above them.

In the belfry.

'Let's get out of here,' Channing said, his voice catching. 'Come on. I think we've done enough for tonight.' *Had she detected the note of fear in his voice?* He didn't really care if she had. He was tired, cold and something else he didn't care to admit. *No, what the hell?* He was frightened. The place made him uneasy at the best of times and now these bloody noises …

'Let's go, Cath,' he said again, more forcefully this time.

She was still gazing at the window, moving towards it as if she had spotted something in the glass which Channing couldn't see.

'For Christ's sake,' he snapped. 'We'll come back in the morning.'

That thud again, and now he knew it was coming from above them.

A rational part of his mind told him it was the door which led into the belfry. The wind must have blown it open and now, with each fresh gust, it was slamming it back on its hinges. That was the answer. He suddenly felt angry with himself for even entertaining any solution but the most logical one. Lack of sleep fuelled the imagination, he told himself, thinking how late at night it was for home-spun philosophy.

Cath was kneeling beside the window now, looking more intently at the face of the child held in the clawed hand. She wiped more dust away from it.

'I'll wait for you in the car,' said Channing irritably, and she heard him clatter through into the main nave.

Cath looked at the face on the window, running the tip of her index finger around it, trying to make out the features.

116

Something …

Channing muttered to himself as he tripped and almost fell over a pew in the nave.

… familiar …

He heard a strident screech ahead of him as the church door opened.

For fleeting seconds he blinked in the gloom, the wind roared outside and the moon broke free of the clouds.

… about the face …

A dark shape filled the doorway of the church.

Dark and massive.

'Oh, Jesus Christ,' murmured Channing, fumbling for his torch.

'Cath,' he called, flicking on the torch, swinging it back and forth.

The church was filled with a smell unlike anything he'd ever encountered before.

A stench of decay.

And it was drawing closer to him, filling his nostrils.

He heard footfalls, sensed movement.

'Cath.'

He backed off.

In the chancel, Cath squinted as she continued to trace the features of the child in the window.

She knew that face.

She heard her voice being called. She smelled the vile stench.

As she heard the scream from inside the nave she looked around.

'Mark,' she called, getting to her feet, taking one last look back at the window. At the face of the child.

As she did the breath caught in her throat.

The face of the child was contorted into an attitude of terror. The child was screaming.

117

But it was no longer a child.
It bore the face of Mark Channing.

Twenty-Seven

She called out his name as she sat up, her body sheathed in sweat.

As she was flung from the nightmare she let out a low gasp, a combination of fear at the images which had invaded her mind and also of relief that the experience had been within the confines of her subconscious.

Now she sat forward, one hand to her throat, feeling the sweat on her fingers.

She almost screamed again when she saw the figure standing beside her bed.

In the semi-darkness, her mind still reeling from what she'd dreamt, she was unable to focus on the figure and the newest intrusion sent her heart pounding even more furiously.

It took her a second to realize that it was Channing.

'Jesus,' she murmured, her hand falling from her throat to her chest. She could feel her heart thudding against her ribs.

'Are you ok?' he asked, looking down at her. 'I heard you shout.'

She swallowed hard and nodded, looking at her watch.

2.14 a.m.

'I'm ok,' she said. 'Just a bad dream. I haven't had a nightmare since I was a kid.' She sucked in a couple of deep breaths, aware that only the sheet around her protected her nakedness from Channing's gaze. She pulled it higher, up to her throat in a gesture of exaggerated modesty. The gesture seemed somewhat inappropriate, considering they had once been lovers. The thought was pushed from her mind rapidly. The images of the dream returned and she switched on the bedside lamp, as if the coming of light would hasten the banishment of those images.

As it illuminated Channing's face she saw how pale and drawn he looked; the rings beneath his eyes were so dark and deeply etched as if a manic tattoo artist had been let loose with dark ink around the blood-shot orbs.

'You look pretty bad, Mark, if you don't mind me saying,' she said, aware of how clumsy the words sounded. 'Sorry if I woke you.'

'I was already awake,' he explained. 'Bad dreams too.'

She shrugged.

'I dreamt I was in the church,' she told him. 'I could see it as clearly as I can see you now.' She looked up at him and he squatted on the edge of the bed.

'What did you see?' he wanted to know.

'The window. Uncovered. At least another part of it.'

'A clawed hand,' he said flatly.

She nodded.

'A clawed hand holding a child,' he continued.

She looked at him, a frown creasing her brow.

All she could do was nod gently. She felt cold.

'What time did we get back from the church tonight?' she asked him, as if her own memory were suddenly untrustworthy.

119

'About eleven-thirty,' he told her.

Outside the wind whipped through the village square, catching one corner of an unsecured market stall awning. It began flapping in the breeze like the wings of a massive bat.

'What else did you dream?' Channing wanted to know.

'We were in the church, it was after we uncovered the window. It started to get colder in there. It was as if I could feel it.' She rubbed one arm where the flesh had risen in goose-pimples. 'There were noises. I saw something on the window. The hand you mentioned, holding a child.' The realization seemed to strike her like a slap across the cheek. 'You saw the hand, too?'

He nodded.

'On the window?' she asked.

'I think so.' He massaged the back of his neck with one hand.

'The noises carried on so you went out into the nave, left me with the window. I saw the child's face in the glass, it seemed to get clearer. I heard you calling me but I couldn't look away from the glass.'

'You felt the cold, heard the church door open.'

These weren't questions, they were statements.

'You heard me scream, you called to me, you were about to come through into the nave when you looked back at the painting and saw that the face of the child was really *my* face.'

She could only look at him blankly.

'We shared the same nightmare, Cath,' he told her. '*I* saw what *you* saw.'

'That's not possible,' she said, but there was no conviction in her voice.

'Then you give me another explanation.'

120

She couldn't.

Outside the wind continued to whip the awning loudly. It sounded like some huge carrion bird coming closer.

Twenty-Eight

ENNISKILLEN, COUNTY FERMANAGH, NORTHERN IRELAND:

He moved the rifle slightly to the right until the cross-threads of the telescopic sight rested squarely on the woman's head.

She bent down and he followed her with the rifle, never losing his aim, his finger resting gently on the trigger of the HK91 rifle.

Maureen Pithers knelt down beside the flower-bed and pulled some weeds from the dark earth, dropping them into the bucket beside her. She carefully worked her way round, removing any offending piece of foliage which spoiled the look of her garden. She enjoyed the task. Her weekly war on weeds, she called it. Now she continued with her own war, unaware of the rifle pointed at her head.

Billy Dolan lowered the rifle for a moment and lit up a cigarette. From where he lay he was well hidden from the house and garden by almost one hundred and fifty yards of gently sloping hillside, tall grass and trees. He'd found the best spot about an hour ago, ensuring that he had the front door of the house in clear view. The house was at the bottom of the slope, a white-painted, red-tiled building that seemed to shine in the sunlight. Nice place, Billy thought as he lit his cigarette, puffing contentedly on it for a moment before rolling over back onto his stomach, resting the stock of the rifle against his shoulder and drawing a bead on the woman once again.

She was in her mid-forties, a little plump, dressed in a green plastic apron to stop the earth from the garden getting on her clothes. He watched her pull vigorously at the weeds, tossing each one into the bucket.

Yes, it was certainly a nice place. Beat the fuck out of his home in the Turf Lodge area of Belfast. Fast approaching his twenty-second birthday, Billy had foreseen for himself the same life as his father. Jobs here and there if he was lucky, sucking up to some fucking Proddy foreman, then on the dole, drawing thirty quid a week if he was lucky.

Billy didn't want that. He didn't want to spend the rest of his days signing on and then drinking the money away in the pub on a Saturday night with the rest of his mates, who were also out of work. Fuck that.

He shifted position on the hillside and drew deeper on his cigarette.

Most members of the IRA had brothers, fathers, grandfathers or kin of some description in the ranks. Or they had followed family members into the arms of the cause. Not Billy. He had made the decision on his own because that was the way he chose to spend his life. Not bowing and scraping to anyone. Fuck the lot of them. He only took orders from one man now.

That man was lying next to him on the hill, gazing at the white house through a pair of binoculars.

James Maguire was about eight years older than Billy, a dark-haired, hard-faced man who was short yet so powerfully built his appearance could almost be described as brutish. He scanned the house and garden with the binoculars, aware that Billy had the woman pinned in the sight of the HK91.

When the time came, he would not miss.

'The car's waiting,' said Maguire. 'There's no hurry. Bring the gun with you when you've finished.'

Billy nodded.

'Company,' said the younger man, spotting a new arrival through the telescopic sight.

Maureen Pithers had stopped her war on the weeds to speak to another woman who had approached the hedge which separated the immaculately kept garden from the narrow country lane in which it stood. The house was about two hundred yards from its nearest neighbour.

Billy began moving the rifle back and forth, fixing first one woman then the other in the sights of the weapon.

'Billy.'

The sound of his own name broke his concentration.

'Front door,' said Maguire, still peering through the binoculars.

Billy looked across and saw a man emerging from the house. He was in his late forties, tall, balding. What hair he had was grey. His face was full, jovial.

Reverend Brian Pithers stood on the front doorstep for a moment, briefcase in hand, smiling across at his wife and her friend, then he crossed the lawn to the women and began speaking animatedly to them.

'I can imagine what he's saying,' said Maguire, a slight smile on his lips. 'We should never have trusted the IRA. I warned everyone about them. Now there'll be a price to pay.'

123

Billy chuckled.

'Have you been reading his speeches, Jim?' he said, squinting down the sight.

'It's all he's been saying since the business at Stormont,' Maguire said quietly.

'It's all he was saying *before* it,' Billy added. This time both men laughed.

Billy was still chuckling when he drew a bead on Reverend Pithers and fired.

The bullet, moving at a speed in excess of two thousand feet per second, struck Pithers just above the left eye, blasting a path effortlessly through his frontal bone before ploughing on through his brain, finally exploding from the rear of his skull, carrying a massive portion of the parietal and occipital bones with it. A thick flux of brain spewed from the wound, propelled by the force of the bullet which lifted the clergyman off his feet and catapulted him several yards backwards. He hit the ground, spraying blood all over his wife's carefully tended lawn.

Both women screamed, Mrs Pithers running to her husband's side, the other woman bursting through the gate and hurtling towards the house. Presumably to call an ambulance.

Save your strength, thought Billy, studying his handiwork through the sight.

Pither's eyes were still open, although blood from the entry wound had run into the left one. It was spreading rapidly around what remained of his head while his wife could only kneel beside him shouting something neither Billy nor Maguire could hear. There were slicks of crimson on her apron, no doubt splashed there when the bullet had first blasted away part of her husband's cranium.

The two IRA men got to their feet and sauntered away, spotting the car which waited for them at the other side of the hill, its engine idling. They'd gone less than ten feet when Maguire took the rifle from Billy and wandered back to the crest.

'Jim, what's wrong?' Billy asked, looking at his companion.

Maguire raised the rifle to his shoulder.

'He's dead,' the younger man protested.

'I know he's dead.' Maguire took aim. 'But I'll tell you something, Billy,' he said quietly. 'My mother always used to say it to me. There's nothing in this world so sad as a widow.'

And he shot Mrs Pithers once in the head.

Twenty-Nine

COUNTY-CORK, THE REPUBLIC OF IRELAND: Night had brought with it the first spots of rain.

David Callahan stood before the huge picture window that ran virtually the length of the sitting-room and glanced out, watching the droplets spattering the glass.

After a moment or two he pulled the cord and drew the thick velvet curtains across, shutting out the darkness and elements. He crossed to the drinks cabinet and poured himself a large brandy, warming it in the large crystal tumbler.

'Do you want anything?' he asked, glancing across at Laura, who was stretched out on one of the sofas in the lounge reading. She shook her head but he poured her a vodka anyway and placed it on the table beside her.

Callahan crossed to the leather chair facing the TV and sat down, glass in hand. He reached for the remote control, pondering whether or not to switch on the set. He decided to finish his drink first.

Laura looked up from her book and caught his pensive expression.

'What are you thinking about?' she asked, reaching for the vodka and taking a sip.

'This and that,' he said enigmatically.

She folded over one corner of the page and tossed the book onto the coffee table.

'You miss London, don't you?' she said.

Callahan smiled.

'Is it *that* obvious?'

'What's there to miss, David? We've got everything here. Money, freedom to do just what we want. To experiment.' She smiled at him over the rim of the glass. 'Besides, it was too dangerous there, you know that.'

He nodded, staring down into the brandy glass. He knew she was right. They'd had no choice but to get out of London. The police had been after him; two other gangs had threatened to kill him. One had even tried. His customers had complained about the quality of the merchandise he'd been supplying. With good reason, he thought, smiling thinly. The last batch of heroin he'd sold had been only thirty per cent pure.

The rest had been made up of vim and talcum powder.

Callahan had no way of knowing how many had died as a result of taking the inferior stuff. He didn't really care, either. He'd made in excess of three million on

126

the load. However, even that was chicken-feed compared to the other rackets.

The gun-running had been so far the most lucrative, with over sixteen million netted in just over a year. When he offset the police pay-offs it still left him with close to fourteen million. The odd two or three million here and there was a small price to pay for being able to run such a lucrative business.

However, with the money came danger. Selling guns to terrorists brought its own risks. A group of French radicals had threatened to kill him over a shipment of inferior Sterling rifles he'd sold them. He'd had trouble collecting money from an over-ambitious group of Chinese youths who'd fancied their chances against one of the Triads in London.

Three of them had finished up decapitated, their bodies found in Soho Square, their heads jammed onto the railings in Leicester Square.

No one ever discovered what became of their genitals.

Callahan smiled at the recollection.

He had seen the signs early enough. He and Laura had slipped out of the country and travelled the world for eight months: the States, the Far East and the Caribbean. Finally they bought the estate in Ireland, where they now lived like throw-backs to a feudal age.

Callahan employed six house staff and four others to work the estate. At first he and Laura had both thought that Ireland, with its relaxed way of life, might be too slow for them. But they had found diversions.

And there were always the drugs.

One thing remained elusive, though. Not so much because of its unavailabilty but because it was intangible.

The ultimate thrill.

The supreme experience.

Callahan had searched for it all his life, experimenting with every substance and experience he could imagine. There were things he hadn't tried, of course, but that time would come.

He and Laura had made it their quest.

It was their Holy Grail.

He chuckled at the analogy. There had been nothing holy about most of their indulgences.

In Laura he had the perfect companion, as devoted, as obsessive in her search for that ultimate thrill as he was. Together they had run the gamut of perversion, exhausting their minds as well as their bodies in their singular quest, never really knowing how close they were to achieving the elusive dream. Neither of them knew which form it would take. They lived in a state of almost constant expectation, existing in a world of heightened arousal.

Callahan knew that the ultimate thrill was not in taking a life.

He'd done that twice before, one by shooting, the other by strangulation. Watching, feeling a man's life ebb away was a powerful sensation indeed but he knew that there must be something beyond it.

Beyond death itself, perhaps.

Callahan smiled to himself and flicked on the TV.

There was a photo of a clergyman behind the newsreader. Something looked vaguely familiar about the man's face. Callahan got to his feet to re-fill his glass, turning the volume up as he did.

'... *earlier today. The shooting happened outside Mr Pither's home in County Fermanagh and was seen by a neighbour ...*'

'David, do we have to watch this?' Laura said wearily.

Callahan raised a hand to silence her, his attention focused on the screen. He made his way back to the chair and gazed rapt at the television.

'... *Reverend Pithers was dead upon reaching hospital. His wife was also killed in the attack* ...'

Callahan sipped his drink slowly.

... '*The attack has been condemned by all sides including the Provisional IRA, who were anxious to stress that none of their men were involved in the killing* ...'

Laura rolled onto her stomach, her chin resting on her arms as she looked disinterestedly at the television.

'... *Coming so close to the massacre at Stormont it would appear that any permanent solution to the military and political problems in Northern Ireland is now fading fast. Police suspect that the same men responsible for the shootings at Stormont were responsible for the killing of Reverend Pithers and his wife* ...'

Callahan took a long swallow from the brandy glass, feeling the amber fluid burn its way to his stomach.

'... *the hunt for the killers continues* ...'

Callahan was on his feet, making for the drinks cabinet again when the maid appeared in the doorway of the sitting-room to announce that dinner was ready. Laura thanked her and got to her feet, preparing to switch off the TV as she passed.

'Leave it,' said Callahan, his eyes still fixed on the screen.

Laura shrugged and wandered out of the room.

The phone rang and Callahan picked it up.

'Hello,' he said, eyes still on the television, flicking it off when he realized the item had finished. 'Hello.'

No answer.

'Who's there?' he said irritably.

There was a click as the phone was put down.

He held the receiver for a second then dropped it back on the cradle and followed Laura through to the dining-room, where they both sat down.

The first course had barely been laid in front of them when the phone rang again.

'Let Julie get it,' said Laura but Callahan was already on his feet and heading for the phone in the hall.

He returned a few moments later, his face a little pale. Laura frowned as she saw his expression.

'Are you ok, David?' she asked.

He nodded briskly but didn't look at her.

'Who was that on the phone?' she wanted to know.

'Wrong number,' he said dismissively.

Laura shrugged and continued eating. As Callahan raised his fork to his mouth he noticed that his hand was shaking slightly.

Wrong number.

He wished it had been.

Thirty

He paused by the entrance to the cellar.

Callahan knew that no one else would be awake in the house at such an hour; he also knew that no one else was allowed access to the cellar. Even so, he stood for what seemed an eternity with his hand on the door knob, looking around him.

The door of the cellar was in the kitchen, and it was through this first barrier that he now passed, locking it carefully behind him. He flicked on the light switch and a narrow stairway was illuminated below him. It smelled of damp down there despite the fact that the walls were relatively free of mould, the paint still uncracked.

He descended the first flight of steps and came to another door.

Selecting a second key, Callahan let himself through and emerged into the room beyond.

More stairs stretched away before him and he snapped on more lights. A bank of fluorescents burst into life illuminating the sub-cellar. It was large, over twenty feet square. On all four sides wooden boxes were piled as high as the ceiling. As he descended he saw the words on the sides of the boxes, sprayed there with the help of a stencil.

Some of the words were foreign.

The writing was Russian. French. German.

As Callahan reached the centre of the sub-cellar he could smell the familiar odour of oil. As he crossed to the box nearest him the smell became stronger. The lid had been partially removed using a crow-bar, which lay nearby. Callahan completed the task, pulling the lid free, removing the straw which covered the contents of the box.

Four Heckler and Koch Model 33 assault rifles lay on top of the straw. Beneath them, four more.

Piled beside the crates were smaller wooden boxes full of ammunition.

Bullets of every calibre imaginable.

.45. 9mm. 5.45mm. 7.62mm. .357. .38. .44 Magnum rounds (half and full metal jacket). Hollow tips. Wad-cutters. Even a case of .223 'Duplex' cartridges.

Every type of bullet to fit every type of pistol and rifle and machine gun.

The crates were storehouses of death.

Combat Magnums, Smith and Wessons, Rugers, Walthers, Berettas, Brownings, Heckler and Koch, Remington.

And the sub-machine guns.

Ingrams, Berettas, Uzis, Skorpions, Steyrs.

The shotguns were there, too. The Ithacas, Brownings and Spas.

For the right price Callahan had always said he could get a tank. Now he smiled and picked up one of the HK33's, working the bolt action as if he were chambering a round. He pressed it to his shoulder and squinted down the sight, peering around the subterranean room.

He squeezed the trigger and the hammer slammed down on an empty chamber. The metallic click sounded thunderous inside the sub-cellar.

He had seen a young lad dressed in a T-shirt once which had borne the slogan, 'Killing is my business ... and business is good.'

It might have been invented for Callahan.

He couldn't begin to imagine how many hundreds of thousands of pounds worth of weapons were stored here below the house; it might even run into millions. Brought to him by private plane or boat from his many contacts around the world. Sent out the same way when they were needed. And there were many who paid for what he had to sell.

He re-cocked the HK33 and held it before him, finally pressing it to his shoulder and bringing the sight to bear on the sub-cellar door.

He knew he would have need of these weapons himself soon.

The time was drawing closer.

132

Thirty-One

BRITTANY, FRANCE:
As she drove, Catherine Roberts caught a glimpse of herself in the rear-view mirror, and what she saw wasn't very pleasing.

She was pale through lack of sleep, her eyes swollen and puffy as if she'd been crying. There were bags beginning to form, she thought, annoyed at this sudden attack of vanity. She ran a hand through her hair and concentrated on the road instead.

Beside her Mark Channing lay back in the passenger seat, his eyes closed as if hoping that the sleep which eluded him at night would come now. And yet he knew that with sleep would come dreams.

Those dreams.

He opened his eyes and rubbed them with his fists, blinking myopically at the passing countryside. Then he glanced across at Cath, who seemed unaware of his gaze. He noted every detail of her appearance and attire. Her thin face with its high cheek bones, her long hair which was whipped by the wind flowing through her open window. She wore a simple plain blouse which successfully concealed her breasts. Her jeans were tight, marked in places with the dust of the church.

The church.

It seemed that he could not escape the building whatever his train of thought and, at the moment, those thoughts were *not* on some relic of the past. They were firmly on the present.

'I don't think I've had time to thank you for coming out here, Cath,' he said, finally. 'I appreciate it.'

She smiled.

'I didn't think you'd come,' he continued, 'after what happened between us. I thought you might find it difficult.' He shrugged.

'What happened is in the past, Mark,' she said.

'Meaning you've forgotten about it?'

'I didn't say that. I haven't forgotten about it. You can't wipe out memories that easily.'

'Do you *want* to wipe them out?'

'Our affair is in the past. We were different people then.'

He looked a little disappointed.

'It was good at the time but that time has gone,' she told him.

'And you don't want it to happen again?' Channing asked, his tone lower.

'No.'

Cath was amazed she'd managed to say it quite so directly. She hoped she hadn't hurt him, but if she had then he would have to learn to live with it.

'Is there anyone at the moment?' he wanted to know.

'Is it important?'

'I'm just curious.'

'You're more than curious, Mark,' she said wearily. 'But in answer to that question, no, there isn't anyone at the moment.'

'Are you going to tell me your work comes first?' he said. She wasn't slow to pick up the hint of sarcasm in his voice.

'What's so bad about that?' she snapped.

'Nothing. I just didn't picture you as a career woman,' he told her, and again there was that edge to his tone she didn't care for. She thought about saying something but resisted the temptation.

'Don't you think we'd be better off discussing the real reason I came here, instead of raking over the past?' she said finally.

Channing was silent for a moment, looking out of the window distractedly. Finally he nodded briskly.

'So give me your *expert* opinion,' he said.

Again that edge to his voice.

'The date of the window and as much as you can tell about its manufacture.' He reached into his pocket and pulled out a packet of Rothmans, offering her one before lighting up himself.

'It's too early to tell without a thorough examination of the glass,' she began. 'But from what little I've seen I'd say that it was early fifteenth century.'

'Which would place it around the time of Gilles de Rais,' he said quietly, a softly-spoken affirmation of his own original theory. 'What I can't understand is, if de Rais was a necromancer, black magician, whatever, why would he have a stained-glass window put into a church he'd already desecrated?'

'From what we've seen of the images in the glass so far the window isn't exactly an offering to God,' said Cath. 'Stained-glass windows were usually offered as dedications to God by the men who commissioned them.'

'Jesus Christ,' murmured Channing. 'Maybe that's what the window is. An offering. An offering to the deity de Rais worshipped.' He sucked on his cigarette. 'Stained-glass windows usually told a story of some kind, right? Perhaps this one does too.'

'I won't know that until we've uncovered it all,' she

135

told him. 'There has to be somewhere else to work, Mark. I need to do more detailed tests on the glass.'

'Where would you suggest? Back at the inn?' he said, acidly. 'The work has to be done inside the church. Also, the fewer people who know about it the better.'

'Jealous of your little discovery, Mark?' she said, and now it was *her* turn to inject scorn into her words.

He didn't answer.

She swung the car around a curve in the road.

The church came into view, momentarily enveloped by deep shadow as a cloud passed in front of the watery sun.

Neither of them spoke as they drew nearer the building; both had their eyes fixed on it, a mixture of anticipation and unease flowing through them.

It was Cath who spotted it first.

'Mark, look,' she said, pointing ahead.

Outside the church, close to the main door, another car was parked.

Thirty-Two

Cath slowed down as they approached the car, able to see that its owner was not in evidence.

'Drive past it and stop,' said Channing, scanning the area around the church.

She did as she was instructed then they both clambered out of the Renault, eyes and ears alert to the slightest sight or sound of movement from the church. Clearly the owner of the vehicle was inside the building.

Channing headed for the door.

He was less than two feet from it when the figure emerged.

Channing took a step back, startled by the sudden appearance of the man. He was in his late twenties, tall and slightly built, with short dark hair. He smiled politely and moved out into the open, nodding a polite greeting to Cath.

'Who are you?' asked Channing.

The man looked stumped for a moment and Cath wondered if he was unable to understand English. Her French wasn't up to much but it might do in a crisis. She took a step forward.

'*Qui êtes vous?*' she asked.

'*Pardon,*' said the man, smiling. 'You may speak English if you wish. I have enough of your language to prevent difficulties.' He smiled again and Cath found herself smiling back, amused at his accent.

'What are you doing here?' Channing said, less charitable in his approach.

'My name is Claude Lausard,' he said, extending a hand which Channing declined to shake. 'I was visiting the church.'

Channing eyed the man suspiciously.

'Have you been inside?' he wanted to know.

'Only briefly ...'

'What did you see?' Channing interrupted.

'What should I have seen? Tell me, Mr Channing, you have spent more time here than most in the past few days. Miss Roberts, too.'

'How do you know our names?' Cath asked him.

'Madame Chabrol, the lady who runs the inn, *she* told me,' Lausard admitted, the smile never leaving his lips.

137

'We still don't know who you are,' Channing said irritably. 'Why have you been prying, finding out our names? What the hell do you want?'

Lausard held up his hands to calm Channing.

'I want a story, Monsieur Channing,' he said, still smiling.

'You're a reporter,' Cath said flatly.

The Frenchman nodded.

'Only from a humble regional newspaper, I admit, but we all have to work. What is the attraction of Machecoul?' he said, motioning to the church, his smile finally fading. 'No one ever comes near this place; you should have known that your work here, I presume it is work, would not go unnoticed by the locals. What happened here may have happened over four hundred years ago but the stigma remains. The name of Gilles de Rais belongs to history, Monsieur Channing. Perhaps for the wrong reasons, but it does nonetheless.' Lausard lit up a cigarette and walked across to his car, leaning on the bonnet. 'What were you hoping to find here?'

'Information,' Channing told him tersely.

'About de Rais? Why?'

'For a book I'm writing. I'm a historian.'

'And you, Miss Roberts? What is your interest here?'

'It isn't really any of your business, Mr Lausard,' she told him flatly.

The smile returned to the reporter's lips.

'You are certainly very protective of your discovery, whatever it may be,' he said, reaching for his lighter. As he held it up to relight his cigarette Cath noticed it was in the shape of a silver horse's head. 'Have you found de Rais' treasure?'

A heavy silence descended, broken finally by the Frenchman.

'I am not here to interfere,' he said, 'but to discover, like you.' He eyed them both. 'Is it the treasure you've found? Don't pretend you don't know what I'm talking about. If you know about Gilles de Rais then you know about the treasure he supposedly had.'

'No one knew what form that treasure took,' Channing said.

'That is what you are here to find out, I presume?'

'Look, why don't you just leave us alone to get on with our work?' snapped Channing.

Lausard continued to smile.

'Don't let me stand in your way. I'll come back when you're not so busy.' He tossed away his cigarette and slid behind the wheel of his car, starting the engine. He wound down the window and looked at the others. 'I will see you again,' he said and drove off, gravel spinning up behind the car as he sped away. Cath and Channing watched the car disappear up the dirt track then around a bend.

'That's all we need,' said Channing wearily.

The sun was sinking slowly when Lausard returned to Machecoul.

He parked his car on the crest of one of the hills which sloped down to the valley floor, got out and sat on the bonnet, looking down at the church. He reached into his pocket, pulled out first a packet of cigarettes then the silver lighter. Lausard sucked hard on the Gaulois, inhaling the smoke, allowing it to burn its way into his lungs.

From his vantage point he could see the Renault parked outside the church. He knew that Cath and Channing were still inside. What they were doing he could only guess at.

A chill breeze had sprung up; it whistled around the car, making Lausard shiver. He decided that it would be warmer waiting inside. He glanced at his watch.

7.26 p.m.

It might be a long wait.

Thirty-Three

It was almost eleven-thirty when Lausard saw the headlights of the Renault cutting through the blackness of the valley floor away from the church of Machecoul. He sat behind the wheel of his car and finished his cigarette, finally tossing the butt out of the window. Then he started the engine and guided the Citroen down the narrow road towards the building.

He didn't put on his own headlamps, relying instead on the side lights despite the unevenness of the road. No point in announcing his arrival, he thought, smiling.

The moon was hidden behind vast rolling banks of dark bilious cloud but Lausard welcomed the darkness. It aided his secretive approach.

He pulled up close to the main door of the church and switched off the engine, sitting there a moment, looking up at the church. It towered above him like some predatory animal. He finally swung himself out of the car, reaching over to the back seat in the process to pick up the camera that lay there. Checking that it was loaded with film he proceeded towards the main door, pausing before it, listening for any sound from inside.

Maybe only one of the English couple had left; perhaps the other one was still inside?

He moved closer, pressing gently against the door which opened a couple of inches.

The smell of damp enveloped him as he stood on the threshold and he stifled a cough, so strong was the odour of neglect.

It was as quiet as the grave.

He was sure he was alone.

Lausard moved into the nave, pulling a torch from his jacket pocket, flicking it on as, for the second time that day, he wandered through the derelict building. The torch beam picked out overturned pews. Dust swirled as he walked, the motes pinned in the roving light like flies on paper. He moved down the central aisle of the church towards the door that led into the chancel.

Christ, it was cold.

His breath clouded in the air as he exhaled. He stopped for a moment to breathe on his hands. It hadn't felt this cold outside, he thought, as he moved closer to the far door.

His inspection of the building earlier in the day had not taken him beyond the nave. In fact he'd been on the point of investigating the chancel when he'd heard the car with Cath and Channing in pull up. Now, however, there was no one to interrupt him.

Keeping the torch at chest height he moved on.

He knew they'd found something inside the church. Otherwise what reasons would they have for being so secretive?

Had they really found de Rais' treasure?

Lausard reached the chancel door and pulled at it, relieved when he found it wasn't locked.

141

As he opened it a blast of cold air hit him like a freezing hammer. It was as if all the warmth had been sucked from his body. He paused for a moment, trying to re-acclimatize himself to the sudden, savage drop in temperature.

The darkness inside the chancel was almost palpable. Lausard felt as if he were drowning in it, as if the gloom was filling him as he breathed. He slowed his breathing and shone the torch around the inner sanctum of the church, picking out the altar, the boarded-up windows, the door which led to the stairs and belfry beyond, the shape ...

To his left was an object draped in a piece of cloth.

An object about six feet high.

He shone the torch over it, unable to make out any contours.

Aware of his own heartbeat thudding more insistently, Lausard moved towards it, reaching out to grip the cloth.

He pulled and it came free.

Lausard frowned.

Was this what they were being so secretive about?

A stained-glass window.

The top third of it had been uncovered by painstaking work and the images seemed to glow in the light of his torch with surprising brilliance. Exactly what they were he didn't know.

Some of them disgusted him.

He moved closer, shining the torch over the glass, gazing long and hard at the features of the creature in the top right-hand panel, then turned away and headed towards the door that led to the belfry stairs. If they'd found something, he reasoned, it had to be more than the window.

Surely.

The door opened with difficulty, its ancient hinges creaking protestingly as Lausard pulled.

A gust of cold wind blew down the spiral stairs and ruffled his hair. He shone the torch up and saw that the stairs curved around to the right, the spiral apparently growing tighter the higher the staircase rose.

He pressed on the first step, putting all his weight on it, satisfied when the old timbers merely groaned under his pressure.

The stairs were safe to climb.

He began to ascend.

Lausard was halfway up when he detected the stench.

It was noxious beyond belief, a nauseating smell which made him feel faint, such was its intensity. He stopped on the stairs, putting one hand across his mouth in an effort to minimize the effect of the choking fetor.

It was then that he realized it was coming from below him.

From the chancel.

He turned on the stairs and headed back down, the torch beam swaying back and forth as he hurried down the creaking steps, almost retching now, such was the vehemence of the stench.

As he stumbled into the chancel itself he felt his legs give way and he fell to the ground, his lighter skidding across the floor.

He didn't attempt to retrieve it.

All he wanted to do was get out of the church, get away from this rancid atmosphere.

He dragged himself to his feet, his torch beam settling briefly on the window again.

The smell was momentarily forgotten as he stood gaping at it.

At ...

Lausard wanted to shake his head, wanted to register some gesture but it seemed as if every muscle in his body was frozen.

Thirty-Four

Callahan was half way up the stairs when he heard the phone ring again.

Callahan called that he would answer it, anxious that Laura should not retrieve the receiver. He snatched up one of the extensions in a spare room, pressing the phone to his ear, his hand shaking slightly.

'Hello,' he said.

The line was crackly, alive with static.

'Who is it?' Callahan repeated, trying to steady the quivering in his voice.

'Callahan,' the voice on the other end said. 'It's me. It's Lausard.'

Callahan swallowed hard and his grip on the phone relaxed.

'What do you want?' he asked.

'I might have something for you,' the Frenchman said.

'What is it?'

'It should fit nicely into your collection,' the Frenchman said.

'Just stop pissing about and tell me what it is,'

Callahan snapped. 'I don't pay you to play games.'

'It's a stained-glass window.'

Callahan didn't speak.

'Did you hear what I said?' Lausard repeated. 'Probably commissioned by Gilles de Rais himself.'

'Who else knows about it?' Callahan wanted to know.

Lausard explained about Channing and Catherine Roberts.

'I want it Lausard. Do you understand? No matter what, I want it.'

'It's going to cost you a lot of money.'

'I don't care how much it costs, I want it.' There was a steely determination in his voice. 'We'll come over as soon as we can.' He hung up.

Callahan smiled to himself.

Gilles de Rais.

The man had murdered over two hundred children, many of them in the church at Machecoul. Ritual killings, the children had been between the ages of four and ten, rarely older. De Rais himself had been burned at the stake as a witch. Again Callahan smiled. He climbed the rest of the stairs to the bedroom, where Laura lay naked on the bed glancing at a magazine.

'Lausard's found something in the church at Machecoul,' he said quietly.

She turned to look at him.

'To do with de Rais?' she said.

He nodded.

'Machecoul.' She said the name softly, with something bordering on reverence.

They had visited it many years ago. Just as they had visited countless other places around the world where murders, and sometimes much worse, had taken place. They visited and they photographed and they studied.

145

Their interest had often taken them far afield but they had visited sites and soaked up atmospheres others would have shunned.

Auschwitz.

Belsen.

10050 Cielo Drive in Los Angeles, scene of the ritual murders of Sharon Tate and four others by Charles Manson's family.

Dealey Plaza in Dallas. (They had stood on the spot in the road where the car had been when President Kennedy had been shot.)

Saddleworth Moor in Yorkshire. (Laura had been excited by the fact that she might actually be *standing* on the grave of one of the victims of Ian Brady and Myra Hindley.)

The German Embassy in Stockholm, fire-bombed by the Baader-Meinhof gang.

Cranley Gardens, Muswell Hill, London. (They had wanted to look inside the flat where Denis Nilsen had killed and mutilated his victims but had been turned away. Still, Laura had taken plenty of pictures of the outside of the building.)

Jeffrey Manor, Chicago. (Richard Speck had killed eight nurses there in one night of madness.)

Buhre Avenue, New York City. (David Berkowitz, known as 'Son of Sam', had shot his first victims there.)

The list was endless. They had travelled the world to sample these delights, bringing back with them souvenirs wherever possible. Pieces of wire from Auschwitz. Turf from Saddleworth Moor. Stones from Buhre Avenue. Usually, however, they were content with photos; they had hundreds in one of the rooms close to their bedroom. It was like a shrine.

146

Laura often sat in there alone, staring around at the walls, surrounded by images of death and pain, excited sometimes beyond endurance.

Sex in that room was beyond belief.

It was pleasure without measure, or equal.

'How many did de Rais kill?' she asked, letting one hand slide across the bed towards Callahan's groin.

'Over two hundred,' he said, feeling his own excitement growing as she rubbed his penis, feeling it stiffen.

'All children,' he continued.

He was fully erect now.

She leant over and took him in her mouth, allowing her saliva to coat his purple glans, licking down the length of the hard shaft to his testicles.

'He killed them slowly,' Callahan said, feeling urgently between her legs, smiling as he felt the hot wetness there.

'How did he kill them?' she asked, swinging herself around, lowering her dripping sex onto his organ with infinite slowness, allowing just the tip to penetrate her, teasing both herself and her husband.

'He cut them at the base of the skull, then he'd masturbate over their bodies,' Callahan said.

She lowered herself sharply, allowing him to slide up inside her. The glorious insertion ripped the breath from her and she moaned loudly, pausing only a second before beginning to move up and down on his rigid erection.

'He timed it so that his own climax would arrive as they died,' she gasped, perspiration beginning to form on her forehead. Machecoul.

The window.

He had to have it.

147

Had to possess it. To put it alongside the pieces of masonry he and Laura had taken from the building on their last visit.

Laura began to come.

Callahan was close behind her.

The window.

He *would* have it.

Thirty-Five

STRABANE, COUNTY TYRONE, NORTHERN IRELAND:

'It's a fucking disgrace.'

Joseph Hagen spat the words out as if they were poison, aware that all other eyes in the room were upon him but revelling in that knowledge.

'These bastards have put back the name of the IRA twenty years,' he continued. 'And after all we've done. All the sacrifices. All the compromises. Something has to be done and done fast.'

There was a babble of agreement from the other men in the room.

It was a small room over the top of a bar called 'The Mean Fiddler'. The pub stood about twenty miles from the border with Donegal. It had been used countless times by the men who sat in it now and by their fathers and grandfathers before them. It was perfect, the location, the surroundings. Jobs had been planned here for as long as anyone could remember. Any hint of police or army interference and they could be back across the border into the Republic within twenty minutes.

But now the members of the IRA high command were meeting for a very different reason. The target was not to be an RUC outpost or an army border patrol.

It was much closer to home in all respects.

Joe Hagen took a hefty swig from the glass of Jameson's and shook his head. He looked down at his large hands.

'I agree with Joe,' said another man, a smaller man with thin, pinched features and the beginnings of a beard. 'We all know who's to blame for what's been going on. The longer we leave the problem, the worse it's going to get.'

Another babble of agreement.

'Jerry, make a decision now. It can't be that hard, especially for you,' Eamonn Rice said. 'Christ, you were at Stormont, you could have been killed along with the others. We all know what has to be done.'

The words were directed at the man who sat in one corner of the room, head down, the collar of his flying jacket pulled up high so that he looked like an owl. When he glanced around the room he saw expectation in the faces of his colleagues.

Gerard Coogan clasped his hands together on the table in front of him and tapped his thumbs together. Mention of Stormont brought pictures flooding back into his mind like forgotten photos dredged up from an unwanted album. The gunmen. The bodies. The blood. Coogan had seen it all before but he'd never been on the *receiving* end before. He was thirty-five, dark-haired, sallow-faced. The most striking thing about him were his eyes, a blue so vivid they glowed as if lit from within his skull. He moved his gaze over the

149

men in the room, those eyes roving like sapphiric searchlights.

'You're right,' he said finally, his voice deep and rumbling. 'I do know what has to be done but that doesn't make it any easier. For as long as I can remember the British Government have been our enemy. It's their soldiers who patrol our streets, it's their policies that govern the six counties. But now, all that's different. The enemy doesn't wear a khaki uniform anymore. We've got no fuss with the British now, or the fucking Protestants. For all I know there are British agents in Ireland already. If there are I don't really care. This is *our* problem and we'll solve it *our* way.' He cleared his throat, using the back of one hand to mask the cough. 'We know Maguire and his men did the shootings at Stormont. We know they killed Pithers and his wife. What we don't know is *why*.' He glanced around the room. 'We need to know who paid them. Joe's right; what they've done, what they might do has damaged the image of the IRA badly. That's why *we* need to catch them. Catch them and destroy them.' He smiled thinly. 'We're not fighting the British anymore. We're fighting ourselves.'

'Who do *you* think was behind it, Jerry?' Rice asked.

'Probably the fucking Protestants,' Hagen snapped.

'Why should they be?' Coogan said challengingly. 'They wanted peace here more than most.' He shook his head. 'I haven't got a clue. I really haven't. Whoever set it up knew what they were doing, though. We're all at the stage of not trusting one another again. If something isn't done quickly then relations will break down and we'll be back to square one.'

'Maybe that wouldn't be such a bad thing,' Hagen rumbled.

150

'Don't talk shite, Joe,' Coogan snapped. 'We couldn't fight this war against the British indefinitely and, besides, our demands had been met. We've all fought too long to get where we are now. Not just us but our fathers and grandfathers too. We'd *won*.' He looked icily at Hagen, fixing the man with the full ferocity of his stare. 'If we get Maguire then all the suffering over the years will have been worthwhile. But we have to get him fast.'

'How many men has he got with him?' Rice asked.

'Four or five,' said Hagen. 'We have their names.'

Coogan nodded and Hagen reeled them off like a roll-call.

'Billy Dolan. Damien Flynn. Paul MacConnell and Michael Black. And Maguire himself of course. There could be a couple more but I doubt it.' Hagen drained what was left in his glass.

'Like I said, the British have probably got someone on their trail too,' Coogan said. 'But it's important that we find them first.' His gaze travelled in the direction of the man in the far corner of the room. So far he hadn't spoken, merely sat listening, his face impassive. His features looked as if they'd been carved from granite. He regarded Coogan from beneath heavy-lidded eyes. The lines across his forehead looked as if someone had drawn a fork through the flesh. There were deep creases around his eye corners, too. He looked older than his twenty-seven years.

'We'll get them,' Simon Peters said quietly. 'I've got men checking them out now; their homes, where they were last seen. We'll get them.'

'And whoever paid them,' Coogan reminded him.

Peters nodded.

'What about the British?' he said. 'You think they've

already got men chasing Maguire. What if they get in the way?'

Coogan stroked his chin thoughtfully for a moment.

'Kill them too,' he said, flatly.

Thirty-Six

The crack of pool balls was scarcely audible above the noise coming from the juke-box.

Sean Doyle sat at the bar of 'The Standing Stones', alternately gazing around at the other drinkers and staring into the bottom of his glass.

To his right two men were playing darts. Behind them one of the two pool tables was in use. The men playing looked like father and son. Both had bright red hair. The pub was relatively busy, most of the booths taken and many of the bar stools occupied. A concentrated buzz of chatter filled the air, competing with the juke-box. There was a television set at one end of the bar, set high up on a shelf, and that too was on but the sound was turned down and images appeared in silence.

The air smelt of smoke and alcohol.

It was a smell Doyle had grown accustomed to during the past two days. Ever since arriving in Belfast it seemed that he'd spent all his time drifting from pub to pub. From the Ardoyne to New Lodge. From the Lower Falls across to Short Strand. Now he found himself in Ballymurphy.

His procedure, such as it was, had been simple and

unwavering in every place. Order a couple of drinks, sit at the bar or close to any large group of drinkers. Just observe and listen.

He was like a gull following a trawler, waiting for any tit-bit to fall in front of him. The talk was the usual pub talk, had been in every one of the places he'd visited so far. Sport. Politics. Women.

Never religion.

Each pub, each face had seemed to blur into one as he'd ceaselessly trekked around the city in search of that elusive piece of information he sought. If any of the locals knew anything about Maguire and his renegades they weren't saying. In fact, they weren't even voicing opinions about it. Not as far as he knew, anyway.

He ordered himself another drink and swivelled around on his stool to watch the two men who were playing darts, but his gaze darted around the bar constantly, alighting on each new face as it entered the bar.

How beautifully simple it would be, he thought, if Maguire were to walk in now.

Doyle smiled to himself.

So simple.

The counter terrorist had a .38 special strapped to his leg in an ankle holster, hidden by his jeans and boots. Yet, if Maguire walked in, how easy it would be to retrieve the pistol. The weapon was loaded with Blazer .357 rounds. Hollow tips to ensure that one or two shots at the most would be enough to stop his quarry. The .44 which he usually carried was too bulky for the ankle holster. It lay back at the hotel along with the CZ automatic and the extra special little item he'd brought along.

Back at the hotel.

Donaldson had fixed both him and Georgie up with

jobs at the Excelsior hotel in Belfast city centre, Doyle as a night-porter, Georgie as a bar-maid. They were posing as an engaged couple.

Since the relaxation of hostilities between the IRA and the British in the last few months, the curiosity and mistrust which newcomers usually faced was not so apparent. Doyle had been able to move unhindered through areas where, twelve months before, he would have been risking his life travelling.

Ballymurphy was one such place. The Catholic stronghold had been infiltrated a number of times in the past by Secret Service men but, more often than not, they were discovered. Their fate was invariably a savage beating and torture; then they were bagged and dumped on waste ground.

Doyle had been working undercover in the same way when he'd been so badly injured in Londonderry two years earlier.

Now he sipped at his drink and continued looking around the bar. Darts continued to thud into the board. Pool balls cracked loudly against each other. The cacophony of conversation grew in volume.

The man next to him had a newspaper laid out on the bar and he was running his index finger down a list of horses, looking vainly for a winner. He picked out a couple of possibles, then folded the paper up and dropped it down, front page up.

MORE MURDERS AS PEACE PLAN FACES CRISIS

proclaimed the headline of the *Evening Herald*. There was a photo of Reverend Brian Pithers' house with an ambulance outside and several police cars. Doyle pulled the paper towards him.

'Do you mind?' he asked the owner of the paper, his

154

Irish accent unfaltering.

'Help yourself,' the man replied, smiling amiably.

Doyle scanned the headline again then quickly read the report on the clergyman's death and that of his wife.

'Terrible business,' said the man next to him, nodding in the direction of the paper.

'He had it coming,' said Doyle flatly, smiling at the man. 'He's been doing nothing but putting down the Cause for the last five or six years.'

'You'll be telling me his wife had it coming too,' said the man irritably.

Doyle shrugged and pretended to look at the paper.

Pick your words. Play it carefully.

'Maybe she did,' he said indifferently. 'Her *and* those fellas at Stormont. Why did they have to interfere, anyway? What makes *them* think they can put the bloody world to rights?'

'Ah, you're bloody crazy,' said the man dismissively.

'What's wrong, George?'

Another voice joined the conversation. It belonged to a tall, brown-haired man who was leaning against the bar as if for support. Doyle could tell from the slight slur on his words that the man had had too much to drink.

Perfect, he thought.

'Your man here,' said the first drinker, hooking a thumb in Doyle's direction. 'He reckons that old Pithers had it coming.'

'Him and the others,' Doyle said loudly. 'Who the fuck do they think they are, anyway? A peace plan. To hell with it. It's a pity the IRA ever sat down at the same table with the bloody Brits and the Proddies. They should have carried on as they were.'

155

'How long have you lived in this city, man?' said the drunken individual, pushing past his companion. 'Long enough to see the fucking bombs going off and people being shot down? There was a chance of peace and these fucking rebels or whatever they call themselves might have ruined that chance.'

Come on, sunshine. The bait's laid, you've picked it up, now I've just got to reel you in.

'So what?' Doyle said, scornfully. 'I hope they kill a few more.' He raised his glass in a toast. 'Here's to the rebels,' he said, smiling.

'You bastard,' snarled the drunken man, lunging at him.

Bingo.

Doyle moved away from the bar, side-stepping the clumsy dive with ease, but the man rounded on him, preparing to throw a punch.

'Cut it out,' shouted the barman, seeing the impending trouble.

'You've got a fucking big mouth,' snarled the drunk, glaring at Doyle.

'Then make me shut it, shithead,' he rasped, waiting for the inevitable onslaught. Doyle took a step backwards towards the unused pool table. Two cues were lying on it.

'Leave him, Tommy,' said someone further down the bar but the drunk was incensed, his reason clouded by the amount of booze he'd consumed.

'I'm going to knock your fucking head off,' he hissed at Doyle.

'Then do it,' he snapped back.

The man ran at him.

From a booth in the corner, Billy Dolan looked on with interest.

Thirty-Seven

The attack was clumsy.

Doyle side-stepped the drunken man's charge with little difficulty, his hand closing around a cue on the pool table.

As the man rose Doyle gripped the long piece of wood tightly and swung it with savage force.

The blow caught the man full in the face as he was rising. The thick end of the cue shattered two of his front teeth as it hit him squarely in the mouth. The enamel disintegrated under the impact, one tooth torn from the gum and forced through his upper lip. Blood poured from the hideous injury and the man dropped to his knees, both hands held to the bleeding cavity, moaning in pain as others came to his aid.

Doyle thought about bringing the cue down on the top of the man's head but finally he threw it to one side, his eyes on the two other men by the bar who'd been with his opponent before the fracas began. One of them took a step towards him but Doyle shook his head, his hand going to his jacket pocket.

The man didn't know there was nothing in there but he backed off nonetheless.

Shouts now filled the pub. Of rage. Outrage.

'Get out of here,' shouted the barman, flipping open the bar and ambling towards Doyle. 'Go on, get out of my fucking pub.'

The counter-terrorist had every intention of doing

so; he even tolerated a half-hearted push from one of the injured man's colleagues. Then, suddenly, he was in the street, the sounds of bedlam closed off as the main doors of the pub shut behind him. He began walking immediately, hands dug deep in his jacket pockets, his pace even and unhurried.

He smiled as he remembered the sight of the drunken man's face after he'd hit him with the cue. It had felt good, all the more amusing to Doyle because he'd inflicted the damage defending the name of an organization he'd spent a good portion of his life fighting. The irony kept the grin on his face as he walked.

He wandered down streets of terraced houses, each one looking as if it had been deposited from the end of a huge conveyor belt. They had a depressing uniformity; the only concessions to individualism were different coloured curtains or front doors.

On the other side of the road there was a shop, a small general-purpose store. Its windows were heavily boarded up. Slogans had been sprayed over the metal guards.

FREEDOM FOR IRELAND
BRITS OUT
GOD BLESS THE CAUSE

A group of children were kicking a ball about, bouncing it off a parked car nearby. The ball spun loose and skidded in Doyle's direction. He trapped it expertly with one foot, flipped it up into the air and began knocking it from one foot to the other then from one knee to the other, finally balancing it on his head as the youngsters watched. He finally flipped it up, caught it on the volley and sent it crashing against a lamp post.

'Flash bastard,' said one of the children as he passed.

Doyle grinned broadly and walked on.

Two women standing in the doorway of a house

looked across at him, perhaps not recognizing his face, wondering who this newcomer to their community was. Life on the estates of Belfast was very insular; everyone knew everyone else's business. There were no secrets. It was as if the whole country were part of one gigantic conspiracy.

He stopped to light a cigarette, tossing the spent match into the gutter.

It was as he turned into Whiterock Road that he realized he was being followed.

He had suspected as much when he stopped to kick the kids' football but he had only glimpsed the man briefly out of the corner of his eye. To a less trained man the tail probably would have been anonymous, as it was intended, but to someone in Doyle's profession the pursuer might as well have been wearing a sandwich board proclaiming the fact.

A friend of the injured man's, perhaps?

A plain-clothes policeman even, suspicious of such open support for the IRA renegades?

A number of alternatives passed through Doyle's mind as he walked on.

He crossed the road, glancing back supposedly to check for traffic.

His pursuer was still there.

Gaining, if anything.

Doyle reached the other side of the road and slowed his pace. Fuck this; he wasn't going to wear himself out for nothing. He dropped to one knee and pretended to adjust his boot, aware how easy it would be to slip the .38 from its holster should he need to.

He heard footsteps quickening behind him.

There were about a dozen people on the street but Doyle didn't care. If he had to he would use the gun.

159

The footsteps drew closer.

'Hey,' a voice called.

Doyle got to his feet, his pursuer now less than ten feet behind him.

'Hey, you,' the voice called again, much closer this time.

Doyle turned, not wanting to be caught off guard.

The man who approached him was in his early twenties, a little shorter than Doyle.

He was smiling.

'I saw what happened in the pub, back there,' said Billy Dolan.

'What if you did?' said Doyle challengingly.

'I just wanted to tell you that if you're in there again I'll buy you a drink.'

Doyle's facial expression didn't change.

'Why?' he asked.

'I heard what that mouthy bastard was saying about the IRA before you put one on him. I wanted to thank you. The Cause doesn't have too many friends right now. One more never hurts.' He smiled that broad, infectious smile again.

'Thanks,' said Doyle. 'I'll take you up on that drink.' He faltered, realizing he didn't know the man's name.

'Billy.'

Doyle extended a hand which Dolan shook warmly.

'Good to meet you, Billy,' he said, looking closely at the man's face, taking in every detail, every furrow and line, every nuance of expression. 'My name's Sean.'

'I'd buy you one now but I've got to be off,' said Dolan. 'But, like I said, if you're in there again the offer stands.' He turned and headed back across the road, raising a hand as a gesture of farewell.

Doyle watched him go, looking down briefly at his

own right hand as if he could still feel the strength of the man's grip.

'Well, Billy,' he said, softly, his Irish accent now gone. 'Maybe I will let you buy me that drink after all.' Then, smiling, he turned and headed towards the bus stop at the bottom of the road.

Thirty-Eight

She wanted to see where he'd died.

That had been her first, irrational, ridiculous thought, looking out of the plane onto Belfast.

She had wanted to see the place where her brother had been murdered.

Now Georgina Willis stood against the window of her room on the tenth floor of the Excelsior Hotel and looked out across the city where her brother had been killed.

It was late afternoon; the sky already dark with approaching rain clouds. The weather forecast even spoke of some localized fog. She pressed her face to the cold glass and sighed, glancing down at the people milling about in the streets below, at the cars and buses which clogged the roads. From here, Belfast seemed like any ordinary city, full of shoppers and business people, tourists and visitors. But since 1969 it had been a battleground. And, just when that conflict had looked like reaching a final conclusion, the threat had risen once more to cloud the minds of those who lived in the province. It seemed as if so much hope was to be dashed, already had been dashed, in the blaze of automatic weapons at Stormont less than a week earlier.

But those that had died at Stormont had been faceless to her in the widest sense. Yes, she knew their names, but their deaths had been unfortunate. Their passing had not touched her life. They had been strangers.

She thought that most of the pain of losing her brother had passed by now, but as she stood gazing out over the city she found the hurt rising again inside her, swelling like a blister on her consciousness. She finally moved away from the window, walking across to the bed. There she sat on the edge and took off her shoes, massaging her aching feet. The shift had seemed unusually long behind the main bar of the hotel. She'd been working for over four hours, pulling pints and measuring shorts, cleaning glasses, chatting with the other bar-staff and customers alike.

There had been little information worth storing, little worth telling Doyle when he returned. If he ever did.

She had seen little of him in the past two days. He had a room next to hers, but when he wasn't posing as a night porter he was out and about in the city. She'd seen him for less than an hour since they'd arrived in Belfast two days before. He was becoming restless, angry that no leads were turning up. It seemed that Maguire and his men had disappeared into thin air after the killing of Reverend Pithers. There had been talk of the latest murder in the hotel and Georgie had probed and cajoled her colleagues to speak their views on what had happened in the vain hope that one of them might have some shred of information worth following up, but so far she had heard nothing.

She unbuttoned her blouse and tossed it onto the bed, slipped off her skirt and threw that to one side as well.

She wandered through into the bathroom and turned on the shower, testing the water with her hand. Then she pulled off her bra and knickers, wrapped a white housecoat around her and padded back into the bedroom. She put her skirt and blouse on a hanger and crossed to the wardrobe.

As she opened the door she looked down at her handbag.

The gun was inside.

While she waited for the shower to heat up she took the pistol from her bag and walked across to the bed with it, where she sat, one leg drawn up beneath her, the gun cradled in her hand.

The Sterling .357 Magnum was surprisingly light; it was one of the reasons she had chosen it. It was chambered for either .38 or .357 rounds. Georgie flipped out the cylinder and spun it, checking each chamber. In her bag she had the ammunition. She was using Blazer rounds, light and hollow-tipped.

She raised the pistol and squeezed the trigger, smiling at the smoothness of the action. The hammer slammed down on an empty chamber, the metallic crack echoing around the room. She replaced the weapon, wandered through into the bathroom, took off her robe and stepped beneath the shower, enjoying the feel of the water on her skin. She adjusted the spray so that the jets stung her skin and stood beneath the spray, eyes closed, allowing the water to bounce off her. It ran over her breasts and down her stomach, through her light pubic hair. The hiss of the shower was loud.

Loud enough to mask the sounds outside her door.

Georgie did not hear the rattle as someone tried to turn the handle.

She stood beneath the shower, allowing the water to wash the smell of smoke and drink from her hair, to scour the tiredness from her muscles.

The door-handle twisted.

She heard nothing beneath the pounding spray.

She reached for the soap.

'Shit,' she murmured, noticing that she had left it by the sink.

She stepped from beneath the shower, almost slipping on the tiled floor as water ran down her legs, one hand wiping moisture from her eyes.

She was about to step back into the shower when she heard the rattle of the lock.

Through the open bathroom door she could see the handle moving very slightly.

Without a second thought she sprinted through into the bedroom, naked, leaving soggy footprints on the carpet as she scuttled towards the wardrobe.

Towards the revolver.

The sounds outside the door had ceased for a moment and Georgie opened the wardrobe quietly, wincing when the hinges creaked. She kept one eye on the door, pulling the gun and ammunition from her bag.

The handle moved once more.

She slid six bullets quickly and carefully into their chambers and snapped the cylinder shut. Then, raising the gun before her, she pressed herself against the wall and moved towards the door, leaving wet slicks against the wallpaper.

She heard a click as the lock was slipped, she guessed with a credit card.

The door began to open.

Georgie steadied the gun in both hands, making sure

that, if the door was pushed, she would still have clear access to the intruder.

The door opened a little more; she saw the outline of a shadow fall across her threshold.

A figure took a step inside.

She lowered the .357, her heart pounding that little bit faster.

The intruder was in now.

Georgie smiled and thumbed back the hammer, pushing the barrel of the weapon against the intruder's head.

'You move and I'll blow your fucking head off,' she whispered.

Thirty-Nine

It took Georgie a couple of seconds to realize what was happening.

To recognize the long hair, the leather jacket.

'For Christ's sake, Doyle,' she hissed, lowering the pistol. 'Couldn't you just knock?'

The counter-terrorist turned to face her, a smile spreading across his lips as he saw that she was naked, her body still dripping water. Georgie suddenly seemed to realize as well and tugged the blanket from the bed, wrapping it around herself. Her cheeks flushed.

'What the hell are you doing creeping around breaking into my bloody room, anyway?' she said, irritably, returning the .357 to the wardrobe. As she turned her back on him he saw that the blanket didn't serve as a very good wrap around. Her buttocks were bare. Doyle raised his eyebrows approvingly. He walked across to the bed and sat down.

'We are supposed to be a couple,' he said, still smiling, stroking the scar on the left side of his face.

It was as he raised his hand she noticed there was blood on it.

'What happened to you?' she asked, nodding towards his hand.

Doyle noticed it now too and shrugged.

'It's not my blood,' he told her. 'It's from some mouthy mick I met in a pub.'

She walked back into the bathroom, pushing the door shut behind her, finishing her shower quickly. She emerged a moment later, dressed in the bath robe, her hair dripping. She wiped it with a towel.

'Have you heard anything?' he asked.

'Just the usual chit-chat,' she said. 'Everyone's outraged by what's happened, can't understand why the killing took place. The usual sort of thing. Nothing to go on. What about you?'

'If anyone knows anything about Maguire they're keeping it bloody quiet,' he said, lying back on the bed, arms folded behind his head. 'No one even wants to admit allegiance to the IRA since what happened.' He paused for a moment. 'Apart from one guy I met today in a pub in Ballymurphy.' He told her briefly what had happened in the pub.

'Who was this guy who followed you?' she wanted to know, running fingers through her hair to dry it.

'His name was Billy. I didn't get his last name, unfortunately. Young. Early twenties, about five-eight, dark-haired, grey eyes. I'm going back tomorrow, see if I can find him. It's not much of a lead but it's all we've got at the moment.'

She finished drying her hair, perched on the end of the bed looking down at Doyle.

'Where the hell have you been for the last two days? I've hardly seen you?'

'Doing my job,' he said. 'We came here to find Maguire, not go on a sightseeing trip.' He regarded her coldly for a moment.

'You don't have to be so hostile, Doyle. I'm on *your* side, remember?' she said quietly.

He swung himself up and prepared to get to his feet.

'If it hadn't been me coming through that door just then,' he said. 'What would you have done?'

'Fired, if necessary. Does that surprise you?' she asked.

'No.' He smiled at her.

'You're off tonight, aren't you?' she said. 'I know because I checked the rotas. I'm off too.'

'Want to go out somewhere?' he asked, almost as if it were a natural thing to do. 'A meal, perhaps? You never know, we might even overhear something.'

She smiled.

'That would be nice,' she said.

He was already heading for the door.

'I'll be back in half an hour, I want to get cleaned up,' he told her. He paused as he reached the door. 'Have you got anything else with you except that Sterling?'

She nodded.

'I've got a PD Star. Why?'

'Bring it,' he said flatly. 'Slip it in your stocking top.' He winked at her. 'Just in case.'

Then he was gone.

Georgie went back to the wardrobe and found the Star in a side compartment of her handbag. At less than four inches in length it fitted into the palm of her hand, but its 9mm calibre meant that, should it be needed, it was more than adequate for bringing down a man. She laid it beside her on the dressing table as she began to apply her make-up.

Doyle was bang on time.

At 8.36 p.m. they rode the lift to the ground floor where he invited her to take his arm.

'We *are* supposed to be a couple,' he reminded her.

Arm-in-arm they walked through the foyer and out into the bustling streets of the city, which was now under a blanket of darkness.

Doyle hailed a taxi and they climbed in.

Neither of them spotted the car which pulled out behind them and settled in traffic two car-lengths behind.

The driver never let the cab out of his sight as he followed.

Forty

The restaurant wasn't very crowded, and for that Doyle was grateful.

It was small, what the tour guides like to call 'intimate'. Subdued lighting, plush seats and mirrors on the wall reflecting the glow from the lamps on each table. Every now and then Doyle would catch a glimpse of himself in the mirrors and avert his eyes, as if the sight of his own reflection was somehow unpleasant.

He sat alone, waiting for the first course to arrive and

for Georgie to return from the ladies room. There were two other couples in the restaurant and one portly man on his own in a corner. He constantly looked round as he ate, although invariably his gaze met Doyle's and he would hastily return his full attention to his meal.

What do you know?

Why are you on your own?

Businessman? Out for a quiet dinner because there's no one at home to cook you one? Had a row with your partner? Wife out with the girls?

Doyle smiled at his own curiosity. Perhaps it was a hazard of the job, he told himself.

A bit like being blown up by suicidal IRA men?

Another occupational hazard?

His musings were interrupted by Georgie's return. Doyle ran appraising eyes over her, liking what he saw.

She wore a tight-fitting black dress open in a 'V' down the back just above the small of her back. It was too tight to allow underwear beneath, something he was convinced of by the way her nipples pushed against the material. She walked with grace on a pair of precipitous high heels.

As Georgie arrived so did the starter and they both began eating. Her clutch bag lay on the seat beside her, the Star automatic nestled inside.

Doyle wore the Charter Arms .44 in a holster around his waist, hidden by his jacket.

'How did you find this place?' Georgie asked. 'It doesn't look like *your* style.'

'And what does my *style* mean?' he said somewhat scornfully. 'You mean you think I'd be better suited to a MacDonalds?'

'I didn't say that,' she murmured, looking a little embarrassed.

'Appearances can be deceptive, Georgie,' he said. 'I mean, look at *you*. You don't exactly look like a counter-terrorist.' He lowered his voice as he spoke the last two words.

'What do I look like?' she wanted to know.

'Tonight?' He smiled. 'You look like a model.'

She was taken aback by his remark. Surprised and flattered by it.

'You're full of shit, aren't you?' she chuckled.

'The best quality bullshit,' he reminded her.

'And do all the girls fall for it?'

He shrugged.

'Some.' He looked at her unflinchingly. 'What about you?'

'If you mean do I fall for bullshit, the answer is sometimes. I'm going to take what you said as a compliment, though. It's probably the closest I'll get from *you*.'

They continued eating.

'So are there any women in your life, Doyle?' she wanted to know. 'Is it true what I've heard about you?'

'Tell me what you've heard and I'll tell you if it's true.'

'You're a womaniser. An irresponsible, violent, disrespectful and possibly disturbed man. You've got a death wish. You treat everyone with equal contempt, men and women. A loner. You drink too much, you're unpredictable, single and, as I said, a womanizer.'

'You've been reading my file,' he said. 'Or is that what Donaldson told you?'

'I read your file *and* your psychological evaluation. When I found out I was working with you I wanted to know more about you.'

'So you found that out and you *still* wanted to work with me. Why?' he wanted to know.

170

She shrugged.

'Perhaps it was a challenge for me,' she said, smiling.

'Now who's full of shit?' he muttered, sipping from the glass of Scotch beside him.

'So *is* it true? What it says in the file?'

'Believe what you want,' he said, flatly.

'What about me? Did *you* check up on *me*?'

He shook his head.

'I didn't feel the need,' he said. 'I couldn't see the point in getting to know about your past and you might not have a future. All that matters is *now*. What's the point in me getting to know you when you could be killed tomorrow?'

'What a cheerful thought. Thanks, Doyle.'

'I'm being realistic, Georgie. You could be killed, we could both be killed. That's why I never look ahead. What's the point in making plans when you could get shot tomorrow? I take each day as it comes. If I'm still alive when I get into bed at night then I've had a good day.' He took another sip of his drink and ordered a fresh one. 'It's just my way of coping with life.'

'Have you only been like this since the accident?' she wanted to know.

'What is this? Twenty questions? What does it matter? And anyway, it wasn't an accident. I was bloody careless. I shouldn't have got that close to McNamara. I should have killed him before he had the chance to spread himself all over the Craigavon bridge.'

She finished eating and pushed her plate away. The waiter came scuttling over and removed their plates, bringing a bottle of wine when Doyle asked. He prepared to pour but Doyle waved him away and did the honours himself, filling Georgie's glass. A moment later the main course arrived and they were left alone again.

'What do your family think about what you do?' Doyle asked.

'I thought you didn't want to know anything about me,' she said somewhat sarcastically.

'I'm just making conversation,' he said flatly.

She nodded.

'I don't have a family,' she told him. 'My mother and father were killed in a plane crash when I was ten. An aunt brought me up. She died the day before my twentieth birthday. My brother, I told you, was killed by the IRA.' She laughed bitterly. 'No one would miss me either if I *was* killed.' She took a sip of her wine.

'What about boyfriends?'

'There've been a few. Nothing serious, though. Perhaps I'm like you in that way, Doyle.'

He grinned.

'Maybe.' He exhaled deeply. 'So we're just two lonely little souls pursuing our own goals. You want revenge for your brother ...' He allowed the sentence to trail off.

'And you? What *do* you want? What do you get out of this? Out of knowing that you could be killed any day? Why do you do it?'

'Because it's all there is for me,' he told her, his face impassive. 'Some days I used to *wish* that I'd get caught in a fight, a gun battle or something.' He smiled. 'So I could go out blazing like some fucking cowboy. Maybe it's because I haven't got the guts to get into a car and drive it into a wall. At least if I get shot or blown up then my death is someone else's responsibility.'

'Why do you want to die?' she asked him.

'Because there isn't a better alternative,' he told her. 'Like it says in the song, "No happy endings like they always promised".' He chewed his steak for a moment.

172

'That's right, you know. Perhaps we do share one thing in common. We're alone in the world. My parents are both dead, too. My mother had a stroke, my father had a heart attack. They both hung on longer than they should have and I watched them die, lying there in fucking hospital beds. There's no way I'm going out like that, Georgie. Better to burn out than fade away, they say. Fucking right.'

She sipped her drink, looking across the table at him, realizing that there was something not only dangerous about him but also something very sad. It touched her deeply. More deeply than it should have done. His arrogance, his anger and his attitude were the qualities which made him attractive to her. She looked across the table at him and she wanted him, wanted to share that rage, that ferocity. But she feared that she couldn't. She wondered if Doyle was already dead as far as his emotions went. Was he capable of feeling anything other than hatred and anger? She wanted to know.

But she knew that now was not the time.

'How are you getting on working as a barmaid?' he asked after a long silence, a slight smile on his face.

'I'm managing,' she replied, also smiling.

The rest of the evening was spent passing good-natured conversation and Georgie was surprised at the occasional warmth that crept into Doyle's tone. For all that, he was guarded about himself. He told her jokes, anecdotes. They swapped stories about their experiences in the C.T.U. They talked business.

They talked about killing men.

It was almost 11.30 p.m. when they finally left the restaurant.

Doyle suggested they walk and she was pleasantly

surprised when he draped one arm around her shoulder. She responded by slipping her own around his waist. *Well, it had to look convincing.*

They spoke quietly as they walked, as if not to disturb anyone.

It was as they passed the City Hall for the second time that Georgie realized they were walking in circles.

She slowed her pace and turned to him, smiling, but Doyle's features were set firm and he was gazing ahead as if at something she couldn't see.

'Sean, we're walking in circles.' she said. 'The hotel ...'

'Just keep walking,' he hissed.

She felt the .44 inside his jacket as she snaked her arm around his waist again.

'Are you carrying your automatic?' he wanted to know.

'Yes,' she told him.

'Good. You might need it. We're being followed.'

Forty-One

'How many are there?' Georgie asked almost nonchalantly, keeping up the same steady pace, not looking back.

'I don't know,' Doyle told her. 'I spotted a car and one guy on foot as we passed City Hall first time. The car went through a red light to keep close.'

'How do you want to play it?'

'Let's keep walking for now, see if they move on us.'

174

'And if they do?'

'We kill them. It could be anyone. IRA. UVF. It could even be one of Maguire's mob.'

'Sean, there's no reason for it to be the IRA or the UVF. Since the peace talks started, guerilla activity has ceased. You know we couldn't have infiltrated as easily as we have otherwise.'

He nodded.

'Then it has to be Maguire,' he said.

They came to a turning in the road.

'Right,' he said, pausing to light a cigarette. 'We'll split up, try to lose them. I'll meet you back at the hotel. Don't forget, Georgie; if you have to, shoot.'

She nodded then snaked her arms up around his neck, drawing him to her, pressing her lips against him. He felt her tongue probing and opened his mouth, allowing it to stir the warm wetness within. They remained like that for long moments, then she pulled away, smiling.

'If you're saying goodnight we might as well make it look convincing,' she told him and turned away.

Doyle smiled and walked off in the opposite direction.

The car followed him.

The man on foot pursued Georgie.

Doyle knew that the driver of the car dared not drive too fast. As far as *he* knew, Doyle was still unaware he was being followed. He didn't know the counter-terrorist was aware of the tail.

He walked briskly but unconcernedly. If his tracker was going to try and kill him then he'd have to pull level with him or, better still, in front of him.

Then Doyle would be able to use the .44.

He smiled at the prospect, but for the moment he

merely kept walking, keeping his pace slow enough to allow the driver to track him.

The time for speed would come soon enough.

Georgie meanwhile was also walking slowly, her high heels beating out a tattoo on the wet pavement. She pulled her jacket around her to ward off the cold, her clutch bag held before her, the comforting shape of the automatic nestled within.

There was an alley up ahead to her right.

She ducked into it.

It ran for about three hundred yards along the back of shops and houses.

It was as black as pitch down there, the only vague light coming from some of the rear windows of the houses or their yards. Dustbins were lined up on both sides of the narrow alley like sentinels.

Georgie scuttled along it, heading for a pile of old boxes stacked high against one of the shops. The place stunk of rotting vegetables and cats' piss but she pressed herself against the wall, eyes fixed on the opening of the alley, watching to see if her pursuer followed her.

She saw his shape loom in the alley entrance.

He paused for a moment, then began walking tentatively down the narrow thoroughfare, cursing when he tripped over the rusted frame of a child's bike.

He drew closer, slowing his pace now, eyes and ears alert for the slightest sound or movement.

Doyle crossed the street, quickening his pace slightly, not even glancing back over his shoulder as he walked. He knew the car was still there, its driver watching him through the windscreen.

There were a set of traffic lights up ahead, showing green.

Doyle paused and lit another cigarette, one eye on the lights.

They changed to amber.

He sucked hard on the cigarette and walked on.

Red.

Doyle broke into a run, hurtling across the junction, narrowly avoiding a car which came from his right. The driver banged on his hooter angrily as the counter-terrorist dived across in front of him.

The man in the pursuing vehicle swore under his breath as he glanced up at the red light then at the figure of Doyle disappearing around a corner on the far side of the road.

He stepped on the accelerator and shot across the junction, ignoring the traffic signal, swerving to avoid a van which was forced to brake hard to prevent a collision.

'You fucking idiot,' the driver of the van bellowed as the other car sped after Doyle.

Doyle himself had ducked into a side-street. He watched as the pursuing car shot past, skidding to a halt at the end of the street, its engine idling as the driver looked around for his quarry.

Whoever was driving was no expert, Doyle thought. A blind man would have known by now that he was being followed. In the glare of street lamps, Doyle could see that there was just one man in the car.

Just the one in the car and the one following Georgie.

He frowned.

Who the fuck *were* these guys?

He watched the car finally turn left and drive off in the direction of Sandy Row.

Doyle waited a moment longer then turned and headed back the way he'd come.

177

Georgie lost sight of the man momentarily as he entered the alley-way, so impenetrable was the darkness. She could hear his footfalls on the cracked concrete but she couldn't see him.

She thought about easing the .45 from her bag but resisted the temptation.

The man was closer now.

Georgie carefully stepped out of her shoes, anxious that the click of her heels should not give away her hiding place.

As she did so she put her left foot into something soft. It felt cold and she winced as she felt it ooze up between her toes. What it was she didn't even *want* to think about.

The man was on the far side of the alley, drawing closer all the time. He pressed against the door of a yard and the hinges creaked loudly.

From inside the yard a dog flew at the door, barking madly.

The sound startled the man and gave Georgie the opportunity she was looking for.

She hooked one hand through a dustbin lid handle and ran at the man who turned, stunned, to meet her charge.

His reactions were too slow.

Georgie smashed the dustbin lid into his face, a loud clang echoing around the alley, joining with the frenzied barking of the dog to create a deafening cacophony.

The man fell back against the gate, his nose broken by the impact, his head spinning.

She dropped the dustbin lid and brought her bare foot up into his crutch with stunning force.

He let out a strangled cry and dropped to his knees.

Georgie retrieved the dustbin lid and hit him again, across the back of the head this time. The blow opened a hairline cut across his scalp. Blood ran through his hair as he pitched forward, his face connecting with the ground, the impact lessened as he fell into the contents of a spilled dustbin.

Georgie prodded him with her foot, dropped to one knee and hauled him over on to his back.

The dog was still barking madly, throwing itself at the gate as if anxious to get through to the people in the alley.

She knew she had to move fast; so much noise would attract attention.

She rummaged through his pockets, finding it difficult to see anything in the pitch blackness. Even his features were hidden from her in the gloom.

She found a wallet in his trouser pocket but nothing other than money inside.

Not even in his jacket or inside pockets.

No I.D. Nothing.

She paused for a moment then wiped her bare foot on his jacket, retrieved her shoes and bolted down the alley-way, the sound of the dog echoing in her ears.

As she reached the other end of the alley she slowed down, breathing deeply to restore her composure, wiping her foot with a tissue before slipping her shoes back on.

She set off at a steady pace, and in fifteen minutes she was back at the hotel.

She wondered what had happened to Doyle.

Forty-Two

The night porter in the Excelsior Hotel nodded politely at Georgie as she passed him heading for the lifts. She returned the gesture, aware that his eyes were following her every movement, his gaze centred on her legs and backside as she entered the lift.

She rode it to the tenth floor and got out, passing two middle-aged men about to descend. One of them said something to his companion and she heard their raucous laughter inside the lift.

She reached her own room, fumbled in her bag for her key and was about to let herself in when the door next to her opened.

Doyle stuck his head out and smiled, motioning her inside. She closed the door behind her as she entered, then walked to the bed and sat down, kicking off her shoes. She sat cross-legged, watching him as he went to the dressing table, poured two glasses of Scotch from the bottle of Haig which stood there and handed her one.

'What happened?' he asked, listening intently as she relayed the story, waiting until she'd finished then stroking his chin thoughtfully.

'And he was carrying no I.D. at all?' Doyle said, perplexed.

'No driver's licence, no credit cards, nothing,' she said, taking a sip of the Scotch. 'What about your bloke?'

'I lost him easily. Maybe *too* easily.' He pulled at the top button of his shirt, loosening it, then pulled off his tie and tossed it to one side. 'You know, the more I think about it the more I reckon they *wanted* us to know we were being followed.'

'You mean, whoever put them on to us was warning us? Letting us know we're under surveillance? It doesn't make any sense, Sean. If it was the RUC they'd have come straight out and confronted us. The IRA or the UVF or any other of the para-military organizations aren't actively functioning at the moment, and if it'd been Maguire and his men they'd have killed us.'

'That doesn't leave many alternatives, does it?'

'It doesn't leave *any*.'

Doyle took a swig of his drink and looked at Georgie still sitting cross-legged on the bed.

'Are you OK?' he asked her.

'I'm fine. Just curious, like you.' She smiled at him, noticing that he was moving closer to her.

'You've cut yourself,' he said, pointing to a graze on her shoulder. He wet the tip of his finger and wiped the dried blood away gently.

'It must have been in that alley-way,' she said as he bent closer, inspecting the small cut.

Their faces were inches apart. She could smell the faint scent of after-shave on him, could feel the heat from his skin close to her.

'Sean ...'

She spoke his name, then whatever words she intended to speak were lost as he turned his face and kissed her. Their lips crushed together, his tongue probing, met by hers with equal if not increased vigour. She uncrossed her legs, allowing one to slip down and her foot to touch the floor. He pushed her back onto the bed as she fumbled with the buttons of his shirt, their mouths still locked together in the kiss.

She felt his left hand sliding slowly, gently, up inside her dress, stroking the smooth flesh of her inner thigh, his fingers brushing briefly against the tightly curled down of her pubic mound. Then the fingers were gone again, tracing paths over her thighs.

He was aware of the warmth radiating from her sex and it seemed to spur him on but there was no impatience in his touch. Only tenderness. A gentleness which seemed almost alien but was all the more arousing because of that.

He took his hand from beneath her dress and stroked her cheek as he lay down beside her.

She fumbled with his shirt, pulling it open.

As he rolled onto his back she saw the scars that criss-crossed his torso.

If they shocked her she showed no signs. Instead she bent forward and kissed his chest, allowing her tongue to flick gently against a scar which ran across his chest, licking it, following it down to his belly where she found another. She kissed it.

And another.

She kissed that too, sucked the white flesh into her mouth, her saliva running into the deep scar, trickling down to the waistband of his trousers which she began to undo.

He pulled her up and kissed her again, more forcefully this time, gripping her head between his hands as if he were going to crush it.

She reached out with her right hand and unzipped his trousers, feeling for his stiffness, aware of the moisture between her own legs, of the aching in her nipples which pressed against the material of her dress almost painfully.

She sat up and pulled the dress over her head, throwing it to one side then, naked, she slid onto him, allowing him to raise one thigh so that it was rubbing against her moist cleft. She left a stain on his trousers as she manoeuvred herself down his body, licking the line of the scars as if they were guides for her. She slipped his trousers and pants off in one movement so that they were both naked.

She saw other scars on his thighs and those too she kissed before trailing her tongue up to his swollen testicles, one of which she took into her mouth, sucking so gently on it. Then she swivelled around, lowering her slippery sex towards his face, offering it to him as she took the head of his penis into her mouth, licking the clear liquid from the swollen glans.

Doyle parted her pink, puffy lips with his index finger and ran his tongue over their outer edges, feeling her shudder as he flicked his tongue deep into her. He stirred her wetness for a moment before transferring his attentions to the hard bud of her clitoris, drawing back the fleshy hood to reach it, raking it gently with the edges of his teeth.

He felt her release his penis and gasp her pleasure as he licked faster, sensing her urgency, sensing her desire for release.

He kissed her inner thighs, brushed his nose through her dewy pubic hair and smelt the musky odour of her sex and she began to suck him once more, her hands rubbing his thighs and testicles, knowing that he too was close.

Doyle grabbed her slim hips in his powerful hands and lifted her off him, slithering around so that he was beside her, looking down onto her.

He raised himself up and she parted her legs to

183

welcome him, moaning softly as she felt the head of his penis probing against her vagina. He inched forward, penetrating a fraction then withdrawing. He repeated the action half a dozen times, each tiny stroke greeted by a gasp of pleasure from Georgie as she raised her hips in an attempt to coax him into penetrating her fully. Instead, he merely moved his swollen organ over and around her slippery sex, placing his glans against her clitoris for glorious seconds before pushing a little more deeply into her.

'Please ...!' she whispered, stroking his face, her breath coming in great racking gasps.

And he slid into her fully.

The feeling was exquisite and she arched her back, both because of the sheer pleasure but also so that he could penetrate her further.

He began to move rhythmically, each thrust of his met by her raising her hips. She gyrated them gently, her eyes now closed. Lost in the pleasure of the moment she was aware only of his penis deep inside her and of the growing pleasure, the feeling which was building inexorably.

He held her breasts gently, running his thumb over the stiff nipples then bending his head to take first one then the other between his lips.

She whispered his name again as she felt the warmth begin to spread across her thighs and belly, at its hottest between her legs.

She raised her legs, locking them around the small of his back, drawing him deeper as the feeling finally reached its peak.

She clawed his back, her nails scratching him, skimming over deep scars which had long since healed. He licked the perspiration from her cheek as he thrust

184

harder, his own release now seconds away.

Georgie called out his name loudly as she climaxed and the sound, coupled with the vibrations he felt beneath him, pushed him over the edge into ecstacy. She moaned more loudly as she felt his thick fluid filling her, his thrusts still perfectly rhythmic as he poured his liquid lust into her, his body trembling.

She kissed him, the feeling only barely subsiding. She was quivering all over.

'Oh God,' she murmured, her legs finally slipping from around him, her eyes still closed.

He licked more perspiration from her cheek, tasting its saltiness, his own pleasure now spent for the time being. He eased himself free of her, their fluids mingling, dampening the sheet beneath them.

He lay beside her, listening to her breathing, his own deep and guttural. Gradually it subsided as the burning became a pleasant glow.

She rolled across to him, looking down at his back, at the scars there too. She kissed one on his shoulder, licking it with her tongue, brushing his long hair away with one hand.

She wondered what he'd looked like an hour after the explosion.

He glanced across and saw her smiling at him.

'What are you smiling at?' he asked, touching her lips with his index finger.

'You. You're full of surprises.'

He looked vague.

'You're very gentle, considerate.'

'What did you expect me to do? Tie you to the headboard?'

She laughed and kissed his back, just above a particularly deep scar over his kidney.

185

'Do they ever give you pain?' she wanted to know.

'Life's full of pain, Georgie. You just learn to live with it.'

He reached out and stroked her blonde hair, feeling how soft it was as his fingers slid through it. She stroked the backs of his thighs, tracing one or two more scars.

He must have bled badly.

She finally shifted around so that she was lying beside him, also on her stomach. He began to run one hand up and down her back, pausing every so often to enjoy the gentle curve of her buttocks. She kissed him softly on the forehead, then the nose, then the lips.

When she felt cold he pulled the blanket over them.

After a while they made love again.

Eventually Georgie drifted off to sleep.

Doyle lay awake gazing at the ceiling, his mind thankfully clear of thoughts. Finally he eased himself out of bed, careful not to disturb her, and walked across to the window. He peered out over the city below, looking down on cars which showed little more than pinpricks of light from their headlamps, moving along roads that looked like the illuminated lines on a map.

Somewhere in that city were the men who had followed them and they had answers which he needed.

Doyle stood by the window and glanced back at Georgie as she lay sleeping. Then he faced the glass once more, seeing his own reflection. He raised his arms, putting one on either side of the frame, resting his head against the cold glass.

Don't let her get close.

He gritted his teeth until his jaws ached and he lowered his head a fraction, as if he didn't want to see his reflection.

Keep her distant.

186

He drew his head back a few inches and slammed it forward against the toughened glass, so hard it made his forehead throb.

'Bastard,' he hissed and headbutted the window again.

And again.

Forty-Three

BRITTANY, FRANCE:

The window was fully exposed.

As if every single piece of stone had been meticulously chipped from around it, as if every panel had been painstakingly cleaned.

The window in the church at Machecoul was as vivid and visible as the day it had been created.

It stood amongst the dust and dirt of the old building like a beacon, the colours in its glass apparently glowing, such was their intensity. Reds looked like liquid fire, blues like sapphires, yellow like freshly polished gold.

The window seemed to be glowing.

Mark Channing stood staring at it, his jaw slightly open.

Catherine Roberts was beside him, her own gaze rivetted on the window, her emotions in turmoil. She felt a curious mixture of elation, bewilderment and two other feelings which she didn't care for so much. One was awe at the sheer magnitude of the craftsmanship in the window.

The other was fear.

When they had left the window the previous night it had been partially encased in stone, its panels still covered by the dirt of ages, yet now it stood in all its original glory.

The question they both wanted to ask was, How?

Yet each knew that to voice that question would merely confuse matters even more. They had the clichés in their minds and on their lips, ready to roll them out like bit-players in a bad B-Movie.

'Who could have done this?'

'What has happened to the window?'

'What we are seeing is impossible.'

They were like atheists trying to explain a miracle.

It couldn't have happened. It wasn't possible.

And yet they saw it.

For a moment Cath wondered if it was a dream, an extension of the nightmares they had shared for what seemed like an eternity. She almost pinched herself.

Instead she took a step towards the window, narrowing her eyes against the brilliance of the colours contained in the glass.

Come on, there had to be more clichés to describe the way she was feeling.

Amazed. Incredulous. Dumbstruck.

The list was endless.

Channing also moved closer, his jaw still slightly open.

Should he look for scientific explanations? Perhaps it *was* a fucking miracle, he thought. Perhaps God had seen fit to restore a window dedicated to him to its full splendour.

One look at the design on the glass told Channing that God did not figure anywhere in this tableau.

If he had seen what the window bore he would have destroyed it, not renewed it.

He wanted to speak but the words would not come. They eluded him with the same stealth as rational thought. He didn't know what to say, he didn't know what to think.

He could only look at the window, take in its details, marvel at its appearance.

If only he could stop shaking.

Cath moved to within a foot of the window, then stepped back lightly, as if to take in every panel, every mullion, every trefoil and quatrefoil. Every line, every colour, every shape. They seemed to converge on her like a manic kaleidoscope, searing her retina, implanting their forms on her mind as well as her eyes.

She felt faint and backed off a little, as if direct confrontation with the window was somehow too overpowering, too difficult to contend with.

The feeling passed gradually and she was able to look once more, mesmerized by the radiance of it.

The sun had pierced the gloom of the church, cutting through the darkness as it fought its way past a broken slat in one of the boarded up windows.

The shaft struck something lying close by the window.

Something silver.

She took another step backwards but kept her eye on the glinting object, not sure if Channing had seen it or not. He mumbled something under his breath about the camera and left the chancel, his unsteady footsteps echoing away within the main body of the church.

And now Cath saw that silver object glinting again and, this time she moved towards it.

It lay close to the base of the window at its left hand

side, almost hidden in dust and crumbled stone. She knelt and picked it up, brushing the grime from it, cradling it in her hand.

It was a cigarette lighter in solid silver, shaped like a horse's head.

Lausard's lighter.

She regarded it impassively for a moment until she heard Channing re-enter the church then, quickly and surreptitiously, pushed it into the back pocket of her jeans.

Out of sight.

Lausard had been here after them, that much was obvious. But why? How had he come to drop the lighter, or, more to the point, to leave it?

Another mystery?

She looked at the window again, feeling the lighter in her back pocket.

Channing didn't notice the slight smile on her lips.

Forty-Four

The creature was almost six feet tall.

It rose in the centre of the window, arms outstretched and upraised. In its left hand sat a child, in its right another, smaller apparition.

It stood on the heads of two humanoid beings which were lying sideways.

Both had been created naked; their large genitals were clearly visible.

Beneath the creature's legs there was a gate, a

portcullis-like affair further adorned with heads. The hundreds of tiny eyes each seemed to reflect the light with unsettling intensity.

The central creature, the largest, was coloured dark blue except for its eyes, which seemed to glow hellish red in the glow of the lamps and the intruding rays of sunshine creeping almost timidly into the transept of the church. The two monstrosities it stood upon were yellow in colour, apart from their eyes which were the same vivid red. Thick tongues had been fashioned to make it appear that they were licking their lips.

Most of the panels contained at least one representation of a child and every one, without exception, carried some letters or symbols. The words were in Latin.

Channing sat by the altar, glancing up at the window, making a note of the words, trying to make sense of them. He couldn't. The only thing that came into his mind when he looked at the window was the uncertainty of how it had come to be uncovered. And uncovered so thoroughly and expertly.

He and Cath had spoken barely ten words to each other since they'd arrived at Machecoul and found the restored window. He had taken a series of photographs of it; she had set to work trying to figure out the design, the date and possibly the creator.

The window was complex in its construction but relatively simple in its illustration. Just the four large creatures surrounded by over a dozen smaller ones and the children.

So many children.

'It's definitely fifteenth century,' Cath said, her voice cutting through the stillness, cutting through Channing's thoughts too. 'This window is perpendicular glass.' She pointed to the mullions which divided each compartment, segmenting every panel. 'There's a lot of white glass in it. It's been painted over, at least the large figure has, not fired like the smaller ones.' She tapped the glass with the end of her pen. 'The figures of the children have been made using a mosaic effect. Tiny pieces of coloured glass pieced together like a jigsaw. The rest of it is peculiar to perpendicular glass. Decorated style, S-pose, ogee arches.'

Channing raised a hand for her to be quiet:

'You're losing me, Cath,' he said, wearily.

'Sorry. It's just that we seem to be straight on at least one thing about this bloody window. Its date.'

'That's about the only thing we *are* sure of.'

'What about the letters? Can you make any sense of them?'

'They're basic Latin, no anagrams, no inversions, thank Christ. It shouldn't take too long to decipher them. It's those symbols I'm not sure about.'

In the top right hand panel there was a hand, severed at the wrist. It was ringed three times. Two panels below was a stone and, below it the word:

COGITATIO

Other words were dotted around the window, not in sentences but at random, almost like graffiti which someone had scrawled on the finished artefact. Other words that Channing had written down:

SACRIFICIUM
CULTUS
ARCANA
ARCANUS

He shrugged.

'They don't make much sense on their own,' he said. 'Thought. Sacrifice. Worship. Secrets. Hidden.' He

192

shook his head.

'A secret,' murmured Cath. 'Hidden in the window, perhaps?' She turned to look at him.

There were more words at the foot of the window.

OPES
IMMORTALIS

Channing looked at the words again, repeating them aloud as he translated them.

'Treasure and Deathless.' He frowned.

The frown suddenly changed to a look of realization.

'Jesus Christ,' he murmured. 'A deathless treasure. A secret deathless treasure. Gilles de Rais was an alchemist. One of the things all alchemists sought, along with the secret of turning base metal into gold, was the secret of immortality. Perhaps that's what these figures and symbols concern.'

Cath was silent for long moments, her attention focused on the window.

'That still doesn't solve the biggest mystery of all, does it? How this window came to be in the condition it's in after just one night.'

Channing exhaled deeply.

'No, it doesn't. It also doesn't explain why an atheist child murderer, a black magician like de Rais would want a stained glass window put in a church in his name.'

'This word here,' Cath said, pointing at one on a panel which was just above the head of the largest creature. 'What does it mean?'

BARON

'It probably refers to de Rais' title,' said Channing. 'He was Baron of Machecoul and the estate around it.'

'Then why is it in English and not Latin?'

Her words hung on the air, drifting as lazily as the

motes of dust caught in the shafts of sunlight penetrating the gloom.

'The Latin for Baron, the title, is *princeps*, isn't it?' she said, eyes still fixed on the window.

'Yes, you're right,' Channing agreed, stroking his chin thoughtfully.

'I think I know what it is and I think I know what this window is meant to illustrate,' she told him.

He looked at her intently.

'One of the most popular images on stained-glass windows in the fifteenth century was a thing called the Jesse Tree. It was the literal representation of Christ's family tree, in glass. The figure of Jesse, founder of the House of David, would lie at the bottom and, from him, vines or branches come, each one bearing one of Christ's ancestors.' She nodded towards the window. 'I think this is some kind of parody of a Jesse Tree. If de Rais was a black magician, what better way to show his contempt for God than by having something like this on view in a church?'

'And Baron?'

'I think it's a name.'

They both stared at the window, at the name. At the creature with the blazing red eyes.

Who but someone as warped as de Rais would have chosen to personalize such an abomination? And if he did, why venerate it so?

'A monument, that's what the window is,' said Cath. 'A monument dedicated to this thing which de Rais called Baron.'

'What did it give him to make him worship it the way he did?' said Channing, his own thoughts now running rampant.

Cath stepped back.

She didn't speak.

She merely gazed at the face in the glass, her gaze held by those blazing red eyes.

Forty-Five

She knew he wouldn't be sleeping.

The need for silence and stealth were paramount. Their rooms were separated by just the landing. *If he heard her leaving ...*

Catherine Roberts pulled her jacket more tightly around her, stood with her back to the door for a moment, then gently eased it open, moving as quietly as she could.

The inn was cloaked in silence and every movement, every sound seemed to be amplified in the stillness. She glanced across at the large grandfather clock which stood on the landing close to Channing's room, its pendulum swinging slowly back and forth.

2.16 a.m.

She headed for the stairs and descended, cursing under her breath when one of them creaked protestingly under her weight. She glanced back towards the door of Channing's room but there was no movement.

She reached the bottom of the stairs and crossed the small reception area.

The front door was locked but not bolted.

Slowly she turned the key, gritting her teeth when it refused to twist, but finally, with a resounding click, the lock opened.

Cath paused once more before opening the door and slipping out.

The chill wind hit her like an invisible fist as she stepped onto the street, ruffling her hair and making her shiver. She pulled up the collar of her jacket, easing the inn door shut behind her and then fumbling for the keys of the Peugeot as she hurried across to it. She slid behind the wheel and started the engine, not caring now if he heard the car. Even if he did he would not think it was her.

He would not suspect her.

The engine caught first time and she swung the car out of its parking space, through the village and out towards the road which would take her to the church.

As the houses slowly seemed to disappear, the countryside took over. So lush and inviting in the daylight, in the blackness of the night it seemed to crowd in on her. She flipped her headlamps on to full beam, the shafts of light cutting through the gloom, illuminating the narrow road which led out of the village.

Trees growing close to the roadside seemed to stretch skeletal fingers down as if to sweep the car up. A strong wind had risen and Cath could hear it gusting around the car as she drove. The moonless sky was like a blanket of mottled velvet.

She tried to concentrate on the road as she drove but the image of the window kept creeping into her mind.

The question still plagued her, all the more so because she hadn't even the beginnings of an answer. How had the window been uncovered? How could it possibly be in such a perfect state of preservation? As she shifted in her seat she felt something digging into her buttocks and she remembered she still had Lausard's lighter in her pocket.

196

It prompted another question.

When had the reporter been inside the church? What had made him leave his lighter behind?

Questions.

And no answers.

There were too many questions. Too much to take in. She turned a corner, guiding the car around a bend in the road, knowing that the church was close now.

Cath felt the hairs at the back of her neck rise.

Just the cold wind.

She told herself it was only that.

As she reached the top of the hill the church was invisible in the valley below, hidden by the darkness.

She guided the Peugeot down the narrow track which led to the valley floor, gripping the wheel as it bounced over the uneven surface.

As she drew closer to the church the headlamps picked out the outline of the building. It seemed to grow from the night itself, hewn from the umbra, carved from darkness.

Something moved close to the door.

Cath swallowed hard and slowed down, now less than thirty feet from the main door of the church.

Whatever had passed before the building appeared to be gone. She squinted into the blackness.

Movement again.

A rat scuttled away from the church and disappeared into the long grass that grew around. Cath exhaled deeply, angry with herself for being so jumpy but knowing that she had at least some cause to feel uneasy about being at this place alone in the middle of the night.

She stopped the car, taking a torch from the glove compartment. As she switched the engine off the lights died with it and the only light in the black was her torch. It seemed scarcely adequate for cutting through such stygian gloom but she scrambled out of the Peugeot and walked purposefully towards the building.

She pushed the door open, the musty smell enveloping her. Even after so many hours spent in the place the odour still made her cough but she passed quickly through the nave and on into the chancel.

To the window.

She shone her torch over it, looking once more at the details, marvelling at the skill which had gone into its construction but also feeling uneasy about the *reasons* for that creation.

She picked out the words with the torch.

ARCANA

ARCANUS

'Hidden secret,' she murmured under her breath.

Hidden in these panels, in these abominations which stared back at her in the torchlight.

Had Lausard seen something of that secret, she wondered, pulling his lighter from her pocket and closing her fist around it?

She knew that it would take a lot of work before the secret of the window was complete but she knew that the riddle must be solved.

God alone knew what it was.

Although she suspected that God had nothing to do with it.

Not the God *she* knew.

She pulled the notebook from her pocket, propped the torch on the altar so that it was illuminating the window, then, slowly, began to write.

As she did she was aware that her hands were shaking.

Forty-Six

BELFAST, NORTHERN IRELAND:

A curtain of cigarette smoke enveloped him as he walked in.

It hung in the air, not dissipating, merely expanding and thickening like man-made smog.

The saloon bar of 'The Standing Stones' was busy as usual. Both pool tables were occupied, men sat around in one corner playing dominos and there was a game of darts well under way. Hardly anyone looked at Doyle as he let the door bang shut and walked across to the bar.

He ordered a whiskey and plonked himself on a bar stool, his eyes studying the reflections in the mirror behind the bar.

As yet, none of the faces looked familiar. He glanced across to the booth where Billy Dolan had been sitting the day before last but it was empty. There were a couple of empty beer glasses on the table but they were quickly whisked away by a barmaid who, having collected some more for washing, returned to her post behind the bar. Doyle smiled at her as she passed him, glad to see the gesture returned. She wore a name tag on her white blouse which he read as she passed.

Siobhan.

He smiled again as she moved to the other end of the bar.

As she disappeared the landlord arrived with Doyle's drink and put it down in front of him.

'I don't want any trouble from you today, or you're out of that fucking door on your ear,' he snapped.

Doyle dug in his pocket, found some change and tossed it onto the bar.

'I don't know what you're talking about,' he said, eyeing the landlord coldly.

'I'm talking about the trouble the last time you were in here.'

'It wasn't me who started it.'

'I don't give a fuck who started it. I'm just warning you.' He stalked off to the other end of the bar to serve another customer who'd just entered. Doyle caught the man's reflection in the mirror but it wasn't the one he sought.

Billy. One fucking name wasn't much to go on if he had to trace the Irishman, Doyle thought, sipping his whiskey. He had a Christian name and a description. It might be enough to run through the RUC files, *if* the man was even in them. If he had a record of some description then there might be a way of tracing him. If not ... Doyle took another sip of his drink. It was a thin lead but it was all he had.

Georgie had come up with nothing at the hotel either. No overheard conversations, no conspiratorial whisperings amongst the staff.

Georgie.

The image of her floated into his mind for a moment. The remembrance of their passion. They had made love that morning, then she had dressed and left him alone in the room with his thoughts.

He took a long swallow of the whiskey, driving the visions from his mind.

He tapped on the bar to attract the attention of Siobhan. Siobhan with the badge on her blouse. On the left breast.

She came across to him, smiling. She was pretty. About five three, dark hair. Slim. Big-busted.

'Put another Jameson's in there, will you?' he said. 'And have one yourself.' He held out a five-pound note. She returned a moment later with the drink and his change. 'What did you have?'

'Just a lemonade. I don't drink while I'm working,' she told him.

'What about when you're *not* working?'

'Depends who I'm with.'

'How about with me?' He fixed her in his gaze. 'What time do you get off work this afternoon?'

'About three,' she said. 'Are you asking me out?' That delightful smile flickered on her lips again.

Doyle sipped his drink, regarding her over the rim of his glass.

'Three o'clock?' He nodded and smiled at her, his gaze momentarily distracted by some movement from behind him. The door opened, Doyle watched the newest customer in the mirror.

Billy Dolan had his collar up and his hands stuffed in his jacket pockets. He nodded a greeting to the landlord and made for the booth in the corner.

Doyle watched him sit down, rubbing his hands together as he waited for his drink to be brought across.

'I could meet you outside,' said Siobhan.

'Maybe another time,' Doyle told her, smiling.

Siobhan with the name tag on her blouse watched as he slid off the bar stool and walked across to the booth where Dolan sat. Her smile had been replaced by an expression of annoyance. She bustled off to the far end of the bar to serve someone else.

'Does that offer still stand?'

201

Dolan looked up as he heard the voice. He smiled that infectious smile as he saw Doyle standing there, glass in hand.

'What are you drinking?' Dolan wanted to know. When the landlord brought his own Guinness over he ordered a refill for Doyle.

'I wondered if you'd come in,' said the Englishman. 'I thought I was going to have to buy my own drinks.'

'I've been busy,' Dolan told him.

'Working?'

Again that infectious grin.

'You could say that. Preparing, more like.'

Dolan lifted his glass.

'Here's to the Cause.'

Doyle did likewise and they both drank.

'What about you?' Dolan asked. 'What do you do?'

Doyle told him about working at the Excelsior.

'When there's fucking Brits staying there and I have to take food up to them I sometimes spit in it first,' he lied.

Dolan grinned.

'What's the pay like there?'

'It's shit but they give me a room.'

Dolan regarded Doyle quietly for a moment and cleared his throat.

'You fancy making some extra cash, Sean?'

'Doing what?'

'A bit of driving. You *can* drive, can't you?'

Doyle nodded.

'It'd have to be on the quiet,' Dolan told him. 'Maybe just picking up the odd parcel here and there, sometimes a person. Think about it.'

Doyle said that he would.

'I've got to be going now,' Dolan said, finishing his

202

drink, getting to his feet. 'I'll see you, maybe.' He raised his hand in a gesture of farewell. He'd reached the door when he paused and looked back at Doyle.

'Hey, Sean. Are you a football fan?' he asked, that infectious grin back on his face. 'If you are there's a game on Tuesday night at Windsor Park. It should be quite something.' Then he was gone.

Doyle looked puzzled for a second but then swallowed what was left in his glass, got to his feet and followed Dolan out of the pub.

There was no sign of the Irishman.

Doyle looked quickly right and left and just caught sight of him turning a corner. He set off after his quarry, the .38 snug against his ankle, hidden by his boots.

He slowed down at the corner, peering around.

Dolan was about twenty yards ahead of him.

Doyle saw the blue Sierra pull up alongside him and spotted the driver motion for Dolan to get in, which he did quite willingly, walking round to get in the passenger side.

Doyle looked at the number-plate, consigning it to memory as the Sierra sped off.

'Shit,' Doyle hissed and ran down the street towards a phone box. He punched the digits quickly, waiting for the connection, waiting for the phone to be picked up. When it finally was he asked to speak to Georgie.

She was a moment or two coming to the phone.

'Georgie, listen to me,' he snapped, barely giving her time to acknowledge who he was. 'We've got to trace a car. Quick. Get in touch with the RUC, get them to run it through one of their computers. I need to know who owns it and where he lives. I'm in a call box. I can't do it from here. Use Donaldson's name when you call, tell them you're with the C.T.U. And tell them to hurry. Ring me back at this number when you've done it, right?' He gave her the number of the public phone and then the car number-plate. Then he hung up, stepped outside the box and propped himself against the wall of a house, eyes on the phone box, waiting for the ring.

Five minutes.

Ten minutes.

'Come on, for Christ's sake,' he muttered, pacing up and down outside the box.

A young woman pushing a pram rounded the corner and made for the phone box.

'It's out of order, love,' Doyle said to her, looking disappointed. 'I just tried it myself.'

The woman shrugged.

The phone rang and Doyle pushed past her into the box.

'Here, wait a minute,' she said angrily, banging on the door.

He snatched up the receiver.

'Yeah,' he snapped.

The woman was still banging on the door.

'Doyle, listen,' said Georgie. 'I checked up on the car.'

The woman outside opened the door and stuck her head in.

'I wanted to use this phone,' she said irritably.

'Look missus, just fuck off, will you?' hissed Doyle and kicked the door shut.

'Ignorant bastard,' she shouted from outside.

'What the hell's going on there?' Georgie wanted to know.

'Never mind. Just tell me about the car,' he said.

'Like I said, they checked it out. It's registered in the Republic. To a Mr David Callahan.'

Forty-Seven

BRITTANY, FRANCE:
'So, Lausard knows about the window. So what?'

Catherine Roberts spat out the words angrily, looking at Channing who was sitting on the edge of the bed, head lowered.

'He's a reporter, *isn't* he?' Channing hissed. 'The bloody story will be everywhere within a few days.'

'He hasn't been back to the church and nothing has appeared in the papers. Perhaps he didn't think it was a good enough story,' she said quietly.

His lighter was still in her handbag.

'There's no reason to think he'll be back. Besides, all we can do is get on with our work. I think we're worrying needlessly.'

'You sound very sure of that,' he snapped.

'Look, Mark, the window isn't *your* property,' she told him. 'Neither of us has any right to keep it to ourself. What were you going to do with it, anyway? Hide it? Take it home with you so only you could see it? If that's what you wanted, why did you call me out here, too? You should have kept the information to yourself.'

'I told you, I needed your help,' sighed Channing wearily.

'My only concern is that window,' she said angrily.

'The work on it is too important to stop now.'

Channing paced the floor for a moment, head bowed.

'What we should be thinking about is how the window managed to become free of the stone,' she said.

As she spoke she glanced across at her handbag, to where the lighter was hidden.

Lausard's lighter.

Stuffed in the side pocket was her notebook, filled with observations from the previous night.

They were not to be shared with Channing.

She got to her feet.

'Where are you going?' Channing wanted to know.

'To the Church.'

'We could leave it for today. I think we both need a rest. I didn't sleep much last night again …'

She cut him short.

'You stay if you want to, Mark. I'm going.'

'It's become an obsession with you,' he said, flatly. 'The window, what it means.'

She picked up her handbag and headed for the door.

'I'll see you later,' she said and walked out.

He heard her footsteps on the stairs. A moment later he saw her walk out of the front of the inn and cross to her car. She slid behind the wheel, started the engine and drove off.

Channing exhaled deeply and ran a hand through his hair, then he fumbled in his pocket for his car keys and also hurried from the inn.

He should be able to catch her before she reached the church.

Forty-Eight

BELFAST, NORTHERN IRELAND:
The roar was deafening.

Doyle glanced towards the pitch in time to see a green-shirted player drive a shot only inches beyond the right-hand post.

The crowd around him seemed to swell for a second, as if each of them had been pumped full of air. As the ball skidded away for a goal kick they seemed to deflate again.

Windsor Park football ground was three-quarters full, the International fixture between Northern Ireland and England not having sufficient pulling power to fill the ground. Nonetheless, it had attracted the largest gate for two years. Both main stands and one end of the terracing were full to capacity. For safety reasons the far end of the ground from Doyle was less than half full. It contained most of the English supporters.

He moved with relative ease amongst those on the terraces, glancing at some of their faces, but mostly content to let his eyes rove over the heaving mass.

He knew the chances of picking out either Dolan or Maguire in a place this size, amongst over 20,000 people, were minuscule. But he had a feeling that they were here somewhere. He had told Georgie it was only a gut instinct; a hunch. Or any other cliché he could think of. But Dolan's remark in the pub the previous day about the football match had set him thinking.

It was the first time the English national side had played at Windsor park for two years. There were obvious attractions to Maguire and his renegades. A large gathering of people, a proportion of them English.

Doyle had a nasty feeling of unease in the pit of his stomach.

It may just have been his imagination; the remark which Dolan had made may have been purely innocuous. Doyle doubted it.

'There's a game on Tuesday night at Windsor Park. It should be quite something.'

Doyle continued to move amongst the crowd, glancing at the pitch every so often.

A long ball had set the England strikers free and two of them were now bearing down on the Irish goal, defenders frantically scrambling back to get goal side of them.

'Break his fucking leg,' shouted an encouraging amateur coach close to Doyle.

Nice to see the spirit of sportsmanship hasn't been affected by the recent mayhem, he thought, smiling.

The player with the ball chose to chip the goalkeeper and his shot flew towards the goal before striking the crossbar and bouncing back into play. An Irish defender nodded it into touch and the crowd relaxed again momentarily as players went forward for the impending corner.

Doyle moved on, eyes scanning the crowd.

'Put it out the fucking ground.'

'Cover the near post.'

Words of encouragement and advice were bellowed from the terraces and stands as the corner was swung in.

The Irish goalkeeper met it with a punch, clearing his area, relieving the pressure.

Doyle paused long enough to light a cigarette, slipping the packet back into his inside pocket. As he did so his hand brushed the shoulder holster and the butt of the CZ-75 automatic. He jammed the cigarette in the corner of his mouth and walked on, wondering if Georgie was having any luck on the other side of the ground.

She wasn't.

She felt even more helpless than Doyle. She only had his description of Dolan to go on and she'd only seen photos of Maguire. The identities of the other renegades were unknown to both her and Doyle. She stopped close to a group of men who were standing watching the match and thought that, for all she knew, she could be watching the renegades now and not even be aware of it.

That was assuming they were even present.

She had gone along with Doyle's hunch about an incident at the match purely and simply because hunches were all they had to go on at present. But she also trusted his instincts.

As she pulled her jacket tighter around her she felt the reassuring bulk of the Sterling .357.

Ever vigilant, she moved on.

Doyle was approaching the tall iron fence which segregated Irish supporters from English.

Despite the progress that had been made in halting sectarian violence in the province over the past few months the fence was a reminder that football violence was almost as insidious an illness and would require treatment of a similarly spectacular nature. He walked up to the fence, wondering if this was what a beast of prey felt like in a zoo. Doyle wandered up and down the length of the fence, glancing at the policemen who formed a further barrier behind the railings on the other side. They were all standing facing the crowd, unable to see the game. Unable to see the Irish winger cutting inside the English full-back.

The crowd roared its encouragement as he left the back for dead then drove in a curling cross which was met by an Irish forward.

The ball sped goalward, past the outstretched fingers of the English goalkeeper, finding the top left hand corner of the net.

The ground erupted as the ball crossed the line and Doyle turned to watch the celebrations on the pitch as the green-shirted players congratulated the scorer and the English players looked at one another incredulously before one of them retrieved the ball from the back of the net and booted it angrily upfield for the re-start.

Men all over the terraces were jumping up and down, hugging each other, hurling scarves into the air. The feeling of jubilation was almost palpable.

Doyle watched indifferently, draining what was left of his tea from the cup and dropping it onto the ground, crushing it underfoot as he looked around.

The small black bag at the foot of one floodlight stanchion almost escaped his attention.

There was no one standing near it, not within twenty feet.

He moved quickly towards it, pushing past a man and his young son who were still celebrating.

The bag was sealed with masking tape wrapped around it several times so tightly that the outline of the shape within the bag was clearly visible. It was rectangular.

Even through the black plastic, Doyle could see a tiny red light winking.

He dropped to one knee close to the package. It was about twelve inches long, perhaps half that in width. From his jacket pocket he withdrew a pocket knife.

The roar of the crowd grew in intensity as Ireland launched another attack, but as far as Doyle was concerned, he may as well have been the only man in that stadium. All that mattered to him was the package.

He took the tip of the knife and, with infinite care, cut the plastic bag, opening a rent about six inches long.

A couple of people nearby shot him cursory glances but their attention was soon dragged back to the game as the Irish won another corner, the ball booted unceremoniously behind by the English centre-half.

The roar began to swell.

Doyle used the tip of the knife to ease open the package, peeling back the black bag enough to see inside.

The winger swung the corner in and it was met by the defender on the near post, who headed it clumsily across his own penalty area. An Irish midfield player running in from the left caught the dropping ball full on the volley and the ball rocketed towards the goal before slamming against the angle of the post and crossbar and flying back into play.

Another massive shout from the crowd.

Doyle could see the device now, the two blinking lights, one red, one green.

He could even smell the familiar marzipan-like odour of the plastic explosive.

It looked like there were at least two pounds of it.

Enough to create havoc, strapped as it was to the floodlight stanchion. If the explosion …

'Jesus Christ,' he murmured as the realization hit him.

The floodlight stanchion.

If the bomb went off the blast would be enough to bring down the towering structure. Enough to bring down over fifty tons of steel and glass onto the crowd and probably a part of the pitch. There was no timer on the bomb. Doyle had seen this kind before. It was detonated by remote control.

As he got to his feet he might have smiled, satisfied that his hunch had been right.

The bomb could only be detonated by a remote *within* one hundred yards.

Somewhere in the crowd, somewhere in the stadium, were Maguire and his renegades. They had to be.

That much pleased Doyle.

It was the knowledge that they could detonate the bomb at any second which made him feel slightly *less* than happy.

Forty-Nine

How long had it been there?

How long before it went off?

These and other questions passed through Doyle's mind as he hurried away from the bomb towards the iron railings and the cordon of police beyond it.

On the pitch the English team, searching for the equalizer, were mounting a sustained attack. Shots rained in, striking defenders or parried by the goalkeeper but the Irish couldn't seem to clear their lines. Just outside the penalty area one of the English wingers cut inside, left two men for dead and, dropping his left shoulder, flipped the ball past two more defenders.

The crowd howled for him to be stopped as he bore down on the goal.

Doyle reached the fence and bellowed something at the nearest policeman.

The man didn't even acknowledge his presence.

A desperate lunge from the Irish centre-half brought the England winger crashing to the ground.

The referee pointed to the penalty spot.

'Hey, you, listen to me,' roared Doyle, his own entreaties completely lost in the shouts of the crowd as they vented their anger on the referee.

'Listen,' he bellowed again, realizing how useless it was. 'Fuck,' he snarled and ran to the bottom of the terrace, pushing past a number of people who had moved nearer to get a better view of the spot kick which was about to be taken.

Doyle leapt at the fence, climbing it quickly and skilfully, finally swinging himself over and landing with a thud on the outer rim of the pitch.

Two policemen hurried towards him.

The kicker ran forward to take the penalty.

Doyle saw the policeman getting closer; he stood and waited.

The English forward connected firmly with the ball and sent it high into the roof of the net.

The crowd responded with a chorus of cat-calls and shouts of derision.

The two policemen reached Doyle, one of them grabbing his arm.

'Get off me, you arsehole,' he snarled. 'Listen …'

'Come on, sunshine. Out,' snapped the first man, grabbing his arm again.

Doyle again shook loose, stepping back a couple of paces.

'You can do this the hard way if you want,' the second policeman said. 'It makes no odds to us.' He reached for his baton.

'There's a bomb in there,' snarled Doyle, pointing at the enclosure from which he'd just clambered.

'Yeah, and I'm fucking Frank Sinatra. Now come on you bastard,' said the second man, the larger of the two, drawing his baton and raising it menacingly towards Doyle.

'What the hell were you doing in there anyway?' said the first policeman. 'The area there,' he motioned behind him, 'is for English supporters. Now come on.'

'Look, I won't say it again,' Doyle rasped. 'There's a bomb in that enclosure. Get the fucking people out now, as quick as you can.'

'You're a real comedian, aren't you?' said the second man, lunging at Doyle with the baton.

The Englishman side-stepped and, his hand went to the inside of his jacket.

He pulled the CZ free of its holster and pointed it at the two uniformed men.

'Now listen to me,' he snarled. 'I'm not going to say this again.' He saw other policemen approaching now, running. 'There is a bomb secured to the floodlight in there. Check it out.'

One of the men reached for his radio.

'Unit two, come in, over,' he said, struggling to

214

make himself heard over the sound of the crowd. 'We require assistance in sector five, armed suspect ...'

Doyle snatched the radio from him.

'Unit two,' he shouted into the set, one eye on the uniformed men. 'Check out the floodlight stanchion in sector five. Suspected bomb found there. Do you read me?'

A hiss and a crackle of static on the set.

'Suspected bomb, we'll check it, over and out,' said a metallic voice.

'Now back off,' said Doyle, the CZ still pointed at the policemen.

Three or four others had arrived now and were gathering around Doyle, trying to cut off his escape routes. Not that he had many to choose from, with his back to the perimeter fence and the pitch blocked off by at least three men.

'Put the gun down,' said the largest of the men, the baton still drawn.

'Fuck you,' said Doyle, the noise of the crowd ringing in his ears.

Some of those close to the fence could see he was carrying a gun and many had moved back, fearing the worst.

'You'll never get away,' said another man. 'Not unless you kill us all and you're not going to do that.'

'Don't count on it, shithead,' snapped the Englishman.

A radio crackled.

'Unit two reporting.'

The words were scarcely audible over the noise of the crowd.

'Unit two, come in, over,' said a sergeant to Doyle's right.

'We've found it. There *is* a bomb here.'

'Get those fucking people out of there *now*,' shouted Doyle, angrily.

Stewards, alerted by the commotion, were already unlocking the gates in the fencing.

The police began filing through onto the terraces.

Doyle swallowed hard and looked towards the floodlight.

Would they be in time?

He wondered if Maguire was watching all this now, his finger poised over the button of the detonator.

Just waiting.

After all, *he* had plenty of time.

Doyle knew that for him and the people close to the bomb, time might have run out.

Fifty

She counted at least a dozen policemen on the touchline near the single figure and, as Georgie squinted across the length of the ground, she realized that it was Doyle.

Moments later she saw more police clambering over the barrier, moving around the side of the pitch towards the area of terracing where Doyle stood. He looked as if he was directing them, standing alongside a tall sergeant.

What the hell was going on?

She had to get round there, help him if she could.

Georgie turned, accidentally bumping into two men as she did.

216

She looked up and apologized.

James Maguire smiled politely and stepped to one side to let her through.

Don't react. Even though you know it's him, don't react.

She moved past the renegade IRA man, taking up a position about ten feet to his right. Each time she glanced past him towards the match, she was able to look at his face.

The square features. The dark hair.

Could she be mistaken?

Maguire stood with his hands dug deep into the pockets of his overcoat, occasionally muttering something to the man next to him, a tall man in his mid-thirties with a pale complexion and short brown hair.

She remembered the photo of Maguire she'd seen back in London, in Donaldson's office.

There was no mistake, this was the man.

But what to do? Pull down on him right here and now in the crowd and risk a shooting match?

Her hand went almost unconsciously to the .357 tucked in the holster beneath her left arm, her fingers touching the butt for reassurance. Then she hooked her thumbs in the pockets of her jeans and stood still.

Watch him.

Her gaze travelled across the pitch to where the police were still flooding onto the terracing.

The game continued, despite some bemused looks from the linesman on that side. Most of the crowd didn't even seem to have noticed the commotion; shouts and roars greeted every pass from the Irish side as they mounted another attack.

Maguire nudged his companion and nodded in the direction of one of the exits. They turned and made their way slowly through the crowd.

Georgie waited a moment before following them.

There was no way of telling Doyle what was going on; she couldn't afford to let Maguire out of her sight now. She had little doubt that he and his companion were armed. If it came to a fight she was ready. The Sterling was full and she carried two speed-loaders as well.

They were drawing closer to the steps which led down to the exit.

Georgie paused at the top of the steps, glancing back at the hordes of police still flooding onto the terracing. She could see Doyle standing on the edge of the pitch looking around.

Perhaps he was looking for *her*, she mused.

With that last thought she hurried down the steps after Maguire.

Others were leaving, too, so her presence wasn't noticeable as she walked briskly along twenty feet behind the Irishman. She followed both of them out into the car park and through the rows of stationary vehicles, aware that her pursuit became more obvious with every step.

Should she try and arrest them now?

There was a massive roar from inside the stadium and Maguire turned slightly.

Georgie walked off to the right, away from him, and headed towards a car, digging in her pocket as if to find her keys.

Maguire and his companion walked on. This time she circled around in a wide arc, trying to see which car they were headed for.

There was a man behind the wheel of the blue Sierra they climbed into. A short, heavy-set, brutish individual who had not used a razor for many days.

218

Georgie moved closer to the car, her eyes narrowed to read the number plate.

There was something familiar about the car.

Something ...

She recognised the number plate as the one Doyle had given her over the phone the other day. This was the car she had traced.

She undid her jacket, ready to pull the .357.

She moved closer to the vehicle, hearing the engine start up.

If she didn't move fast they were going to get away.

To her right she spotted a man opening the door of his Cavalier.

Georgie took a few steps towards him, glancing back at the Sierra. It wasn't moving. The bloody thing was just sitting there, engine idling.

What the hell were they playing at?

She could see them through the back window.

All three were checking their watches.

Fifty-One

They would never do it in time.

Doyle was convinced of that. He watched countless uniformed men flooding onto the terracing, shepherding the spectators away from the bomb. He heard garbled messages over radios that an army bomb disposal unit was on its way. But he was sure that they would never clear the scene in time. In his mind's eye

219

he could see Maguire standing watching the pande-
monium, finger poised over the button that would
detonate the device.

If you're going to push it, push it now, you bastard.

The crowd in that sector of the ground were moving
swiftly, co-operating with the police, bewildered by
what was happening but convinced that it was in their
own interests to evacuate the area.

Men ushered their children away; some carried their
off-spring. The evacuation was orderly, considering the
imminent danger.

Doyle wondered why nothing had been announced
over the public address system. He wondered why the
game was still going on. There could be other devices
in other parts of the ground. Why take chances?
Evacuate the whole bloody ground!

He scanned the faces of the spectators as they left,
looking pale and frightened. The exodus from this
particular part of the stadium must have been noticed
by others in the ground by now, surely. Others would
be asking questions, wondering what was happening.

Some would realize.

He saw many in the stand on the other side of the
pitch out of their seats, looking across towards the area.
For many the match itself was becoming something of a
sideshow.

He glanced back at the terracing behind him.

It was almost empty.

The police had done their work well. Doyle felt a
momentary rush of expectation. Perhaps the bomb
would not cause any loss of life.

A thin smile touched his lips.

Perhaps he'd got to the bomb before Maguire had
anticipated. Thwarted him. Doyle's smile broadened as

he heard word come over a radio that the terraces were clear and cordoned off.

'Fuck you, Maguire,' he murmured. 'Not *this* time.'

He turned to look back across at the main stand, at the spectators still gazing at the now-empty terracing.

It was then that the explosion came.

The blast was massive, ripping through the main stand, sending seats, pieces of concrete and plastic, metal and bodies flying into the air.

So enormous was the explosion that, even a full pitch width away, Doyle felt the concussion blast. Felt the wave of heat which followed the gigantic eruption.

He saw bodies flung skyward, some trailing blood like grotesque fireworks.

A searing red and white ball of flame filled the stand, momentarily blinding Doyle. It was followed by a secondary blast and reeking clouds of black smoke which rose above the scene of devastation to form a thick noxious mushroom cloud which rose into the sky, lifted on tongues of flame which leapt a full thirty feet.

Portions of the stand roof, blasted away by the fearful explosion, fell to the ground, huge sheets of twisted metal crashing down on those not already killed or maimed by the initial blast. As the thunderous roar of the detonation died away Doyle heard screams of pain and terror.

He set off across the pitch, past players who stood dumb-struck, gazing at the carnage, past others who had thrown themselves to the ground. Others were running towards the tunnel, towards the terracing. Anywhere to escape the horror.

There were bodies on the pitch, flung there by the ferocity of the discharge.

Doyle passed a man with one leg missing, torn off at

221

the hip, blood spouting madly from the stump.

Another had been decapitated by the blast, his lifeless body spread-eagled on a pitch now slicked heavily with crimson.

A hand, most of the arm still attached, lay close to the touchline. Two or three paces to the left was the body of a child, the back of the skull sheared off, the spine exposed between the shoulder blades.

Others still moved.

A man with his arm torn off above the elbow tried to drag himself away from the blistering flames. A woman ran screaming from the remnants of the stand, her hair and clothes alight.

Doyle grabbed her, singeing his hands in the process, and rolled her on the grass to extinguish the flames. She rolled onto her back, skin blackened by the incredible heat. He saw blisters actually rising on her face. Rising then bursting, spilling their sticky contents over her charred features. She coughed and smoke puffed from her mouth. As he stood up he knew she was dead.

Debris littered the ground everywhere, some of it red hot. Doyle looked up into the blazing wreckage and saw other bodies lying across seats; unable to move, they could only wait to be devoured by the flames which still leapt and danced in the cool night air and now brought with them a new stench.

The sickly sweet odour of burning flesh.

Doyle turned and saw policemen and ambulancemen dashing towards the scene of devastation. They were helping the wounded, comforting the dying. Some were lifting the dead and carrying them to the edge of the pitch.

A young boy, his face a mask of blood, stood over his

222

dead father, crying softly as he looked down at the eviscerated corpse. An ambulanceman tried to usher him away but the boy wouldn't go.

'Jesus Christ,' muttered Doyle through clenched teeth. He could feel the sweat on his body, could feel the heat as he stood looking into the flames which still blossomed from the stand. His ears were filled with screams and moans, his hearing still slightly impaired by the aftermath of the massive blast. He fixed his eyes on the crying child, its sobs echoing inside his head.

Doyle wished he'd been completely deafened.

He spun round to look back across the field at the section of terracing which had been cleared.

Cleared so effectively, people ushered away so efficiently from what was now, he realized, merely a decoy. The package had been placed there in *order* to be found.

He kicked at the ground angrily, his frustration spilling over into rage.

Behind him the stand continued to burn.

The wounded continued to moan in pain.

The child continued to cry.

Fifty-Two

The Sierra pulled away as the explosion ripped through the stand.

Georgie spun round, ducking down instinctively as she heard the thunderous roar, saw the screaming funnel of fire rocket into the air. She didn't wait to watch the mournful black smoke rising like a vast shroud over the scene of devastation. She turned in time to see the blue car pulling smoothly out of its parking space. No speed, no haste. They had no reason to hurry now, their job was done. They'd be clear of the stadium before the first ambulance even arrived.

The owner of the Cavalier was still sitting behind the wheel, rear-view mirror tilted towards him as he combed his hair. That simple act, however, had also been interrupted by the explosion. All eyes in the car park had turned towards the source of the blast and now looked on in horror and awe as the flames took hold.

It seemed the only ones not looking at the aftermath of the blast were the three men in the blue Sierra and Georgie who, by now, had reached the Cavalier.

She pulled open the driver's side door with one hand, reaching for the Sterling with the other.

'What the hell are you doing?' the driver snapped angrily, but the annoyance soon faded, transformed to fear as he saw the .357 drawn from its holster.

'Get out,' snapped Georgie, pushing the weapon into his face, motioning with her head.

He didn't need telling twice.

He raised his hands in surrender and slid from behind the wheel, his bowels loose. Helpless, afraid he was going to fill his pants, he watched as Georgie got into the car, stuffed the .357 back into its holster and started the engine. She pulled away smoothly, eyes searching for the blue Sierra.

It was about thirty yards ahead of her, turning out of the main entrance to the car park. The security guards and police who had been manning the entrance were running towards the stadium, presumably thinking that

224

their duties now lay within. The IRA men slipped out unchallenged.

Georgie followed, shifting her position in the driving seat, angry when she found that the chair was uncomfortably far from the pedals. Still, no time to stop now, she'd have to manage.

As she pulled out into traffic behind the Sierra she heard the first wail of sirens, saw the first of the emergency vehicles come screeching around a corner and hurtle towards the stadium. Red and blue lights filled her eyes but she blinked the glare away, more intent on not losing sight of her quarry.

The Sierra was approaching a set of traffic lights.

Georgie kept a reasonable distance between herself and the other car, glancing down at the Cavalier's fuel gauge, relieved to see that the needle was hovering on a mark just below full. She had no idea how long this was going to take.

What was she hoping for?

That they would lead her to their hideout?

Perhaps to the man who hired them in the first place?

Another police car went flashing past, sirens screaming.

The Sierra crossed the junction with the lights on amber.

'Shit,' hissed Georgie, knowing what she must do.

They were going to spot her sooner or later anyway.

Hold tight.

She put her foot down and the Cavalier sped through the red lights. A car coming the other way swerved, narrowly avoiding her, the driver slamming hard on his brakes, hitting his horn at the same time.

In the Sierra, the driver, the thick-set man with a heavy growth of whiskers, looked back and glimpsed the

Cavalier in the rear view mirror.

'I think we've got company,' he said quietly.

Maguire turned and looked out of the back window.

'Police?' asked Paul Maconnell, swinging the car around a corner.

'I don't know,' said Maguire, squinting through the window to get a better look at their pursuer. 'Lose them.'

Maconnell nodded and put his foot down.

The Sierra shot forward as if fired from a cannon.

Georgie knew now that they'd spotted her. At least now she knew what to do.

She stepped hard on the accelerator, the needle on the speedo nudging seventy.

Ahead of her the Sierra took a corner doing nearly seventy-five, the tyres squealing as they struggled to grip the road. The car skidded, spun then shot off once more, leaving tread marks for at least ten feet behind it. She smelt the burning rubber as she hurtled after it, the wind rushing through her open side window.

More traffic lights ahead.

Red.

Fuck it. Both cars roared straight through, Georgie forced to guide her car up on to the pavement to avoid a Metro which had stalled ahead of her. She felt the Cavalier bounce up onto the kerb, the jolt throwing her against the door, almost knocking the wind from her.

Another corner and the Sierra took it approaching eighty.

Georgie tried to coax more speed from the Cavalier, gripping the wheel tight as she wrenched it hard to guide the car around the corner. The street she came into was narrow and she saw the Sierra directly ahead.

It scraped the side of a parked car, sparks flying from the chassis. Maconnell controlled the vehicle, though, swinging it away from the parked car, allowing it to screech across a corner of the pavement. It hit the kerb and rose a couple of feet, slamming down again, skidding violently. But the Irishman regained control and drove on.

Georgie also took the short cut across the pavement, the wheels thumping the kerb so hard she thought for one terrible second she'd had a blow-out, but the Cavalier continued on and she leant forward, as if to put more pressure on the accelerator.

Ahead of her on the left was a supermarket, shoppers filling parked cars from trolleys.

The Sierra managed to swerve in time to avoid the trolley which rolled in front of it.

Georgie tried but couldn't.

The wheeled basket was catapulted into the air by the collision, twisted into scrap by the impact. It skidded off the roof and fell back into the street.

Georgie kept her foot on the gas pedal, her palms moist now on the wheel.

More sirens, behind her this time. She glanced into the rear-view mirror and saw a police car.

Maconnell saw it too.

'The fucking law,' he hissed, twisting the wheel violently as he took another corner.

'Fuck the law,' said Mick Black from the back seat. 'Who's this comedian that's chasing *us*?'

Maguire said nothing; he merely glanced again at the oncoming Cavalier. He reached into the glove compartment and took out a gleaming object.

A loud metallic click filled the car as he slammed in the magazine of the Skorpion machine pistol. Then, as quickly as he could, he slid over the passenger seat and into the back with Black.

'Slow down, Paul,' said Maguire, winding down one of the rear windows. 'Let the bastard get a bit closer.'

Maconnell nodded and did as he was instructed.

Cold air rushed into the car as Maguire wound down the window, steadying himself on the back seat.

Georgie saw the sub-machine gun a fraction of a second before it was fired.

She hit her brakes, the Cavalier skidding madly.

Maguire opened up.

The staccato rattle of automatic fire filled the evening and bright flames spewed from the barrel of the Skorpion as it spat out its deadly load. The single burst of 9mm ammunition spattered the front of the Cavalier.

Bullets screamed off the bonnet, tearing off a wing mirror. Three or four hit the windscreen.

Georgie was lucky. The fact that the Cavalier had spun to one side ensured that the high velocity slugs didn't hit directly. Two merely whined off the glass but the others shattered it. The windscreen spider-webbed. It was like looking through ice.

She eased her foot slightly on the accelerator, slowing down a little as she struck at the shattered glass, managing to punch a hole in it. Wind rushed in, blasting into her face, but she kept punching until all the windscreen seemed to fold in upon itself. Some fragments merely collapsed and were blown off the bonnet of the car as they fell outwards. Others, blown by the wind, were flung back into the car.

Georgie hissed in pain as one needle-like sliver sliced her cheek. She felt blood running down her face. The cold wind screaming in through what was left of the windscreen seemed to deaden the pain. She saw that Maguire was steadying himself for another burst of fire.

Georgie pressed her foot down as hard as she could on the accelerator and the Cavalier rapidly closed the gap on the Sierra. Closed it, cut it and ...

She slammed into the back of the fleeing vehicle, smashing one of its tail lights. Pieces of glass and plastic housing skittered away on the road. She rammed it again, the jolt throwing her back in her seat, but she gripped the wheel more tightly, watching with satisfaction as Maconnell struggled to keep control of the Sierra.

A third time she rammed it, seeing Maguire knocked off balance by the impact.

Now. Do it now.

Using one hand to steer, she reached into her jacket and pulled the .357 free, resting it against the window frame ahead of her for support. She knew there'd be one hell of a kick; she needed all the help she could get. She thumbed back the hammer, feeling the six pound pull on the trigger as she squeezed it.

The Magnum bucked in her fingers, the butt slamming into the heel of her hand, making it tingle. But she fired again. The retort was deafening, mingling with the howling wind and the scream of tyres as the Sierra skidded again.

The first bullet blasted away the remaining rear light on the fleeing car, the second punched a huge hole in the back windscreen. Glass was sent flying into the car by the explosion and she saw the two men on the back seat dive for cover.

Behind her another police car had joined the chase but Georgie was concerned only with what was ahead of her.

A car reversing out into the street.

The Sierra swerved, slamming into another car on the opposite side of the road.

Georgie hit the tail end of the reversing car so hard the Chevette turned almost one hundred and eighty degrees. A massive jolt shook the Cavalier; she grunted as the steering column struck her in the chest. She almost dropped the .357, the breath momentarily knocked from her.

Behind her the blaring of sirens was deafening.

She drove on.

Maguire was up on the back seat again, steadying the Skorpion.

He fired two quick bursts.

The first peppered the radiator of the Cavalier. The second was aimed low, bullets screeching up off the street.

Both her front tyres were shot out.

She heard the bangs, felt the car begin to slide out of control. Knew she'd never control it around the corner, which was coming at her like something on a fairground ride gone mad.

She wrestled with the wheel but lost the battle. The Cavalier hit the kerb doing sixty-five. It flipped, rose into the air, spinning, before finally crashing down on its passenger side, the door punched in. As it continued to roll Georgie gripped the wheel tight, shoulders drawn up, her head sunk low to avoid any damage to her neck as the car spun like a toy a petulant child had tossed away.

It felt as if someone had taken her by the lapels and was shaking her. She closed her eyes tightly, not wanting to see the world spinning round through the shattered windscreen.

The car finally came to a halt, flopping down on its roof, turning slightly.

She felt sick. Her head was spinning. She tasted blood in her mouth but didn't know where it came from. Perhaps she was bleeding internally. There was no pain, though. Just the nausea, waves of it washing over her. There was a ringing in her ears.

She managed to push open the driver's side door and fall out onto the pavement, her face pressed to the cool concrete.

She heard sirens.

Saw people running towards her.

Then there was only darkness.

Fifty-Three

The wound on her cheek was a superficial one; she probably wouldn't even have a scar to show for it. Georgie was more concerned with the constant pounding inside her skull. It felt as if ten men with pneumatic drills were trying to tunnel their way out.

The headache had grown steadily worse during the questioning, the fluorescents in the main interview room of Hastings Street police station adding to her discomfort. She sat forward at the desk, shielding her eyes as the barrage of questions were directed at her.

She couldn't remember how long they'd kept her there; all that she could remember was the chase, the gunfire and the crash.

The officers questioning her seemed to be in another

dimension, their questions floating towards her as if spoken by disembodied inquisitors. Georgie kept her eyes closed most of the time, irritated by the fluorescents, angered by the splitting headache.

Angered, too, by the fact that Maguire and his men had escaped.

They had brought Doyle in around eleven o'clock, and threatened to charge him with illegal possession of a firearm.

Or anything else they could think of.

Georgie had been told she was likely to be charged with a breach of the peace, causing an affray, endangering lives, reckless driving. The list seemed to go on and on until it reached attempted murder.

They had been questioned separately, then together.

When she next looked at her watch it was approaching two in the morning. She felt tired, irritable and dirty. The blood she had tasted in her mouth when the car crashed had run down from the cut on her cheek. One tooth was cracked as well, she discovered, probing it with her tongue.

The two counter-terrorists allowed their captors to question them, never replying to any of the enquiries.

It was Doyle who finally decided he'd had enough.

He gave them Donaldson's telephone number in London and waited while they rang it.

He had merely shrugged at Georgie as the RUC man went off to make the call, returning about ten minutes later with a disappointed look on his face.

They were, he told his superiors, indeed British counter-terrorists. Their identities had been confirmed from London.

Within thirty minutes they were released, their weapons restored to them.

Anxious to get the English agents away from the police station, the RUC put them in separate cars and had them driven back to the Excelsior.

On the way back Doyle asked if a figure had been put on the number of casualties at the Windsor Park blast. He was told that so far more than thirty people had been killed and four times that number injured, many critically.

Doyle asked to be dropped off about two hundred yards from the hotel. Not that it really mattered any more.

When he finally entered the foyer he found Georgie sitting, head in hands, on one of the seats close to reception. They rode the lift together to the tenth floor. She told him she was going to shower.

He told her to come along to his room in ten minutes.

Doyle's small case was packed when Georgie entered the room, dressed in just a towelling robe. She wandered across to the bed and sat down, glancing at the case and at what lay on top of the carefully folded clothes.

It was an MP5K sub-machine gun.

Despite being only eight inches in length, the sub-gun was capable of firing over 650 9mm rounds a minute in the right hands and, she concluded, they didn't come much better than Doyle.

He sat down on the bed facing her and flipped the case shut.

'The bastards tricked us,' he said. 'That fucking bomb ...' He allowed the sentence to trail off.

'Your hunch was right, though.'

'Fat lot of good it was to the poor sods who got blown up, eh?'

She nodded.

'So what now?' she wanted to know.

'They know we're after them,' he said. 'This incident tonight has blown what little cover we had anyway. There's no point in staying in Belfast. I think it's time we moved into the Republic. Fight the bastards on their home ground. Besides, I think it's time we found out who this Mr David Callahan is. I'd like to know what the IRA are doing driving around in his car.'

'Fake name?' she suggested.

'More than likely, but we've got to check it out.'

'What makes you think they'll move into the Republic?'

'They've pulled too much exposure here. They need to lie low for a while, too.' He got to his feet, walked around the bed and touched her cut cheek with the back of his hand. He smiled.

'You got too close to them. I think you scared them,' he told her.

'I would have killed them, Doyle,' she told him.

He nodded, then bent and kissed her lightly on the lips.

When he straightened up he turned away from her, looking towards the window.

'I bet Donaldson didn't appreciate being woken up at that time in the morning,' she said, smiling.

'We're lucky he verified who we were. We'd have been right up shit creek if he hadn't.' Doyle turned to face her again.

'How long will it take you to pack?' he wanted to know.

'Ten minutes.'

He nodded.

She got to her feet and made for the door, leaving Doyle to gaze out of the bedroom window, out over the city. He was glad she was all right, relieved that she hadn't been injured but he didn't tell her, wouldn't tell her.

Couldn't.

Don't drop the barriers now. No need.

Keep that distance.

He sucked in a weary breath.

Ten floors below, seated in a car parked across the street from the hotel, other eyes were also watching.

But they were watching the hotel entrance, waiting for Georgie and Doyle to appear.

They didn't know how much longer they'd have to wait, they'd already been sitting there for over two hours.

They had played this waiting game before.

It was only a matter of time.

Fifty-Four

Simon Peters took one final drag on his cigarette and tossed the butt out of the window. He held the smoke in for a moment, then blew it out in a long blue stream.

The whole interior of the Ford Escort was full of smoke.

Beside him Joe Hagen puffed away at a Dunhill. In the back seat Eamonn Rice and Luke McCormick were also smoking. It was like sitting in a mobile ashtray.

They were parked on a hill overlooking Milltown cemetery. The sun was rising slowly in the morning sky, dragging itself reluctantly towards the heavens, spreading an orange glow over the countryside. A thin film of mist still hung in the air, like dry ice. As Peters stepped out of the car it swirled around his feet. The grass was slippery underfoot but he walked with assurance, breathing in the crisp morning air, clearing his lungs of cigarette smoke.

It was so peaceful up here at this time, he mused, watching the sun climb higher in the sky. He had often driven up here and sat for an hour or so, watching over the city as it woke from its slumbers. The sound of early morning birds twittering in the trees only served to reinforce the beauty of the scene. He sometimes thought that the newsmen who came to the province to report on the violence should see scenes like this, should watch the sun staining everything gold. Should hear the birds singing. But they weren't interested in the beauty of Northern Ireland. None of them. They could see no further than the troubles in the Falls Road. The bomb blasts in Londonderry. The sniping in Clonard. They saw what they wanted to see. They saw his country being crushed into the ground by years of bigotry, hatred and jealousy.

Many victims of that conflict lay below him in Milltown now. The cameras came there when there was a funeral. They came to record death with a relish Peters found obscene. And he had seen enough death during his time in the IRA to know it for the vile thing it was. But death was a necessary part of the province. Just as violence had been for the last twenty years. He had caused some of those deaths himself: soldiers, security men, civilians when necessary. But it all had a purpose. His was not the campaign of a psychopath. He had no more time for the slaughter than those he had fought against, but for Simon Peters it was a way of life.

The only way to free the country he loved.

No one had been happier than he when the Stormont peace summit had finally gathered, but the promise of an end to the bloodshed, the hope of a united Ireland had been dashed. Blown away in a hail of bullets by men who dared to call themselves members of the very organisation to which he was so proud to belong.

Those same men had been responsible for the deaths of over sixty people at Windsor Park the previous night.

Men like James Maguire.

Peters knew Maguire well; he had even worked with him on a number of jobs during the past few years. He knew some of the men he had with him, too.

Men like Billy Dolan and Mick Black.

Even the thought of them set the knot of muscles at the side of his jaw pulsing angrily.

He would not let them destroy his own dreams. He would find them before they could do so.

Find them and kill them.

Joe Hagen climbed out of the car and wandered over to join him, hands dug into the pockets of his trousers. Dew darkened his suede boots as he walked across the long grass.

He stood beside Peters, watching the sunrise and the city coming to life beneath it as if coaxed into stirring by the warm rays.

'My father used to say that the sunrise was the colour of the gold on the tricolour,' Hagen murmured reflectively. 'When people used to talk about the gold meaning the Catholics and the green meaning the Protestants he'd say it was the bit in the middle you had to worry about. The part where the two colours could never join.'

'Quite a philosopher, your old fella,' Peters nodded, smiling.

'He was that. I wish he could have lived long enough to see a United Ireland.'

'If we don't find Maguire soon then none of us will see a United Ireland, because things will go back to how they were before,' Peters said, his smile fading.

On a branch nearby a thrush chirped contentedly, then flew off, its outline a black arrowhead against the brightening sky.

'I spoke to Coogan this morning,' said Peters. 'There's at least one English agent on Maguire's tail, too. The RUC are looking for him as well. Belfast is too hot for him and his men right now. They've probably already crossed over the border.'

'Who's the British agent?' Hagen wanted to know.

'James Bond,' said Peters flatly. 'How the fuck do I know?'

'He could get in the way, Simon.'

'God help him if he does. This is *our* business, not the bloody Brits'.'

He sucked in another lungful of crisp air, turned and began walking slowly back towards the car.

'I think it's time we paid a visit to some of the families of these … *renegades*.' He emphasized the word with contempt. 'If Maguire and his men have crossed the border, someone might know where they've gone. Someone close to them.'

'And if they won't talk?' Hagen wanted to know.

Peters smiled.

'They'll talk. I guarantee it.'

Fifty-Five

BRITTANY, FRANCE:
They weren't reporters.

Channing knew that much from the moment the couple stepped from the car. The new arrivals were too smart to be press.

The man wore a light grey suit, immaculately pressed and tailored. He was powerfully built, his shoulders broad, his features heavy.

The woman with him was dressed in a black dress which came to just above her knees, hugging her fine figure tightly. She had a red leather jacket draped around her shoulders. The slight breeze stirred her shoulder-length brown hair as she walked.

Channing drew a hand across his forehead and sighed, eyeing the couple suspiciously as they drew nearer. The man was smiling.

'Good morning,' he said, nodding at Channing.

He returned the greeting, still running appraising eyes over the couple.

'What can I do for you?' he asked warily, expecting the answer even before it came.

'We want to see the window,' David Callahan told him. 'We've come from Ireland; we flew in last night.' He introduced himself and Laura.

'Why do you want to see it?' Channing asked.

'I have an interest in artefacts like this.' Callahan looked the other man up and down. 'Who *are* you, anyway? How come *you're* here?' There was an edge to Callahan's voice that Channing wasn't slow to notice.

'My name is Mark Channing. I'm the one who found the window,' he said.

'Good for you,' Callahan countered acidly. 'May we see it?'

'I am here trying to work. All I want is some peace and quiet.'

'That's fine by me, Mr Channing, but we have a right to see the window if we want to. You can't keep us from it.'

'Why do you want to see it?'

'You've already asked me that.' Callahan's temper was beginning to fray.

'We know something about the man who had this church built,' Laura interjected.

'We've been here before,' added Callahan. 'Probably before *you*.' He was breathing heavily and a vein in his temple throbbed angrily. 'You don't own this land, do you, Mr Channing?'

He shook his head.

'Then there is nothing you can do to stop us going inside that church and looking around. You found the window; you're not its protector, the judge of who should or shouldn't look at it.'

Channing still blocked their path to the main door but he could see the anger in Callahan's eyes, could hear it in his voice.

'We came here out of *genuine* interest,' said Callahan. 'I've made a study of Gilles de Rais. This window you've found is of concern to me and I don't intend leaving here until I've seen it. Now you can take us and show us the window, step aside and let us in or you can carry on being difficult. But I warn you, Mr

240

Channing, I'm not leaving here until I've seen what's inside that church.'

'Are you threatening me?'

'I'll do more than threaten you if you don't get out of the way,' snarled Callahan, taking a step forward.

'What's going on?'

All heads turned as Catherine Roberts appeared in the doorway of the church.

'They want to see the window,' Channing told her.

Cath nodded slowly.

'Come on, I'll take you through,' she said wearily.

Channing shot her an angry glance.

Callahan smiled thinly and he and Laura followed Cath into the church.

As they entered both were struck by the smell of damp and decay and Laura had to tread carefully, cautious not to trip over any of the pieces of rotting wood which littered the stone floor. Dust several inches deep rose up like puffs of smoke each time they put their feet down. It was like walking on a bed of ashes.

'I apologise for my companion,' said Cath as they moved through the nave. 'He's become a little over-protective where the window is concerned. It's important to him.'

'It's important to me, too,' Callahan told her. Then he remembered he didn't know her name. Hasty introductions were exchanged.

'What's your interest in the window, Mr Callahan?' Cath asked.

'You could say I'm a collector,' Callahan said, smiling.

Cath, puzzled, opened the door which led through to the chancel.

Shafts of sunlight which had managed to force entry

241

through broken slats on the far side of the chancel now struck the window, illuminating its colours so vividly it seemed to be glowing.

Callahan and Laura entered.

'Jesus Christ,' murmured Callahan, gazing in awe.

Laura stood as if mesmerized, her eyes never leaving the glass.

Callahan moved closer, reaching out to touch the panel which showed the clawed hand holding a child. The glass was cold against his fingertips.

Channing entered the chancel and looked at the two newcomers, then at Cath. He reserved the same look of distaste for all three.

'What do the words mean?' asked Callahan, pointing at the Latin legends within the glass.

'We're still working on that,' Cath told him.

'Who's paying you?' Callahan wanted to know.

'No one,' Channing said. 'This is research.'

Callahan smiled.

'It can't be comfortable working in these conditions,' he said.

'We manage,' Channing snapped.

'You don't have to *manage*. I'm offering you the chance to work at your own pace, in private, without press interference in a controlled environment. Anything you could want.'

'How?' Cath sounded intrigued.

'Work for me,' said Callahan quietly. 'It's your choice. But if you don't then someone else will, and I warn you now I want this window. And what I want I get.'

Channing smiled.

'What are you going to do? Wrap it up and put it in your suitcase?'

'No. I'm going to have it flown out by private plane back to my estate in Ireland.'

'You can't.'

'Are *you* going to stop me?'

'How much would you be willing to pay for the work to continue on the window?' Cath asked.

'You can't ...' Channing hissed but she raised a hand to silence him.

'Fifty thousand pounds. More, if you want it,' Callahan said flatly.

'You can't buy this window and you can't buy our expertise,' Channing said.

'The window doesn't belong to you, and if you don't want to work on it that's your business. If you want to throw fifty thousand back at me that's your business, too.' He looked at Cath. 'What about you, Miss Roberts? The offer stands.'

'Make it a hundred thousand,' she said.

'Cath, for God's sake,' snarled Channing.

'Right,' Callahan agreed. 'One hundred thousand it is.' He looked at Channing. 'And you?'

'No. I won't let you take the window.' He turned and wrenched open the chancel door. 'I'd rather see it destroyed.'

They heard his footsteps as he stalked off through the nave.

Callahan looked at the window, then at Cath.

He was smiling.

Fifty-Six

Channing paced the floor of his room agitatedly, occasionally stopping to look at Cath, who stood by the window watching him.

'All Callahan's offering us is better working conditions,' said Cath softly.

'You make him sound like a factory boss.'

'Don't be so bloody ridiculous. You know what I mean. There's nothing more we can do on the window in its present position or location. Besides, I'm sick of working inside that church.'

'He has no right to take the window. It isn't his.'

'And it isn't *ours*, either,' she reminded him. 'Work with him, Mark, not against him. You want to find out the secret of the window. So does Callahan, and he's prepared to pay money to find it.'

'You told him about it, then? About the secret?'

'*He* mentioned it. After you'd gone he said something about the treasure, about some kind of secret de Rais had. Callahan's no fool, Mark.'

'So just because he happens to have read a couple of books about Gilles de Rais, you're impressed with his knowledge, eh? For that you'll allow him to take the window? For that you'll sell your talents and your skills to him to help him find the secret?'

'It's not just for *his* benefit,' she snapped. '*I* want to know what that window means, what it meant to de Rais. *I* want to know and I intend to find out. You said

244

I was obsessed with it; well, perhaps you're right. I'm not going to stop working on it until I find out.'

'You bargained with him,' said Channing scornfully, 'like a whore doing a deal with a customer. Fifty thousand wasn't enough, so you pushed him to a hundred. A whore's bargain.'

She took two steps towards him and slapped his face hard.

Channing looked at her angrily, his cheek stinging from the blow.

'Don't ever call me that,' she hissed.

'I won't let you do it, Catherine,' rasped Channing.

He swung at her, his fist catching her across the jaw, a blow which sent her sprawling. She tasted blood in her mouth as he advanced on her.

'I won't let you take the window,' he repeated, and grabbed her by the hair, tearing a great chunk from her scalp. She screamed in pain as he ripped it free, staring at the clump for a moment before lunging at her again.

Cath tried to roll to one side, to escape him, to reach the door of the room but Channing was too fast for her. As she made a dive for the bed he grabbed her leg and pulled her back, throwing all his weight on her, pinning her down.

He fastened his hands around her throat and began to squeeze, his thumbs digging into her larynx.

She struck at him, raking his cheek with her nails, pieces of his skin coming away. Blood dripped onto her face from the deep gashes but the pressure on her throat didn't ease.

'I won't let you go,' he hissed, shaking her now, exerting more pressure, driving his thumbs deeper until she thought he must begin to crush her spinal cord.

White light danced before her eyes and she could not

245

get her breath. It felt as if someone were sucking every last drop of air from her lungs as Channing pressed down harder.

She hooked her legs around him and tried to bring her heels down hard into the small of his back. For brief moments, with Channing lying between her legs, her own limbs around him, they looked to be in some kind of murderous coital embrace, but then her legs seemed to lose their strength and slip to either side. Waves of nausea swept through her. She realized with horror that she was losing consciousness. The blood pounded in her ears. Through eyes blurred with pain and fear she saw Channing's face above her. There was spittle on his lips, his teeth gritted together.

He looked like a madman.

In her last few moments of rational thought she guessed that madness had indeed finally taken him.

She couldn't breathe. His thumbs were gouging even more deeply into her throat.

She realized with unshakeable certainty that she was going to die.

One last effort.

She forced strength into limbs she had thought incapable of movement.

Summoning every last reserve of will she managed to bring her left knee up with terrific force, driving it into his groin.

The grip on her throat weakened noticeably.

She heard Channing's strangled cry of pain and brought up her knee again, this time so hard she felt it connect with his pelvic bone.

He rolled off her, groaning and clutching his testicles.

She fell from the bed, hit the floor hard. Holding her

bruised throat with one hand, her breath coming in choked gasps, she made for the door.

She'd almost reached it when she felt the hand on her shoulder.

Channing, his face still contorted with pain and rage, grabbed her by one arm and swung her round with such force that she was catapulted across the room. Unable to stop herself she smashed into the dressing table, her head snapping forward, striking the mirror with sickening force. The glass shattered, great long shards of it spraying out around her.

She slid to the floor, blood pouring from the savage wound on her forehead.

Through a mist of semi-consciousness she saw Channing coming towards her, bending to snatch up a particularly long, rapier-sharp piece of shattered mirror. The jagged edges cut his hands but he seemed to ignore his own pain.

'You won't take the window,' he hissed, his face twisted and bloated.

He looked like something embodied in the window, Cath thought.

Something monstrous.

It was her last thought before he drove the razor-sharp length of glass into the top of her skull.

She didn't scream.

Cath merely sat bolt upright in bed, her entire body coated with perspiration.

She looked frantically around, her eyes wide, still unsure for a second if she was immersed in the nightmare. Her hand went to her throat and she felt no marks, found that she could swallow without pain. There was no blood on her face. No wounds.

247

'Jesus,' she murmured and swung herself, naked, out of bed, feeling the sweat dry on her skin as she crossed to the door. She stood there for a moment, the residue of the dream still seared onto her retina like the muzzle-flash of a gun. Then, quickly, she locked the door and went back to bed, but it was a long time before she slept. Instead she watched the curtains billowing in the breeze like the wings of some gigantic moth.

Across the landing Mark Channing also lay awake, only shortly having emerged from the nightmare.

The nightmare in which he had murdered Catherine Roberts.

He lay motionless for long moments, then climbed out of bed and crossed to the wardrobe where his case was. He pulled it out and rummaged about inside.

The knife was almost eight inches long, double-edged and sharp as a razor. He examined it in the gloom, feeling the edges with his thumb. The blade itself was scratched and worn from many years' use: whittling, prising rocks from the ground.

It was a useful tool in his field work. His father had presented him with it just before he'd died and Channing treasured it for that as much as for its practicality and usefulness.

He scraped the pad of one thumb across the edge a little too hard and drew blood. He wiped the crimson droplet away.

He hefted the knife once more, glancing towards the door, wishing he could see beyond it. Into Catherine Roberts' room.

He turned the knife slowly in his hand and slid it carefully back into his case.

Fifty-Seven

BELFAST, NORTHERN IRELAND:
Number Forty Glenarvon Road was as unremarkable and as uniformly ordinary as most of the other houses on the Turf Lodge estate.

It was terraced, with a blue-painted front door which was blistered and in need of redecoration. The window frames were in a similar condition. There were slates missing off the roof, as there were on many of the other houses on the street.

The early morning sunrise, which had spread its orange glow through the sky and made even the worst areas of the city look inviting, had passed. The sun itself had disappeared behind banks of clouds which periodically spattered the earth with rain. The sky was grey. The street was grey. Even the people in it looked grey; colourless entities who led grey lives.

There was movement behind the curtains of Number Forty.

Simon Peters watched quietly, drumming on his knee.

'Someone's at home,' said Luke McCormick. He flicked on the windscreen wipers every now and then to clear the spots of rain from the glass and to give the men an unobstructed view of the house.

There were just the two of them in the car. Hagen and Rice were a few miles away in Ballymurphy, checking on the whereabouts of Michael Black.

The four men were to meet up at the Divis flats in two hours' time.

Peters continued to watch the house, moving slightly in his seat every now and then. As he did he felt the weight of the Browning Hi-Power against his left side. Tucked in his belt was a Charter Arms 'Pathfinder', a .22 calibre pistol.

The use to which the IRA put .22 pistols was limited.

But the smaller calibre weapons served their purpose admirably.

After all, anything larger would mean the whole of the lower leg being blown off, and why do that when a knee-cap was sufficient?

The curtain of Number Forty moved again.

'I wonder if young Billy is home,' said Peters.

'Perhaps he is and he's seen us,' McCormick suggested.

'If he'd seen us, Luke, he wouldn't be standing there looking out of the window at us, would he, now?' Peters observed, smiling. 'He'd have legged it.'

Peters glanced down at the clock on the dashboard, checking it against his own watch.

9.26 a.m.

The door of Number Forty opened and a tall youth dressed in jeans and a denim jacket nosed his way out, looked both ways then turned back to peer into the house. He was speaking to someone.

'Is that Billy's brother?' McCormick said.

Peters shook his head.

The youth waited a moment longer then wandered out, slammed the door behind him and ran off down the street, disappearing round a corner.

Peters pushed open his door and climbed out.

'Come on,' he said quietly, and his companion

250

joined him as they moved slowly across the street from the parked car.

A woman cleaning her front step looked up and saw them. McCormick waved to her and she waved back, continuing with her task.

As they reached the door of Number Forty Peters slid one hand inside the jacket. With the other hand he knocked.

No answer.

He tried again.

There was a hasty movement behind the door and it was opened a fraction.

Maria Dolan looked out at the men, her hair tousled, her face flushed, with only a towel wrapped around her.

'Who are you?' she asked, brushing a strand of blonde hair from her forehead.

Peters ran appraising eyes over her. She was in her late teens, not particularly pretty, a little on the thin side. Her legs needed shaving, he noted, seeing the shadows on her shins. The dye was beginning to grow out of her hair and the dark roots were showing where it was parted.

'Is your brother in, Maria?' Peters asked.

'Who wants to know?'

'Is he here?' McCormick added. 'We just want to talk to him.'

She regarded both men warily, her brown eyes flicking back and forth between the two of them.

'Are you with the RUC?' she wanted to know.

Peters grinned.

'No, we're not. We're friends of Billy's. We just want to speak to him.'

'He's not here,' she said and tried to push the door shut.

Peters saw what she was doing and managed to get one foot across the threshold.

'Open up, come on. If Billy's not here we'll have to talk to you,' he said, his hand gripping the pistol in his belt.

'Fuck off,' she said, trying to shut the door again.

Peters pulled the pistol free and, keeping it hidden, aimed it at her stomach.

'Open the door, you little tart. Now.'

She obeyed instantly, allowing them both inside. McCormick closed it behind them.

The sitting room was small and untidy. There were clothes lying around on the sofa. Peters noticed a pair of knickers on the arm of a chair. In an ashtray on the small coffee table there was a condom wrapped in tissue paper.

'Been entertaining, have you, Maria?' he said, smiling and pushing the .22 back into his belt.

She pulled the towel tighter around herself, the colour drained from her face. The bravado had gone from her voice.

'Who are you?' she asked quietly.

'Like I said, we're friends of your brother.' Peters looked around the room. A painting of Mary Magdalene stared back at him from one wall, encased in its plastic frame. On another wall there was a crucifix. Over the fireplace hung a calendar showing different views of Ireland. It was a month out of date. He crossed to it and turned it to the correct month.

'Parents out, too?' he observed.

'Dad's on the early shift, Mum left about two hours ago,' she said.

'So you invited your boyfriend round?' he chuckled.

McCormick looked into the small kitchen, then left

the sitting room and Maria heard him walking about upstairs.

'You're not going to hurt me, are you?' she said softly.

Peters shook his head.

'We just want to talk to you,' he told her. 'Has anyone else been here to see you in the last few days?'

She shook her head.

McCormick returned from upstairs, looked at Peters, shook his head and went into the kitchen.

Peters picked up the jeans from the sofa and a T-shirt, threw them to Maria and turned his back.

'Get dressed,' he told her, gazing out of the small front window. She did so hurriedly. When he thought she was finished he turned to face her again. She stood quivering before him like a naughty child in front of a headmaster.

McCormick returned from the kitchen.

The carving knife he carried was over ten inches long, broad-bladed and wickedly sharp.

Maria took a step backwards towards the picture of Mary Magdalene.

'You said you weren't going to hurt me,' she blubbered, tears filling her eyes.

'We're not,' Peters reassured her, stepping closer.

He grabbed her by the arm and pulled her close to him, one hand going across her mouth to stifle the scream she tried to release. He gripped her hard, one arm bent up her back.

McCormick advanced towards her, the knife levelled.

It was as he was reaching for her that they heard the key turn in the front door.

253

Fifty-Eight

Frank Dolan shrugged off his jacket and closed the front door behind him without looking up.

'Mr Dolan.'

The voice made him jump and he looked up, frozen by the tableau before him.

Two men held his daughter, one of them with a knife close to her face, the other holding a gun. A gun that was pointing at *him*.

'What's going on?' Frank Dolan said, his voice a mixture of fear and outrage. How dare these men come into his house? And what were they doing to his daughter? Anger began to filter into his emotions but it was beaten down rapidly by the fear. The barrel of the .22 was unwaveringly pointed at his chest.

'Sit down,' Peters told him, moving away from Maria, leaving McCormick to hold her.

Dolan did as he was told.

He was in his late forties, his face thin and pale, the skin looking as though it had been pulled taut over his high cheek-bones. His nose had been broken in a fight many years before. Beneath thick eyebrows his eyes were wide and alert, darting to and fro around the sitting room.

'You're supposed to be at work, aren't you?' said Peters conversationally.

'The Union called an unofficial strike,' Dolan said. 'Sent us all home.' He swallowed hard. 'You know why

I'm here; would you mind telling me why *you* are?'

Peters smiled thinly.

'Your son, Billy. Where is he?'

'How the hell should I know? I haven't spoken to him for a couple of months now.' He glanced across at Maria who stood silently, the blade held to her throat. Her cheeks were stained with tears.

'Please let my daughter go,' he said, looking at Peters.

'We've already said we're not going to hurt her. We're not,' the IRA man reassured him. 'I just want to know about Billy.' He knelt down in front of Dolan and looked into his face. 'You know who we are?'

The older man shook his head.

'You know why we want Billy?'

Again a shake of the head.

'You know what he's done?'

'I can't be doing with your bloody guessing games, for God's sake. Just tell me who you are and what you want.' Dolan's voice was strained, the fear seeping into it.

'You follow the news, don't you?' Peters said. 'You heard about the shootings at Stormont, the murder of Reverend Pithers, the bombing at Windsor Park?' He looked into Dolan's eyes. 'Your Billy was involved in them all. Him and his friends. They used to be *our* friends.'

The realization hit Dolan like a hammer.

'IRA,' he said, flatly.

'Have you seen him lately?' Peters demanded, the warmth disappearing rapidly from his voice.

'No, I swear it. Not for a couple of months, like I said,' Dolan said.

Peters turned briefly and nodded towards McCormick.

The other IRA men took hold of a hunk of Maria's

255

hair and, in one swift movement, sliced through it, dropping the dyed mass onto the floor.

'Oh, Christ,' Dolan murmured.

Maria couldn't scream; it was as if her vocal chords were frozen. Even as McCormick carved more of her hair away she stood motionless, tears streaming down her face.

'Where's Billy?' Peters asked again, his voice low and even.

'Let her go,' Dolan protested. 'Please.'

'Where is he?'

'I don't know, I've told you.'

McCormick carved away more of Maria's hair. There was a small pile of it at his feet now.

'Do you know what he's done, that fucking son of yours?' said Peters. 'The damage he's done? Not just in human lives but in the work he's destroyed. Work that's been going on for years.'

'I don't know where he is,' Dolan wailed.

McCormick tugged hard on Maria's hair and carved away a huge hunk of it, exposing one ear, nicking it accidentally in the process.

She let out a small whimper of pain but other than that the only sound she made was a low sobbing.

'What about his friends?' Peters asked, still squatting in front of Dolan, still glaring into his eyes. 'Did you ever meet any of them?'

'No,' the older man said, tears forming in his own eyes now. 'Leave my daughter alone, please. I'm telling you the truth. Please.'

'Do the names James Maguire, Michael Black, Damien Flynn or Paul Maconnell mean anything to you?' Peters asked, calmly.

McCormick cut away more of Maria's hair.

'No,' shouted Dolan. 'I don't fucking know them. Any of them.'

Peters drew the Pathfinder but kept it low at his side.

'You've almost convinced me,' he said, thumbing back the hammer.

Dolan was so intent on seeing that no harm came to his daughter he hardly noticed the gun.

'Do you do much walking in your job, Frankie?' Peters asked.

Dolan looked puzzled.

Peters smiled.

'Because if you do you'd better learn how to use crutches,' he said.

The last word had barely left his lips when he raised the .22, pressed it against Frank Dolan's left knee and fired once.

The retort of the weapon was almost as loud as the sickening crack as Dolan's patella was shattered by the bullet. The knee splintered as the bullet tore through his leg, ripping its way from the back, severing the cruciate ligaments. Blood began to soak through Dolan's trousers as he shouted in pain and clutched at the pulverized joint, crimson running through his fingers.

As she saw her father crippled by the bullet, Maria at last found the breath to scream.

McCormick didn't try to stop her as she ran to him, her stomach somersaulting as she saw the blood running down his leg and staining the carpet.

Peters stepped back, pushing the pistol into his belt, and motioned for his companion to join him. They headed for the front door.

'When you see Billy, tell him we want to talk to him,' Peters said, as if their departure required some form of etiquette.

Dolan was groaning in agony. Maria was sobbing as she gaped at the wound.

'I'd call an ambulance,' Peters advised, opening the door.

Then they were gone.

They walked back unhurriedly to the car and climbed in.

If any of the neighbours had heard the shot or the screams, they weren't exactly rushing to the Dolans' assistance. A couple of front doors were open, their occupants peering out into the street.

'Let's get out of here,' said Peters. His companion started the car and drove off.

'Do you think he was telling the truth?' McCormick asked. 'About Billy? That he hadn't really seen him?'

Peters nodded.

'I wonder where the bastard is.'

'Ireland's not a very big country, Luke. He can't run forever. We'll find him. *And* Maguire *and* the others. Count on it.'

Fifty-Nine

BRITTANY, FRANCE:
There was no sound from inside his room.

Catherine Roberts stood on the landing and listened for movement within but there was none.

She knocked once and waited.

Perhaps he was still sleeping. Neither of them had enjoyed a good night's rest since arriving; they had both been forced to content themselves with naps here and there. Deep sleep brought the nightmares.

There was still no sound from inside.

'Mark,' she called, knocking again.

This time when he didn't answer she pushed the door and walked in.

The bed was made, the room tidy. None of Channing's personal belongings were on the dressing table. She crossed to the wardrobe and opened it.

His case was gone.

Cath frowned and moved over to the window, peering out at where the Renault should be parked below. She was not surprised to find it gone. She hurried out of the room and down the stairs to the reception area, pausing at the desk and banging the little bell.

The plump woman who owned the inn emerged from a room at the rear wiping her hands on her apron. She smiled broadly at Cath.

'Have you seen Mr Channing?' Cath asked.

She was told he had checked out that morning about an hour ago.

'Where did he go?'

The woman had no idea.

Cath hesitated a moment. Then, thanking the woman, she dashed back up the stairs. The plump woman watched her, shrugged, and disappeared into the back room.

Upstairs Cath snatched up the keys to the Peugeot and hurried back down the steps and out into the square. Opening the door she slid behind the wheel and started the engine.

Where the hell was Channing?

Why had he left without telling her?

As she drove through the village she wasn't even sure where she was going but she felt she must try the obvious place first.

She swung the Peugeot onto the road to Machecoul.

As she did, Channing's words echoed in her mind;

'I won't let you take the window. I'd rather see it destroyed.'

He sat cross-legged, staring at the window as if mesmerized.

Mark Channing had been in that position for the last thirty minutes.

Staring. Dazzled, awestruck by the designs, the colours and the sheer artistry. It seemed to hold an even more potent spell over him than when he'd first seen it.

The eyes of the creatures depicted in the window, and the eyes of those who surrounded them, millions of eyes it seemed, all met his gaze, held it and fixed him in their own unblinking stare. He looked at the words, spoke some of them aloud:

'Sacrificium. Cultus. Opes. Immortalis.'

Even though he whispered, the words still seemed to echo around him.

Finally he rose, aware of the stiffness in his joints, of the chill in the air. His breath frosted as he exhaled.

A ray of sunlight struck the window, reflecting its colours even more vividly. The red eyes of the largest creature looked like puddles of boiling blood.

Channing gripped the piece of wood in his hands. It was heavy, about four feet long and five inches thick. Solid. He gritted his teeth as he raised it above his head and advanced towards the window.

It was growing colder.

He stared into the eyes of the glass monstrosity, steadied himself and brought the lump of wood down with incredible force.

He may as well have struck stone.

The thick wood slid off, the impetus of his swing causing Channing to overbalance. He went sprawling in the dust on the floor. Even as he rose he looked at the window, his eyes wide with disbelief. He dragged himself upright, raised the wood again and struck with even greater force, yelling loudly, as if the exhortation would give him the added strength needed to shatter the glass.

The wood connected but seemed to bounce off.

Channing shook his head and struck again.

And again.

Despite the cold inside the church he felt perspiration beading on his forehead from his exertions. He beat at the window relentlessly, unceasingly, until his strength seemed to drain away.

The window remained intact.

The eyes of the largest creature still stared at him.

Were they mocking him?

He dropped the wood, picked up a piece of stone and hurled it at the glass.

It too bounced off.

Channing was panting now, his chest heaving.

He stepped towards the window and leaned close to the glass.

It was unmarked.

No scratches. No marks. Nothing.

He picked up the stone and prepared to strike again. But before he could do so, he heard a thin keening wail, building slowly in volume, deepening too, growing louder, to unbelievable proportions.

He tried to move back from the window, tried to look away.

He opened his mouth to scream but no sound would come.

His eyes bulged madly in their sockets; the blood roared in his ears, ears that were already bleeding from the deafening cacophony of sound that filled them.

And it was the source of that sound which made him shake his head in disbelief.

On the window, every creature, every severed head, every child had its mouth open. And it was from the window that the wall of sound was coming.

Channing stood motionless, the rock still held in his hand, waiting for the dream to end, waiting to be catapulted back from the nightmare.

The roaring continued, the mouths open, screaming, shouting.

He raised the stone once more then brought it down with incredible ferocity against the window.

The screams rose in pitch, joined by one other.

It was Channing's turn to scream.

Sixty

She saw the Renault parked outside the church.

As Cath guided the Peugeot along the narrow road which led to Machecoul she spotted Channing's vehicle parked on the gravel surrounding the old building. The bright sunlight reflected off the roof and windows. The car looked as though it was on fire.

262

As she drew closer she managed a smile; her hunch had been right. Perhaps Channing just wanted one last look at the window before he left.

Perhaps.

She brought the Peugeot to a halt and climbed out, walking briskly across to the other car. She peered through the driver's side window. His camera was lying on the passenger seat. Cath wondered how long he'd been here. She turned and headed for the door of the church, pushing it hard to gain entry.

The silence was almost palpable.

'Mark,' she called, her voice echoing off the walls.

She walked briskly through the nave towards the door that would take her through into the chancel.

To the window.

He had to be there.

She was about to open the chancel door when she noticed the smell.

Cath hesitated a second, repelled by the stench. It was a cloying, thick, pungent odour which clogged in her nostrils as surely as the dust which her footsteps had disturbed. She rested her hand on the ornate knob, feeling how cold it was.

'Mark.' This time she spoke his name, low, under her breath.

She opened the door.

The stench rushed to meet her, enveloping her, but she didn't notice it; the sight before her filled her senses.

She stood rigid in the doorway, staring into the chancel.

The window was there.

Untouched.

Channing was there, too.

She stood for interminable seconds, waiting for the nightmare to end, waiting to drag herself upright and free of this dream. But as she felt the cold surrounding her and became aware of the stench once more, she knew there was to be no release from this particular nightmare.

Mark Channing lay in the middle of the chancel, a few feet from the window.

At least, that's where his legs and torso were.

One arm, she noted with disgust, was lying close to the door.

A leg, severed just below the knee, was over by the belfry door.

The whole chancel was covered in blood; the walls, the floor. There was even some on the window.

Cath put one hand to her mouth. Her breath was coming in short gasps. Her throat felt as if someone had filled it with sand. She couldn't swallow. All she could do was stare dumbly at what remained of Channing's body.

It took her a couple of seconds to realize why it was lying at such an unearthly angle, then she gritted her teeth and moved closer.

The body looked as if it had been twisted in half at the waist, the head and upper torso turned completely around, facing backwards. There were dozens of deep lacerations on Channing's face, neck and chest. Some of the cuts on his neck were so deep that the head had been almost severed. His clothes were bloody rags; portions of his jacket and trousers had been ripped away and lay scattered around like crimson confetti with other pieces of tissue, which she realized were flaps of skin.

One eye was missing from the socket.

It hung by the optic nerve, dangling in the blood and dust on the floor. Channing's other eye was open, wide and staring. As she approached his corpse, Cath tried to look away from it, disliking the blind stare. She did notice, with renewed revulsion, that his upper eyelid was missing.

She was careful not to slip in so much blood. It stuck to the soles of her shoes, still uncongealed in many places. Had she been able to manage rational thought she might well have realized that he had not been dead that long but rational thoughts eluded her when faced with the destruction of a human body as comprehensive as this. Cath knelt down a couple of feet from him, looking more closely at the pulverized corpse, cursing that infernal eye which hung from the dripping cord of nerve like a bloodied ping-pong ball. The eye seemed to be staring at her.

She tried to ignore it, aware again of the overpowering stench.

Cath felt light-headed, the combined effects of her grisly find and the odour which seemed now to be permeating her pores. She stood up and backed away, turning at last to look at the window.

Blood had spattered across it in several places, over the figure of the child held in the large demon's hand and also across the mouth of the demon itself.

Cath exhaled deeply and shook her head.

What had happened?

Channing had been killed (that seemed a reasonably safe assumption, considering the state he was in) but by who? And why?

Questions whirled in her head, her mind spinning almost as violently as her stomach.

Callahan?

He had known Channing's reluctance to let the window leave Machecoul.

But even if it had been Callahan, why would he destroy Channing's body in such a way? Why leave it for *her* or anyone else to find?

She shook her head again, her eyes drawn to the mutilated, twisted remains of her former colleague. His appearance made her feel sick. She thought she was going to faint and made for the chancel door, leaning against it until the feeling passed. She could feel the perspiration on her forehead and back, despite the chill in the air.

As Cath stepped back she noticed that blood from the door was now on her hand. She pulled a tissue from the pocket of her jeans and scrubbed the crimson liquid away, scraping frenziedly, as if she feared she would be marked with it forever. Slowly she turned to look at Channing once more, wondering what she should do.

Call the police?

Call Callahan?

She swallowed hard, her stomach churning less violently now, her composure returning slowly. She sucked in a long, deep breath, tinged as it was with the scent of death, held it for a moment and released it slowly. Her mind began to clear.

She wished that dangling eye would stop staring at her.

She knew she had to think.

What was she going to do?

Come on, get a grip.

A thought occured to her. Struck her like a hammer blow.

What if Channing's killer was still in the church?

The thought sent her heart racing, thudding so hard against her ribs she feared it would burst. She listened for any sounds from the nave. From the belfry above her. Perhaps she should leave the church, go now, pretend she'd never been here, just get out, leave the country. Anything to be away from this place, this carnage that lay around like the work of some careless butcher.

The killer would have no need to stay around, she reasoned, her heart slowing its frantic pace a little.

What should she do?

She looked at the body once more.

Something was glinting just inside the pocket of Channing's jacket.

Cath moved towards him, trying not to inhale too deeply, attempting to minimize the vile stench.

She reached for the glinting object and pulled the car keys from his pocket, holding them tightly in her fist.

The car. Someone would find his car eventually.

She stepped back again, glancing at the window, at the slicks of blood which covered it. Pulling another tissue from her pocket she fastidiously wiped the crimson liquid from the glass where it covered the figure of the child.

What would happen to the window if Channing's murder was discovered?

The church would be closed, the window lost to her forever.

The secret would be taken.

She looked at the car keys and gripped them tightly in her hand.

The secret.

She turned back to face the window, to wipe away the blood that had covered the mouth of the largest demon.

It was gone.

Not a trace of the sticky fluid remained on the glass.

Cath stared into the blazing red eyes of the creature,

267

then turned back to look at Channing, his own blank eyes fixing her in that blind stare.

She felt the car keys cold against the warm flesh of her palm.

And she knew what she must do.

Sixty-One

'Channing's dead.'

Catherine Roberts didn't wait to be either formally greeted or welcomed into the hotel room of the Callahans. She told David Callahan as soon as he opened the door and stepped past him into the room. Laura was sitting on the bed dressed only in a thin robe, unconcerned that her breasts and also the dark triangle of her pubic hair were visible through the diaphanous material. She looked at Cath indifferently.

Catherine Roberts was angry. The drive from Machecoul to St. Philbert had not served to calm that fury. She had found the hotel where the Callahans were staying without any trouble, asked which room they were in and rode the lift to the appropriate floor while the concierge was still attempting to alert the guests of her presence.

Now she stood in the room, looking calm, wiping a stray hair from her forehead, but seething inside.

Callahan's attitude to her announcement further irritated her. She may as well have announced that smoking could cause lung disease for all the reaction she elicited from the man. He merely looked at her and shrugged.

'Did you hear me?' she snapped. 'I said Mark Channing is dead. Murdered.'

'How do you know he was murdered?' asked Callahan.

'Because I saw his body,' she hissed. 'Believe me, it wasn't suicide.'

Callahan offered her a drink and she accepted.

'What happened?' he wanted to know.

She told him the story as briefly as possible. She even mentioned her nightmare. When she arrived at the part about reaching the church she paused and sipped at her drink. Laura was watching her intently.

'His body was …' Catherine struggled for the words. 'He was mutilated. Very badly.'

'How?' Laura wanted to know.

'I told you, I don't know.'

'I mean, what kind of injuries?' asked Laura quietly.

'He was cut very badly,' Cath said wearily, the recollection of the sight she'd seen making her feel queasy once again. She sipped her drink. 'I don't know how to describe it without sounding stupid.' She looked at each of them in turn. 'He'd been torn to pieces. His body was smashed, broken.' She lowered her gaze, content to look into the bottom of her glass.

'What did the police say?' Callahan asked.

'They don't know,' Cath told him. 'No one knows. No one *will* know.'

'What makes you so sure?' he wanted to know.

She downed the remainder of the drink and put down the glass a little too heavily.

'Because I took his body out of the church.' She looked at Callahan. 'I dragged it out to his car and put it in the boot. Then I drove the car into the woods nearby and covered it up. It'll be ages before anyone

269

finds it.' She sighed. 'After that I walked back to the church and cleaned it up inside as best I could. Then I drove back to the inn, washed, changed, packed and came here.'

'You did well,' said Callahan, smiling.

'I didn't come here for bloody praise,' Cath snarled. 'I want to know if *you* killed him.'

Callahan shook his head.

'Why should I?'

'He said he was going to destroy the window,' Cath reminded him.

'Where's the window now?' Callahan asked.

'Still inside the church.'

He nodded.

'I've arranged for it to be picked up tomorrow,' he said. 'Some men will come and pick it up in a truck. Colleagues of mine will fly it back to Ireland in a private plane. I'll be there to meet it, then it'll be taken back to my estate. You can carry on your work on it there.' He smiled. 'Laura and I are flying back today. I thought you might stay on and supervize the loading. You can travel back in the plane with the window. To keep an eye on it.' He smiled that condescending grin again.

'How do we know *you* didn't kill Channing?' Laura asked. 'You've accused *us*. *You* had as much reason.'

'You didn't want the window destroyed any more than we did,' Callahan reminded her.

'I didn't kill him,' Cath snapped.

'Why did you hide his body?' Callahan enquired.

Cath swallowed hard.

'I knew that if the police were involved there was no chance of getting the window out of the church. Their enquiries would have held up my work for too long.'

Callahan smiled.

'You're as obsessed with it as I am,' he said flatly.

She had no answer.

'Who do *you* think killed him?' Laura asked.

'I don't know,' Cath told her. 'It was the *way* he was killed that was so bizarre.' She shook her head, the images coming once more into her mind. Images of the blood, of the body twisted at the waist, the severed limbs. That eye dangling, staring blindly. She put her hands to her face and exhaled deeply. Callahan smiled.

'You realize that what you did makes you an accessory?' he said.

'What the hell are you saying, Callahan?' she snapped.

'Just telling you what I'm thinking,' he answered. 'It's a good job you *are* leaving France soon. You'll be safe on my estate.'

'You make it sound as if Interpol are after me,' said Cath sardonically.

'Could someone have found out about the window?' Laura mused aloud. 'That it was going to be removed, I mean. Perhaps someone who didn't want it taken away killed Channing.'

Callahan shrugged.

'It's possible, I suppose,' he added. 'That may be true. If it is then whoever killed Channing is going to be after *us*, too.'

PART THREE

'You know you'd have gone insane if you saw what I saw.'

— Iron Maiden

'He clings firmly out of defiance to a cause which he has seen through – but he calls it "loyalty".'

— Nietzsche

Sixty-Two

DUNDALK: THE REPUBLIC OF IRELAND:
Doyle woke early, glanced at his watch and tried to
sleep again, but the more he tried to relax the more
impossible he found it. It was just after six a.m.

He rubbed both hands over his face and exhaled.

Georgie was asleep with her head resting on his
chest. As he lay there he watched the rhythmic rise
and fall of her shoulders as she breathed. He could feel
the softness of her hair against his skin. For a moment
he found himself stroking the silky blonde locks, but
then he withdrew his hand hastily, as if he'd touched
something hot. Instead, he propped both arms behind
his head, supporting himself against the headboard.
Only a sheet covered them; Doyle could see the outline
of Georgie's body beneath the thin material. He
followed it with his eyes.

It had been she who had pulled the sheet over them
after their love-making the previous night.

The ferocity of their passion, the intensity of their
coupling had exhausted them both. Perhaps it was their
way of releasing the tension of the past few days, Doyle
thought.

*Or perhaps it was because there was something deeper
than just physical attraction between them.*

Doyle pushed the thought angrily from his mind and
decided it was time he got up. He eased himself free of
Georgie, slipping out of bed, trying not to disturb her.

She murmured something in her sleep but then rolled onto her stomach and was quiet again.

Doyle walked to the bathroom and filled the sink with cold water. He splashed his face, finally lowering it into the water, scooping more up over the back of his neck. He stood up, moisture coursing down his features, rivulets of water running over his torso. He regarded his reflection in the mirror, touching the scar on the left side of his face, tracing its length with one index finger. He ran a hand through his hair, dried himself and wandered back into the bedroom with just a towel wrapped around him.

He crossed to the wardrobe and took out the small case. He set it on top of the dressing table and flipped it open.

He laid the MP5K on the floor beside the bed, lifted the CZ and the .44 from their holsters and put them beside the sub-gun. Then he sat down, cross-legged, his back against the bed, looking at the weapons. Using a piece of rag he'd also taken from the case he began cleaning the .44.

He and Georgie had crossed the border into the Republic late the previous evening. They'd stopped at a small hotel on the outskirts of Dundalk, booking in under the names of Taylor and Blake, ignoring the knowing glances the proprietor gave them as he told them where their room was. Doyle had stopped him when he'd offered to carry their small cases.

They had undressed together and climbed into bed together. It had all seemed so natural, as if sex between them was part of the job. Doyle glanced down, as he cleaned the gun, at the scars which criss-crossed his body.

Emotional scars run deeper.

276

He snapped the cylinder back into the .44 and laid it on one side.

As he reached for the CZ he heard murmurings from behind him and movement. Georgie yawned and stretched, then slid across the bed and kissed Doyle's shoulder.

'Good morning,' she whispered sleepily. 'How long have you been up?'

'Not long. I tried not to disturb you.'

'You're very thoughtful,' she told him and began stroking his back with her fingertips, feeling the indentations of his scars.

Doyle, his back to her, closed his eyes tightly and finally edged away from her. Away from her touch.

He continued cleaning the automatic.

Georgie regarded him silently, then crossed her arms and rested her chin on them.

'You didn't move away from me last night,' she said.

'That was last night,' he said sharply, working the rag around the inside of the barrel.

'What are you afraid of, Sean?'

'I don't know what you're talking about.'

'Scared that the mask is going to drop?'

Doyle pulled back the slide and continued cleaning.

'You're like Dr Jekyll and Mr Hyde,' she persisted. 'Sometimes you're warm and caring, other times you're cold. It's like being with two different people.'

Doyle pressed the slide release and the metallic crack reverberated around the room.

'I thought we'd been through all this shit before,' he said.

'I had your home-spun philosophy about life and death, if that's what you mean,' she said acidly.

'What more do you want from me, Georgie?' he

asked. 'We're here to find and kill some men, not start up a big fucking romance.'

'We sleep together. Doesn't that mean anything to you? Doesn't it make us closer?'

'Do you want it to?'

She sighed.

'I don't know,' she whispered. 'I know how you feel about ...'

He cut her short.

'You don't know how I feel about anything,' he told her, his tone a little too vehement.

'I'm not asking you to fall in love with me, for Christ's sake,' she said angrily. 'I just want to know what frightens you about people getting close to you? Why does it matter so much? Why won't you let anyone get close?'

'Because the closer they get the more painful it is when you lose them.'

She was silent for a moment, her eyes never leaving his broad back.

'You're always so sure you're going to lose them,' she said softly.

'Nothing's permanent. *You* should know that. Ask the families of the people killed at Windsor Park. Think about your own brother. Did you ever think it'd be *him* who got killed? No. It was always going to be some other poor sod, wasn't it? Well, death makes no exceptions, Georgie, and today or tomorrow it could be you or me they load into a fucking body bag.' He put down the CZ. 'Like the song says, *Live for today, tomorrow never comes.*' He turned to face her, kissing her lightly on the lips. 'That's the only way I can live.' He touched her cheek with his hand, feeling how smooth her skin was.

She lay there for a moment longer then swung herself out of bed, naked.

Doyle ran one hand up the inside of her thigh as she stood before him and she sucked in a quivering breath, smiling as his fingers brushed against her pubic hair.

'I'd better get dressed,' she said softly, smiling down at him.

He nodded, watching as she padded off into the bathroom.

Doyle held the CZ before him, satisfied at its condition, then reached for the sub-machine gun and began cleaning that.

From behind him he heard the sound of splashing water as Georgie washed.

He gripped the MP5K in one fist, his thoughts turning to Maguire and his men.

He squeezed the trigger of the machine pistol, the hammer slamming down on an empty chamber.

Soon.

Very soon.

He knew the time was coming.

Sixty-Three

'I don't like graveyards.'

Damien Flynn looked around him at the uneven rows of stone crosses and headstones as he picked his way carefully over the wet grass.

'Remind you that you'll end up in one yourself one day, eh, Damien?' James Maguire said, careful to step over a freshly-laid bouquet.

'I've been to too many bloody funerals,' Flynn observed, glancing over his shoulder towards the path that cut through the cemetery.

Billy Dolan was guiding the dark blue Ford van up the narrow path, its wheels crunching gravel. He saw Flynn looking at him and waved happily, his infectious grin lighting up his face. Flynn stepped on a plot, apologising quietly to its inhabitant as he did so.

The cemetery was about two miles south of the town of Navan, on the Boyne river, the resting place of so many inhabitants of that small community. It was on a slight rise; in clear weather, the ruins of Bective Abbey could be seen further to the south. However, Maguire and his men weren't on a sight-seeing trip and Flynn's preoccupation with where he put his feet prevented him taking all but the most perfunctory interest in his surroundings.

Ahead, the church was built on a slight incline, its bell-tower thrusting up towards the overcast sky, a weather vane turning gently in the breeze. To their left were more graves; much smaller plots, these. The resting places of those who chose to be cremated.

To their right was the mausoleum.

It was about twelve feet in height, its stonework weather-beaten, scarred by time. Cracks in the outer walls had been infested with moss, which filled the rents like gangrene in septic wounds. Weeds grew high up the walls, some clinging to the stonework so thickly they looked as though they would pull the edifice over. Flynn noticed the remains of a bird's nest on the top of the mausoleum.

More weeds grew thickly around the door, which was secured by a padlock. It was brand new and looked incongruous against the aging stonework.

Maguire fumbled in his jacket pocket and pulled out a key which he fitted into the padlock, turning it and snapping it loose. The chain fell away and he pushed the door, which opened with relative ease apart from a squeal of protest which came from hinges that hadn't tasted oil for many years.

A stench of neglect and damp swept out into the early morning air, making Flynn cough as he inhaled the dank odour.

Billy Dolan turned the van and reversed it up to the door of the mausoleum, then climbed out and threw the back doors open. Maguire pulled the torch from his belt and entered the ancient edifice, closely followed by Flynn. It was as black as pitch inside, the beams of the torches scarcely cutting through the tenebrous gloom. Ahead of them was a short flight of steps, slippery with mould. The walls were also stained green, and in several places the stone had been breached, allowing rain through to further erode the construction. As Maguire moved towards the steps, Flynn shone his torch around the inside of the small tomb. There were at least five coffins, each one lying on a ledge protruding from the wall. Flynn half-expected to see rats sitting up on the coffin lids but there were none. There were only one or two dusty cobwebs on the boxes, too. He seemed almost disappointed.

'Damien, come down here.'

Maguire's voice, lancing through the darkness, startled Flynn, but he regained his composure and scuttled towards the short flight of steps, using his torch as a guide. Careful not to slip on the mould he made his way down to where Maguire was standing.

He was leaning against one of half-a-dozen crates, each one about six feet by three. The wood was new;

Flynn could smell its tangy odour even through the mustiness of the tomb. A crowbar lay on top of one of the boxes and Maguire used it to prise the first one open. Inside there was a layer of straw. The IRA man pulled some of the straw away and dug his hand in, smiling as he raised his find like some kind of prize.

'Jesus,' murmured Flynn, shining his torch on his companion and the Sterling-Armalite rifle which he held.

There were more in the box.

Flynn put down his torch so that the beam was pointing at one of the other crates and used the crowbar to open the large container. Inside there was more straw. More weapons. He lifted the Armalite out of its packing and pressed it to his shoulder, squinting down the sight.

'Billy,' Maguire called, 'let's get these loaded up and get out of here.'

Flynn squeezed the trigger and heard a dull thud. He frowned.

'Wait a minute, Jim,' he said, lowering the rifle. 'Hold that torch over here.'

Maguire shone the beam in the direction of the weapon, watching as Flynn skilfully and quickly removed the top portion of the rifle and peered at it.

'What's wrong?' Maguire wanted to know.

Flynn didn't answer. He put down the partly-disassembled weapon and reached for another, cocking it and squeezing the trigger.

He heard that same dull thud.

He reached for another and another.

His reaction was the same every time.

'Fucking bastard,' he snarled, hurling the gun to one side. He looked at Maguire, his face contorted with

282

anger. 'There's no firing pins in these guns. They're bloody useless.'

Maguire was about to say something when Dolan's voice cut through the blackness.

'You'd better get up here quick,' called the younger man. 'We've got company.'

Sixty-Four

The car carrying the two Garda officers moved slowly up the gravel path towards the stationary blue van.

About twenty yards away it stopped and both men stepped out. One remained beside the car. The first, a tall, broad-shouldered man with greying hair, began walking purposefully towards the van.

Billy Dolan took a step backwards, his hands dangling at his side, the 9mm Bernadelli tight against his left side.

Not yet.

From inside the mausoleum Maguire could see the uniformed officer. He eased the Browning Hi-Power from its holster and gently worked the slide, chambering a round.

Officer Gary Farrow slowed his pace slightly when he came to the end of the gravel pathway. The big man fixed Dolan in his gaze, taking in details of his features, trying to see if there was anyone with him. He noticed the door to the mausoleum was open. Farrow also glanced at the number-plate of the van.

Behind him, at the waiting car, Officer Christopher

Page was also taking a note of the number. He moved away from the car, peering around the cemetery as his companion drew closer to the van.

'Can I ask what you're doing, sir?' Farrow enquired, his voice even.

Dolan smiled.

'I was looking for the priest,' he said gaily.

'I don't think you'll find him in there,' Farrow answered, nodding in the direction of the tomb. 'Could I have your name, please?'

From inside the vault Maguire raised the pistol and steadied himself, watching as Farrow drew closer to the van.

'What about the other one?' whispered Flynn, spotting Page standing by the car further down the pathway.

'Your name, sir, and I'd like to see your driver's licence, too,' Farrow said, moving closer to Dolan.

Maguire prepared to fire.

'Fuck you,' snarled Dolan, and plunged a hand inside his jacket, gripping the Bernadelli.

He fired twice as he pulled it free.

The first shot sliced through empty air, the second struck a gravestone, blasting a chunk of it away.

Farrow threw himself to the ground, rolling onto the gravel, trying to find cover.

'Shit,' hissed Maguire, emerging from the tomb like a vengeful resurrected corpse. He gripped the Browning tightly and squeezed off three rounds, two of which hit the Garda car. A wing mirror was torn off; another bullet holed the windscreen. Page ducked down behind the open door, scrambling to pull his own gun free.

Farrow was still rolling, trying to get to his feet, to find some cover.

Dolan fired another four rounds from the Bernadelli, the savage recoil slamming the weapon back against the heel of his hand until it felt numb. The stench of cordite filled the air.

Farrow was hit in the back, the bullet macerating one kidney, travelling upwards to shatter and bounce off a rib before lodging below one lung. He grunted in pain and felt the strength draining from him along with so much of his blood. He crawled towards a headstone as more bullets struck the ground around him, sending up geysers of earth and gravel.

Another shot struck him in the side of the face, pierced both cheeks and pulverized three of his back teeth, carrying portions of enamel away through the gaping exit wound. Blood filled his mouth, but he kept crawling.

'Kill him, for fuck's sake,' snarled Flynn, leaping into the back of the van, watching as Maguire fired a full magazine towards the car.

Bullets struck the body work, the windscreen, the tyres.

Two hit Officer Page.

One tore through his left calf, ripping away most of the muscle there, snapping his shin. As he sprawled on the ground another bullet struck him in the face, just above the chin. His bottom jaw seemed to disintegrate, portions of bone and shattered teeth falling to the ground, propelled by the gushing blood which erupted from the wound. He lay still until a third shot caught him in the chest and sent him rolling over onto his back, his sternum destroyed. Blood flooded over his lips, bubbling as he exhaled. He felt incredible pressure on his rib cage, as if someone had put heavy weights on it. When he tried to breathe the pain prevented all but the smallest of gasps. He felt unconsciousness beginning to creep over him.

The fourth bullet which hit him tore off most of the left side of his head.

'Start the fucking van,' shouted Maguire, pushing Billy towards the vehicle.

He himself hunched low to the ground and scuttled towards the headstone where Farrow was sheltering.

There was a loud retort and Maguire actually heard the bullet sing past his ear, no more than two or three feet away. Farrow fired again, his hand remarkably steady as he pumped the trigger of the .38.

Maguire hurled himself down, rolled over and, using a marble cross as support, squeezed the trigger again. The slide shot backwards to signal that the Browning was empty and Maguire dug in his jacket pocket for a fresh magazine which he slammed into the pistol butt. He wrenched back the slide and fired again.

Farrow was hit in the shoulder, the bullet shattering his collar bone. The impact flung him backwards, the revolver flying from his hand.

As he lay on his back staring at the sky he heard footsteps coming closer to him and saw Maguire looking down at him, the barrel of the Browning yawning massively.

Maguire smiled and shot Farrow in the temple.

Billy Dolan guided the van back onto the gravel path, pushing open the passenger side door for his companion to get in. As Maguire clambered into the van, he put his foot down. Gravel was sent spinning into the air as the wheels skidded on the surface, finally gaining purchase. The van sped off past the Garda car and the body of Officer Page towards the gates of the cemetery.

Dolan swung it left onto the road.

'What about the rifles?' he said, his eyes fixed on the road ahead.

'They were no fucking good,' Flynn rasped from the back.

Dolan glanced across at Maguire as if for verification.

The older man didn't speak. He merely continued thumbing 9mm shells into an empty magazine, his features set, the knot of muscles at the side of his jaw throbbing angrily.

'What are we going to do about the rifles?' Dolan persisted.

'I'll take care of it,' said Maguire quietly. 'Just drive.'

Sixty-Five

Doyle tapped impatiently on the wheel as he drove, eyes on the horse-drawn cart which blocked the road ahead of him. He thought about hitting the Datsun's horn – anything to clear the bloody cart out of the way – but decided against it. He wound down his window, one arm draped over the edge. The sun was warm against his skin and the countryside smelt fresh and clean after the light shower which had fallen just half an hour earlier.

Georgie looked across at him and caught the impatience in his expression. She smiled thinly. Doyle glanced at her and noticed her grinning.

'What's so funny?' he wanted to know.

'You,' she told him. 'You're so impatient. Life's slower out here, Doyle. This isn't London, you know.'

'If it was any slower it'd be fucking comatose,' he said, shaking his head, relieved to see that the horse and cart were turning off to the right into a field. Doyle put his foot down and accelerated past.

A sign announced that Dublin was just under twenty miles away.

'So where do we find this Mr David Callahan?' asked Doyle. 'If he's leasing cars to the IRA I think we ought to talk to him.'

'He lives on a private estate in County Cork,' Georgie announced, consulting the notes she had scribbled on a pad. 'He's lived there for the past two years. Used to live in London. Married. No kids. He employs about six staff.'

Doyle chewed his bottom lip contemplatively.

'You know there's something familiar about that name,' he said. 'Has he got any form?'

'If he has he was never convicted. He's got no criminal record of any description, as far as I could find out.'

'So what are the IRA doing driving around in his car?' Doyle mused.

'There's no reason why Callahan should be mixed up with them. The car could have been stolen; *this* David Callahan may even be a completely different person. Maguire and his men probably just used a false name when they bought it.'

'Coincidence, though, isn't it? There can't be that many David Callahans living in the Republic who own a blue Sierra.' He smiled. 'Or used to, until you shot it to pieces.'

'Just doing my job.' She chuckled.

Doyle reached across and fumbled with the dials of the radio, flicking from station to station. He found a

288

Gaelic speaking station, a pop channel, then some news.

'...*early this morning. One officer was killed in the gun battle.*'

Doyle turned up the volume.

'...*There were no witnesses to the shooting and the bodies were only discovered by a visitor to the cemetery, which has now been closed off by the Garda pending investigaton into the shootings.*'

Georgie looked across at Doyle, who was listening intently.

'*The wounded officer, whose name has not been released, was taken to hospital in Mullingar where his condition is said to be critical.*'

'Where's Mullingar?' Doyle snapped, flicking off the radio.

Georgie hesitated a moment, then reached for the map which lay on the parcel shelf. She ran her finger over it, searching for the location.

'About six miles west of where we are now,' she told him. 'Doyle, you don't even know if these shootings are anything to do with Maguire ...' Her words were cut short as Doyle quickly checked his rear-view mirror then pulled hard on the wheel, swinging the Datsun around in a U-turn.

'Two Garda officers shot,' he said. 'It's worth checking out. Especially if one of them is still alive.'

'How the hell are you going to get to him?' Georgie asked. 'By the sound of it, the poor devil is almost dead anyway. What can he tell you?'

'He can tell me who shot him,' said Doyle flatly.

Georgie shook her head.

'I thought we were supposed to be going after Callahan,' she said.

'We are.'

'I'm telling you, Doyle, you'll never get near the guy who was shot,' she repeated.

'I know. *I* might not be able to.' He glanced across at her. 'But *you* can.'

Sixty-Six

The flight had been smooth enough, but David Callahan had been glad to touch down all the same.

Their car had been waiting at Shannon airport and they had climbed in gratefully, relaxing in the plush seats of the Mercedes as they were driven home.

The drive took less than two hours. Laura smiled as the car finally came to a halt outside the house. She and Callahan got out, their luggage was brought into the house and the car was put in the double garage. It was as if they'd never been away, thought Laura, as she made her way up the stairs. The thought of a bath made her smile.

Callahan joined her upstairs carrying two drinks.

They kissed as they waited for the bath to fill, the sound of running water filling the bathroom.

'Do you think the window will be safe?' Laura asked, slipping out of her clothes and walking naked from the bathroom to the bedroom, where she sat in front of the dressing table and began combing her hair, finally putting it up into a bun.

'Sure it will,' Callahan said. 'It's only got to be taken from the church. It'll be picked up. I don't see why there should be any problems.'

'Do you trust that woman?'

'Why shouldn't I? She's got more to lose than us if anything happens to the window. Don't forget, she was the one who covered up a murder.'

Callahan pulled his shirt off and stepped out of his trousers. He stood naked for a moment, then pulled on a bathrobe.

'What you said about Channing's killer coming after us,' Laura said quietly. 'Do you think it *is* possible?'

Callahan could only shrug.

There was a knock on the bedroom door.

Laura called out, 'Come in,' and they both looked up to see one of the maids standing there. She smiled at them, told them she was glad they were back, asked briefly about their trip.

'Did anything exciting happen while we were gone, Trisha?' asked Laura, smiling, heading towards the bathroom to turn off the taps.

'There were some phone calls,' the maid said, brushing her long blonde hair from her face. 'I made a note of them.' She handed Callahan a pad which he scrutinised, nodding as he looked at the names.

'Thanks, Trisha,' he said.

'Someone else called,' she said. 'But he wouldn't give his name. He called four or five times while you were gone. He wanted to know where you were, but when he wouldn't give his name I didn't tell him.'

'You did the right thing,' Callahan assured her. 'What did he say? Did you recognise the voice?'

She shook her head.

'When I wouldn't tell him where you were he got a bit abusive. Mary answered the phone to him a couple of times and he was the same to her,' Trisha told him.

'When did he last call?' Callahan's face darkened.

'A couple of hours before you got back. He still wouldn't leave his name.'

Callahan swallowed hard as the maid continued.

'All he said was that he had something to discuss with you and that he'd be seeing you very soon. Then he hung up. If he calls again, do you want to speak to him?' she enquired.

Callahan didn't answer.

'Mr Callahan, I said if ...'

He cut her short.

'I heard you. No. If he calls again tell him I'm not back yet.'

She nodded and left.

Callahan took a sip of his drink, rolling the crystal tumbler between his hands.

'Be seeing you very soon.'

He would be ready.

Sixty-Seven

Doyle replaced the receiver, pushed open the door of the phone box and walked unhurriedly back towards the waiting car.

'This will never work,' said Georgie as he slid back behind the steering wheel.

'Oh ye of little faith,' he said, not taking his eyes from the hospital entrance.

There were two Garda cars parked outside the main doors, uniformed men in both.

The building itself was small, a four-storey concrete

and glass affair which looked as if it could do with some modernisation. An ambulance was parked close to the other vehicles. It was empty, as far as the two counter-terrorists could see.

'I wonder why he was shot,' said Georgie.

'That's what we've got to find out,' Doyle told her.

'And if it's nothing to do with Maguire and his men?'

He shrugged.

'Then we carry on looking. This is worth a go, Georgie. Anything is, no matter how remote. If it means getting to Maguire it's worth trying.'

Doyle reached onto the back seat and retrieved the bunch of flowers they'd bought a couple of streets away.

'Let me carry them,' she said. 'You don't look like the caring *type*.'

Doyle raised one eyebrow quizzically and handed her the flowers. They both climbed out of the Datsun and walked across the street towards the main entrance of the hospital, moving slowly, apparently oblivious to the uniformed men in the cars on either side of the short flight of steps to the main doors of the hospital. They passed unchallanged and wandered through into the reception area.

It was cool in there, the air-conditioning set a little too low. On their right, as they entered, was the hospital shop and Doyle saw a woman there buying chocolates. There were several rows of plastic chairs set next to a large picture window that looked out onto a small enclosed garden. About half a dozen people sat in the chairs, one man with his head bowed, hands clasped on his lap. Doyle nodded almost imperceptibly to Georgie, who went and sat on one of the seats. To his left there was a vending machine. A weary-looking man not much older than Doyle was feeding coins into it.

293

Doyle crossed to him, standing close behind him.

As the man turned from the machine, Doyle stepped closer to him.

The man couldn't help himself and spilled hot coffee on Doyle's hand.

'Christ, I'm sorry,' he said.

'Don't worry about it,' Doyle told him, wiping the hot liquid with a handkerchief. He patted the man on the shoulder. 'I shouldn't have been standing so close. I'll get you another one.'

'It's ok.'

'No, please,' Doyle insisted, already pushing coins into the machine.

The man smiled thinly and discarded the half-empty plastic cup.

'I hate hospitals,' Doyle said. 'I'm here visiting my wife. She was in a car accident. Broke a leg and an arm, shook her up badly.'

'I'm sorry about that.'

'How about you? Who are you here to see?'

'My father. He had a heart attack a couple of days ago. They moved him out of intensive care yesterday, though. He seems to be on the mend. Tough old sod.'

'My wife's mother was in intensive care here,' Doyle lied. 'I didn't like the doctor at all. Didn't seem to know what he was doing. Tyrone, I think his name was. That's not who's looking after your old fella, is it?'

The man shook his head.

'It's Doctor Collins. He's a nice guy.'

Doyle nodded and sighed theatrically.

'Well, I'd better go,' he said. 'Sorry about the coffee,' he added, shrugging, managing a smile.

The man said goodbye, finished his drink and wandered out of the hospital. Doyle watched him go then walked across to the reception desk, his face emotionless.

'Excuse me,' he said earnestly, not returning the smile the receptionist gave him. 'Doctor Collins spoke to me on the phone this morning. He told me that I could see my brother, that they'd operated on him.'

'Doctor Collins is up in intensive care at the moment, sir,' the receptionist said. 'What's your brother's name?'

'Jonathan Martin.'

The receptionist looked down at a list of names pinned to a clipboard, following the column with the end of her pen.

'There's no one here under that name, sir,' she said, puzzled.

Doyle sighed.

'Could you please check again. Doctor Collins said I could see him.'

'When was he admitted?' she wanted to know.

'Last night.'

'His name might be on another list of admissions. This one,' she tapped the clipboard with her pen, 'only covers those brought in today.'

Like Officer Gary Farrow, Doyle thought.

The receptionist got to her feet and wandered into an annexe beyond her desk. Doyle leant across the low partition and scanned the list of names.

FARROW. G. I.C. 4.

He spun round and walked away, tapping Georgie on the shoulder as he reached her.

'Fourth floor,' he said as they walked to the lifts. Doyle jabbed the call button and the lift arrived. The doors slid open, disgorging three passengers, one of them a uniformed Garda officer.

Doyle and Georgie got in and Doyle pressed 3 and 4.

The lift began to ascend.

It stopped at 3.

Doyle got out and headed for the stairs, scurrying up the stone flight, trying to time his arrival on the fourth floor with that of the lift.

He reached the landing and peered through the small window in the door, watching as Georgie emerged holding the flowers. To her right was a desk and switchboard with a nurse seated behind it. Standing close to this desk was a Garda officer. He saw Georgie approach the man. He couldn't hear what she was saying but he could see the Garda officer nodding.

Doyle slipped through the door, moving almost soundlessly, eyes still on the tableau at the end of the corridor. He saw Georgie offering the flowers to the uniformed man. There were about five doors facing him, each one closed, but they all had a small square window. He moved hurriedly from one to the other, peering in.

A woman, old, dying.

A man in an oxygen tent. Forty years old. It was hard to tell from looking at his pale skin and sunken features. Doyle moved to the next window.

The man's face was bandaged heavily, with only his eyes showing. There were intravenous drips attached to both his arms and tubes ran from his nose and mouth. Doyle could see the blip on the oscilloscope beside the bed moving in lazy waves.

He glanced down the corridor to where Georgie was still speaking with the uniformed man and the nurse, then at the door of the room.

STRICTLY NO ENTRY TO UNAUTHORISED STAFF

This had to be the one.

He slipped inside, recoiling immediately from the

antiseptic smell. The blip of the oscilloscope was audible now, as was the man's laboured breathing. Doyle noticed that he had a catheter attached to him, the bag half-full of dark fluid.

He knew he had to move quickly.

'Farrow,' he whispered.

No reaction.

'Farrow,' he said again, touching the man's shoulder this time.

The injured man's eyes flickered open for a second, closed and then opened again.

'Listen to me,' said Doyle. 'The man who shot you,' he fumbled inside his jacket, pulled out a small photo of Maguire. 'Was this him?'

The blip of the oscilloscope.

The laboured breathing.

'Was this the man who shot you?' Doyle persisted.

He heard footsteps in the corridor. Heavy footfalls.

'Was this the man?' he continued.

The blips increased in rapidity.

Farrow blinked at the image of the picture. Doyle realized that the footsteps were coming closer.

Come on, come on.

He gripped Farrow's hand.

'This man shot you, didn't he?' Doyle said. 'Squeeze my hand if he did.'

Footsteps drawing nearer. Had Georgie's ruse failed?

The blips increased in speed. Doyle shot a glance at the bouncing green dot.

'Was this the man who shot you?'

Farrow squeezed his hand once.

The door opened.

Doyle spun round, pulling the CZ from its shoulder holster.

297

The door swung. He caught sight of the Garda officer standing there, looking back down the corridor.

Doyle had time to straighten up and take a couple of steps back, ducking behind the door as it opened. He held the automatic close to him and waited.

The Garda officer entered. Doyle didn't hesitate.

He struck him hard across the back of the head with the butt of the pistol, catching the man before he could drop, easing him to the floor. Then he turned and slipped out again.

The corridor to his left and right was empty. He sprinted for the door which led to the stairs, took the steps two at a time until he reached the second floor, then sucked in a deep breath, wandered calmly towards the lifts and rode one to the ground floor.

Georgie was sitting in the Datsun when he emerged from the main entrance of the hospital.

He slid behind the wheel, started the engine and drove off.

'It *was* Maguire who shot him,' he said flatly. 'I fucking knew it was.'

'I thought they were going to catch you,' Georgie told him. 'I managed to stall him as long as I could. I said I'd heard what had happened, that my husband had been in the Garda, that the IRA had killed him and I wanted to pay my respects.'

Doyle seemed unimpressed with her story.

'Maguire must be close,' he said, his eyes narrowed. 'I can smell him.'

He drove on.

SACRIFICE

It was cold like the grave.

The chill seemed to penetrate his very bones.

His very soul.

He huddled in the centre of the room, shivering in his nakedness, his body sheathed in sweat despite the cold.

Candles were arranged in a circle around him. Their dull glow did little to cut through the darkness. When he looked around their tiny flames seemed to flicker in his wide eyes.

Gradually he stood up, his shivering diminishing. The stone floor was wet beneath his feet, the dark stains quite black in the dull glow of the candles.

He held the knife in his right hand for a moment, inspecting its razor sharp edge.

He glanced only briefly at the small bundle at his feet.

The other occupant of the room watched impassively as the tall man took the knife and rested it gently against his chest, the blade cold against his flesh. He pressed the point against his left breast then pulled it away, the pin-prick causing a tiny indentation in his skin.

The other did not move.

The tall man held the knife to his chest once more, pressing harder this time, gritting his teeth as he pushed the point with infinite slowness into his pectoral muscle. Blood began to bubble from the small cut, flowing more rapidly as the knife was drawn easily through the slippery skin. A cut about four inches long was opened up on his chest. He relaxed as he withdrew the knife, feeling the blood running warmly down his chest.

He reached for the large goblet which stood at his feet.

Lifting it, he inspected the contents.

The human eye which lay in the cup stared back at him, tendrils of nerve still attached to it.

He smiled and glanced down at the body at his feet.

The body with the left eye missing.

The tongue was also gone. That too was in the cup.

The tall man smiled and held the goblet to his chest, feeling the coldness of the gold against his hot breast. He looked down to see his blood dribbling slowly into the receptacle.

He opened another cut on his chest, slightly deeper this time, and the blood flowed much more swiftly, half-filling the goblet, running over the gouged eye and the severed tongue.

The man grunted in pain but gritted his teeth and remained standing, watching as the dark fluid rose almost to the top of the container.

He took it away from his chest, feeling his own life fluid dripping down his torso, over his belly and into his pubic hair, onto his throbbing erection. Some dribbled from the end of his penis like crimson ejaculate. He watched the droplets fall and strike the ground, splashing in the puddle of gore he stood in.

He held the goblet at arm's length, feeling the already unbearable chill deepen.

His breath frosted in the air and his heart began thudding faster against his ribs.

The other drew closer until the tall man felt his hand enveloped by another.

It was like being touched by fingers of ice.

The goblet was taken from his hands. He smiled, pleased that his token had been accepted, happy that the offering was satisfactory.

300

He watched as the other held the goblet, steam rising in the cold room, wisps of it floating from the hot blood in the goblet.

The other was satisfied with the offering.

The tall man smiled again.

It was a small price to pay.

Gilles de Rais was satisfied, too.

Sixty-Eight

BRITTANY, FRANCE:

Catherine Roberts yawned and rubbed her eyes. The notes looked blurred for a second, but as she blinked myopically at them they gradually swam back into focus. She looked around the hotel room, vacated by the Callahans, which she now occupied.

The ticking of her watch, lying on the dressing table beside her, sounded loud in the silence of the night. It was almost 11.48 p.m. The curtains stirred gently, blown by a cool night breeze which had also brought with it the first spots of rain. Cath looked up and watched the rain spitting against the glass for a moment.

Glass.

She reached forward and touched her reflection in the mirror on the dressing table.

Glass.

Her whole life seemed to be like a piece of glass at the moment; brittle and about to shatter if too much pressure were applied to it. She was at this place because of glass, because of the window and now she sat staring into glass, staring at the tired face reflected there. Notepads were spread all around her, scribblings about Machecoul, about Gilles de Rais. Written on a fresh sheet of paper were the words she had seen on the window.

COGITATIO – Thought
SACRIFICIUM – Sacrifice
CULTUS – Worship of the gods
ARCANA – Secrets
ARCANUS – Hidden
OPES – Treasure
IMMORTALIS – Deathless

They made as little sense to her now as they had when she'd first seen them. She tapped on her pad with the end of her pen, running her free hand through her hair.

The part about the hidden treasure was almost self-explanatory. Something in the window in Machecoul unlocked the secret to a vast fortune, of that she had no doubt. De Rais had been a remarkably wealthy man; perhaps the window held the key to where some of his vast fortune was hidden. She shook her head. He had died relatively penniless, bled dry by charlatans and con men who had promised to help him look for the *real* treasure he sought. That of eternal life.

IMMORTALIS.

'Deathless,' she said aloud.

She paused for a moment, her eyes fixed on one of the words;

CULTUS

Worship of the Gods

She chewed the end of her pen thoughtfully.

But worship of which gods? Not her god, that was for sure.

Satan?

She dropped her pen and rubbed her eyes again. Her neck was beginning to ache from constant leaning over. Her head was throbbing with the persistent strain of so much thought. She felt as if she were trapped in some kind of maze, unable to find her way out, not even sure of what she sought.

Gilles de Rais was not immortal; he had not gained immortality. He had been strangled and then ordered to be burned, after being found guilty of many crimes including murder, invocation of demons, sodomy, bestiality, conjuration and …

Conjuration.

He had been accused of witchcraft, of summoning demons. Perhaps he had actually been successful. She almost laughed, realizing that she was clutching at straws. She reminded herself that she was supposed to be approaching her subject with a scientific mind, not relying on superstition and legend.

She thought about Mark Channing.

The vision of his mutilated body came into her mind unbidden, forcing its way into her consciousness and sticking there like a splinter in skin. Who had killed him? And why? Whoever it was had done so in a manner she could never have imagined. Channing had not been murdered so much as destroyed. Destroyed by someone extremely powerful.

'Something beyond our understanding.' She chuckled humourlessly, remembering a cliché from a hundred bad horror films. Thoughts of Channing made her shudder and she tried to push them from her mind but they persisted.

Had he found something before she arrived at the church that day? Something which would unlock the secret of the window?

She got to her feet and walked to the window. The breeze blew droplets of rain into her face and she closed her eyes, hoping that the night air might clear her head. It didn't. She felt as tired as she could ever remember feeling. A heavy, almost numbing exhaustion which had sucked her energy like some kind of invisible leech. She realized that she could work no more this night and she began to peel off her clothes, stopping for one last look at the column of words written on one of her notepads. At the words which she had copied from the window. The key? Her eyes were drawn to the one word which didn't belong.

BARON

It *had* to be a name. But whose?

Charges against Gilles de Rais included conjuration of demons ...

She pulled off her skirt and sat at the dressing table in just her panties. She felt perspiration beading on her back despite the cold breeze blowing through the window.

De Rais was an alchemist. He sought the secret of turning base metal into gold. Each alchemist had a familiar, a creature which would give him that secret.

A demon?

She remembered her own words:

'*A monument, that's what the window is.*'

ARCANA

ARCANUS

IMMORTALIS

And the name: Baron.

BARON.

'A familiar,' she whispered. She was sure of it now, BARON was a name. The name of de Rais' familiar.

That was why he had venerated it so. The window had been built in its honour. Because it had given him a treasure without equal. She sighed.

It had to be the answer.

Cath got to her feet, her eyelids feeling leaden. She crossed to the bed, slipping off her panties as she reached for the edge of the sheet.

She pulled it back.

Lying there, one eye still dangling from an empty socket, was the body of Mark Channing. Blood had soaked into the bedclothes around his remains and she could smell the stench of blood.

The head turned and smiled at her.

She screamed.

Screamed and woke up.

Cath struggled from the bed, her body covered in perspiration. She almost fell as she hurried to get out. She ran to the door, then pressed her back against it and stared at the bed.

It was empty. No mutilated corpse. No grinning head.

She swallowed hard, feeling sick. She crossed to the bathroom, snapped on the light and spun the cold tap, scooping water into her hand. She drank then wiped the remaining moisture over her face and chest, trying to slow her breathing. Her heart was hammering against her ribs. She took a couple of deep breaths and gradually felt the calmness returning. Even so, she couldn't resist a glance back at the bed to check that it was unoccupied.

There was nothing there, just sweat-sodden sheets.

She knew she wouldn't be able to sleep again that night. Pulling a bathrobe around her she sat down at the dressing table with her notes. She picked up a pen and began writing.

It was 3.36 a.m.

Laura Callahan sat bolt upright in bed, her eyes bulging, the scream still locked in her throat.

It took her a moment or two to realize where she was.

Home. Safe in bed.

In bed.

She looked across to the side where her husband usually lay, but he wasn't there. She hauled herself naked from the bed. She had to tell him about the nightmare. About how she had seen Catherine Roberts pull back the sheet to find Mark Channing's mutilated body, and how the body had been twisted in half at the waist, lacerated on every inch of skin.

As she left the bedroom she glanced at her watch.

2.36 a.m.

She wondered why the name Baron had suddenly entered her mind.

Sixty-Nine

She didn't know the men. She didn't know where Callahan had found them. She didn't really care.

Catherine Roberts watched in silence as the four men gathered around the window in the church of Machecoul. It was secured firmly inside a large packing crate, protected inside by another smaller box and wedges of padding. Each panel had been covered with transparent tape then blockd with styrofoam. The men

306

had arrived with all the equipment. They had been at the church before her that evening. They had said little as she pulled up in the Peugeot, one had watched her a little too intently as she climbed out of the car, her skirt riding up around her thighs. He had looked at her but he hadn't smiled.

She had given them their instructions about moving the window, about taking care with it. If they had been listening then they certainly gave no indication that they were. All of them had been too preoccupied with looking at the window. When the time came to begin preparing it for its journey from Machecoul, the men had worked quickly. As if they were anxious to be rid of the window, away from its presence.

Cath leant against the door of the chancel, watching the men. Her eyelids felt heavy, swollen through lack of sleep. She rubbed her face every few minutes, flexing her shoulders every so often to try and relieve the ache.

Outside the trunk which would carry the window had already arrived. The driver sat in the cab smoking, waiting for his colleagues to emerge from the church. Even from inside the church Cath could hear the steady drone of the engine.

She watched now as the four men prepared to lift the window, each one getting a grip on a corner of the crate. They were talking amongst themselves and she feared that her pleas to them to be careful were in vain. She watched as they lifted the crate.

One of them shouted something Cath didn't understand and they hurriedly lowered the crate again, stepping back away from it.

She asked what was wrong and walked across to the box.

The oldest man muttered something under his

307

breath and held out a hand.

On the palm was a burn about the size of a large coin. The skin was red and a blister was already forming, rising up from the mottled flesh.

Cath frowned and reached out to touch the box.

It was freezing cold, like touching a lump of ice.

The oldest man wrapped a cloth around his hand and then he and his companions began lifting again. Cath watched as they manoeuvred it towards the chancel door.

She was aware of a chill filling the room, growing in intensity.

They edged the crate through, careful not to trap their hands against the door frame in the process. Cath blinked hard and stared at the box.

There was a dark patch on one side of it, like a burn. As if some source of heat inside were being pressed against the wood. The mark was growing larger by the second.

She rubbed her eyes.

The mark was gone.

Get a grip on yourself, she thought angrily. It was only a shadow on the crate.

She waited a moment until the men had moved the crate through into the nave then she followed them out. The acrid smell filled her nostrils as she passed through the chancel door.

A smell which reminded her of scorched wood.

They loaded the crate onto the lorry without difficulty, then three of the men climbed into the back of the vehicle with the box while the fourth joined the driver up in the cab. The driver finished another cigarette, tossed the butt out of the window and prepared to start the engine.

Inside the church Cath took one final look around the chancel, shuddering as she glanced at the place where she had found Mark Channing's body. But she pushed the thought from her mind. The dust was thick on the ground except for the place where the window had stood. The silence was oppressive and Cath turned and headed out of the chancel, out of the church to the waiting truck. She checked with the driver that he had his instructions right. He would drive, she would follow in her car and, when they arrived, the crate would be loaded aboard the aircraft Callahan had chartered. The instructions were understood. The driver started the engine and pulled away. Cath watched the truck move slowly away up the narrow track towards the road then she slid behind the wheel of the Peugeot and twisted the key in the ignition.

She glanced in the rear-view mirror, catching sight of her haggard reflection. She reached into her handbag and pulled out her sunglasses, anxious not to look at her own red-rimmed eyes. She slipped on the glasses and looked at herself again.

The visage which stared back at her was that of Baron.

Reflected in the rear-view mirror was the face of the creature on the window.

In place of her own dark, shrouded eyes, the eyes of boiling blood glared back at her. The mouth was open, leering, the long tongue lolling wolfishly from the gaping maw.

Cath only just managed to stifle a scream.

As she pushed herself back in her seat she closed her eyes, feeling cold pressure at the back of her neck.

When she looked in the mirror again she saw only her own face.

What was happening to her?

Not enough sleep. When she reached Ireland she would rest. She promised herself she would sleep. It was the pressure of the past few days, the lack of rest, what had happened to Channing. There was a logical explanation to it all. She nodded and started the car, winding down her window, allowing fresh air to blow in, hoping it would clear her mind.

She glanced at the rear view mirror again and saw only her own reflection.

She frowned and reached up to touch the mirror. The breath caught in her throat.

From one side of the mirror to the other was a crack. Right across her eyeline.

Seventy

She heard the bang.

Gunshot loud, it startled her badly. The next thing she knew the car was skidding across the road.

Cath struggled to keep control of the vehicle, slamming on the brakes and finally bringing it to a halt at the roadside. She sucked in a deep breath, relieved that there had been no traffic coming in the opposite direction. She pushed open her door and walked around the car. The front offside wheel was holed, punctured by a piece of sharp stone. She stood with her hands on her hips for a moment, surveying the damage, then glanced up the road to where the lorry carrying the window had stopped. They had obviously seen what happened. Even as she watched one of the men jumped down from the cab and ran back towards her.

He offered to help her change her wheel, saying that they would wait for her, but Cath shook her head and told him that the lorry must continue. The window must reach its destination at the appointed time so that it could be loaded aboard the plane which was waiting for it. The window was the important thing, she told him. She could manage the tyre on her own. The man looked at her, then at the wheel, and nodded, running back to the waiting lorry which pulled away.

'Damn,' snarled Cath and angrily kicked at the tyre.

She watched the lorry disappear around a bend in the road. Then she walked to the boot of the car and opened it, checking the spare tyre.

There was no way now that she would reach the plane in time to travel with the window. She would have to catch a commercial flight.

A car drove past, the occupants giving her a cursory glance as she removed the jack and the spare wheel from the boot. She wondered how long it would take her to change the tyre. Perhaps she should have allowed the man to stay and help her, she thought as she pulled her hair back and tied it up, ready to begin her task.

She would ring Callahan when she reached the airport.

The plane was a Cessna 560, over forty-eight feet in length and with a wing span of fifty-two feet. It stood motionless, the pilot glancing out of his window as the lorry carrying the crate drew up alongside.

The cabin, which usually held seven passengers, had been modified, the three aft-facing seats removed to increase the capacity of the hold.

It was into this hold that the crate containing the window was carefully placed then secured by the three-man crew of the plane with the help of the men from the truck who, once the task was completed, clambered back into their vehicle and drove off.

'I thought we were supposed to have a passenger too,' said the pilot. 'A woman.' John Martin stroked his chin thoughtfully and shrugged.

'Looks like we're out of luck,' Nick Cairns said, smiling. 'Just the box.'

Martin nodded again.

'What's in it, anyway?' asked the third member of the team, a tall Scot called Gareth James.

Martin shook his head.

'I didn't even think to ask,' he said. 'But it's supposed to be valuable, whatever it is.'

Cairns raised his eyebrows quizzically. They were used to a diversity of cargo, human and otherwise. They owned the plane jointly and had done for the last year. Martin had been a civil pilot for more than five years prior to going into business with his two colleagues, both of who had been engineers. Cairns had experienced a short spell in the R.A.F. ten years before. He was the eldest of the trio.

Their business was smuggling.

The hold had been converted for that reason, to carry more contraband. They had carried most things in their time, from drugs, to clothes, to guns. People were their cargo too, if necessary. They had taken criminals to countries where they could not be traced. Flown men out of places where they'd been sprung from

312

prison. As long as the money was right they would do the job.

The money had certainly been right for *this* job.

Martin could not think what could make the contents of one box worth £250,000 to the man who had chartered the plane, but wondering wasn't his business. Flying was.

Cairns checked the instrument panel as Martin seated himself.

The pilot glanced at his watch and stifled a yawn. They should be at the drop-off point in about three hours.

The final checks were completed and he allowed the plane to taxi for a moment, bringing it into take-off position. Then, when he was ready, the twin Pratt and Whitney engines began to roar and the Cessna sped off.

The sound of the turbo-fans grew to a crescendo as the plane finally left the ground, climbing at a rate of 3,650 feet a minute. In fifteen minutes they were at 35,000 feet. Only when he drew close to the Irish coast would he bring the plane down low enough to elude radar, ena :.ng them to reach their drop point undetected. For now he settled back in his seat and gazed out at the clear night sky. They were promised good weather all the way, even over the Irish sea. But for a little cloud cover it was a pleasant, humid night.

Odd, then, that it should feel so cold inside the plane.

Seventy-One

COUNTY CORK, THE REPUBLIC OF IRELAND:
Doyle guided the car through the massive open gates
that led onto David Callahan's estate. He slowed
down, looking around him at the sprawling, green
land, the thickets of trees. The long driveway snaked
through the grounds for a good two miles until finally it
curved to the right and the house came into view.

'Christ,' murmured Georgie. 'Look at the size of it.'

Doyle slowed down a little more, looking with even
closer scrutiny at his surroundings. To the left he
noticed some movement: a horseman.

The man rode towards them on a large bay which he
reined in as he rode closer to the car. Doyle ran
appraising eyes over him and noticed a large bump
inside the man's coat beneath his left arm.

Probably armed.

Little wonder, too. On a place this size Callahan
would need security.

The horseman guided his mount around to Doyle's
side of the car and looked down at him. The
counter-terrorist slowed the car to a crawl.

'Can I help you?' asked the horseman.

'We're here to see Mr Callahan,' Doyle told him.

'Is he expecting you?'

'Not really. We just want to talk to him.'

'You're not from around here.'

'You're quick,' said Doyle, smiling thinly.

314

The man caught the sarcasm in the Englishman's voice and glared at him. Doyle held the look for a moment then pressed his foot slightly on the accelerator, revving the engine. The bay whinnied nervously and moved away, the rider struggling to keep control of the animal. Doyle pressed harder on the gas and the Datsun moved away swiftly. The horseman rode after them.

'You should sue them, Doyle,' said Georgie, shaking her head.

He looked vague.

'Your charm school,' she said flatly.

'Very funny,' he murmured without looking at her. In his wing mirror he could see the horseman riding up alongside. By now they were at the house and Doyle brought the car to a halt outside the massive building. Both he and Georgie got out.

'I'll tell him you're here,' said the horseman.

'No need. We can manage,' Doyle assured him, striding towards the front door. He rang the bell and waited, looking at the horseman who was still glaring. The door opened and Doyle found himself confronted by a pretty young woman, he guessed in her early twenties. Shoulder-length brown hair, highlighted. She wore little make-up. Doyle smiled at her.

'Good morning,' he said. 'My name is Sean Doyle and this is Georgina Willis. We're here to see Mr Callahan.'

'Do you have an appointment?' the girl asked.

'Do we need one?' Doyle asked, still smiling.

'Who are you?' she persisted.

'Is something wrong, Trisha?'

Georgie saw Laura Callahan first. Dressed in jeans and a sweatshirt, her hair freshly washed, she was inspecting the two newcomers.

'You want to see my husband?' Laura said.

'I don't know who they are, Mrs Callahan,' Trisha said.

'British Counter-Terrorist Unit,' Doyle said, his smile fading. 'This is official. Where is your husband, Mrs Callahan?'

'Do you have identification?' Laura wanted to know.

'No, we don't, but you'd save everyone, your husband included, a lot of trouble if you'd let us speak to him.'

'How do I know you're who you say you are?' Laura persisted. 'My husband is a very rich man. You could be anyone. You might want to kill him.'

Doyle sighed.

'If I wanted to kill him I wouldn't have rung your fucking doorbell, would I?' he snapped. 'We just want to talk to him about a couple of things, then we'll go.'

There was an uneasy silence, then Laura finally nodded. Both she and the maid stepped aside. Doyle and Georgie entered, Georgie looking around at the huge hallway.

'It's all right, Trisha,' said Laura Callahan. 'You can go back to work now. I'll take care of these people.' The maid nodded and disappeared up the stairs. Laura led them along a carpeted corridor to her right towards the sitting room. She pushed open the door and walked in.

David Callahan turned as they entered, his brow furrowing as he caught sight of Doyle and Georgie.

Introductions were swift and cursory.

'They're with the police,' said Laura.

'Not quite,' Doyle corrected her. 'Counter-Terrorist Unit.'

'Would you like a drink?' asked Callahan, smiling.

Georgie accepted an orange juice, Doyle a whiskey.

'What can I do for you?' Callahan wanted to know.

316

'I won't beat about the bush, Mr Callahan,' Doyle told him. 'Just under a week ago in Belfast there was an explosion. The men responsible were driving a car which was registered to you. They were members of the IRA. We wondered if you could tell us how three IRA men happened to be driving *your* car.'

'The Sierra?'

Doyle nodded.

'It was stolen a couple of weeks ago,' Callahan told them.

'Did you report it?'

Callahan shook his head.

'Why not?'

'The police around here aren't too bright, Mr Doyle.' He smiled. 'Besides, it's only a car.' Callahan looked at his watch.

'You've lived here for two years, right?' Doyle said.

'A little less than that, actually,' Callahan told him.

'And before that?'

'Here and there.'

'London, for instance?' Doyle said, a slight smile playing on his lips.

'We lived in London for a time, yes.'

'And ran some businesses there?' Doyle persisted.

'Look, if you've got something to say then say it,' snapped Callahan, looking at his watch again. 'I've got to leave soon. I haven't the time to stand around here playing games with you.'

'Where are you going?' Doyle wanted to know.

'That's none of your business.'

'Maybe not, but finding out how the IRA got hold of your car is my business.'

'I told you, it was stolen.'

'Yeah, and you never reported it. Bollocks.'

'Look, Doyle, I don't have to listen to this crap. If you've got something to say then come out and say it. If you're who you say you are then show me some bloody I.D. to prove it. If not, you and your ...' – he looked at Georgie – 'your *companion* can get out of my house. Now.'

'The Flying Squad in London questioned you about an arms deal about five years ago, didn't they?' Doyle said. 'Selling weapons to a number of terrorist organisations. The IRA included.'

'Get out of here now,' snapped Callahan.

'It's true, isn't it?' said Doyle. 'You were questioned about selling arms to the IRA?'

'Questioned, but never anything more,' Callahan told him smugly. 'It was guesswork, Doyle. New Scotland Yard wanted me, and gun-running was the only charge they thought they could make stick. But they couldn't do it. I haven't got a criminal record, as you doubtless already know. Get out now,' he snapped, walking to the door of the sitting room and opening it.

Doyle got slowly to his feet.

'We'll be back, Mr Callahan,' he said, handing the millionaire his empty glass.

'If you come back onto my estate you'll be treated as trespassers and my staff would have every right to shoot you. Now get out.'

'I'll be back,' Doyle assured him. He and Georgie headed for the front door escorted by Callahan, who opened the door for them, ushering them out.

'If you've got nothing to hide, why are you so jumpy?' Doyle wanted to know.

'Get off my land, Doyle,' Callahan snapped.

He watched as they walked to the car, climbed in and drove off. Only then did he shut the door and lean against it for a moment breathing heavily.

As he headed back towards the sitting room the phone rang.

'Stolen my arse,' snapped Doyle. 'He knew where that fucking car of his was *and* who was driving it.'

'We've got to prove that,' said Georgie.

'No problem,' Doyle told her, putting his foot down.

'We're going to have trouble getting back in, Doyle,' she said.

He didn't answer.

Doyle finally swung the car out of the huge gates which marked the exit from the estate. He spun the wheel to the left, guiding the car along the narrow road in the direction of the nearest town.

Neither of them saw the vehicle parked in the trees at the roadside behind them.

Its driver lit his roll-up and glanced at his watch.

Give them two minutes, he thought. Then follow.

Seventy-Two

He'd been forced to kill the man.

There had been no time to think, only to act. The hold had been full of weapons at the time, a batch of brand new AK-47's. The guard had insisted on searching the plane. John Martin had been given no choice. He'd drawn his pistol and shot the guard twice. The pilot had taken off immediately, grateful to escape Libyan air space without attack. But then, he reasoned,

319

there had been no one else at the air strip that day to report what had happened. The arms had been bound for a terrorist group in France. They had paid well for them and they had paid John Martin well to collect and deliver them in the same Cessna 560 in which he now cruised, glancing at his instrument panels every now and then, wondering why he should suddenly think of the incident with the Libyan guard. It had been eight months ago. Perhaps it was because the man had been the first he'd killed.

They'd been in the air for over two hours, a journey untroubled by turbulence or bad weather.

Yet there was still that chill in the cabin.

He checked the temperature and the mercury was at a steady sixty-eight degrees.

Why was it so bloody cold?

He felt like blowing on his hands. This was crazy.

'You ok?' asked Cairns from his co-pilot's seat.

Martin nodded.

'Cold,' he said flatly. 'I have been since we took off.'

'Join the club,' Cairns said, rubbing one hand over his forearm which was bristling with goose-pimples. 'Turn the heating up.'

The plane dropped like a stone.

It was as if some invisible hand had torn both of the aircraft's engines free in one clean movement. They had no power.

The plane plummeted earthward.

'Jesus Christ,' hissed Martin, struggling with the controls. He glanced at the altimeter and saw the needle spinning madly, like a coil winding down as the miles sped past and the distance between the plane and the ground lessened by the second.

The cabin door opened and James stuck his head in.

'What's going on?' he shouted, his face pale.

'We must have lost an engine,' Cairns said, his eyes darting around in search of the problem.

'No, we're still on full power,' Martin told him, struggling with the controls.

The descent stopped as suddenly as it had begun.

The Cessna levelled out again at 22,000 feet and Martin allowed it to cruise at that height for a few minutes while he and his two companions regained their composure.

'What the fuck is happening?' James wanted to know. 'Could it have been turbulence?'

'No,' Martin said flatly. 'Turbulence or any downward thermo-draft wouldn't cause us to drop *that* far *that* quickly. It was as if the power just failed completely.'

'But it didn't because the instruments were still working,' Cairns reminded him.

Martin didn't answer. He merely gazed around at the inside of the cabin, looking for any blinking warning light, some clue as to what had made the Cessna behave in such an aberrant manner. The other thing he found curious was that the plane had not gone into a dive as it should have done if power had cut out. It had dropped still in its flight position. As if suddenly released from the strings of a giant puppeteer.

'I'm taking her back up to 35,000 feet,' he announced and the Cessna began to climb steadily once more into the clear blue sky. As it levelled out again he shuddered, not so much from the chill in the cabin this time, he thought, although that was still growing.

'We'll check her out when we land,' Martin said.

The altimeter needle began to waver again.

'Look,' snapped Cairns, pointing at it.

The plane continued to cruise.

The altimeter continued to register that they were losing height.

The needle began to hover over 35,000 once more.

'I just can't understand what's happening,' Martin said. 'The instruments were checked before we took off, the whole bloody plane was given the once over a month ago. It doesn't make sense.'

Just like the chill in the cabin. That didn't make sense either.

'Why don't you check out the radio,' Martin said.

Cairns nodded and reached for it.

He flicked the switch to transmit. A hiss of static erupted from the radio. Cairns held it away from him as if it were some kind of venomous reptile. The static didn't abate but merely kept up its hissing rasp, filling the cabin with nerve-grating sound.

The two men looked at each other for a moment then Cairns switched the set off.

'I don't *know* what's going on,' said Martin, answering his companion's unspoken question.

'Drop her anyway,' said Cairns.

Martin nodded and the plane began to descend.

It was as he felt the first bumps of turbulence that Gareth James noticed the wisps of thin smoke rising from the hold.

'John,' he called, his eyes still fixed on the slowly rising plume. 'There's something wrong in the hold.'

'If there is it's not registering on any of the instruments,' Martin told him, checking the rows of lights and expanse of dials. 'What is it?'

'I think it's a fire,' James told him, snatching an extinguisher from the wall and advancing towards the rear of the plane.

322

As he stood over the hold he could smell the gossamer vapour as it rose.

It smelt rancid, corpulent. It wasn't the acrid smell of smoke. That much he was sure of.

Then what?

'I'm going to have a look,' he shouted back, unfastening the catch that secured the hold doorway. He put down the extinguisher and used both hands to lift the flap, feeling how cold the metal was against the flesh.

'Is it a fire?' Martin called from the cabin.

James was staring down into the hold, peering through the malodorous fumes, his eyes bulging so wide in their sockets they threatened to burst from his skull.

'Gareth,' Martin bellowed. 'Is it a fire?'

James was shaking violently, his eyes still riveted to the holds entrance and to what lay beneath.

The vapour rose around him, swirling and enveloping him like ethereal arms, closing tighter.

Seventy-Three

She fought off the tiredness, determined not to let herself drift off to sleep.

Catherine Roberts glanced down at the notes spread on the small table-top before her and peered out of the plane window. She'd been lucky to get a seat on the flight, the last seat, she'd been told. It had been in the smoking area but she could put up with that for the three hours it would take to reach Ireland, even if it did

323

seem as if the man sitting next to her was determined to consume as many Marlboro as possible before the flight terminated. She coughed, waved a hand before her face and looked down at her notes once again.

She had no way of knowing whether the window had been loaded aboard the plane chartered by Callahan. She just hoped everything had gone smoothly. It should arrive a couple of hours before her if everything went according to plan.

She rubbed her eyes, trying to fight off the tiredness. Cath wanted to sleep, to push aside the notes and lie back in her seat and drift away into oblivion for a couple of hours, but she knew she couldn't because with sleep came dreams.

Those dreams.

Even so she felt the weariness pressing down on her like a palpable force, a parasite draining her resolve and her consciousness. She put her head back and immediately felt her eyelids growing heavier. She closed them for a moment and a wonderful feeling of release flowed over her.

She snapped her eyes open again just as quickly, wanting to sleep but not daring to.

There was a child seated in front of her, a young boy kneeling on his seat peering over at her. Cath looked at him wearily and managed a perfunctory smile. The child looked on indifferently, staring at her then looking down at the notes spread out in front of her. She tried to work, to ignore the unblinking gaze of the child.

BARON

She wrote the word in capitals and gazed at it, looking up briefly to see that the child had tired of staring at her and had slumped down in his seat once again.

She had no doubt that Baron was a familiar, summoned by Gilles de Rais to impart to him the secret of turning base metal into gold.

But how to carry out that summons?

SACRIFICIUM.

A sacrifice.

De Rais had murdered over two hundred children in his time. What better offering to his own particular deity than the lives of so many so young?

She rubbed her forehead with her fingers.

Did she really believe that? Did she really believe what she had written? Demons were the products of superstition and fear. She was meant to be a professional, an expert in her field. She dealt with facts, not with legends and hearsay. Horror stories had no part in her world. The idea of a demon was ridiculous and yet the window, everything that had happened so far, all seemed to point at least to a belief in such an entity. Perhaps even to its existence.

She thought about Mark Channing.

Could a human being have done to his body what was perpetrated?

But if not a human being, then who?

Had Channing somehow discovered the way to release Baron?

She sighed and sat back in her seat once more, aware that the man next to her was lighting another cigarette. More smoke began to drift across her. She closed her eyes.

There had to be a rational explanation for what was happening.

There had to be.

She felt herself dozing; she tried to wake herself up but found the effort was growing more each time.

'Baron,' she whispered as she felt sleep slipping over her.

Logical explanation ... had to be one ... Demons don't exist ...

Don't exist.

She shivered as she dozed.

She was cold.

Seventy-Four

David Callahan checked his watch as the Mercedes pulled out of the main gates of his estate. The drive should take less than two hours. The plane may even have arrived by that time. He sat back in the rear seat of the car, glancing ahead to the flat truck driven by one of his workers. Once the window was unloaded from the plane he'd chartered, it would be placed on the truck and returned to his estate.

Callahan lit a cigarette and puffed agitatedly at it. He felt uneasy. The clash with Doyle had left him feeling angry and a little edgy. The counter-terrorist was a little *too* inquisitive for Callahan's liking. Mind you, the girl with him had been nice. Attractive. Callahan took another drag and forced thoughts of Georgie from his mind. He was more concerned with other matters now.

As the Mercedes turned a bend in the road, the estate began to fade into the landscape, the house itself now hidden behind high hedges and trees.

*

'Do we follow him?' asked Georgie, as the Mercedes passed them.

'No,' said Doyle. 'We wait awhile and then we go back in.'

'I think we'd be better off talking to Callahan,' she offered.

Doyle shook his head.

'We'll get nothing out of him. Not yet. But his wife, she's a different matter.' He checked his watch. 'Not long now. Let him get clear.'

The truck pulled up beside a thickly wooded area overlooking a long flat stretch of land. Callahan's Mercedes pulled up alongside and the millionaire stepped out, sucking in the crisp night air, gazing up at the sky.

He lit a cigarette, wondering how long it would be before the plane arrived.

Behind him his two workers stood chatting idly while the Englishman drew slowly on his cigarette, holding the smoke inside for a moment before blowing it out in a bluish-grey plume. He watched the smoke slowly dissipate.

Not long now, thought Callahan. Again he looked at his watch.

She saw it.

Saw the plane.

Saw the twin-engined Cessna rocking lazily in the air as it began its descent.

Catherine Roberts stirred in her sleep aboard the Air France flight, murmured something under her breath and clenched her fists.

Somewhere in that dream she thought she heard laughter.

Laura Callahan sat at the bedroom window looking out over the grounds, which were practically invisible in the gloom. In the darkened bedroom she could see her own reflection in the glass as she stared out. But when she closed her eyes she could see something else.

She could see a small, twin-engined plane approaching a dark clearing.

She could hear its engines as it bore down on its destination.

Laura opened her eyes and found that her breath was coming in gasps. There was perspiration on her brow.

She felt frightened.

More frighened than she could ever remember.

Seventy-Five

The plane was going to crash.

As Callahan watched the Cessna come hurtling out of the night sky he was convinced of that fact.

It was going to crash.

Like some unguided missile it rolled and swooped on the air, its nose dipping violently every few moments.

As it passed overhead he could see that the undercarriage was down.

What the hell was happening?

It turned and he watched as it cut across the black canopy of night, only the landing lights on its very

328

wingtips glowing. Apart from those twin pinpricks of red the rest of the Cessna was a floating black hulk.

Callahan frowned as he saw it level out once again, preparing to land on the flat piece of ground below him. He took the cigarette from his mouth and tossed it aside, his attention now riveted on the plane which was dropping lower by the second.

One hundred feet and it would be able to touch down.

Callahan still couldn't shake the conviction that it was going to crash.

Fifty feet.

The window.

Thirty feet.

If it should crash, the window would be destroyed.

Fifteen feet.

He tried to push the thought from his mind.

The plane hit the ground, seemed to bounce back into the air momentarily then skidded for about thirty feet, the wheels unable to gain purchase on the slippery grass. Finally, it came to a halt.

Immediately Callahan ran down the slope towards the stationary craft. His workers followed him.

He was about fifty feet from the Cessna when the pilot appeared.

In the darkness Callahan could see how pale he was. He gripped the frame of the door, hanging on with difficulty.

The millionaire slowed his pace as he drew nearer.

'What is it?'

The words came from Martin. He was pointing towards the rear of the plane. Towards the hold.

'What's in that fucking box?'

His voice was low, quivering.

'Get it off my plane now,' he gasped without waiting for the millionaire to answer. 'Quickly,' he shouted.

Callahan called for the truck. The two men hurried back up the slope and jumped into the cab. The driver guided the lorry down the slope and along the shallow valley until it was beside the Cessna.

Cairns, his face white, his eyes wide and staring, clambered down from the plane and unlocked the hold.

'Get it out of there,' Martin called breathlessly.

Callahan's men did as they were told, easing the box containing the window onto the back of the flat truck.

Cairns was already climbing back into the plane.

'Just give me the money and let us get out of here,' snarled Martin.

As Callahan passed him the briefcase full of notes the pilot's hand brushed against his own and the millionaire felt how numbingly cold the man's flesh was.

'Check it,' Callahan said.

Martin shook his head and slammed the door shut. Immediately the Cessna's engines roared into life. Callahan scurried for the bank as the aircraft turned swiftly and began building up speed, as if the crew couldn't wait to be away from this place. The aircraft rose into the air and, in a matter of seconds, had disappeared into the blackness, swallowed by the night.

Callahan touched the back of his own hand where it had brushed against Martin's flesh and shuddered as he recalled the icy feel of the other man's skin. He looked across at the flat truck and the large box now firmly secured to it.

He had the window at last.

As he walked to the waiting Mercedes he *too* felt a chill envelope him.

Seventy-Six

Doyle banged the door hard and kept banging until it was opened.

The good-looking maid he remembered as Trisha stood before him, frowning.

'We're here to see Mrs Callahan,' said Doyle, pushing past the Irish girl.

'You were told to stay away from here,' she protested as Georgie stepped over the threshold. 'I'll call the Garda.'

Doyle smiled thinly.

'I don't think your boss would appreciate it,' he said cryptically. 'Where's Mrs Callahan?'

'She's upstairs,' said Trisha, regarding them both angrily.

Doyle took the steps two at a time in his haste to reach Callahan's wife. He pushed open doors as he emerged on the landing, finally discovering Laura in the master bedroom. She was lying on the bed dressed in just a bathrobe watching the television at the foot of the bed.

'What the hell are you doing here?' she rasped as Doyle entered, followed by Georgie.

'I tried to stop them, Mrs Callahan,' Trisha interjected, her way into the room barred by Georgie.

'It's all right, Trisha,' Laura said, eyeing the counter-terrorists warily. 'I'll be fine.'

The maid paused, then closed the door. Doyle heard her footsteps as she padded down the stairs.

'You have no right coming back into this house,' said Laura.

'We have every right,' Doyle snapped. 'Your husband wasn't very co-operative. I hoped you might be a little more reasonable.'

'What do you think *I* can tell you that David couldn't?' she wanted to know.

'Couldn't or *wouldn't?*' Georgie said.

Laura got to her feet, pulling the bathrobe more tightly around her.

'I don't know why you're asking me about my husband's business,' she said. 'I don't know what he gets up to. I'm not interested.' She poured herself a drink from the cabinet.

'Selling guns to the IRA is a serious offence,' Doyle said. 'Being an accessory should get you at least ten years.'

'I don't know what you're talking about.'

'I'm talking about the shit that's been happening in Northern Ireland for the last few weeks,' he snapped. 'I'm talking about the murder of politicians at Stormont, the assassination of a clergyman, the bombing of Windsor Park football ground. Your husband was involved in all of those incidents.'

'That's rubbish,' Laura said.

'Is it? Then how come the fucking IRA were driving a car owned by your husband when those incidents happened?'

'He told you, the car was stolen.'

'Bullshit. They were driving one of his cars, using weapons he sold them.'

There was a heavy silence.

'How much did he pay Maguire to go on this fucking killing spree?' the counter-terrorist persisted.

Laura sipped her drink.

'How much?' he roared, taking a step towards her.

'I don't know anything about it,' said Laura, a flicker of fear in her voice.

'Who's he working with?' Doyle rasped. 'Come on, this is too big even for someone as rich as your old man. Who's backing him? And why?'

'Where is he now?' Georgie interjected.

Laura said, 'He's meeting a plane.'

'Who's on it?' the counter-terrorist wanted to know.

'Nothing of interest to you. A stained-glass window.'

Georgie looked puzzled.

'Fuck the stained-glass window,' snapped Doyle. 'Where are the weapons? When is he next trading with Maguire?'

'I don't know what you're talking about,' Laura shouted.

'I'm going to search this house,' Doyle told her, 'search it until I find what I want. And I don't care if I have to tear it apart in the process.'

He turned and dug both hands under the mattress of the bed. With a grunt he overturned it.

Laura shouted something he didn't hear. She took a step towards him but Georgie stepped in front of her, pulling the Sterling .357 from its holster.

Doyle overturned the TV which promptly expired in a sputter of sparks and a plume of smoke.

He grabbed the drinks cabinet and hauled it over, crystal glasses and bottles of drink crashing to the carpet, liquor spilling over and soaking into the deep pile.

'Stop it,' shouted Laura.

'Where are the guns?' Doyle responded, gripping the curtains and tugging hard. They were torn free, falling to the floor with a thud.

'When is he supposed to contact Maguire again?' He swept his arm along the dressing table. Expensive perfume and ornaments were sent hurtling to the floor, delicate bottles shattering.

'I don't know what you're talking about,' Laura told him, watching helplessly as he continued to destroy the bedroom.

Finally he tore open the door and stormed out onto the landing. There was a large vase on a dresser close by. Doyle swept it to the ground, watching as it shattered.

'If I were you I'd tell him what he wants to know,' said Georgie quietly. 'Otherwise he'll get mad.'

Doyle headed down the stairs. As he reached the bottom he roared up to Georgie to join him.

'You take the West wing, I'll take the East,' he said. 'Turn everything over if you have to.'

'And what if you're wrong?' she offered.

'Just do it,' he snapped and they headed off in opposite directions.

Laura appeared at the top of the stairs.

'Stop it, you bastards,' she bellowed. 'My husband will kill you when he gets back.'

'Let him fucking try,' Doyle roared back.

'Car,' said Georgie, hearing a sound from outside. She nodded in the direction of the front door.

They both listened, heard footsteps. Running. Approaching the door fast.

What the hell was going on?

Three shots.

Doyle pressed himself back against the wall as bullets tore holes through the door, blasting the handle of the front door away. Then he heard voices outside and, as he watched, the door was kicked open.

Standing in the entrance, a Skorpion machine-pistol gripped in his fist, was James Maguire.

Seventy-Seven

It was as if time had stood still.

A frame of film momentarily frozen.

Maguire standing in the doorway, the sub-gun gripped in his hand, only his eyes moving as he took in Doyle and Georgie's presence.

The two counter-terrorists staring at the IRA man, Doyle with his back pressed to the wall, Georgie already ducked low.

Then the film was running again.

Maguire opened fire, raking the hall, bullets blasting lumps of plaster from the immaculately-decorated walls. Two shots struck a vase close to Doyle, shattering it. Ricochets screamed off the bricks as the Irishman fired another short burst.

Doyle threw himself to one side, pulling the CZ from its holster. He hit the ground and rolled twice, ending up on his belly. He fired three shots, the automatic bucking in his hand. They all missed but one tore away part of the door frame close to Maguire's head.

Georgie also fired, her two shots ploughing into the door itself, blasting great lumps of wood and paint away. She scrambled towards a nearby door as Maguire raked the hall with fire once more.

Doyle heard a crash from the rear of the building.

Paul Maconnell and Michael Black were blasting their way through the huge picture-windows of the Callahans' sitting room. They blundered about in the darkness until Maconnell saw the strip of light beneath the door which led to the hall beyond. They advanced towards it.

Doyle threw himself through an open door to his right, slamming it behind him. He kept low, his breath coming in short gasps. He heard more fire from the hallway and then shouts.

There was a scream.

Georgie?

He wrenched open the door and looked up to see Maguire and Black hurtling up the stairs towards the landing.

Towards Laura Callahan.

She bolted for her bedroom but Maguire caught her by the hair and jerked her back, slapping her hard across the face.

Doyle sprinted across the hall, firing upwards as he ran. Bullets blasted part of the banister away. Maconnell appeared to his left and fired. Doyle threw himself to the floor as one 9mm shell blasted a chunk out of the ground close to him. He rolled over and fired one-handed, pumping the trigger until the slide rocketed backwards.

He dropped the empty CZ and pulled the Charter Arms .44 from his belt, now crouched behind a leather chair which stood in the hallway.

Where the fuck was Georgie?

Maguire leaned over the banister and let off a burst of fire from the Skorpion. Doyle shouted in pain and annoyance as a bullet clipped the top of his left ear. Another passed through a fold in his jacket without

336

touching skin. He could smell the odour of cordite and burnt material. To his left was Maconnell, above him Maguire and Black.

That left two more.

He heard shots from outside, heard the crash of breaking glass.

Georgie had slipped out of the house through a window in the room to which she'd retreated. Now, standing on the gravel drive outside the building, she steadied herself and fired three times from the .357. The pistol bucked in her grip as the weapon spat out its lethal load. The first bullet blasted away the offside headlamp of the car, the second missed and the third hit the radiator, staving in most of the grille as if it had been struck with a sledgehammer.

From inside the Orion Billy Dolan leant out of the driver's side and fired off a burst from an Ingram M-10. The sub-gun spattered off two dozen shots, its muzzle-flash illuminating the area in front of the house. Spent cartridge cases spewed from the weapon in a brass arc, clattering down on the gravel. He dropped the gun onto the passenger seat and reversed, the rear wheels spinning on the rough ground. Pieces of stone were sent flying into the air by the ferocity of his manoeuvre. The car shot backwards and Georgie ran after it, firing off her last two shots.

She ducked behind one of the stone pillars in front of the main door, flipped the cylinder from the Sterling and ejected the shell cases. Then, moving with practised precision, she pulled one of the quick-loaders from her pocket, jammed the slugs into the chambers and snapped the weapon closed again.

Dolan put his headlights on full, snatched up the Ingram and drove straight at her, swerving past at the

337

last moment, raking the front of the house with fire.

Georgie squeezed herself against the pillar for cover, wincing as bullets drilled into the concrete around her. One blasted away a piece of stone only inches from her face, the dust flecks filling her eyes momentarily.

'Who the fuck is that?' roared Damien Flynn from inside the car.

Dolan didn't answer but swung the car around and drove towards the pillar again, firing as he went.

'Come on, you fucker,' he bellowed.

Georgie waited until the car had passed, then sprang out and fired at the back of the Orion. Her second shot exploded one of the rear lights.

Inside the house, Maguire knew that the only way out was through the front door and past the fucking maniac in the hall, whoever he was.

'Get her to the car,' he told Black, nodding at Laura Callahan who was firmly held by the IRA man. He had one hand over her mouth; the other held her arms. 'When I tell you to move, you move, right?'

Black nodded, thinking how far down he had to go, how long a staircase he had to descend. He suddenly seemed miles from his goal. The door yawned open invitingly but he could still hear gunfire from outside.

Maguire slammed another magazine into the Skorpion and looked at his companion.

'Set?' he muttered.

Black nodded.

'Come on,' roared Maguire and opened fire.

Doyle ducked down as a concentrated burst of fire blasted the chair behind which he was crouching to atoms. He threw himself towards the nearby door, looking round to see that Maguire, Black and their captive were making for the front door. Maconnell was following, also firing.

Doyle steadied himself and fired off one round from the .44.

It struck Black in the left shin, pulverizing the bone, ripping through his calf muscle, crippling him immediately. He screamed in pain and fell, letting loose his grip on Laura, but Maguire grabbed her and hurried her through the front door.

Maconnell dragged his companion through after them, leaving a thick trail of blood from the man's shattered leg.

Dolan saw them come out and sent the Orion speeding up alongside. Flynn flung open the doors and they clambered in, Black only scrambling inside with some difficulty, yelping in pain as he banged his injured leg on the door frame. Georgie took her chance and fired off another couple of shots, one of which punched in the nearside rear window, showering those in the back with glass.

Dolan spun the wheel and the Orion spat more stones into the air.

'Go, go,' bellowed Maguire and the car hurtled off down the driveway.

Doyle dashed from the house and saw the single tail-light disappearing into the night. He was half-way to the Datsun already.

Not this time.

I've got you this time, you bastards.

He wrenched open the driver's side door and slid behind the wheel. Georgie hurled herself into the passenger's seat and was flung backwards as Doyle stepped on the accelerator. The car was catapulted forward, wheels spinning for a second before gaining purchase, then it was off, the needle on the speedometer touching sixty as Doyle pressed down harder on the accelerator.

'In the glove compartment,' he hissed and she fumbled for what he wanted.

The MP5K was only inches larger than the .357 she herself carried, but it was capable of firing over 650 rounds of 9mm ammunition a minute. Doyle cradled it across his lap, both hands locked on the wheel as he followed the fleeing Orion.

The lead vehicle hit a bump in the drive and all four wheels left the ground before it slammed back to earth, skidding violently as Dolan regained control of the wheel.

The gateway to the estate was approaching. In his haste to escape the pursuing Datsun, Dolan drove too close to the stone wall. There was a high-pitched squeal as sparks spattered from the side of the vehicle, the paint stripped off as surely as if someone had turned a blowtorch on it. Then the car turned sharply to the right onto the main road. For precious seconds it seemed as if the vehicle must turn over but Dolan kept it under control and it roared on.

In the back Laura Callahan's scream was cut short as Maguire struck her in the face with the butt of the Skorpion. She fell across Maconnell, her lip split, blood weeping from the cut.

Doyle followed, his face set in harsh lines as he struggled to control the Datsun. He took the turn too sharply, one of the wing mirrors being torn from the car as he collided with the wall, but he ignored the minor inconvenience and drove on.

Beside him, Georgie was pushing more shells into the Sterling.

Neither of them noticed the car which pulled out of the trees to their left and began following *them*.

Seventy-Eight

The road that led away from Callahan's estate was so narrow in places it barely allowed two cars to pass one another.

Doyle didn't seem to care. He floored the accelerator of the Datsun in an attempt to get up alongside the fleeing Orion.

He could see the tail light tantalisingly less than twenty yards from him. As they reached a straight stretch of road he picked up the MP5K and, steadying himself, gripped it firmly in one hand and fired off a burst. The muzzle-flash lit the night, momentarily blinding him, but he kept his foot pressed down, the needle on the speedo never dropping below seventy.

Bullets spattered the road and some drilled into the rear of the Orion.

'Laura Callahan's in there, Doyle,' Georgie reminded him.

'Fuck her,' he rasped. 'I want Maguire.'

He fired again, shouting his pleasure as the sub-gun flamed.

The back window of the Orion was peppered, the glass spider-webbing then crashing inwards onto the occupants.

Shots came from the rear of the fleeing vehicle, one of them cracking the windscreen of the Datsun.

Georgie fired from her own side, trying to hit a tyre, but in the dark and moving at such speed it was almost impossible. She heard one shot sing off the rear of the Orion.

As she eased herself back into the car she caught sight of the third car's headlamps in the wing mirror. She turned in her seat to see the Mazda close.

'We've got company,' she told Doyle, who checked his rear-view mirror.

'Police?' he wondered aloud, catching sight of the headlamps.

'I don't think so,' she said quietly, holding on to the seat as the Datsun ran dangerously close to the edge of the roadside ditch. She squinted through the gloom, trying to see how many people were in the car, but it was impossible; the glare from the pursuing vehicle's headlights made it a futile cause.

Up ahead the Orion turned a corner, crashing through a wooden gate and skidding across a field.

Doyle followed without hesitation.

The Mazda followed too.

'Who the fuck are they?' he hissed, glancing once more into the rear-view mirror.

A burst of fire from up ahead interrupted his musings.

Bullets struck the front of the Datsun, two of them blasting out a headlamp. Doyle swung the car back and forth to make it a more difficult target to hit. Simultaneously he fired another burst from the MP5K, his hand numb from the prolonged and powerful recoil. The stench of cordite filled his nostrils despite the gust of cold air pouring through the side window.

'Could they be more of Maguire's men?' Georgie mused aloud, peering over her shoulder again at the oncoming car.

342

'They'd have taken us out by now,' Doyle said with an air of certainty. 'Probably have been sitting there with a fucking rocket-launcher waiting for us.' He glanced into the rear-view mirror, frowning. The Mazda didn't appear to be making any attempt to catch up with them, but was maintaining a steady distance. *Tracking it as well as following* he thought.

The cars were bumping over deep ruts in the ground now, bouncing and skidding every few yards, yet they didn't reduce their speed but roared on through the night, across the field, the occasional shot flying back and forth between the two vehicles.

There was a hedge on the far side of the field. Dolan put his foot down and sent the Orion crashing through.

Doyle followed suit.

So did the Mazda.

The road they found themselves on was wider now and Doyle saw his chance to get up alongside the Orion. He floored the accelerator, slamming into the rear of the escaping vehicle, dropping back immediately. Then he repeated the move, smashing the other tail light of the Orion, smiling to himself as he saw the vehicle skid. He drove up alongside it, twisting the wheel, slamming the Datsun into the other car.

He could actually see Billy Dolan's face, the Irishman yelling at him angrily as the two cars collided once more.

Dolan raised the Ingram and fired.

Doyle hit the brakes a fraction too late and bullets ripped into the side of the Datsun, punching holes in the bodywork. He dropped back then shot the car forward again, coming up on the other side of the Orion, bringing his own sub-gun to bear on the vehicle.

343

He'd fired half a dozen shots when the hammer slammed down on an empty chamber.

'Shit,' Doyle snarled, tossing the weapon to Georgie. She reloaded it, punched open the sun roof and stood on the passenger seat, her head and shoulders through the top of the car. She took aim and fired, the spent cartridge cases flying back at her, hurled by the wind. Red hot, they singed her skin and she winced.

Both side windows were blown inwards, bullets drilling across the side and roof of the Orion.

Dolan twisted the wheel and sent the vehicle crashing through another hedge into another field.

Georgie dropped back into her seat as Doyle followed, glancing once more at the ever-present Mazda behind.

Doyle felt like telling Georgie to riddle the fucking thing with bullets, just to get it off their tail, but for now his attention remained locked on the fleeing Orion.

The burst of fire which took out his windscreen was lethally accurate.

The glass was blasted inwards as surely as if a maniac with a sledgehammer had been standing on the roof of the Datsun swinging wantonly at the screen. Pieces of glass flew back at Doyle and Georgie, cutting them and causing Doyle to swerve.

Another shot caught him in the fleshy part of the shoulder.

The pain was sudden and unexpected and Doyle felt a dreadful numbness spreading rapidly through his left arm. His hand slipped from the wheel for precious seconds, long enough for him to lose control of the car. It spun round, fish-tailing suddenly. With a feeling of rage and apprehension he realized that it was going into a roll.

It spun viciously, twisting over more than a dozen times, finally ending up on its roof.

The Orion sped off into the night.

The Datsun lay still like some stricken beast, its occupants unmoving.

The Mazda pulled up a few yards behind, headlamps pointed at the upturned car. Slowly both its occupants clambered out and walked towards the Datsun, watching for any sign of movement.

Both men carried guns.

Seventy-Nine

As she stared out of the window, Catherine Roberts' reflection looked back at her, mirrored against the blackness of the night sky.

The plane moved silently through the low clouds, its engine apparently muffled by the darkness which seemed to envelope it like a velvet glove. Every so often it would judder slightly as it passed through an air pocket.

She looked down at the papers and notes spread out on the table in front of her.

In that maze of jottings and jumble of papers lay the answer to the riddle she and Channing and probably hundreds more before them had sought to find.

She had the riddle of the window solved.

Cath glanced at her watch, wondering how much longer it would take to reach Dublin. Once the plane set down she still had to reach Callahan's estate.

He had to know about the window. *Had to know everything.*

She sighed wearily and glanced out of the window again. There was nothing to see but blackness. Cath looked down at her notes, eyes flickering over the scrawled sentences and drawings. There was a page of latin, a sketch of the window with arrows drawn to point out meanings in the different panels.

Callahan would have to see these.

The child sitting in front of her peered over its seat and looked at her again. The man next to her was still smoking, wreathing both of them in a cloud of bluish fumes.

Cath tried to ignore them and concentrate on her notes. She pulled a pad from her bag and began transcribing some of the less legible sentences onto a fresh sheet of paper, aware all the time of the child's gaze upon her.

How much longer before they reached Dublin?

As if in answer to her unspoken question, the voice of the Captain suddenly filtered over the radio and told the passengers they would be landing in approximately thirty minutes.

Cath glanced at her watch.

She had to reach Callahan as quickly as possible.

The child tired of staring at her and slipped down into its seat. Cath continued writing, stopping every now and then to re-read what she'd written, wondering perhaps if there had been some mistake.

Wondering?

Could she have been wrong somewhere along the line? Wrong with her translation of the words? Wrong with her understanding of the window? Wrong, perhaps, in her reading of the stained glass? But the more she looked at the findings before her, the more she re-checked her work, the more certain she was that there had been no errors. Her findings were correct. She had found the secret, of that there was no doubt.

As she looked at her watch she realized she was not *wondering* if she'd made a mistake.

She was *hoping*.

At Dublin Airport she rented a car. The drive, she knew, was not going to be easy, her speed hampered by little knowledge of the roads and also by the need constantly to consult a map.

She felt tired, both because of the lateness of the hour and the incidents of the past week or so. She felt as if all the energy had been drained from her. She had to fight to keep her senses alert, winding down her window to allow cold air to sweep over her face.

Beside her in a briefcase on the passenger seat were her notes. Answers to questions.

Twice she had to stop and consult the map given her by the rental company, pulling into the side of the road and tracing the routes with her index finger, conscious all the time of her own slow progress. If only she could pull into one of the hotels and book a room for the night. Sleep. She could continue with her journey in the morning refreshed. But Cath knew that she could not do that. She had to keep driving, despite the crushing weariness.

She had to reach Callahan, and the window, no matter what.

He had to know.

Cath tried to coax more speed from the car.

She hoped she wasn't too late.

347

Eighty

There were pieces of bone protruding through the pulped flesh.

Mick Black looked down at the savage wound in his left leg and howled in pain again. Blood was still oozing from it, running down to stain his sock. It was matted in the hairs on his leg. On the back seat beside him, still unconscious, was Laura Callahan, her bathrobe dotted with blood. Her own and Black's.

'What the fuck was that bastard firing out of that gun?' Maconnell wondered aloud, looking down at the massive destruction Doyle's shell had wrought on his companion's leg.

Maguire didn't answer.

Black continued to moan softly, his pain intensifying.

'We've got to change cars quick,' said Maguire, glancing over his shoulder. 'If we run into any Garda we've had it.' He looked at Dolan. 'Dump this fucking thing as soon as you can. Find something else.'

The driver nodded, his youthful features sheathed in perspiration. There were flecks of blood on *his* face too from a couple of slight gashes he'd sustained when flying glass had exploded into the car.

'Who the fuck were they?' he wanted to know.

'How do I know?' Maguire said irritably. 'Probably the same ones who were after us in Belfast.'

'We've lost them twice. We might not be so lucky

the third time,' Damien Flynn offered.

'There won't *be* a third time,' snapped Maguire.

Black's teeth were gritted against the waves of agony that racked his body. He had lost a lot of blood. He felt sick. The back window was open and the cool night air washed over him, yet still he felt nausea sweeping through him in unrelenting waves.

'We've got to get him to a doctor, Jim,' said Maconnell, glancing down at Black's wound again. The other man was slumped back in his seat. Even in the darkness his features looked waxen. 'That bullet nearly took his fucking leg off.'

'We'll dump *her* first, then see to Mick,' Maguire said, nodding in the direction of Laura, sprawled unconscious across Flynn's lap. 'I want to get rid of this car.'

They passed a sign that proclaimed:

KINARDE 2 MILES.

'First car we see, we take it,' Maguire continued. The road curved around to the right, flanked on both sides by trees and hedges which looked as if they had been formed from the night itself, so dense and impenetrable were they. About two hundred yards ahead a car was parked in what passed for a lay-by.

'Kill the lights,' said Maguire and Dolan obeyed, cruising up to within ten feet of the stationary Citroen Estate. He pulled up.

The car was in darkness, with no tail lights on, no hazard warning lights. Nothing. Of the driver there was no sign.

Maguire got out of the Orion, sliding the Browning Hi-Power from its shoulder holster, keeping it low by his side as he approached the car. He moved around it, saw that the dashboard was illuminated, tried the door and found that it was open. Movement in the hedge behind him made him spin round.

The man, who Maguire took to be the driver of the car, was still doing up his flies as he emerged from his position behind the hedge. He raised his hands in an attitude of surrender, the colour draining from his face. Despite the fact that he'd just relieved himself, urine suddenly darkened the front of his trousers as he saw the automatic in Maguire's hand.

Maguire fired once.

In the silence of the countryside the sound was thunderous. The 9mm bucked in his fist as he pumped the trigger, the bullet catching the man in the face just below the right eye. The impact propelled him back through the hedge, where his body lay twitching. Maguire stood over him, watching as the last muscular spasms racked the body, then prodded the corpse with his toe and turned back towards the Orion. His companions were already scrambling from it, Maconnell supporting Black, Flynn carrying Laura bodily. Maguire watched as he laid the woman across the back seat and slid in beside her.

Black was burbling incoherently as Maconnell half-dragged, half-walked him to the waiting Citroen.

'I'll take him,' said Maguire. 'You get in the front.' Maconnell nodded and eased his companion towards Maguire who snaked one arm around Black's shoulder, supporting him. 'It'll be ok, Mick,' he said. 'We'll get that leg sorted out.'

Black nodded and groaned, afraid he was going to vomit. The pain from his leg was intolerable.

Maguire looked down at the wound and saw the portions of bone poking through the torn flesh.

'It's bad,' he said, shaking his head.

350

With that he pressed the Browning to the base of Black's skull and fired once.

Again the sound reverberated in the stillness, the harsh blast mingling with the wet slop of exploding brains as the roof of Black's skull was blown away, the skull resembling a volcano as it spewed blood, fragmented bone and grey matter into the air. Maguire stepped aside, allowing the body to fall into the grass at the roadside, then slipped into the back seat and slammed the door.

'There was nothing we could have done for him,' he said.

Silence greeted the remark.

The reaction was a combination of shock and acceptance. There was a cold logic to it.

Maconnell nodded thoughtfully.

'Let's get out of here, Billy,' said Maguire.

Dolan nodded and started the car, pulling out of the lay-by, leaving the two bodies where they had fallen.

Eighty-One

Doyle heard the soft footfalls drawing closer but lay still.

Next to him in the overturned Datsun, Georgie had her eyes closed. As he swivelled his eyes, he could see a thin ribbon of blood coming from beneath her hair, some of the crimson liquid dripping onto her cheek. There was a dull pain in his left shoulder where the bullet had clipped him and his neck was throbbing.

The ache was beginning to fill his skull. When he tried to draw in a deep breath it felt as if his chest was constricted but there was no pain. He concluded that he had no broken bones.

The footfalls drew nearer, muffled by the grass in the field.

Doyle reached with infinite slowness across his body, allowing his fingers to touch the butt of the .44, ensuring he could reach it if he had to.

Right, you bastard, keep coming.

He allowed the arm to rest across his chest, then lay still again.

A torch was shone into the car.

'Get them out.'

The voice was English.

He heard hands scrabbling at the doors, tugging open the buckled panels. Then he felt himself being hauled from the upturned vehicle and pulled onto wet grass, which soaked into his sweatshirt and jeans as he lay on the ground. He could smell petrol, and wondered if the Datsun's fuel tank had been ruptured in the spin.

'Is she alive?'

The same voice.

'Yes, she's just dazed.'

The second voice was English too.

Doyle smelled tobacco smoke, felt himself being pulled upright, pushed back against the car.

'Doyle.'

The sound of his own name surprised him. Startled him into opening his eyes.

'Doyle,' the man said again, shaking him slightly.

The counter-terrorist blinked myopically, exaggerating the extent of his confusion.

352

He didn't recognise the man who stood before him glaring into his eyes.

A hand crashed against his cheek.

'Come on, snap out of it,' the first man hissed, shaking him again.

Doyle groaned and allowed his head to drop forward onto his chest. The man gripped his chin and raised it so that he was staring into his face again.

'Where did Maguire and his men go?' the man asked.

What the fuck was going on here?

They knew Doyle's name, they knew who he was chasing.

Garda? No, the voices were English. And they were in plain clothes.

'Come on, you bastard, wake up. Talk to me.'

Doyle was slapped again.

He gazed at the man blankly, satisfied that his pretence was working.

'Where's Maguire?' the man insisted angrily.

Doyle was pushed back harder against the car, the man bringing his face closer. The smell of cigarettes was strong on his breath.

'Talk,' rasped the man.

Doyle opened his eyes wide and, for a fleeting second, the man who held him realized that the counter-terrorist was vividly conscious.

Doyle drove his head forward with terrific force, the snake-like speed catching the man unawares. There was a harsh crack as his nose was broken. Blood burst from the shattered appendage and now it was Doyle's turn to grab him. He butted him again, this time letting his body fall as he reeled from the impact, sprawling on the grass. Doyle reached for the Bulldog and pulled it from the holster, aiming it at his fallen

353

foe. The man tried to rise but Doyle drove a foot hard into his crutch. The man doubled up in agony and lay writhing on the grass, clutching his throbbing genitals.

The counter-terrorist spun round to see that the second man was approaching him from the other side of the car. He held Georgie in front of him. Doyle could see that she was conscious but still groggy.

'Drop the gun, Doyle,' the second man said, pointing his own Beretta automatic at the younger man.

'Fuck you,' Doyle hissed, steadying himself. He raised the pistol until the barrel of the .44 was aimed at the man's head.

'Drop it or I'll kill the girl,' the man said as Doyle took a step towards him.

'So kill her,' Doyle said flatly, thumbing back the hammer.

'I mean it,' the man snarled, pressing the barrel of the Beretta against Georgie's cheek, pulling her in front of him as a shield. 'I'll shoot her.'

'Let go and drop your own gun,' Doyle told him. 'Or I'll fire. You've got three seconds.'

'You'll hit her not me,' the man said defiantly.

'Do you know what I've got in here?' Doyle said, indicating the .44. 'Glaser safety slugs. They'll put a hole in a brick wall at fifty feet. I'll shoot straight through her. And you *know* I will.'

The man swallowed hard, lowered the Beretta a fraction.

'Two seconds,' Doyle reminded him. 'Let her go.'

The man pushed Georgie away from him, dropped the Beretta and raised his hands in a gesture of surrender. Doyle walked across to him and looked into his face. Then, with one swift movement, he struck him with the butt of the pistol. The blow split his bottom lip and loosened two of his front teeth. He dropped to his knees.

'Who are you?' he demanded, the .44 pressed against the man's head.

The man raised one hand to his torn lip, seeing the blood on his fingers.

'Fuck you,' he hissed, the words emerging with a slight whistle through the gap in his teeth.

'Suit yourself. You're wasting my time.'

His finger tightened on the trigger.

Eighty-Two

'Wait.'

Doyle heard the voice but didn't turn. He kept the Bulldog pressed against the man's skull.

Georgie rubbed her head and exhaled deeply, joining her companion, looking down at the helpless figure who knelt before them in what looked like an attitude of supplication.

'I recognise him,' she said.

Doyle frowned.

'That night in Belfast, when we were followed? He's the one who followed me. Remember, I said I went through his pockets but there was no I.D.'

Doyle eased the hammer forward on the .44, gripped the front of the man's shirt and dragged him to his

'Who the fuck *are* you?' he snarled.

Georgie turned to see that the first man w

painfully to his feet, one hand clutching his throbbing testicles, the other dabbing at his broken nose. She pulled the .357 from its holster, wiped blood from her eyes with the back of her hand and fixed the man in the sights.

'Stay where you are,' she told him.

'I'm getting sick of this game,' Doyle said through clenched teeth, lifting the man higher until it seemed he would propel him into the air. 'I'm going to ask once more who you are, then I'm going to blow your fucking head off.'

'Tell him,' called the first man, forced to breathe through his mouth as blood clogged his nostrils.

'We're British agents,' said the man Doyle held.

'Bullshit,' he snarled

'It's true,' the other man said. 'Donaldson and Westley sent us.'

Doyle released his grip on the man, pushing him back a few paces. If the news was a shock it didn't register on the counter-terrorist's face. His features still bore the stamp of rage.

'And you've been following us since we arrived in Belfast?' said Georgie, the revelation catching her somewhat by surprise too. 'Why didn't you contact us? Why the cloak and dagger stuff?'

'We had orders not to,' said the second man.

'This doesn't make sense,' Georgie mused aloud.

'What *were* your orders?' Doyle wanted to now.

'To tail you, keep a watch and observe until you ked down Maguire,' the first man told him.

d then what?'

were to take over.'

nodded.

'Let us do the dirty work, let us risk our fucking necks, then stroll in and take all the glory. Why?'

'Westley and Donaldson didn't trust you to bring Maguire in alive. They were frightened you'd kill him.'

'We had to get to him first anyway,' said the second man. 'There are a unit of Provisional IRA men on his tail, too. They've got orders to kill him and his men. We have to reach him before *they* do.'

'Popular bloke, isn't he?' said Doyle cryptically. He kept the gun aimed at the second man.

'You said you were supposed to "take over" once Maguire had been found,' Georgie interjected. 'What were *we* supposed to do? Just stand aside and let you bring him in? What if we hadn't co-operated?'

Neither of the men spoke.

'You had orders to kill us,' Doyle said, the words coming out as a statement rather than a question. 'Didn't you?'

Still no answer.

'Didn't you?' he roared, raising the gun so that it was level with the second man's head again.

He nodded.

'Yes. Orders from Westley. He wanted you dead. Both of you.'

'I can't say I blame him,' snarled the first man.

'So who are you? Your names?' Georgie wanted to know.

'Rivers,' said the first man.

'Todd,' the second added.

'Why?' Doyle asked. 'Why did Westley want us killed?'

Neither Rivers or Todd spoke.

Doyle raised the pistol and advanced a pace.

'He wanted to protect ...'

357

'Shut up,' Rivers bellowed, noticing the fear on his companion's face.

'To protect who?' Doyle insisted, his back still to Rivers, the Bulldog still aimed at Todd's head. 'Who, you bastard? Tell me or I swear to Christ I'll kill you.'

'Don't tell him anything,' shouted Rivers.

Doyle spun round and, in one fluid movement, raised the Charter Arms .44 and fired off one shot. It hit Rivers squarely in the chest, the thunderous retort of the pistol drowning out his shout of pained surprise as the slug exploded inside him, the impact throwing him several feet backwards. He hit the ground with a thud, blood spreading rapidly around him. His body twitched once then was still.

'Jesus,' gasped Todd as Doyle rounded on him again.

'Talk, you fucker,' he hissed. 'Tell me what you know. Everything. Who was Westley trying to protect?'

'All right, I'll tell you,' Todd said, his face now sheathed in perspiration.

Doyle motioned him towards the Mazda and glanced at Georgie.

'Are you ok to drive?' he asked her.

She nodded.

'Get in the back,' he snapped at Todd, who obeyed. Doyle clambered in beside him, the Bulldog pressed into the other man's groin. Georgie started the engine, flicking on the headlamps. They illuminated the body of Rivers.

'Where to?' she asked.

Doyle glanced at his watch.

11.22 p.m.

'Get us to a phone,' he said flatly.

358

Eighty-Three

Peter Todd shifted uncomfortably in the back seat of the Mazda. Every time he moved he felt the barrel of the .44 pressed harder against his groin. Doyle's stare was unwavering.

Todd had read files on the man and had spoken to others who'd worked with him. It had frightened but not altogether surprised him when the younger man had shot Rivers. He was as unpredictable as he was dangerous. What was more he seemed to enjoy what he did. Todd had guessed early on that there was no room for heroics where Doyle was concerned; with the gun probing against his testicles, he certainly didn't intend being obstructive. To hell with Donaldson and Westley. *They* weren't the ones close to a .44 calibre vasectomy.

'I told you earlier I'm sick of bloody games,' said Doyle. 'I'm going to ask you questions and I'm going to ask you once. Tell me what I want to know, got it? Otherwise you'll wish it was *you* I'd shot, not Rivers.'

'I told you I'd talk,' Todd reminded the counter-terrorist.

Doyle re-adjusted his position on the seat, wincing at the dull ache spreading from his shoulder wound.

'Why did Donaldson and Westley send you to tail us?' he began.

'I told you, they didn't want you to kill Maguire.'

'So when did you intend "*stepping in*" to take over?'

359

'After you'd tracked him down.' Todd swallowed hard.
'That was when we were supposed to kill you both.'

'You said that Westley was trying to protect someone. Who?'

Todd licked his lips, aware that they were dry.

'His name is David Callahan.'

Even Doyle looked surprised.

'What the hell has *he* got to do with all this?' he asked quietly.

'You know him?'

Doyle nodded.

'Callahan *was*, still is, a gun runner,' said Todd. 'Westley knew him, knew where he lived and that he was still trading. He sold guns to the IRA, among others. When the plans for the Stormont summit were first put forward he realized that he'd be losing a sizeable chunk of his income. With peace in Northern Ireland the IRA would have no need of weapons; he'd lose a lot of money.'

'What has this got to do with Westley and Donaldson?' Doyle wanted to know.

'They were in partnership with Callahan.'

'They knew he was selling arms to the IRA?' Georgie interjected.

'They supplied him with some of them to sell,' Todd told her. 'They've been in business with him for a very long time. They've been making money out of the troubles for years and they don't want it to stop. Callahan paid Maguire a million pounds and supplied him with weapons. There was supposed to be a campaign in England, too, but *you* broke that up when you raided that house in Hammersmith.'

Doyle nodded at the recollection.

'Maguire got out of hand,' Todd continued. 'He

exceeded his orders. That's when Westley and Donaldson called *you* in. They knew you'd be able to find him but they didn't want you getting to him in case you found out about the conspiracy, found out that they were involved.'

'Then why didn't they just leave us alone? If they were so sure we were going to kill Maguire they shouldn't have had anything to worry about.'

'Westley wanted you dead, anyway.'

Doyle smiled.

'Isn't it great to be wanted?' he said cryptically.

'Westley and Donaldson were going to say that you two had been killed in a shoot-out with Maguire and his men, after Rivers and I had shot you.' His voice dropped to a whisper.

Doyle glared at his captive.

'What was Callahan getting out of this, apart from money?' the counter-terrorist wanted to know.

'Immunity from extradition. As long as the fighting went on in Northern Ireland, as long as there was no peace settlement, it meant that diplomatic relations between Britain and Ireland were still rocky. If there'd been a settlement then criminals from the Republic would lose their protection. Callahan thought the British police were after him.'

'Why was Laura Callahan kidnapped?' Doyle said. 'That couldn't have been part of the plan.'

'It wasn't. When Westley and Donaldson saw how powerful Maguire was becoming they decided to slow him down. Callahan was supposed to sell them a batch of weapons, deliver them to a place near Bective Abbey in Meath.'

'That's where those two Garda officers were shot,' said Georgie.

'The weapons were faulty, but Maguire had already paid for them.'

'That's why Laura was taken, then?' Georgie offered. 'Revenge?'

'If it's a kidnapping, Maguire's going to have to get in touch with Callahan,' Doyle said. 'Turn the car round, head back to Callahan's place.'

'It'll be swarming with police after what happened,' she protested.

'Just do it,' Doyle snapped. 'Besides, I'd like a word with Mr Callahan when I see him.'

'No one knew they were going to snatch his wife,' Todd added.

Georgie turned the car and headed back the way they'd come.

'You said there were a bunch of Provos after Maguire, too,' Doyle remembered.

'They want him dead.'

'They're not the only ones,' the younger man said, running a hand through his hair. He spotted a phone box up ahead and told Georgie to pull in. Jabbing the gun into Todd's stomach he forced him out of the car, pushing him towards the phone box. Once inside he fumbled for change, fed it into the phone and dialled. And waited.

It rang and rang.

'Yes,' a sleepy voice finally said.

Doyle held the receiver tightly in his fist.

'Who's there?' the voice asked.

'Westley, did I wake you?' said the counter-terrorist, his face expressionless.

'Who the hell is this?'

'It's Doyle.'

Silence.

362

'I know everything. About you and Donaldson, about Callahan. About the conspiracy. One of your dogs told me.' He shoved the receiver into Todd's face, pressing the .44 against his head with the other hand. 'Say hello.'

'He *does* know,' Todd blurted. 'I ...'

Doyle pulled the receiver away from him.

'I just thought you'd like to know that when I've finished with Maguire I'm coming for you, you cunt.' Doyle slammed the receiver down. He shoved Todd out of the box. The agent began walking back towards the car. 'Wait,' Doyle told him. 'Is there anything else I should know?'

'I've told you everything, I swear,' Todd insisted, a note of fear in his voice.

'Everything?' Doyle repeated.

'I swear it.'

Doyle shot him twice, the massive impact of the bullets blasting holes in him large enough for a man to get two fists into. The counter-terrorist walked back to the car and slid into the passenger seat, holstering the Bulldog.

'Why did you kill him?' Georgie wanted to know. 'He told you what you wanted to know.'

Doyle dabbed at his injured shoulder and winced slightly.

'That's right,' he said. 'He had nothing more to tell me. I didn't need him any more. Come on, let's go, I want to talk to Callahan.'

'Are you going to kill *him*, too?' she wanted to know.

Doyle continued looking straight ahead.

'Eventually.'

Eighty-Four

'Drive on.'

Doyle spotted the Garda car parked at the entrance to Callahan's estate, and two uniformed men standing beside it. They glanced impassively at the Mazda as it passed, Georgie swinging it around a corner out of sight.

'Keep going,' Doyle told her.

'I told you it'd be swarming with police,' she said.

'We've still got to get inside,' he murmured, stroking his chin and glancing at the high stone wall which rimmed the estate grounds. About two hundred yards further on he told her to pull up. She stopped the car and switched off the engine.

'And if we do get in? What then?' Georgie wanted to know.

'Come on,' Doyle said, clambering out of the car. He crossed to the wall and stood beside it, locking his fingers together to form a stirrup into which Georgie put one foot. Doyle steadied himself then lifted, giving her the added momentum to reach the top of the wall. She got a grip and held on, looking down at him.

'Are the grounds clear?' he wanted to know.

Georgie looked around. It was difficult to see in the blackness. Trees grew thickly over most of the estate. They would mask their approach.

'It looks safe,' she told him. 'How the hell are you going to climb this bloody wall with an injured shoulder?'

Doyle didn't answer. He took a couple of paces back then ran at the wall, launching himself and hooking his fingers onto the stonework. He gritted his teeth and pulled himself up inch by inch until he reached the top. Georgie grabbed one of his legs to aid him in the final surge. He lay panting for a moment, massaging the wound. It had started bleeding again. Georgie pushed a handkerchief towards him and he stuffed it inside his sweatshirt, pressing it against the wound.

'The bullet went straight through,' he told her. 'It would have been worse if it'd chipped the bone.'

They sat on the wall for a moment, contemplating the drop. Perhaps twelve feet, Doyle thought.

He went first, landing well, rolling over in the damp grass, cursing when he caught his shoulder on a fallen tree stump. He straightened up and urged Georgie to join him. She too jumped and Doyle helped her to her feet, brushing a dead leaf from her hair.

'You ok?' he asked quietly.

She smiled at him and nodded.

They set off towards the house.

The driver of the lorry saw the Garda car blocking the entrance to the estate and slowed down. Behind him, the driver of the Mercedes saw his brake lights flare and followed suit.

Callahan stuck his head out of the rear window to see what was happening. He saw the Garda officer approach the lorry and talk to the driver.

'Officer,' the Englishman called. The uniformed man made his way over to the Mercedes. 'What's happening?'

'Are you Mr David Callahan?' the man asked.

The Englishman nodded.

The officer began explaining what had happened as best he could, using as much tact as he could muster. Well, he thought, how can you *delicately* tell a man that his house has been shot up and his wife kidnapped? Callahan demanded to be let through. The car blocking the way reversed and the Mercedes and truck passed onto the estate, the car speeding past the larger vehicle as Callahan urged the driver to hurry.

From the trees Georgie heard the sound of roaring engines and squinted through the gloom to see headlamps piercing the night. She nudged Doyle and pointed to the speeding car.

'I think Mr Callahan is home,' he said softly, a slight smile on his face. 'I hope he's still in the mood for entertaining.' They pressed on, close to the house now but still hidden from its approaches by the trees.

They saw the Mercedes pull up outside the main door. Callahan leapt from the vehicle and ran inside.

He slowed his pace as he passed the bullet-riddled entryway, his heart thudding hard against his ribs. In the hall there were more bullet holes. There was blood on the carpet, pieces of shattered porcelain and blasted brick. Motes of dust still swirled in the air from portions of plaster blown away from the walls and ceiling. Callahan rushed upstairs, his passage halted halfway by the appearance of a Garda sergeant. The man was broad, his hands like ham-hocks. He carried a radio in one of them.

'Where's my wife?' Callahan demanded, his face pale.

'We don't know that yet, sir,' said the sergeant, still descending.

'Who took her?'

'We don't know that, either. We spoke to your

servants but they didn't see much; they were too frightened. I can't say I blame them. We've got them in town now, in a hotel. They didn't want to stay here. If I were you I'd leave, too. Just for tonight. Give us time to go over the place …'

'I'm staying,' Callahan said, interrupting the man. 'I want you and your men out of here now.'

The sergeant opened his mouth to say something but Callahan raised a hand to stop him. 'Just leave me, please,' he said wearily. The sergeant nodded reluctantly and wandered downstairs, talking into his radio. Other Garda men emerged from other rooms below and waited in the hall.

'We've been ordered to keep up a guard on the house, sir,' he called from the bottom of the stairs. 'If you need anything my men will be nearby.'

Callahan nodded and watched as they filed out, closing the bullet-riddled front door behind them. The house suddenly seemed very quiet. He gripped the banister and looked over into the hall.

At the blood stain on the carpet.

He walked into their bedroom, where some of Laura's clothes were draped over the back of a chair. Callahan picked up her blouse and held it to his face, inhaling her scent. He closed his eyes, his teeth gritted. He murmured her name and replaced the blouse gently. Crossing to the drinks cabinet in the bedroom he poured himself a large whiskey and downed it in one. The liquid burned his stomach. He sucked in a deep breath, eyes closed again, hand tightening around the glass. Suddenly, with a shout of rage and frustration, he threw the glass across the room. It hit the far wall and shattered, crystal spraying in all directions.

'Not part of the plan, was it?'

367

The voice startled him. He spun round to see Doyle standing in the bedroom doorway, Georgie close behind him.

Callahan could see blood on the counter-terrorist's shoulder. He took a step towards the bedside cabinet.

If he could reach the .38 in there, perhaps take them by surprise ...

'You shouldn't have double-crossed your Irish friend,' said Doyle, a smile on his lips. 'This wasn't part of the deal, was it?'

'How did you get in?' Callahan asked, edging closer to the cabinet.

'I told you we'd be back,' Doyle said flatly, glancing across at the cabinet. 'If you've got a gun in there,' he nodded towards it, 'I'd forget about trying to get hold of it.' He pulled the .44 free of its holster and pointed it at the millionaire.

Callahan shrugged and sat down on the edge of the bed, head bowed.

'How do you know?' he asked wearily.

'That's not important. What does matter is that we *do* know. Everything. Your involvement with Maguire, with Westley and Donaldson. The pay-off to the IRA. About the only thing we don't know is what time you have a shit in the mornings.'

'We were here when Maguire took your wife,' Georgie told him.

'Did they hurt her?'

'I don't know, but they seemed pretty keen on hurting *us*.'

'Help me,' Callahan said. 'Help me get her back. I'll pay you as much as you want. You know I've got money.'

Doyle shook his head.

368

'I don't think Maguire would be very happy to hear you trying to make a deal with us, Callahan.' He glared at the millionaire. 'Besides, not everyone can be bought.'

'So there is some morality inside you, is there, Doyle?' the millionaire said, smiling bitterly.

'I couldn't give a fuck if they slice up your old lady and send her back piece by piece. I want Maguire for my own reasons and I'm going to get him. If you want your wife back you might be able to help.'

It was then that the phone rang.

Once. Twice. Three times.

Callahan looked at it dumbly, then picked it up.

'Hello,' he said, his throat dry.

'Callahan.'

He recognised the voice immediately, jabbed a button and switched the call to speaker-phone.

James Maguire's voice filled the room.

'We have your wife, Callahan. Think about it. I'll call back in an hour.'

And he hung up.

Eighty-Five

She slowed the car down when she saw the Garda vehicles parked across the entrance to Callahan's estate. As Catherine Roberts drew closer one of the uniformed men approached the car and signalled for her to wind down the window.

He asked for some I.D.

369

She produced a driving licence which he pored over like a valuable antique, looking at her occasionally as if the name on the licence was suddenly going to transform itself into a photo to verify the truth of her identity. Handing the licence back he asked why she was at Callahan's place.

'I've got some business with Mr Callahan,' she said. 'He *is* expecting me.'

The officer wanted to know what kind of business.

'I work for him,' she said, glancing around furtively.

Did Callahan always have this kind of security?

He told her she couldn't go through.

'It's important,' she insisted. 'I have to see Mr Callahan. If you let him know I'm here ...'

The officer cut her short, telling her that the estate was sealed off, no one was to enter.

'Please just call him, let him know I'm here. He'll see me, I'm telling you.'

The officer looked at her for a moment, then pulled the two-way from his belt and flicked a switch. Catherine watched and listened as he contacted one of his colleagues. He gave the other man her name and waited. He told Catherine she would have to wait while the officer inside the grounds checked with Callahan himself.

Another officer wandered over and asked her to open her boot.

'What for?' she demanded.

Security check, she was informed.

Reluctantly she got out of the car and did as she was instructed, waiting impatiently as the Garda officer rummaged around inside. Satisfied that there was nothing offensive he slammed the lid down and wandered around to the front of the car.

'What now?' she said irritably. 'Do you want to check under the bonnet too?'

He did.

'For Christ's sake,' Catherine snapped. 'What's going on here? Just let me through, will you?'

Neither of the Garda officers spoke. The one at the front of the car merely stood waiting for Cath to release the bonnet. Then he began peering inside that, too, shining his torch over the engine.

'Does Mr Callahan know I'm here yet?' she asked angrily.

The officer could only shrug.

She continued to wait.

Georgie dabbed gently at the last smears of congealed blood around the wound in Doyle's shoulder and dropped the cotton wool into the sink.

He had been lucky. The bullet had passed straight through without damaging either bone or nerves. It ached, and the area around the wound stung like hell, but apart from that he had little discomfort. The hole, large enough to push the tip of an index finger into, was already beginning to close up. Georgie pressed a gauze pad to it and began bandaging, her eyes drawn again to the maze of scars on Doyle's torso. He caught sight of her looking in the mirror but said nothing.

'Do you think they'll kill her?' asked Georgie, continuing with the bandaging. 'Laura Callahan? Do you think Maguire will kill her?'

'I wouldn't doubt it,' Doyle answered. 'But not yet. If they'd wanted her dead they'd have shot her when they first broke in here. Maguire wants something, that's obvious.' The counter-terrorist glanced at his watch.

'Another twenty minutes before he rings back. *If* he keeps his word.'

Georgie finished bandaging the wound and tied a neat bow in the dressing. Doyle reached for his sweatshirt.

As he did so, Callahan walked into the bathroom. He saw the patchwork of scars on the other man's body and winced. Doyle caught his reaction in the mirror but ignored it, slipping his sweatshirt back on.

'Keep out of the way,' Callahan told them. 'There's a policeman at the door. I don't think the Garda would appreciate it if they knew you were in here.'

'What does he want?' Doyle asked.

'He says there's someone to see me. I've been expecting her.'

'Do they know that Maguire phoned here?' asked Doyle.

Callahan shook his head.

'Not yet.'

'Don't tell them.'

'They might be able to get her back,' snapped Callahan, 'which is more than you're doing.'

'Ok, tell them. But if you do, I can guarantee your wife will be dead within the hour. The Garda will go thumping all over the countryside looking for her. If Maguire thinks you notified them he'll kill her.'

'How can you be sure he won't kill her anyway?'

'I can't,' said Doyle flatly.

'Who's the woman who's come to see you?' Georgie enquired.

'She's doing some work for me,' Callahan said sharply. 'Now, like I said, keep out of the way until I tell you it's clear.'

Doyle watched as the millionaire left, then touched

his bandaged shoulder lightly, satisfied with the dressing. He looked at Georgie and smiled.

For a second she thought she saw some warmth in the gesture but it quickly faded.

She could go up to the house.

The first officer told Cath that she had been cleared. She muttered something under her breath, started the engine and drove through the gates to the estate, past the two vehicles parked on either side.

The long driveway was rutted in places and the car bumped unceremoniously over it. When she finally came within sight of the house she had time to be impressed by its size and appearance before she brought her car to a halt. There was another Garda car parked about a hundred yards to her right, the men inside watching her as she walked across to the front door of the building and knocked. She was slightly perturbed by the bullet-holes in the wood.

The door was opened a moment later by Callahan, who ushered her in.

Pleasantries were exchanged briefly, then he led her through into the sitting-room and poured them both a drink.

'I have the window here,' he said. 'It's in a room in the West Wing.' He sipped his drink. 'You can begin work on it as soon as you like.'

'I don't need to,' she said. 'I didn't come here to continue work. I came here to warn you about the window.'

Callahan frowned.

'There is a treasure connected with it,' she told him. 'But the treasure is guarded.'

Callahan looked vague.

373

'What are you talking about?' he said irritably.

'Do you remember the figure on the window, the large figure in the centre of it?'

He nodded.

'*That* is the guardian: a demon called Baron. Gilles de Rais worshipped it. That's why he had the window constructed in the first place, to honour it and to thank it for giving him the secret he wanted so badly. I worked out that the panels of the window hold that secret.'

'Do you know how to release it?' Callahan demanded.

Cath looked at him incredulously.

'This creature, this force, whatever you want to call it, would be unstoppable if it was released now.'

'What is the secret that it guards?'

'Immortality,' she said flatly.

Eighty-Six

The silence seemed interminable.

Callahan stood in the centre of the room looking towards one window while Cath stared at him. It was as if neither wanted to disturb the stillness. Finally Callahan spoke.

'Are you trying to tell me this creature can materialize?' he asked softly.

Cath nodded.

'The guardian will be released if a sacrifice is made,' she told him. 'The death of someone will release it. De

Rais used children.' She got to her feet. 'Mr Callahan, I never thought I'd say this but you must destroy that window.'

He laughed.

'Destroy it? I have no wish to destroy it.'

'If Baron *is* released, you can't hope to control him.'

'He will give the secret to whoever summons him, correct?'

'Yes, but –'

'Correct?'

'I told you, there has to be a sacrifice.'

He looked at his watch.

Maguire would be ringing in a few minutes with news about Laura.

Laura.

Callahan looked at the phone, willing it to ring.

They would kill Laura.

'Destroy that window,' Cath said forcefully.

Ring, you bastard.

'If you don't I will,' she threatened.

'You stay away from it,' snarled Callahan. 'I thought you wanted to know its secrets as much as I did.'

'I did, until I found out what they were.'

'You were obsessed with the window. Don't tell me you wouldn't want to witness the materialization of that creature; don't tell me you wouldn't want to learn from it,' he hissed. 'You've been to far more elaborate lengths than I have to protect it. You were the one who covered up a murder, not me.'

Cath glared at him.

'That was before I knew the truth,' she snarled. 'If I'd known then I'd have *helped* Channing destroy it.'

'But I told you, it *can't* be destroyed. It mustn't be.'

'So who are you going to kill? I told you there has to be a sacrifice.'

'*I'm* not going to kill anyone,' he said quietly.

Cath looked puzzled.

It was then that the phone rang.

Callahan looked at it for long moments, then took a step towards it.

Upstairs Doyle and Georgie looked at the phone by the bedside.

It rang. And rang.

'What the hell is he doing?' muttered Doyle.

Callahan finally picked up the receiver and pressed it to his ear.

'Yes. Who is it?' he said.

'You know fucking well who it is,' Maguire hissed. 'You've had an hour to think about it, to wonder what we're doing to her. Or what we *will* do to her. Now listen to me.'

Upstairs, Doyle carefully switched the phone to speaker. He and Georgie listened intently to the conversation, Georgie picking out not just the words that were exchanged but also the sounds in the background. She could hear a low rumbling growing steadily louder.

'I want one million pounds,' said Maguire. 'Paid within twenty-four hours. No interference from the law. I'll call you again to tell you where to leave the money.'

'I can't get hold of that sort of money in twenty-four hours,' said Callahan.

'Bollocks,' snapped Maguire. 'One million or I swear I'll cut her fucking head off myself and send it back to you.'

Callahan didn't answer.

'You shouldn't have crossed me, Callahan,' the Irishman snarled.

Georgie could here the rumbling in the background growing louder. It built to a crescendo then faded slowly away again.

'Twenty-four hours,' Maguire repeated, then slammed the phone down.

'What's going on?' asked Cath, bemused.

'The IRA have my wife,' he said quietly.

'Oh God, I'm sorry,' she said.

Callahan smiled thinly.

'It'll be all right,' he said. 'After all, sacrifices have to be made.' The smile broadened into a grin.

She understood.

'No,' Cath murmured, shaking her head. 'You can't do it.'

'For years my wife and I have searched for the ultimate thrill. The realization of that dream is here now; do you think my wife would deprive me of it?'

'You're going to let them kill her,' Cath said, her voice a low whisper.

'It seems I have no choice. I can't get a million pounds together in the time they've given me.' He looked at her for a moment. 'There's nothing I can do.'

'You're insane,' she said, her voice catching.

'Insane to want knowledge? Insane to want a secret men have dreamt about since the beginning of time? Insane to want immortality?' He shook his head. 'I'd be insane *not* to want it.' He gripped her arm. 'Now come and show me what the window means.' He smiled. 'I need to know.'

Eighty-Seven

She could see nothing. The piece of tape across her eyes ensured that.

She couldn't speak because of the rolled-up length of cloth they had stuffed into her mouth, secured by a tightly-knotted cord which cut into the soft flesh of her neck. Her lip still throbbed where it had been split.

All Laura Callahan's senses could take in was the babble of voices close by, the smell of damp and the bare boards of the floor on which she sat, some of them mildewed. She jerked as she felt something scuttle across her bound hands. In the blindness of her captivity she imagined all kinds of things, all manner of noxious creatures crawling over her skin. Spiders. Cockroaches. Ants. She wanted to scream, then to ask them to remove the tape, to loosen the bonds cutting into her wrists. But she could not ask, could not beg, could not implore because of the gag which filled her mouth. It tasted stale, like an unwashed handkerchief; she realized with revulsion that was what it probably was. The thought caused her stomach to contract, and for a second she feared she would vomit. But would they remove the gag then or leave her to drown in her own puke? She had heard them threaten her with death and had no doubt they would carry out the threat if they were not given what they wanted. She felt like crying, but her fear prevented even that release of emotion.

378

She heard footsteps crossing the room towards her. Heavy footfalls which echoed on the bare boards. With her eyes covered she was able to pick out sounds much more clearly, just as she had done earlier with the train when it had passed by, its low rumble shaking the room. Now the footsteps came closer and she was aware of someone close to her. She could smell cigarette-tainted breath on her.

The tape which covered her eyes was torn away with one tug. The pain was startling. Portions of her eyebrows and some of her eyelashes were ripped away with the sticky covering. Again she wanted to scream, but again the gag prevented her.

A face leered into her own, hard-featured, cold-eyed.

The man's face was impassive.

'Take a look,' he said, holding the back of her head and ensuring she could see every detail of his features. 'If your husband doesn't pay what we asked for, I'll be the one who'll kill you,' Maguire said tonelessly. 'You probably didn't know much about his business, did you? Probably didn't know he sold us a batch of duff guns, did you?'

She tried to shake her head.

'Well, because of his stupidity, you could probably die,' the Irishman continued. 'I just hope he has more compassion than he has common sense.' He released her hair and stood up, motioning for Dolan to come over across and join him. As the younger man sauntered over, that ever-present grin on his lips, Laura looked around the room. It was about twelve feet long, perhaps ten feet across. There was a sink at one end and a small two-burner stove. A kettle stood on it now, steaming. She saw another man pouring the contents of the kettle into a tea pot. She could still not make out what the place was. There was a door to her left, firmly closed. She wondered if there were more men inside. She heard another rumbling sound. It approached quickly and passed.

A train. Just like before.

'Watch her,' said Maguire and wandered down to the far end of the room.

Dolan smiled down at her, his eyes fixed on the gap in her house-coat. He could see most of her left breast. His smile broadened. He leant forward, pulling the house-coat open a little more until both her breasts were visible. Then he cupped one in his right hand, feeling the warmth of the plump orb.

'Get your fucking hands off her.'

Maguire's voice lanced across the small room.

Dolan released his grip and stepped back, his grin fading rapidly.

'What do you think this is? A game?'

'Sorry, Jim,' the younger man murmured. 'But what the hell? She'll be dead soon.' The smile started to return.

'So will you if you don't keep away from her,' Maguire said. 'Now just watch her.'

Dolan nodded.

When he looked at Laura again, she was crying.

He knew it was nearly over now.

The hunt had taken them from Belfast deep into the Republic but they had never once lost the trail of their quarry and now they were closing in.

They had heard that there were two British agents on Maguire's tail too. To hell with them. They would die too if they got in the way. This was a personal thing

380

and it always had been. Outsiders had no place in it, just as they had no place in the country.

The car moved swiftly through the darkened country lanes, its four occupants sitting silently, three of them checking weapons. Pistols, rifles and sub-machine guns. They had used stealth to track down their opponents but now the time for cunning was over. Force was the next step. Pure, unbridled, unstoppable force. Force which would see the destruction of Maguire and his men and anyone else who got in the way.

The hunt was nearly over. The killing was about to begin.

Simon Peters and the other three men in the Provisional IRA unit rode in silence. There was no feeling of excitement or anticipation, merely the knowledge that they had a job to do.

And they intended completing it, no matter who got in the way.

Eighty-Eight

The room had been specially prepared for the window.

To the rear of the house it was about thirty feet long, and half that in width. Cath wondered if, at some time, it might have been a sitting room. Every stick of furniture had been removed, the carpets taken up and the floor covered with tarpaulin. There were marks on the walls, slight discolorations where pictures and paintings had once hung.

The window itself was in the centre of the room, propped up on three large and sturdy trestles about three feet high. There was a small work bench beside it. Callahan had certainly been thorough, thought Cath, as she walked into the room, the millionaire still holding onto her arm but with less force now.

In the glow of the overhead lights the window seemed to be lit by some inner radiance, its colours more vivid than she had ever seen them. Together they walked across to it, Callahan smiling down at the artefact as if he were greeting a long lost friend.

'It's magnificent,' he said quietly, a note of awe in his voice.

Cath's eyes flickered over details here and there. The heads of the children. The figures held in the taloned hands of Baron. And Baron himself. Those glass eyes seemed to bore into her, the deep red hue still reminding her of boiling blood.

'I want to know about it,' said Callahan. 'Everything.' He walked slowly around it, glancing up at Cath. 'Everything *you* know. I want you to tell me. What do the words mean?'

'Is it really important?' she snapped. 'I told you the secret of the window. I warned you of its danger.'

'You were willing to risk that danger, otherwise you wouldn't have kept working on it,' he told her. 'And don't tell me you're not as intrigued as I am to see the materialisation of this ... demon or whatever the hell it is.' He stood by the head of Baron, the red light from the eyes shining upwards, lighting his face with a hellish crimson glow. 'You're as obsessed with finding the truth as I am.'

'Not if it involves someone dying, I'm not,' she countered.

382

'Mark Channing died; that didn't stop you working, did it? That didn't sting your morals to the point where you abandoned the project.'

She heard the scorn in his voice and knew she had no defence.

'But I told you, Callahan, if this creature, this force does materialise, then there's no way of knowing what form it will take. Or, more to the point, how powerful it will be. It could destroy you, you and anyone else it comes across.'

'I'm willing to take that chance,' he said flatly, looking down at the multi-hued panels.

'What's this?'

Doyle's voice cut across the room and Callahan looked up to see him standing in the doorway, Georgie close by him.

Callahan smiled and performed the introductions with the calm formality of a cocktail party host.

'We heard the call from Maguire,' said Doyle. 'When are you going to pay?'

'I'm not,' Callahan said.

'He'll kill her. You should know him well enough by now to realize he's not fucking about. If you don't come up with that money your wife is dead meat.'

Callahan merely shrugged.

'What the fuck is wrong with you?' snapped Doyle. 'They're going to kill her, don't you understand that?'

'You must save her,' Cath interjected.

'Shut up,' snapped Callahan.

'Why is it so important to *you*?' Doyle wanted to know.

'It's not just me,' she told him. 'If Mrs Callahan is killed then her death will release the guardian of this window.'

383

Doyle smiled thinly.

'Guardian?' he said. 'What is this shit?'

'Something you'd never understand, Doyle,' Callahan told him. 'Something beyond your grasp, beyond your intellect.'

'Fuck you. Just tell me what this window has to do with what's going on here.'

'You're used to dealing with weapons, Doyle,' Callahan said. 'We both are. Look on this window as the ultimate weapon. It contains a power, a force unlike anything created by man.'

'You've been watching too many bad horror films, Callahan. You're talking like a fucking mad doctor. I'm not interested in all this voodoo bullshit or whatever the fuck it is.'

'Then leave,' said Callahan. 'Go now.'

'You must find Mrs Callahan,' Cath said. 'Save her. If she dies ...' She allowed the sentence to trail off.

'I'm getting sick of these games,' Doyle rasped. 'And I'm sick of you, Callahan. Start making sense.'

'What kind of force?' Georgie asked.

'Don't *you* start,' Doyle snapped irritably. 'I've got enough with fucking Boris Karloff here.' He nodded in Callahan's direction. 'You want her back, we'll get her back, but I can't guarantee she'll be alive.'

'She *has* to be,' snapped Cath.

'The sounds in the background when the phone calls were made,' said Georgie. 'It sounded like trains. Are there any stations near here?'

'There's a signal box,' said Doyle. 'About twelve miles East, close to the village. The IRA used to keep arms or money there. I tracked a couple of their men to it about five years ago.'

Georgie spun round, heading for the door.

384

'Stop there,' shouted Callahan.

He had pulled the .38 from his belt and now had it aimed at Georgie.

'Go,' Doyle urged her.

'I'll kill you all,' Callahan said, raising the pistol so that it was level with her head.

'The place is surrounded with Garda,' Doyle reminded him. 'One shot and they'd be in here quicker than flies round a fresh turd. You're fucked, Callahan. Give it up.'

'Take off your guns, both of you,' the millionaire said. 'Do it.' He watched as first Georgie then Doyle pulled off their holsters and laid them on the floor, the weapons still inside. 'Now move. Slowly. You too.' He motioned for Cath to follow them.

He forced them out into another narrow corridor and along towards a room further up, close to the hallway. One by one they filed in, then Callahan locked the door behind them.

The room was a study, the walls lined with books. There were just two windows, both small, both high up on the walls.

'You must get out,' Cath said. 'You must save her.'

'I'm going to kill that bastard when I get out of here,' snarled Doyle, punching the wood of the door.

'Didn't you hear what I said?' Cath shouted angrily.

'Look, we've got a job to do,' Doyle told her. 'You take care of your *demons*,' he emphasised the word with scorn. 'I'll take care of Callahan and the fucking IRA.'

'You don't understand, do you?' she said wearily.

Somewhere in the house a phone rang.

Callahan picked it up.

'Time's up,' James Maguire said. 'Here's how we want the money.'

'Fuck you, Maguire,' said Callahan.

'You really are a stupid man, aren't you? You think I won't kill her?'

'So kill her,' Callahan told him and slammed down the phone.

He smiled thinly, looking at the telephone as if waiting for it to ring again. Finally he swept it from the table, allowing it to smash on the floor.

He headed for the cellar.

Eighty-Nine

James Maguire slammed the phone down and stalked across the room to where Laura Callahan lay, still bound and gagged. He dropped to one knee, easing the Browning from its holster and pressing it against her face.

'Do you know what he said?' snarled Maguire, watched by his companions. He tore away the cord that held Laura's gag in place, allowing her to spit it out. She coughed.

'Do you know what your fucking old man said?' the IRA man snarled at her. 'He said he won't pay the ransom. He told me to kill you.'

She shook her head, tears of fear and bewilderment now filling her eyes.

'Why won't he pay?' Dolan demanded.

'How the fuck do I know?' rasped Maguire.

'Let me speak to him,' Laura implored, trying to twist her head away from the barrel of the pistol pressed tight against her neck.

'I'm sick of talking and I'm sick of your fucking husband,' Maguire snarled. 'First he fucks us up with that batch of guns and now this.'

'Kill *him*, not her,' Dolan said half-heartedly.

Maguire glared at him.

'I'm going to kill him, Billy, you can bet your life on that. But I said I'd kill her too if he didn't pay up, and that's just what I'm going to do.'

'Killing *her* won't solve anything. Let's get to Callahan now, make that bastard pay.'

Maguire smiled.

'Just because you've touched her doesn't mean you can have her, Billy,' he sneered.

'Let me speak to my husband,' Laura interjected. 'I can persuade him to pay you.'

'I don't want his fucking money now. I just want his life,' Maguire said quietly.

'If you're going to do it then get on with it, for God's sake,' shouted Damien Flynn. 'Shoot her.'

'No,' Billy Dolan interrupted. 'Leave her. It's Callahan we want.'

'You're going soft, Billy,' said Maguire, standing up. He took a pace backwards, thumbing back the hammer on the automatic.

Laura tried to scream but her throat and mouth were dry.

She could only shake her head as Maguire levelled the pistol. His finger tightened around the trigger.

'There's someone outside.'

The shout came from beyond the closed door, from Paul Maconnell.

For interminable seconds Maguire stood still, the Browning aimed at Laura's head, then he eased the hammer forward and re-holstered the gun, heading for the other door. As he reached it he turned to Dolan.

'You keep away from her,' he snapped. Then he passed through into what had once been the signalman's box. The levers which had once controlled the tracks were still there, now covered in a layer of dust and cobwebs. The huge glass front of the building offered a clear view over the flat countryside beyond. To the right there was a clump of trees. To the left the ground was flat and overgrown.

'I saw someone there,' said Maconnell, indicating the trees.

'Garda?' Maguire wanted to know.

Maconnell shook his head.

'No uniforms,' he said.

To the right another figure moved through the tall grass, appearing momentarily before disappearing once again like a spectre.

Maguire frowned.

Who the hell were they?

In the sub-cellar of the house David Callahan moved swiftly around the stacks of boxes, pulling out the weapons he required.

A Spas Automatic shotgun and some shells which he stuffed into his pocket.

An Ingram M-10 sub-machine gun. He selected half a dozen magazines to go with the weapon, each holding thirty-two rounds.

Callahan smiled to himself. He made his way back upstairs, straining under the weight of the weapons. He carried them to the top of the stairs and ensured that each one was loaded. From the landing he could cover all possible entrances to the hall. There was only one way to reach him and that was up the stairs.

He pushed cartridges into the magazines, thumbed bullets into the .38 and jammed it in his belt.

He was ready at last for the time he had known for so long was coming.

They were all in position.

The signal box was covered. There was no way out.

Simon Peters gripped the Uzi sub-machine gun tightly in his hand and glanced at his watch. Two hours before dawn. When this was over he would watch the sun rise.

Peters gave the order for his men to attack.

Ninety

Doyle took a firm grip on the bookcase and pulled, stepping aside as it crashed to the floor, spilling its contents everywhere. With help from Georgie and Cath he pushed it upright once more, so that it was close to one of the small windows in the study.

Georgie began to climb, using the shelves as rungs, until she finally reached the top and the window. Steadying herself, she kicked out at it, smashing the glass.

'Can you get through?' Doyle asked.

She knocked away some jagged shards which surrounded the frame, trying to work out if the gap was large enough for her to crawl through. She decided that it was.

'Take this,' said Doyle, pulling the .38 from the holster on his ankle. He handed it up to Georgie.

'They're hollow tips in there. They'll stop most things that get in your way.' He even managed a thin smile.

'What about you?' she asked. 'Callahan's armed.'

'I'll worry about Callahan. Just get a move on. Get to his wife,' he told her.

'My car is parked at the front of the house,' Cath told her. Georgie opened her fist, looking down at the keys to the BMW.

'If any of those bloody Garda try to stop you, shoot them,' Doyle said flatly.

He and Cath watched as Georgie gripped the side of the window-frame, wriggling through. The night air greeted her, cold on her face. There was a drop of about six feet to the ground. Looking round, she could see no signs of movement and reasoned that the room must be at the side of the house. Her problems would come when she got round to the front, but for now her only concern was to get out.

She hauled herself the last few inches, realizing that she was going to fall headfirst onto the ground. She was grateful that the house was flanked by lawns. Georgie gritted her teeth and dropped.

Even though the grass provided a relatively safe surface to land on, the impact still knocked the wind from her and she rolled over, groaning under her breath, feeling a sharp pain in one shoulder. She hauled herself upright and, pressing her back to the wall, made for the front of the house. Much to her dismay, it was brightly lit.

Two Garda cars were parked about one hundred yards from the building. She could see their occupants quite clearly.

Catherine Roberts' car was closer. Perhaps twenty yards.

A short sprint.

She gripped the keys in one hand and the .38 in the other, her eyes constantly scanning the front of the house. She watched as one of the Garda officers clambered out of his vehicle, looked around and hurried off towards a tall bush to relieve himself.

Ducking low, Georgie scuttled towards the BMW.

She reached it unseen, pushed the key into the lock and eased the door open, sliding behind the steering wheel. She put the key in the ignition and twisted it.

The engine burst into life first time and she stuck it in gear, reversing, swinging the car around so that it was facing the two Garda cars.

She stepped on the accelerator and the car shot forward, gravel flying up behind it. The BMW sped past the other two cars before their drivers could even start their engines. She saw them fading away behind her in the rear-view mirror. The needle of the speedometer touched sixty as she sped down the long driveway, not flicking on her headlamps until she saw the gates.

There were two cars parked across the exit, nose to nose.

Georgie gripped the steering wheel tighter, hunched over it and floored the accelerator.

She saw men struggling out of the cars as she bore down on them.

There was an almighty crash as she smashed through the makeshift barrier. The jolt slammed her back in her seat but she kept her foot down, only easing up as she reached the road, slamming on the brake to prevent the car hurtling into the ditch on the far side. She twisted the wheel, trying to keep the wheels on the tarmac. They screamed as they tried to retain a hold, smoke rising from the back pair. For one terrible second she thought she was going to turn over but the car held and she drove on.

No one followed.

Twelve miles to the signal box.

She pressed down on the gas again.

'I've got to destroy that window,' Catherine Roberts said.

'We've got to get out of here first,' Doyle reminded her. He glanced at her a moment. 'You really believe that shit about the window? This force, or power, whatever you call it?'

'It exists, Mr Doyle. It has done for hundreds, perhaps thousands of years.'

'Then what makes you think *you* can stop it?' he asked.

She had no answer.

Ninety-One

The first prolonged burst of fire from the Uzi blasted in the glass front of the signal box.

Shards flew into the room and bullets tore into the walls, some ricocheting wildly, screaming off the wood and concrete.

The attacker could only be seen by the blinding muzzle-flash which came from the weapon as he fired.

Maguire and Maconnell threw themselves down as the bullets shattered the windows and parted the air above them. Then Maguire, keeping low, headed for the other room, the Browning already free of its holster.

'What the fuck is happening?' snapped Damien Flynn as the staccato rattle of automatic fire filled the night.

'Someone's trying to kill us,' snarled Maguire. 'Cover that door,' he told Flynn, jabbing a finger. Flynn opened it a fraction, and immediately a hail of bullets shredded the wood, one of them catching him in the thigh. He fell to the floor clutching at the wound, relieved to see that the blood flow was relatively small. The bullet had missed his femoral artery. He cursed, recovered his own Skorpion machine-pistol and fired off several short bursts in the direction of the muzzle-flash. Spent cartridge cases flew into the air and soon the room was thick with the stench of cordite.

'Help Paul,' Maguire said, pushing Dolan towards the other room. The younger man hesitated a moment, then scuttled through to join his companion who was blasting back at the attackers with an MP5. Smoke was drifting in noxious clouds across the bullet-blasted windows.

'How many are there?' asked Dolan, forced to raise his voice to make himself heard above the incessant chatter of weapons.

Maconnell had no idea. It seemed as if there were hundreds out there. More bullets spattered the room, one catching him in the left forearm, shattering the ulna. The crack of the breaking bone was audible even above the rattle of fire. He fell back, a portion of the bone poking through the flesh. Gripping the sub-gun in one hand he stood up and fired a sustained burst, hoping to hit the one who had shot him, his anger overriding his common sense. He kept his finger tight on the trigger, the weapon bouncing in his grip as the savage recoil slammed it back against the heel of his hand. Wreathed in smoke, his face lit by the muzzle-flash, he looked like a creature from a nightmare. Then the hammer struck an empty chamber.

In that split second a bullet caught him in the right eye.

It drilled the socket empty, lifting him off his feet, smashing the sphenoid bone and erupting from the back of his head with a huge portion of pulverized cranium. Blood, brain and bone splattered the far wall as Maconnell went down, crashing into the wall, his face a bloody ruin, crimson gushing from the yawning hole where his eye had been. A dark stain spread rapidly across the front of his trousers as his bladder released its load and Dolan smelt the pungent odour of excrement. A soft spurt as the sphincter muscle gave out.

He scrabbled towards Maconnell, not attempting to touch the body. Why search for signs of life? Most of the poor fucker's head was plastered over the wall. Dolan grabbed the MP5 and slammed a fresh magazine into it, then crawled over to the shattered window, knelt up and began firing short bursts into the trees.

A dark shape moved and he fired at it, gratified to see it stumble and remain still. He fired at it again, a longer burst this time, rewarded by a cry of pain.

In the other room Maguire pulled Laura Callahan to her feet and pressed the gun to the side of her cheek, leaving a grease mark on her soft skin.

'Who are they?' he demanded. 'Are they from your husband?'

'I don't know,' she whimpered. 'Believe me. I swear to you, I don't know who they are.'

Maguire nodded slowly.

'You know something?' he said softly. 'I *do* believe you.'

And he shot her in the face.

Even Doyle felt it.

Inside Callahan's house it was as if the air had suddenly been charged with electricity. He felt the hairs on the back of his neck rise.

Catherine Roberts groaned and fell against the wall, one hand pressed to her head, her eyes closed.

Doyle spun round and saw her, aware that the air seemed to be cooling. He felt goose-pimples rising on his flesh. It was as if someone had sucked all the warmth from his body.

'What's wrong?' he asked Cath, snaking an arm around her waist to support her.

At first she mumbled, her eyes still closed, but then she blinked hard, as if she were emerging from a deep sleep. She looked directly at Doyle and he saw the fear flicker behind her eyes. She tried to suck in a deep breath but the chill in the room seared her throat as she inhaled.

'It's started,' she murmured.

Luke McCormick was dead. As he bent over his colleague, Simon Peters had no doubt of that fact. The other man was lying on his stomach, several large bullet holes in his back. One shot had caught him in the nape of the neck. That was the one which had killed him.

Peters scuttled across to the trees where Eamon Rice

crouched, the Uzi gripped tightly in his hands. He was peering up at the signal box, watching the occasional muzzle-flashes from inside.

'We've got to get inside,' said Peters. 'Where's Joe?'

'Round by the stairs,' said Rice, nodding towards the building.

Peters nodded.

'Give me two minutes, then open up on the window. Just keep firing. They've no way of knowing how many of us there are. It'll give Joe and myself a chance to get through that door.'

'Two minutes,' Rice repeated, checking his watch.

Peters disappeared into the darkness once again.

Georgie could hear the stutter of sub-machine guns, the crack of pistols and rifles. Their sounds carried far on the stillness of the early morning.

She tried to coax more speed from the car, praying that she wasn't too late.

As she drew closer the gunfire filled her ears more insistently.

She reached almost unconsciously to touch the butt of her .357.

The signal box was less than half a mile away now.

The gunfire continued.

Ninety-Two

The room was getting colder.

The chill was intensifying.

'We have to get out,' Cath said, her face as white as

milk. 'I must get to that window and destroy it. There has to be a way.'

Doyle glanced at the door which barred their way to freedom. He crossed to it, tugged on the handle, took a step backwards and kicked hard against the white panelled barrier. The wood creaked but held firm, even when he kicked again. And again.

He paused for a moment, perspiration beading on his forehead despite the growing cold. Then he directed his fury at the door handle itself, kicking furiously at it, cursing when it wouldn't give. There was a large glass paper-weight on the desk to his left. He snatched it up, pulled off his sweatshirt and wrapped the weight in it.

Cath winced as she saw the patchwork of scars on his torso, but Doyle did not see her look of distaste; he was more concerned with the door. He gripped the paper weight in both hands and brought it down on the handle with incredible ferocity. He maintained his hammer blows, the muscles in his arms and shoulders throbbing, the veins standing out.

'Come on, come on,' he snarled, driving the weight down with ever greater strength.

The handle started to come away from the wood.

Encouraged by his success Doyle struck again, his face set in an attitude of determination. He was oblivious to all around him as he battered away at the door.

His own frantic banging masked the sound of movement on the other side of the door.

One last blow.

The handle came free. The door opened a fraction. Doyle grinned crookedly and tossed the paperweight to one side, pulling his sweatshirt back on. He pulled open the door and dashed out.

397

He had to reach the room with the window, had to retrieve the .44 Bulldog.

Had to find Callahan.

Callahan was standing in the doorway of the room opposite, the Spas automatic shotgun levelled and ready.

Doyle saw it. Saw the yawning barrel.

Callahan fired once.

The discharge was massive, blasting a hole almost twelve inches across in the door as Doyle threw himself frantically to one side.

Callahan emerged from the room, working the slide, firing again.

The second shot blasted away some plaster from a wall above Doyle's head.

The counter-terrorist knew he hadn't much time. Eventually Callahan would get lucky and one of the massive blasts would strike him. He hurled himself at a door opposite and found to his relief that it was open. He crashed into it, rolling still, into the room beyond.

In the study behind him Cath pressed herself against the wall, praying that Callahan would not step in. It seemed he was more preoccupied with killing Doyle.

If she could find some way out ...

Doyle ran towards the window, leaping at the glass.

He met it as Callahan stepped inside, firing off two more blasts in quick succession.

One struck the window at the same instant as Doyle.

There was a deafening explosion of shattering glass as the counter-terrorist smashed through, pieces of the crystal cutting him as he landed heavily on the grass outside. He felt a searing pain in his left calf and realized that some of the shot from the Spas had hit him. As he stood up he saw blood on his jeans and a ragged hole in the material, but he gritted his teeth and scuttled along towards the window of the room at the rear of the house.

Where his gun lay.

Cath heard the shattering glass, heard the retorts of the shotgun and realized that Callahan must be pursuing Doyle.

She stepped out into the corridor.

Callahan moved back, swinging round to face her. For interminable seconds she froze.

Callahan was smiling.

Even when he fired.

The discharge hit her squarely in the chest, staving in her sternum, tearing through her lungs before portions of the lethal shot erupted from her back. She was lifted into the air by the impact and thrown several feet down the corridor as blood sprayed out from both entry and exit wounds. She landed heavily, dead even as she slumped against the wall, spilling her life fluid onto the carpet.

Callahan ran to her and looked down into her blank eyes. He stepped over the body and headed for the hall as he heard banging on the front door.

Someone shouted his name.

He heard the door being forced and scuttled up the stairs, picking up the Ingram, pulling back the slide to cock it. Then he stood at the foot of the stairs and waited.

The door burst inwards and two Garda officers careered into the hall.

Callahan cut them down with two bursts from the sub-gun. Outside he saw a third man turn and run back towards his car. The millionaire fired again, the weapon bucking in his hand, cartridge cases spraying from it. His burst was accurate. The Garda officer was hit in the back, pitching forward onto the gravel drive, where he lay still.

Doyle heard the shots too, but he paused for only a second before using a stone to smash his way into the room where the window lay. It was not, however, the ancient artefact which interested the counter terrorist, but the Charter Arms Bulldog that lay close to it. He snatched up the weapon, smiling as he felt its weight in his fist. He flipped open the cylinder and smiled as he saw that the chambers were full.

Glancing down at his injured leg he gritted his teeth.

'Now, Callahan,' he hissed under his breath, 'it's Party time.'

The Garda sergeant had seen his men shot down. The sight had shaken him badly but he snatched up his radio and flicked it on.

'I need reinforcements, quick,' he barked into the two-way. 'The Callahan house. Tell them to bring guns.'

Ninety-Three

Ten seconds.

Eamon Rice checked the second hand on his watch, counting off the moments, steadying himself.

Eight seconds.

He checked that he had enough spare clips of ammunition.

Six seconds.

The firing from inside the signal box had all but ceased now; there was just the odd single shot every now and then. Both sides, it seemed, were waiting.

Four seconds.

He raised himself up slightly, ready to fire.

Three.

He hoped that Hagen and Peters were in position.

Two. One.

He opened up, bullets drilling a path across the front of the signal box, blasting in yet more pieces of glass that had somehow stayed untouched.

On the other side of the box Simon Peters made a dash for the bottom of the wooden stairs which led up to the first level. He could see the shape behind the door; he swung the Uzi up and fired off a long burst. Bullets struck the door and the frame.

He heard a scream from inside, knew that the man who'd been guarding the door had been hit.

He motioned Hagen forward and the other man scuttled up the steps, pausing at the top, the MP5 levelled at the door.

Inside, James Maguire stood looking down at the body of Damien Flynn. Two bullets had penetrated his chest and the third had punched a hole in his throat, shattering his larynx. There was surprisingly little blood. Flynn lay on his back, his eyes still open, flecks of dust settling on the blank orbs. Maguire gripped his own pistol in one hand, the Skorpion machine pistol in the other. He waited.

'Come on, you bastards,' he shouted, raising his voice to make himself heard above the chatter of sub-gun fire behind him. Billy Dolan fell into the room, his face sheathed in sweat, the sub-gun empty in his hand.

'They're moving in, Jim,' he gasped.

Maguire didn't answer; he had his eyes fixed on the door.

It burst open.

There was a deafening explosion of fire as bullets from automatic weapons tore back and forth in the small room. Cartridge cases clattered onto the floor, the smell of cordite filled the air and a reeking bluish-grey haze of fumes billowed upwards as the firing continued.

Dolan was hit in the chest and shoulder.

Maguire took one in the stomach but remained upright, oblivious to the pain spreading through his lower body. Blood ran down his shirt and the front of his trousers.

As Hagen crashed through the door the bullet from a 9mm pistol hit him in the cheek, ripped through and exited on the other side, carrying several teeth with it. He went down firing, raking the inside of the signal box, putting two more shots into Dolan. One of which caved in the left side of his head.

Simon Peters was hit in the leg, his knee shattered by the impact. He fell forward, his finger still on the trigger. He saw bullets strike Maguire in the chest and upper arm, saw him stagger back as another smashed his right collar-bone. Blood was gushing from the wounds. He felt his own lung collapse as a bullet pierced it, erupting from his back with pink gobbets of lung tissue. It was as if someone had applied a very tight tourniquet to his chest. He found it difficult to breathe.

Dolan was lying on his side, twitching madly, a purple foam dribbling over his lips as more bullets hit him. He finally rolled onto his back, slops of brain spilling from the massive holes in his skull.

402

Maguire managed to move into the other room, trailing blood and urine behind him. He could scarcely breathe and it felt as if his upper body was on fire, but he slammed a fresh magazine into the Skorpian and waited. Framed against the blown-out windows of the signal box, his silhouette quite visible, he didn't even see Eamon Rice drawing a bead on him.

'Come on, Peters,' he gasped, waiting for his foe. 'We'll fucking go together.' He chuckled, blood spilling over his lips.

Rice opened up.

Half a dozen bullets from the burst hit Maguire, catapulting him across the room and slamming him into the far wall, where he seemed to remain standing for long moments before sliding down leaving a huge crimson smear.

The Skorpion was still in his hand.

Peters dragged himself into the other room, past the bodies of Laura Callahan and Billy Dolan. He saw Maguire lying there and nodded slowly.

Behind him Hagen coughed, his mouth hanging open slackly, blood from his punctured cheeks and shattered jaw running in a steady torrent from his mouth. Peters tried to suck in a breath and felt cold air hiss through the lung wound. He winced and clapped one hand to it, gritting his teeth against the pain, raising himself up with great difficulty. He looked down at the corpse of his adversary, then back at Laura. Peters shook his head and dug the toe of his shoe into Maguire.

'Animal,' he murmured, then closed his eyes as a wave of pain swept through him. For a second he thought he was going to collapse but the feeling passed. He turned to look at Hagen.

He was unconscious.

'Eamon,' Peters called, the effort making him wince. 'It's finished.'

Outside, Eamon Rice lowered the Uzi and took a step forward.

All he heard was the click of a hammer being pulled back as a gun was pressed to the back of his head.

'Drop the gun,' Georgie told him.

He did as he was told.

'Who the fuck are you?' Rice asked, puzzled that the voice was not only English but also female.

'British agent,' she told him. 'Was that Maguire and his men in there?'

'It *was*,' said Rice.

'Go on,' Georgie snapped, pushing him before her. He led the way to the stairs and ascended slowly, the agent behind him.

'Company, Simon,' he called as they reached the door.

Georgie pushed him inside and looked in at the carnage. She saw Laura Callahan immediately, her face blasted away by the close range discharge which had ended her life.

'We knew you were coming,' said Peters quietly.

'Who killed the woman?' Georgie asked.

'She was dead when we got here,' wheezed Peters. 'You wanted Maguire, didn't you?'

She nodded.

He smiled thinly, a ribbon of blood running from the corner of his mouth.

'It was none of your business,' he told her. 'Never was. We take care of our own.'

'So I see,' she said quietly.

'It's over,' Peters told her.

Georgie looked at the wounded IRA man, at the bodies.

At Laura Callahan.

Over? As she ran back to her car she had but one thought.

She had the most terrible feeling it had barely started.

Thirty of them.

All armed with AR-180 Sterling semi-automatic rifles.

Ten in each van.

The Garda men were briefed as they drew closer to David Callahan's house.

No one was to enter. No one was to leave. Several armed and dangerous suspects were believed to be inside the house. If they couldn't be taken alive they were to be shot dead.

Ninety-Four

The room looked as though it were full of smoke. Great thick bands of it swirled around the window, writhing along the ground like ethereal tendrils, poking beneath the door and reaching towards the window, stirred by the breeze that swept into the room.

Yet through that grey mist there was a radiance, a glow which seemed to build in intensity until the window itself shone. The room was dark; the glass of the window might have been sucking in the light, digesting it like some living thing then disgorging its feast in the form of brilliant-coloured hues.

The trestles that held it in place creaked and groaned, as if the weight of the window had suddenly become too much for them. The wood bowed and split, threatened to collapse.

And still the greyish-white vapour poured out of the very glass itself.

The colours grew more vivid within the heart of the cloud.

A low rumble began, growing in volume.

A chill so intense it left frost on the walls shivered through the entire house.

Then came another sound.

Like that of cracking glass.

Doyle moved from room to room, the .44 held before him, his ears and eyes alert for the slightest sound or movement.

Just step out in front of me, you fucker.

He reached the door which led through to the hallway.

Lying up against it, a gaping hole in her chest, was Catherine Roberts. Doyle gritted his teeth and looked around quickly, checking that Callahan wasn't skulking in either of the rooms to his left or right. Satisfied that it was safe he knelt beside Cath, resisting the temptation to feel for a pulse. The Spas had been lethally effective. The portions of her lungs and spine that still stuck to the wall testified to that fact.

He moved closer to the door, peering through a crack up towards the landing.

There was no sign of Callahan.

Just because you can't see him doesn't mean he's not there.

The counter-terrorist opened the door a fraction, his thumb on the hammer of the Bulldog, ready to cock it. With a fourteen-pound pull on the double-action trigger he couldn't risk the massive recoil, couldn't risk missing Callahan.

He might only get one chance.

Still, he comforted himself, one was all he'd need. If he hit Callahan with one of the Glaser safety slugs there was no fear of him getting up.

He edged forward a little, ducking low, seeing that he had a distance of about twenty feet to cross before he reached the door on the opposite side of the hallway.

As he looked across he saw the bodies of the two Garda officers leaking blood onto the expensive carpet.

Why the fuck had Callahan killed them, too?

Doyle shuddered involuntarily, aware of the biting cold now. He had to cross the hall, had to search the rest of the house in order to find Callahan. But the place was huge. It could take an age.

Unless he finds you first.

Doyle glanced up at the landing again and down at his own injured leg. The wound was throbbing but it didn't hamper his movement. He sucked in a deep breath and pushed the door a little more.

Come on, you can't stand here till daylight.

He ran as fast as his injured leg would allow across the hall, hurdling one of the dead Garda officers.

No shots were fired.

There was no sign of Callahan.

Doyle pushed open the door and stepped back, waiting for the blast of gunfire; it never came. The corridor beyond was in darkness. How many rooms lay hidden in that darkness he could only guess at.

Only one way to find out.

He pressed on, aware now that the cold was becoming almost unbearable.

Callahan had watched the counter-terrorist rush across the hall.

He'd had him in the sights of the HK33 the entire time. How tempting it would have been to have pulled the trigger, but a moving target was always more difficult and Doyle was a dangerous man. A head shot would have been preferable but difficult. Better to let him pass. He waited a moment, then picked up the assault rifle and began to make his way down the stairs, slowly and cautiously.

When he reached the bottom he raised the rifle to his shoulder and sighted it on the door through which Doyle had disappeared. The counter-terrorist didn't appear and Callahan moved stealthily across the hall.

He smiled to himself.

By the time Doyle found him it would be too late.

Much too late.

He also felt the numbing cold but he, unlike Doyle, welcomed it. He knew what it signified.

Ninety-Five

She guessed she was less than three miles from the house now.

Georgie kept her foot on the accelerator, her eyes fixed on the road. Another few minutes and she would be at Callahan's place again. She felt a shiver run up her spine. What would she find when she returned? She tried to push the thought from her mind, suddenly overcome with a feeling of great sadness as she thought of Laura Callahan lying back there, half her head blown away. Georgie felt a crushing weariness; there suddenly seemed to be a ridiculous futility to everything. To her mission with Doyle; to this whole business. It seemed there was only one way for it to end and that was in death.

She sucked in a deep breath, clutching the wheel more tightly, feeling the .357 in its shoulder holster against her ribs.

How many more deaths before this affair was concluded?

She swung the car round a corner and onto the road which led to the main entrance of Callahan's estate.

As she rounded the corner she saw the large black transit vans parked close to the gates. There were men clambering out of them.

She saw that they carried rifles.

For one fleeting second her thoughts turned to Doyle.

Let him be alive.

The thought passed as quickly as it had come. Her attention was re-focused on the men who climbed from the vans. There were three of them parked outside the entrance, but as she watched two drove on and into the grounds, heading for the house.

What the hell was happening in there?

She had to know.

First she had to get past the riflemen.

The leading van hurtled up the long drive towards David Callahan's house, its occupants sitting quiely in the back, automatic rifles clutched across their laps.

One or two were checking that the magazines were full, the others waited patiently until the vans came to a halt and they were ordered out. The chill night air met them like a cold wall.

It was unnaturally cold, a deep biting crispness that caused the hairs on their flesh to rise.

They were deployed in the bushes around the house, behind the cars. Anywhere that offered adequate cover.

The marksmen waited for orders.

The house was in darkness except for the porch light. It glowed feebly, the dull glow illuminating the body of their dead colleague sprawled on the gravel in front of the building.

When the time came, if necessary, they would storm the house. All they needed now was the order.

They waited.

A door up ahead.

Doyle pressed his back to the wall and moved towards it, treading as softly as he could, his eyes constantly darting to and fro in the blackness. He held the .44 in his right hand and reached for the handle with his left. He turned it and pushed. The door swung open. He ducked low and stepped across the threshold.

The kitchen.

He glanced around but there was no sign of Callahan. No sign that he'd been in here recently, either. Doyle backed out of the room, shivering now from the intense cold. He blew on his hands, transferred the Bulldog to his left hand and rubbed the palm of his right against his thigh in an effort to restore circulation. *Christ, it was cold.* He moved across the corridor to another door, paused and then pushed that one open too.

Again the room beyond was empty, but as Doyle

410

moved into it he glanced out of the large picture window and saw movement outside. Keeping low, he scuttled across the room towards the window and looked out.

Two Garda officers were taking up firing positions in the shelter of some trees about two hundred yards from the house.

Glancing round he saw more of them, all with rifles trained on the house.

'Shit,' he murmured under his breath and moved away from the window, edging back into the corridor, making his way back towards the hall.

He would have to search for Callahan upstairs. As he paused at the hall door he saw the risks. To ascend that staircase was to invite death. There was no cover, should Callahan be waiting at the top. If he opened fire there was nowhere to hide. And yet how else could he reach the first floor?

Doyle pushed open the door a fraction, peering up at the gloom of the landing. Even if Callahan was up there now he was invisible in the darkness.

Garda outside, Callahan inside.

This was going to be one hell of a fucking party.

Doyle edged out into the hall, not even looking at the dead Garda officers. He moved to the foot of the stairs, the Bulldog held before him in readiness. No sounds from above.

He began to ascend.

Callahan stood mesmerised, the vapour swirling around him. He held the HK-33 at his side, his attention focused on the stained-glass window, on the brilliant radiance that emanated from it. The walls of the room were thick with ice now, layers of it gathering and clinging as the vapour continued to roll across the floor like fog. There was a smell which reminded Callahan of bad meat; like the cold, it was growing more intense.

He took a step towards the window, watching the tendrils of mist snaking upward towards the ceiling, watching the multi-hued effulgence swelling as if it were being pumped up, throbbing like some rainbow-coloured growth.

The crack of breaking glass was like a whiplash in the silence of the room. It made him jump; his heart thudded against his ribs.

Another crack, louder this time.

A portion of the glass seemed to fly upwards, as if from an impact beneath it. But that could not be so; the window was suspended on trestles, there was nothing beneath it. But Callahan watched the piece of glass rise into the air in slow motion, twist in the mist and fall to the ground, where it lay in small fragments.

A series of cracks. Low rumbling.

Callahan's teeth were chattering, so intense was the cold. He kept his eyes fixed on the window, eyes which were bulging not only in wonder and exhilaration but in fear.

Ninety-Six

She saw the two officers waving for her to stop.

Two of the marksmen were close by, rifles held across their chests, ready to swing them up into a firing position if necessary.

Take it easy.

A hundred yards from the main entrance Georgie slowed down. She could feel her own heart beating hard as she drew closer, could hear her own breathing, rapid and harsh.

Drive through them.

She tapped her fingers on the wheel as she guided the car nearer.

Get closer.

Fifty yards now. She had slowed to a crawl but her foot was poised over the gas pedal. It was just a matter of timing. She had to get through. Had to reach the house. The first Garda officer was still motioning for her to slow down, to stop now. Get out of the car.

Twenty yards.

The gap between the vehicles parked across the entrance was just about wide enough.

Georgie gripped the wheel tightly and glanced at the marksmen. The officer called to her to stop the car and get out.

Ten yards.

She sucked in a deep breath and held it, teeth gritted.

She pressed down hard on the accelerator and the car hurtled forward, dirt spinning up behind it. It slammed into the Garda officer, catapulting him into the air. His colleague dived to one side as she sped towards the cars which blocked the entrance to Callahan's estate. She crashed through them, the impact throwing her back in her seat. The BMW skidded but she gained control of the wheel, glancing in the rear-view mirror. She saw three of the marksmen taking aim. Seconds later bullets began to hit the car.

Georgie put her foot down as the first of them blasted off a wing mirror.

413

The second punched a hole through the rear windscreen, glass showering the back seat. More 7.62mm slugs tore into the fleeing vehicle, one blasting a hole in the dashboard, destroying the speedometer. Another took out part of the windscreen.

Georgie drove faster, anxious to escape the deadly salvo but it continued unabated, bullets striking the car, others ricocheting around it, blasting up small geysers of earth when they struck the ground.

She felt an incredible impact in her back, just below the right scapula. It was as if someone had struck her with a massive red-hot hammer. The contact slammed her forward against the steering wheel. For a second she let go of it, one hand clapped to the huge exit wound in her chest. The bullet had punctured a lung and shattered several ribs before blasting its way out through her right breast. Portions of flesh and slicks of blood spattered the wheel. She gasped in pain.

Another thunderous impact, this time in the small of her back.

She saw dark blood spurting onto the seat, realized that the shot had destroyed part of her liver. Georgie tasted blood in her mouth. It felt as if the lower part of her body was on fire. She gripped the wheel as tightly as she could, foot still pressed down hard on the accelerator. The house was coming into view and so too were the other Garda officers. Red-hot pain filled her body, as if someone had pumped molten metal into her veins. She found it hard to breathe now. Her eyes clouded alarmingly and she blinked hard to clear her vision.

Ahead of her were more men with rifles.

The house was coming up fast.

Blood ran from her wounds, pain filled her body.

Several shots struck the front of the car, one smashing in the radiator grille. Another blew out a headlamp. More smashed the windscreen. Georgie felt one nick her left ear, slicing off the lobe. More blood. She felt it splash her cheek.

She guided the car towards the windows of the sitting-room and clung on, cold air blasting through the remains of the windscreen keeping her conscious, although it was a battle she knew she must lose.

The harsh crack of more rifles filled the air.

She was hit again. In the shoulder. In the chest.

With a despairing wail she let go of the wheel, slumping forward as the car sped towards the house, her foot now jammed on the accelerator.

Her last thought was of Doyle.

Then the car hit the side of the house.

Georgie was flung through the remains of the windscreen, through the window of the sitting-room as the BMW simply folded up against the wall, the metal buckling and bending until the impact ignited the petrol tank. There was a thunderous blast as the car went up in a blinding white ball of flame, the heat sending a rolling blanket fully fifty feet back, making the Garda men shelter momentarily as the wreckage flamed and great clouds of black smoke belched from the ruins. They stood back and watched as the twisted chassis turned white hot beneath the searing flames.

The order came across the radios the Garda carried.

'*Prepare to move in.*'

Ninety-Seven

Doyle was almost at the top of the stairs when he heard the explosion.

The entire house seemed to rock under the thunderous detonation. Then, from outside, he heard shouts. Orders. He spun round, glancing up at the landing, as anxious now to discover the source of the blast as to find out where Callahan was. He turned and hurried back down the stairs, wincing when he felt pain from his injured leg. He could feel the heat from the fire the car had started. As he entered the corridor it washed over him like a wave. Ahead, one of the doors had been blown open by the explosion. Doyle slowed his pace slightly, gun held before him, then ducked low and peered around the frame into the room.

Flames from the wrecked car were still leaping in through the shattered window and the curtains were ablaze. Thick smoke filled the air.

Georgie was lying on her stomach in the centre of the room, her body twisted into a foetal position, one arm crushed beneath her. Blood had spread in a dark puddle around her.

As Doyle looked at her he could see the bullet wounds in her body and gashes in her face where she had been thrown through the window. Her blonde hair was matted with blood, plastered across her face as if she'd showered in the crimson fluid. Her eyes were closed.

'Oh Christ,' he whispered, moving slowly towards the body. He knelt beside her, touching his hand to her cheek. When he brought it away it was smeared with blood. Her eyelids were open a fraction so Doyle reached forward and gently pushed them shut. Seemingly oblivious to the fire that raged in the room he remained beside her, keeping up his vigil for a moment longer before finally retreating back into the corridor, closing the door behind him. It should contain the fire for a time.

At least until he found Callahan.

He stood with his back to the wall, staring at the door behind which Georgie lay, and felt great weariness. It was as if someone had sucked all the life from him. For the first time in his life he felt not the horror or inevitability of death but the sheer futility of it. Or perhaps it was the futility of *life* that he felt more profoundly.

And if life was futile why prolong it?

He shook himself free of the lethargy and strode down the corridor, intent again on finding Callahan.

The sound of shattering glass came from up ahead.

Doyle quickened his pace until he reached the room, the room where he knew the stained glass window was. The door was still firmly shut. He took a step back and prepared to kick it in. If Callahan was in there waiting for him then so be it.

He drove one foot against the door and it flew back on its hinges, slamming against the wall.

Doyle rushed in, the Bulldog held before him.

Callahan was in the room, but he was not alone.

'Jesus,' muttered Doyle through clenched teeth, his eyes wide with disbelief as he looked at the other occupant of the room.

417

The creature towered over Callahan, its red eyes burning insanely as it looked around, finally focusing on Doyle, who could only stand as if frozen to the spot, gawping at the monstrous apparition. Conflicting emotions clashed inside his mind. Bewilderment. Disbelief. Fear. Revulsion.

What the fuck was it?

Callahan still had his back to Doyle, looking up at the creature in awe. Had Doyle been able to see the millionaire's face he would have seen the smile on his lips.

'Get away from it,' Doyle shouted, his eyes riveted on the monstrosity. He raised the Bulldog and steadied himself, then squeezed off two shots.

Both struck the creature in the chest, the shells exploding and the glaser slugs opening up inside their target. A thick mixture of blood and pus spewed from the wounds but the creature only swayed slightly as the massive impacts rocked it.

'No,' roared Callahan and spun round, the HK33 levelled at Doyle.

He fired twice.

The first shot missed. The second caught the counter-terrorist in the side. It punctured his torso just above the right hip but, fortunately for him, tore through the fleshy part of his body without damaging any vital organs. The impact, however, sent him spinning, blood running from the wound. He fell to the ground, his eyes still fixed on the creature. Doyle dragged himself to his knees and aimed once more. This time at Callahan.

He fired once.

The .44 calibre shell, moving at a speed in excess of 1,500 feet a second, hit the millionaire in the back. It tore easily through his shoulder blade, opening up immediately, spreading its lethal contents inside as it exploded. Doyle saw the other man lifted off his feet by the shot. He fell at the feet of the creature, which looked down at him and then at Doyle. By this time the counter-terrorist had managed to scramble to his feet and was propped up against the door frame preparing to fire again.

Callahan's body was twitching slightly. He was finished. Doyle had to kill this other fucking monstrosity.

It took a step forward and he fired.

The bullet struck it in the stomach but barely halted it. It bent down and swept Callahan up in one huge clawed hand, dangling him before it as a child might hold a doll. Then it placed its other hand on his face. Doyle saw its mouth open, saw its lips flickering as if it were speaking. Then it gently lowered Callahan to the floor where he lay still, his eyes closed.

The creature backed off towards the stained-glass window, pieces of which now lay all over the floor like glass confetti.

Doyle thumbed back the hammer of the .44 once again and fired.

This shot hit the creature squarely between the eyes and he watched with satisfaction as its face seemed to fold inward, the skull collapsing under the massive impact of the shell. The monstrosity swayed uncertainly for a moment and Doyle fired again. Again into its head. The entire skull seemed to explode, gobbets of yellow and red matter flying about the room as if someone had placed an explosive charge inside the beast's skull. Portions of bone hurtled through the air, propelled by the massive impact of the glaser slugs and also projected by the streams of foul-smelling fluid which erupted from the ruined head.

The creature stood perfectly still for long seconds then fell to the ground.

Doyle saw it falling.

Saw the ground rushing up to meet it.

Saw it hit the floor.

Saw it disappear.

As he looked on in stunned disbelief, the creature vanished. All that remained were the puddles of vomit-like discharge which had been spread around the room.

Doyle shook his head.

That wasn't possible.

He wondered if he'd blacked out momentarily.

The creature couldn't disappear. *Couldn't.*

He stood panting, propped against the wall, blood running from the wound in his side, his eyes still bulging wide, staring at the place where he had seen the creature fall. It had hit the ground beside Callahan's body. Fallen, dying, beside the man who had summoned it. Fallen ...

Callahan sat up.

Doyle shook his head.

This is fucking crazy. I'm fucking crazy.

He watched as Callahan scrambled to his feet, his flailing hands reaching for the HK33. The millionaire turned around, looking at Doyle.

As he opened his eyes, Doyle could see that they now glowed red, like those of the creature.

And he understood.

Callahan raised the HK33 and fired.

Ninety-Eight

The weapon was on automatic now. The salvo raked the walls, blasting chunks of plaster free. Doyle tried to dive to one side but he was too slow. A bullet hit him in the shoulder, shattering his left collar-bone. Another caught him in the chest, punching through his lung before exiting, carrying bloodied pink tissue with it. He was thrown back against the wall by the impact, blood spattering against the stonework. He fell to the side, dragging himself through the doorway and out into the corridor.

He tried to rise, fumbling in his pocket for more slugs, knowing his own pistol was empty. He found some and pushed them into the empty chambers as Callahan advanced.

'Immortality, Doyle,' the millionaire called. 'What greater treasure could there be than that?'

He rounded the door, his red eyes bulging as he looked down on the wounded counter-terrorist.

Doyle fired twice, upwards into Callahan's stomach.

The blasts lifted the other man off his feet, throwing him back several feet, blood jetting from the massive holes blasted in him by the Bulldog bullets.

Doyle scrambled to his feet, breath hissing through his lung wound.

He ran to the end of the corridor and out into the hall, heading for the stairs.

He was half-way up when Callahan came staggering

into view. He swung the assault rifle up to his shoulder and fired off another burst.

Doyle was hit again. In the back of the leg. In the small of the back.

Searing pain filled his body and he cried out as the bullets ripped a path through his flesh and muscle. More blood flowed from the wounds. Doyle felt pain unlike anything he'd experienced before. No. He shook his head. He had felt worse than this. He had felt agony the like of which no man should be forced to endure.

For a moment he thought he was lying on the street in Londonderry again.

Not a bomb blast this time, but several high velocity bullets had destroyed his body.

Had killed him?

He turned on the stairs, raising the .44 again.

Callahan was coming closer.

He was smiling.

Doyle didn't wipe the smile off his face. He blew it off.

One shot from the .44 caught Callahan in the face, powering through his teeth, exploding from the back of his head. Pieces of enamel were driven back into his mouth, carried through the hole in the base of his skull by the massive force of the bullet. He was lifted into the air as if jerked by invisible wire, his body flying like an unwanted puppet before he finally crashed to the ground at the foot of the stairs, smoke rising from his face, or what remained of it.

Doyle peered down at the body through eyes which were clouding over.

Callahan wasn't moving but Doyle had to check. He tried to stand but the effort made him cough, bright red blood spilling over his lips. His legs felt as though they would give way as he dragged himself upright and made his way tortuously down the steps towards the motionless body of his foe.

He kept the Bulldog trained on him the whole time, ready to fire.

Waves of pain so intense he thought they would make him black out swept over him and he had to pause, trying to draw air into lungs holed by bullets. He could feel an enormous pressure on his chest every time he tried to swallow. When he exhaled the air hissed through the torn lungs like punctured bellows.

He drew closer to Callahan.

'Move in'

The order came and the Garda men scurried towards the house, slowing down as they reached the front door.

Those at the rear and sides of the building crashed through windows in their haste to get inside.

Half a dozen of them waited outside the front door, rifles at the ready.

Doyle heard them on the porch but his attention was focused on Callahan.

The millionaire's face was a bloody ruin, his mouth still open, portions of his upper jaw blasted back into his palate.

Doyle stood over him, fighting off unconsciousness, wanting only to lie down. To rest.

To die if necessary.

Callahan grabbed his left leg and pulled him over.

Doyle felt the incredible strength in the grip, felt himself being pitched forward, hurled across the hallway as Callahan rose and turned on him.

He was smiling, the remains of his face twisted into a sickening mask.

The front door burst open and the first two Garda men came crashing inside. Doyle watched as they swung their weapons round, bringing them to bear on Callahan, but the millionaire was too quick for them. He cut them down with one burst of the HK33. Then, with incredible agility, he sprinted up the stairs.

Doyle could only watch as he reached the top, turning as the remaining Garda marksmen burst in.

They opened fire simultaneously.

Doyle was deafened by the massive fusillade of fire which seemed to go on for an eternity, the hallway filling with fumes as they pumped more and more bullets into Callahan. Bullets hit him in the chest, legs, stomach, face. One even blasted off his nose. The impact hurled him back against the wall with savage force, then he staggered forward again, crashed into the banister and toppled over it, his body falling the twenty or so feet to the hall where it landed with a sickening thud.

This time he did not move.

'This one's still alive,' shouted one of the Garda officers, crossing to Doyle who had rolled onto his back. 'Get an ambulance, quick.'

What's the rush? Doyle thought. He looked across to where one of the Garda was prodding Callahan's body with the toe of his boot.

Doyle opened his mouth to speak, choking on his own blood but managing to force the words out.

'He's still alive,' he croaked feebly.

The Garda officer shook his head.

'He's alive,' Doyle insisted, his entreaty dissolving into a coughing fit which sent fresh spasms of pain

424

through him. 'Believe me, he's alive. For fuck's sake, I'm telling you, he's alive.'

There was fear in his voice now as his words grew weaker.

'Alive,' he whispered.

Blood spilled over his lips.

'Where's that ambulance?' one of the Garda shouted angrily.

It didn't seem to matter, thought Doyle.

He closed his eyes.

Ninety-Nine

Another twenty minutes and his shift would have been finished. If they'd been twenty minutes later some other poor sod would have had all the work. As it was, Paul Rafferty pulled another of the bodies from the gurney and laid it out carefully on the metal-topped slab. Another policeman.

Where the hell were they all coming from? He'd heard something on the news earlier that morning about a gun battle, but he'd never expected anything like this. He'd seen the victims of road accidents, house fires and those who had succumbed to old age or disease during his time as a morgue attendant in Kinarde hospital, but never anything like this before. No sooner had he laid out one corpse than they brought in another. They must have a bloody conveyor belt out there beyond the green double doors, he thought as he removed the clothes from the policeman, noticing the savage bullet wounds in his torso as he did. All the clothes were put into separate black plastic bags and tagged with the name of the former owner. Rafferty attached the necessary identification tags to the left big toes of each of his new arrivals.

The next was a woman, a blonde woman in her late twenties, he guessed. He also guessed that in life she had been pretty but now, with her body and face disfigured by bullet wounds and lacerations, she was a travesty of her true self. There had been another woman too, older, attractive he thought in life. She had been the one with the shotgun wound in her chest.

He began undressing the blonde woman, administering a swift mental rebuke when he allowed his gaze to dwell a fraction too long on her breasts. One had been pulverized by a bullet, anyway. He pulled the green sheet over her, covering her face, then paused for a cigarette, looking over at the remaining gurneys that stood by the door. He took a couple more drags on his cigarette then wheeled the first of them over to the assigned slab and placed the body on it. He looked at the face, or at least what remained of it. He knew this man, recognised him. Rafferty nodded to himself. It was David Callahan, the Englishman who lived on the large estate not too far from Kinarde.

His body was shredded by bullets; hardly a portion of his body was unpenetrated by rounds. Again Rafferty wondered what had happened. How had so many people come to die so violently? He pulled off Callahan's clothes and dropped them into the bag he'd set aside. Then he folded the dead man's arms across his chest and pulled the sheet up over him, crossing to the last gurney and its occupant.

Behind him, he didn't notice that one of Callahan's

arms had slipped from his chest and now dangled at his side.

Rafferty pushed the last gurney over and performed his task one last time. Then he washed his hands, scrubbing the blood away, watching as it swirled around the plug-hole before disappearing.

As he turned he noticed Callahan's arm dangling.

Muttering to himself Rafferty returned to the corpse and pulled the sheet back, peering into the face for a moment. Then he gripped the arm and folded it back into position.

The fingers flexed slightly.

The temperature must be too high inside the room, he thought. It was a phenomenon that happened whenever the temperature rose above fifty degrees. Heat seeped into the dead pores and appeared to reanimate particular limbs. He remembered how, during his first week in the job, the cooling system had packed up completely. To his absolute horror, one of the corpses he'd been cleaning had sat up. Now he merely smiled and crossed to the thermostat on the wall, easing it down a few degrees.

Behind him on the slab Callahan's fingers twitched again.

Rafferty returned to the body, pressed the arm back across Callahan's chest and pulled up the sheet again.

He glanced at his watch. Where the hell was Riley? His replacement was late. Rafferty wanted to get home. He hoped to Christ that the coming night was quieter.

Behind him the bodies lay on their slabs, each covered by a green plastic sheet.

He could feel the air temperature dropping noticeably. The thermostat was starting to do its work. Rafferty smiled, pleased with his handiwork.

427

When the sheet covering David Callahan moved again he ignored it.

Maybe it needed to go down a few more degrees, he thought. Strange that just the one body should be affected, though. Rafferty shrugged and thought nothing more of it. He picked up his paper and sat down behind his desk, waiting for Riley to arrive.

Again movement. Again from Callahan.

Rafferty continued reading.

One Hundred

They were buried together, as had been specified in their wills.

In the same grave, dug twelve feet into the ground, beneath a huge oak tree in the grounds of the estate.

David and Laura Callahan were lowered into their final resting place watched by only a handful of onlookers. Two or three of their staff and the priest attended as they were placed in the hole that would house them for the rest of eternity.

After the ceremony the onlookers drifted away. They went home. The priest stood by the graveside for a moment composing himself, then he too went. The gravedigger was left alone to fill in the hole, something he did quite happily and with no haste. He had no fear of the dead. He had been in the job too long for that. Besides, what was there to fear from a dead man? He whistled happily as he refilled the hole, finally patting down the top soil before replacing the carefully cut

428

sods. It would take a few weeks for the grass to grow back fully. By the end of the month the only evidence of the grave would be the small marble headstone that bore the names of David and Laura Callahan.

When the man had patted the sods down he stood by the grave and lit a cigarette, leaning against the tree and looking up into the sky. The sun was shining brightly, spreading its warmth over the land. Only beneath the leaves of the oak tree was it still a little cool. Eventually he moved away from the green canopy, glad to feel the sunshine on his skin. He carried his spade over to his van, put the tool in the back and slid behind the steering wheel. He swung the car out onto the long driveway.

Behind him the grave was silent.

A blackbird settled on the freshly-turned earth, snatching up a worm that had been disturbed by the gravedigger. The bird took off with its prize, soaring high into the blue sky.

The grave remained in shadow, untouched by the sun.

EPILOGUE

The Beginning

Darkness.

Darkness and pain.

He was aware of them both at the same time. He tried to sit up but his head connected with the lid of the coffin and he slumped back down again.

David Callahan sucked in a deep breath and tasted stale air.

He tried to reach up, to touch his eyes, to feel the stitches which had sewn them shut, but he could not move in the confines of the casket. He tried to open his mouth but his jaws had been wired together with the same care and attention to detail with which his eyelids had been stitched shut.

And there was the pain.

Excruciating, mind-numbing pain that filled every pore of his body. His now living body.

The secret had been his, still was his. The treasure was his, would always be his.

But he had the pain to go with it.

A pain he could not endure but knew he must endure. A pain he would know forever.

Had he been able to smile he might have done so, smiled at the supreme irony of the situation. He was immortal. He could not die. It didn't matter if the stale air inside the coffin ran out. He would not die. He could not die.

The realization grew on him gradually. The understanding that he was twelve feet below earth packed so tightly he could never claw his way through, even if he managed to free himself from the coffin.

The knowledge that no matter how long or hard he screamed no one would ever hear him.

The remembrance that whoever had worked on his body in the funeral parlour had sewn his eyes and mouth shut, had filled in the bullet holes in his body with morticians' wax.

Had sucked out every drop of blood and replaced it with embalming fluid.

That was what caused the excruciating pain.

A pain he must learn to live with because live was exactly what he would continue to do.

The agony seemed to grow upon that realization.

He was immortal.

He had the secret forever.

And he had the rest of eternity to enjoy his agony.